Writing Displacement

Writing Displacement
Home and Identity in Contemporary Post-colonial English Fiction

Akram Al Deek

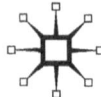

WRITING DISPLACEMENT
Copyright © Akram Al Deek 2016

All rights reserved. No reproduction, copy or transmission of this publication may be made without written permission. No portion of this publication may be reproduced, copied or transmitted save with written permission. In accordance with the provisions of the Copyright, Designs and Patents Act 1988, or under the terms of any licence permitting limited copying issued by the Copyright Licensing Agency, Saffron House, 6-10 Kirby Street, London EC1N 8TS.

Any person who does any unauthorized act in relation to this publication may be liable to criminal prosecution and civil claims for damages.

First published 2016 by
PALGRAVE MACMILLAN

The author has asserted his right to be identified as the author of this work in accordance with the Copyright, Designs and Patents Act 1988.

Palgrave Macmillan in the UK is an imprint of Macmillan Publishers Limited, registered in England, company number 785998, of Houndmills, Basingstoke, Hampshire, RG21 6XS.

Palgrave Macmillan in the US is a division of Nature America, Inc., One New York Plaza, Suite 4500, New York, NY 10004-1562.

Palgrave Macmillan is the global academic imprint of the above companies and has companies and representatives throughout the world.

ISBN 978-1-137-58091-7 hardback
ISBN 978-1-349-95319-6   ISBN 978-1-137-59248-4 (eBook)
DOI 10.1057/9781137592484

Distribution in the UK, Europe and the rest of the world is by Palgrave Macmillan®, a division of Macmillan Publishers Limited, registered in England, company number 785998, of Houndmills, Basingstoke, Hampshire RG21 6XS.

Library of Congress Cataloging-in-Publication Data
Names: Al Deek, Akram, 1984–
Title: Writing displacement : home and identity in contemporary
    post-colonial English fiction / Akram Al Deek.
Description: New York : Palgrave Macmillan, 2016. | Includes
    bibliographical references and index.
Identifiers: LCCN 2015030570 | ISBN 9781137580917 (hardback)
Subjects: LCSH: English fiction—20th century—History and criticism. |
    Identity (Psychology) in literature. | Displacement (Psychology) in
    literature. | Postcolonialism in literature. | Immigrants' writings,
    English—History and criticism. | Exiles' writings—History and
    criticism. | Collective memory in literature. | BISAC: LITERARY
    CRITICISM / Caribbean & Latin American. | LITERARY CRITICISM /
    European / English, Irish, Scottish, Welsh. | LITERARY CRITICISM /
    Middle Eastern.
Classification: LCC PR888.I3 A4 2016 | DDC 823/.91409353—dc23 LC
    record available at http://lccn.loc.gov/2015030570

A catalogue record for the book is available from the British Library.

To my newly born nephew, in the hope this will speak to your generation.
Welcome home, welcome to exile you little displacee!

Contents

Acknowledgments	ix
Placing Displacement: An Introduction	1
1 Writing Displacement	17
Section 1: Debunking the Nomadic Rhizome	17
Section 2: What Is Displacement? Answering by the Example of *Nuzooh*	23
Section 3: Nostalgia and Memory between Melancholy and Celebration	38
Section 4: Contrasting Palestinian Exilic Displacements and Jewish Diaspora	46
2 Displacing Cultural Identity	57
Section 1: Cultural Identity between Ghettoization and Displacements	58
Section 2: Racism and Immigration	67
3 The Windrush Generation: Remapping England and Its Literature	79
4 Masala Fish: Cultural Synthesis and Literary Adventuring	117
Promoting Cultural Diversity/Multiculturalism Post-9/11: A Conclusion	165
Notes	183
Bibliography	189
Index	197

Acknowledgments

I thank the following, whose asset has been immense and whose contribution has been of great help in finishing this work:

My family for love and patience, friends and students for believing in me, and those who died for a home, for both their aspiration and inspiration.

This also goes to the resting soul of my uncle, may he rest in peace, who taught me how to ride a donkey, plant onions, and be careful in dealing with the colonizer; to the resting soul of my cat, whose purring kept me awake and sane during sleepless nights of research; to Al Jalil Football Club (Irbid Refugee Camp, Jordan) and Newcastle Panthers FC (Newcastle, UK) for reminding me what it means to be part of a group, to belong; to my father who taught me poetry, discipline, different types of figs, and punctuality; a German passport which allowed me crossing frontiers; to the resting soul of architect and friend Yousif Khatib, for sharing my daily existential madness and daydreaming; to the resting soul of photographer and friend Muhammad Al Zyoud, who taught me laughter during unbearable schooldays; my mother for teaching me pickling olives, the alphabets, ironing, and compassion.

I would also like to thank Dr Kathleen Kerr-Koch for her impetus, guidance, and thoughtfulness, for being an invigorating tutor and a caring friend; Dr Barry Lewis for several interesting conversations and channeling opinions; and Dr Geoffrey Nash for motivational support. I also thank the Culture and Regional Studies BEACON for its financial support and thriving academic enterprise, Dr Anastasia Valassopoulos, Dr Peter Dempsey, and Professor Peter Rushton for their instructive opinions, annotations, and criticism. Many thanks are also due to Professor Patrick Williams to have taken time despite and through illness to review my work; to my production editor, project manager, and editorial assistants and publisher at Palgrave Macmillan for their advice and cooperation.

Placing Displacement:
An Introduction

I

Using cultural and literary theory and contemporary metropolitan post-Second World War postcolonial fictions, the concept of displacement is revisited here allowing for an affirmation of the specificity and beginnings of displaced writers' identities and for a reassertion of the significance of their starting points meanwhile resisting, precluding, and falling into the dangers of cultural and mental ghettoization and defensive and/or vulgar nationalism. Burdened with colonial history and being "out of place," writings by displaced writers with their hyphenated identities have altered the literature of England in its language and cultural identity. This has promoted the rediscovery, as in the Freudian psychoanalytic context, of materials that have been repressed or "pushed aside" in cultural translation, but which surely continue to cause trouble and restlessness in the perpetual journey of displacement.

Displacement also troubles the ideas of citizenship and national belonging and offers to the noncitizen the freedom to be "out of place," out of the familiar and status quo, which opens doors for cultural translation and filtration. Displacement falls therefore somewhere between nationalism (Oedipal, rigid, imposed, created, and closed) and nomadology (anti-Oedipal, open, flexible, creative, and free), allowing critical and aesthetic distance and balancing the central authority between past and present, tradition and modernity, by translating (between) them. Revisiting displacement is a study that produces therefore an oscillation between the two at will. Displacement as it is understood here celebrates multiplicity and hybridity/syncretism without falling into the anti-memory and history-free, spatially attenuated, free-floating, aloof, and ontologically rootless concept of nomadism, or the nomadic rhizome. In revisiting the concept of displacement, this study is skeptical of nomadology's total and complete transcendence of national and Oedipalized territorial frameworks.

Displacement is not therefore ghettoized in Freud's Oedipal territory, nor is it free-floating and attenuated in nomadic deterritorialization. Revisiting displacement recognizes the importance of starting points and beginnings[1] without sliding into nomadology's aloofness.

This study spans across a time frame that starts with Selvon's *The Lonely Londoners* in 1956, to 2003 which is marked by Monica Ali's *Brick Lane*, which manifests, to a certain qualified extent, a new ethnicity: black British. The two generations discussed here, the Windrush Generation (1956–1976) and the so-called Masala Fish Generation (1976–2003), with its army of displaced migrant writers, mark a shifting boundary that problematizes the frontier of the modern nation-state and engenders a synthesis of cultures and a peaceful celebration of living in the potential radiance of Babylon. This celebration, however, is often precluded by racism and vulgar nationalism among other obstacles.

The structure of this generational division suggested here traces different shifts in the uninterrupted emphasis on beginnings, the different representations of home, and the politics of identity and their changing interrelationship with place and memory; it also reveals the changing nature of the representations and politics of home and identity through a contemporary study of metropolitan english[2] fiction. This study eventually concludes that in both generations the specificity of identity and beginnings is always present and recognized not as a moment of departure only but also as an inventive resource from which perpetual displacements feed an incoherent identity in flux. Although location or locale in this book is kept from being reduced to a mere geographical place on the geopolitical map of the world, locality is always present in the fictions analyzed here. Whether imaginatively constructed or nostalgically romanticized through memories, beginnings are always referenced, referred to, and frequently deferred from. Multiple identities therefore may seem to be directionless; nevertheless, they are not without a concept of home, nor are they forgetful or without history.

This project also concludes that an access to historic memory is always significantly important because it provides the context for politically fruitful invention. Thus, it attempts to semantically expand the concept of displacement by contextualizing it through personal understanding of its nature as it has emerged and emanated from my Palestinian experience of exilic dispersions. The Colonized Territories of Palestine are hence foregrounded here as an example, particularly as represented in the works of Edward Said and Mahmoud Darwish, because, first, of the current and ongoing strife for self-determination under Israeli colonialism; second, because of the Palestinians' enduring struggle in preserving memory and thus the nation; and lastly for Palestine's historical and regional association with the semantic as well as the alienating and dislocating nature of the concept of displacement, or *Nuzooh* (evacuation in Arabic), subsequent to the Catastrophe of 1948. And although the Palestinians' historic circumstance and color of skin is different compared to the Indians or Pakistanis, the Indians of the Afro-Caribbean diaspora and the West Indians, they all share a history of oppression as postcolonial subjects whose so-called homes become artificial and imaginary constructs and whose identities are still burdened with a British colonial history, ongoing racist discriminations, and a persistent, troubling national identification. The Palestinian example is also invoked here because it mirrors other struggling national groups; it is invoked here because it represents a momentous example of postcolonial nationalism and emerging national consciousness,[3] the importance of preserving memory and thus the nation, melancholic nostalgia, and a changing conception of identity over sixty or so years of life under siege and in exilic displacements.

II

Reading about displacement in contemporary post-Second World War literary theory and criticism, a few studies have featured or thoroughly emphasized the concept of displacement in their debates and discussions. The concept of displacement has not been circulated widely enough within literary and cultural studies either. It has not, for example, been semantically expanded or defined. Some studies have discussed the concept of displacement in relation to gender and/or sexuality, cinema and/or music, within the context of one or two writers, or in relation to one specific geographical location over a particular historic time. This project, however, revisits and resuscitates the concept of displacement as it, expands it semantically, and produces an extensive analysis that adds to the already existent body of critical work.

In recent years, studies that have tackled the concept of displacement within the context of literary theory and contemporary British fiction, or post-Second World War literary writings in English seem to have started by using the concept in the Routledge edition of *The Empire Writes Back* in 1989. In "Place and Displacement," the editors highlight the fact that both place and displacement are "major features of post-colonial literatures" (Ashcroft *et al*: 2002: 8); in their brief introductory section, the focus is being laid on the importance of language and its articulation in relation to place. Another work that recognizes the concept of displacement as an exilic narrative in literary studies is a compilation of essays also published by Routledge in 1994, entitled *Travellers' Tales: Narratives of Home and Displacement*. The essays investigate experiences of traveling, tourism, exile, and expatriation; and yet none of the articles adopts or discusses the concept in the book's title, displacement, in depth. All the writers' concerns seem to be exploring narratives of displacement without thoroughly discussing the dynamism of the concept and its politics. Their concern is rather focused on the future of traveling in a world whose boundaries are constantly shifting. Accentuating the concept of tourism and the tourist identity, displacement then is only mentioned when violent images of war, drought, and ethnic cleansing are brought into the narrative. Evidently, displacement is associated with Cambodia, Palestine, Kurdistan, and Bosnia among other devastated countries. Displacement therefore is granted a negative implication, which will be revisited and reversed in this book. And although traveling is presented as a mode of dwelling, there seems to be no distinction between "travel writing" as such and "traveling for pleasure."

In his writings on culture and literary criticism, Edward Said, who, it is worth noting, is a Palestinian exile and an American intellectual, also uses the term with an unsurprising emphasis on the metaphor of "exile" as in "exilic displacement" in *Culture and Imperialism* (1993) and in *Representations of the Intellectual* (1994). In the latter, he states that, "[f]or the intellectual an exilic displacement means being liberated from the usual career, in which 'doing well' and following in time-honored footsteps are the main milestones" (Said: 1994b: 46). Homi Bhabha, again, a Parsee-Indian displaced intellectual in London, defines the term in *The Location of Culture* (1994), among other various definitions, as "the fragmented and schizophrenic decentring of the self," indicating displacement's hybrid/syncretic, dual, and bipolar nature and its continuous deferral (Bhabha: 2005; 1994: 310). A similar indication is carried in another study entitled *Displacements: Cultural Identities in Question* (1994), a compilation of essays aiming to, collectively and individually, "grasp its multivalent complexity" since "the plural of the title of the volume indicates the multiple resonances of displacement [as] both point of departure and site of inquiry" (Bammer: 1994: xiii). The work, however, focuses on linguistic displacement and is framed by two fictional works only. A similar theme is expressed throughout a subsequent compilation of essays in *Displacement, Diaspora, and Geographies of Identity* (1996), where the writings demonstrate "a constant shuttling between reversal and displacement; they track resistances that are both or at once arboreal and rhizomic, sometimes nomadic and sometimes sedentary" (Lavie and Swedenburg: 2001: 13). This particular study defines identity as "an infinite interplay of possibilities and flavors of the mouth" (Ibid: 3). It also encourages the establishment of a multicultural community where "[e]veryone came equally 'different,' despite specific histories of oppressing or being oppressed" (Ibid). While this study suggests considering identity as an open possibility, celebrates the hybrid figure as decentering products of master codes, and encourages multicultural mingling and racial equality, its "shuttling" between rhizomic and nomadic points and arboreal and sedentary points seems to slip more into nomadology and a celebration of a free-floating world. Culture, for example, in the context of that study is "a multicoloured, free-floating mosaic, its pieces constantly in flux, its boundaries infinitely porous" (Ibid). Words such as rhizomic, free-floating, shuttling, and nomadic reoccur more often than their opposites. It is clearly stated, however, that the essays in that volume "wish to stake out a terrain that calls for, yet paradoxically refuses, boundaries, a borderzone between identity-as-essence and identity-as-conjuncture" (Lavie and Swedenburg: 2001: 13). Although poor in its literary references, and although its thesis of "shuttling" back and forth and its oscillation between two points seems to slip into the aloof, anti-memory, history-free, and spatially attenuated nomadic rhizome, Lavie's work contains a significant set of contributions to the field of cultural theory and the politics of identity.

Elsewhere, and resembling his professional and personal identity as a second-generation Afro-Caribbean British writer, Caryl Phillips's *A New World Order* (2001) is divided into four units: the United States, Africa, the Caribbean, and Britain. Written as an anthology, the concept of displacement is optimistically and expectantly enlisted under the Caribbean section as The *Gift* of displacement (my italics). Listing the concept under a Caribbean section is no coincident, however, simply because "the Caribbean artist is better prepared for migration than most" (Phillips: 2001: 131). The division and multiplicity of locations in the book also suggest a multiplicity of displacements Phillips has gone through, psychologically, culturally, and geographically, and which he considers to be celebrated as a gift as opposed to be lamented as melancholic instabilities.

In this book, I write to answer some questions, in the process asking some more than with which I started:

What does it mean to be displaced? What is displacement? How does displacement alter one's being? How does it resuscitate one's becoming? What is the difference between exile, traveling and, say, expatriation? How can displacement be melancholic and/or celebratory? How thin is the line between nationalism and racism? How imaginary are our homelands? Are we nomads and belong no-where? Or do we always have central gravitation now-here? How does memory and nostalgia intensify our exilic displacement? How much of the past is shadow? Is the Palestinian exile uprooted or unrooted? Is s/he homeless or homesick? What is home? Which is harder: to forget or to remember? How much of language is alienating and how much is informative? If return is irredeemably irreconcilable, "where do birds fly after the last sky?"[4] How do you rewrite displacement?

Motivated not only by my own displacements[5] but also by the lack of answers on displacement, I rewrite my own displacements, highlighting the local experience of Palestinian exile in a postcolonial, global context, expanding the concept of displacement semantically, focalizing specific characterizations of an extensive body of metropolitan literatures written in English, investigating the changing politics of identity, emphasizing celebration of beginnings across 47 years of writing fiction, memoirs, and (semi-)autobiographies, two generations of displaced writers, and various representations of home, making it therefore the more significantly dynamic.

III

In a conversation with Salman Rushdie, Edward Said states the following: "Whether in the Arab world or elsewhere, twentieth-century mass society has destroyed identity in so powerful a way that it is worth a great deal to keep this specificity alive" (Rushdie: 1991: 183). This project draws on this idea of keeping the specificity of identity alive and not allowing it to dissolve into the aloofness of nomadology, transnationalism, or total dislocation. Displacement, as it is described and understood here, oscillates between Freud's Oedipal territoriality and what Deleuze and Guattari call the nomadic rhizome. It therefore challenges the claim that nomadology can freely transcend national and territorial frameworks as well as the fact that human beings, nomads or otherwise, can be free of history and/or of memory. This notion of displacement falls therefore somewhere between nationalism (Oedipal, rigid, imposed, created, and closed) and nomadology (anti-Oedipal, open, flexible, creative, and free), allowing for a critical and aesthetic distance, and balancing the central authority between past and present, tradition and modernity, by translating (between) them. The revisiting of displacement here simultaneously proposes an argument for viewing it as an oscillation between the two which also promotes cultural translation. From this perspective displacement can be understood as a celebration of multiplicity and hybridity/syncretism, but one that does not lead into the anti-memory, history-free, spatially attenuated, free-floating, aloof, and ontologically rootless characteristics implied by the concept of nomadology. This will be discussed further in the opening section of Chapter 1.

The experience of displacement does not belittle the role of the present (culture, affiliation, now and here, the acquired, the creative, the new and changing). On the contrary, past and present act in tandem in the displaced's articulation of identity. Ideally, a postcolonial identity is that which survives the nostalgic, magnetic pulling of the past and the seductive, mimetic pushing of the present, and, most importantly, translates between them. As Salman Rushdie notes, the word translation "comes, etymologically, from the Latin for 'bearing across'. Having been borne across the world, we are translated men. It is normally supposed that something always gets lost in translation; I cling, obstinately, to the notion that something can also be gained" (Rushdie: 1991: 17). An identity should resiliently take what Stuart Hall calls a "cultural turn." Hall defines a cultural turn as one that "is neither an ending nor a reversal; the process continues in the direction in which it was travelling before, but with a critical break, a deflection" (Hall: 2001: 9).

Hall's concept of a cultural turn suggests two main things. One, it suggests that everything starts somewhere and has what he calls a "pre-identity" (Ibid: 36); in other words, identity does not emerge from nowhere for there is no identity that is self-sufficient or whole within itself. Two, it suggests that an identity does not have to abandon a past, or a tradition; it can rather simultaneously build on and break from it in dialogic fluctuation. It does not restore a past, but rather takes a turn from it. For to be locked up in the attic of the past (there and then, created, filiation, nature, the traditional, familiar and familial) is to miss the opportunities the present has to offer; it is to miss what comes after the break, after the turn. In other words, to be locked up in the attic of the past and tradition is to live with(in) what Rushdie calls a "ghetto mentality." To be mentally ghettoized is to "forget that there is a world beyond the community to which we belong, to confine ourselves within narrowly defined cultural frontiers" (Rushdie: 1991: 19). This will be discussed further in the first section of Chapter 2.

This revisiting of displacement however allows for an analysis of the different shifting arenas within which the routes of displacement progress and develop: geographical, cultural, linguistic, and psychological, tackling in the process major difficulties such as racism and ghettoizing, vulgar nationalism. This will also be discussed further in the second section of Chapter 2.

Revisiting displacement explores different visions and versions of home and hence multiple rerouted identities across a span of time from 1956 to 2003. In fact, this time frame covers a large variety of displaced generations: namely the Windrush Generation,[6] students on scholarships, females through arranged marriages and family reunions, sons and daughters of the Windrush Generation, those brought at a very early age and remained in England, those who are the product of one English parent and a non-English parent, and those who were born and bred in England to non-English parents. The selected writers in this study do not necessarily represent each group; nevertheless, they reflect the various permutations of the politics of home and identity of their time. Condensed here into two generations to facilitate an examination of displacement in the context of the politics of home and identity, these writers include what is known as the Windrush Generation (1956–1976), discussed in detail in Chapter 3, and what is described here as the double-caste "Masala Fish"[7] Generation (1976–2003) in Chapter 4 and the conclusion.

The writers tackled in these two groups are either students (e.g., Farrukh Dhondy, Salman Rushdie, and V. S. Naipaul), or were brought along with their families at a very early age (e.g., Monica Ali, Timothy Mo, and Caryl Phillips), or were double-caste, born and bred English (e.g., Hanif Kureishi and Zadie Smith). They, or their parents, all came from metropolitan cities such as Trinidad, Mumbai/Bombay, or Hong Kong and resettled in London. Although this "army of metaphors" as Bhabha calls them has had different ways of representing home and identity, they all write about and are stimulated by displacement. While the Windrush Generation is an already established category (Sam Selvon, George Lamming, V. S. Naipaul, and although she was not on the same SS Empire Windrush ship, Jean Rhys), what is described here as a Masala Fish Generation had to be envisaged as comprehensively as possible. Writings by the Windrush Generation diminished significantly during the mid-1970s, during which time Farrukh Dhondy emerged and wrote about a new subject matter: the young, second-generation immigrants of the time. In addition, and while Salman Rushdie contrasted East and West and introduced magic realism throughout the 1980s, Timothy Mo addressed the Chinese immigrant living in England, Hanif Kureishi introduced a new ethnicity during the 1990s, Caryl Phillips took and followed on the steps of Lamming and Selvon, while Zadie Smith and Monica Ali injected the scenery with a fresh image of a multi-generational and multicultural London at the end of the twentieth century and post-9/11, respectively. Although Mo differs from other "ex-colonial" writers such as Dhondy and Rushdie, he is still a part of "a multi-cultural but incoherent Britain" (Wong: 2000: 12) brought about by the forces of globalization. Mo's presence as a non-English writer also coincides with literary production which was at the time moving toward a multicultural society and a celebration of cultural diversity.

The two groups, therefore, are divided according to subject matter and chronological sequence. Studying the two groups comparatively reveals that this generational division traces different shifts in identity politics and their changing interrelationship with home and place, that is the changing nature of the politics of identity and representations of home in contemporary metropolitan english fiction. This book will conclude that in both generations the specificity of identity is always present and recognized not only as a moment of departure but also of a resourceful past to and in the moment of the now and here.

It is difficult, however, to articulate a generic theory across various migrant generations and to offer answers to what it exactly means to be black *and* British, to pinpoint a displaced writer's identity, and to isolate a singular conception of what and/or where the question of home resides. Such difficulty is due to the phenomenon of rapid acceleration and the speed of change that impinges upon migration and displacement in the modern context. In a study of *Contemporary British Fiction Since 1970*, for example, Childs states that

[t]he number of works of fiction published each year doubled between 1950 and 1990; currently, about 100 new British novels are released each week. Approximately 130 works of fiction are submitted for the Booker Prize, while around 7000 novels eligible for the prize are published in Britain and the Commonwealth annually.

(Childs: 2005: 3)

Furthermore, Bhabha, in *The Location of Culture*, observes that, "the last two or three decades have seen more people living across or between national borders than ever before—on a conservative estimate, 40 million foreign workers, 20 million refugees, 20–25 million internally displaced peoples as a result of famine and civil wars" (Bhabha: 2005: 16). The sheer variety and rapid increase in numbers of people becoming part of transforming diasporic communities thus reflects a growing diversity and pluralism in identities. It has been rightly suggested therefore that all fiction is homesickness and reversely, all homesickness is fiction.[8]

Such unhomely fictions have been chosen here to reflect such homesickness and fictionality; they have also been chosen because they significantly shaped what is suggested to be termed as a postcolonial literary displacement. The adjective postcolonial here, however, does not suggest an exclusive time frame after the Second World War. Hall makes clear, for example, that the prefix "post" in this requires some qualification: "the prefix 'post' in post-colonial does not mean 'after' in a sequential or chronological sense, as though one phase or epoch or set of practices has ended and an absolutely new one is beginning" (Hall: 2001: 9). It is evident that postcolonialism would have never happened without colonialism or decolonization; postcolonialism therefore is a movement that preceded and continued throughout and developed after. "Post" in postcolonial therefore "refers to the aftermath or the after-flow of a particular configuration" (Ibid). A postcolonial literary displacement, moreover, means that postcolonial writing (literary theory and fiction in the context of this book) displaces the authority, meaning, and reality of the colonial text and offers an-Other reading, "the Other side of the story" as it were; it narrates another experience: an experience that bears the burden of the colonial experience but which also narrates independently after it: displacing it. This postcolonial literary displacement is thus narrated throughout and is demonstrated in two ways: in language and in subject matter: primarily but not exclusively exile, migration, home and identity, memory and nostalgia. Section 3 of Chapter 1 will discuss the disruptive nature of human memory and demonstrate how the displaced's restless and relentless memory debunks Deleuze and Guattari's memory-free nomadic rhizome and how memory as well as nostalgia can be celebratory and not exclusively melancholic. It will furthermore show how displacement rather intensifies through memory and nostalgia.

"Whether in linguistics, philosophy, or literary theory, post-colonial theories operate recursively and subversively to dismantle preconstituted assumptions in European theories. The complexities occluded by unitary assumptions of monism and universality are unraveled by the constant pull of marginality and plurality, so that through displacement, theory is 're-placed'" (Ashcroft *et al*: 2002: 152). A new Empire indeed writes back against the old one, from within the center. In terms of writers' homes and identities, however, whatever is shifted or changed is not replaced but rather displaced and rerouted in a new experience. In other words, the "there and then" is not replaced by the "here and now." As Bammer states, "what is displaced—dispersed, deferred, repressed, pushed aside—is, *significantly, still* there: displaced but not replaced, it remains a source of trouble, the shifting ground of signification that makes meaning tremble" (Bammer: 1994: Xiii; my italics).

The fictionalized writings discussed here in Chapters 3 and 4 are therefore the so-called unhomely fictions,[9] the (semi-)autobiographical novels, the multiply located chronicles, the centrally metropolitan, doubly conscious narratives, the magically realistic inventions, and the nonlinear accounts of stories of scattering, home, and identity. As aforementioned, the story timeline of this project starts with the father of the folk stories, the East Indian Trinidadian emigrant Sam Selvon and his masterpiece *The Lonely Londoners* (1956) and concludes with Monica Ali's post-9/11 *Brick Lane*. Other writings across a very vibrantly active 47 years of (re)writing also include Naipaul's *The Mimic Men* and *A House for Mr Biswas*, Rhys' *Wide Sargasso Sea* and her unfinished autobiography *Smile Please*, Kureishi's *The Buddha of Suburbia* and *My Beautiful Laundrette*, Lamming's *The Emigrants* and *In the Castle of My Skin*, Dhondy's *Bombay Duck* and *East End at Your Feet*, and Rushide's *The Satanic Verses* and *East, West* to name but a few. These writings are referred to in the title of this book as "contemporary post-colonial english fiction." The word *english* emphasizes the linguistic characteristics shared by these writers as opposed to its racial and ethnic attributes. The appropriation of English serves the displaced writer's own purposes and shoulders his postcolonial, exilic experience. This english displaces the traditional and colonial English language because it is dipped in Indian chutney and sweetened with Caribbean sugar; it dances to the rhythms of reggae and bhangra[10]; it is wounded by a colonial past and history yet healed by a postcolonial present and continuity. The displaced writer's english is a postcolonial voice.

Ahmad, in his book *In Theory*, suggests that, in the case of India, for example, "[o]ne cannot reject English now, on the basis of its initially colonial insertion, any more than one can boycott the railways for that same reason" (Ahmad: 2008: 77). English is certainly one of India's uniting factors, and it has long been assimilated into its social texture. The fictional works of literature are written in (black) english by Britain's formerly colonized subjects, and their succeeding generations, to reach a wider audience, to contain the displaced's postcolonial experience and to rewrite what was perceived once as the Western discourse of the Other. Finally, the unhomely fictions discussed here are *metropolitan* since the majority of the works of fiction studied here have the formerly imperial headquarters, the currently metropolitan city of London at their heart. London is thus the open space as opposed to the rigid, preimposed hierarchy "back home." Hence, in these works of fiction London functions as a prime setting to and with which Other cultural locations are contrasted, presenting multiple locations that reflect the displaced's identity whose meaning is deferred and which functions through a process of multiple displacements. In this sense, displacement acts as a "counter-hegemonic cultural practice to identify the spaces where we begin the process of revision" (hooks: 1989: 15).

On the other hand, the writers discussed in this book follow in the steps of such foreigners and émigrés as Conrad, James, T. S. Eliot, Pound, Yeats, and Joyce who Eagleton once considered "the most significant writers of twentieth-century English literature" (Eagleton: 1970: 9). Caryl Phillips also echoes Eagleton in that "the most radical innovators of form in English literature," namely Joseph Conrad, T. S. Eliot, Lawrence Durrell, Doris Lessing, and Wilson Harris, "are born outside of Britain." Phillips takes his lead from Eagleton's view "that writers with 'access to alternative cultures and traditions' have an opportunity to respond in a more vigorous manner" (Phillips: 2001: 291). Phillips's concern, however, is this: *what* is it in British society that the foreign writer is responding to? His proposed answer is that the foreign writer functions as a "disrupter" to Britain's promotion of itself "as a homogenous country whose purity is underscored not only by race and class, but, perhaps more importantly, by a sense of continuity. The sentiment is as straightforward as this: we are who we are because we've always been who we are" (Phillips: 2001: 291–92). First generations of displaced writers in England are therefore disrupters of national continuity and of what Philips calls the "conventional narrative order." Being outsiders, their work always questioned and reinvented the mainstream.

Eagleton points out, however, that conventional English culture was not able to produce great literary art "of its own impetus" (Eagleton: 1970: 9–10); he focuses therefore primarily on the contribution and general problems raised by the exile and émigré and their disruption. A similar theme is exercised in this study: the new subject matters of home and identity that the postcolonially displaced writer has problematically and playfully introduced into literatures written in English. Through what Bhabha calls "the transnational dimension of cultural transformation—migration, diaspora, displacement, relocation," a new history has been written and the British culture is no longer exclusively white, neither is the nation's identity racially constructed; it is through those who "have suffered the sentence of history—subjugation, domination, diaspora, displacement—that we learn our most enduring lessons for living and thinking" (Bhabha: 2005: 246–47), that is, those who engage with culture as an unfinished product and take nothing for granted. Lessons from the migrant, the diasporic, and displaced teach one, therefore, to deny an absolute, monochromatic culture and to reject pre-given and positioned references: that after the gloom of displacement (loss and alienation, change and instability) creativity flourishes. The displaced finds solace in, and is compensated by the dreamlike, poetics of displacement. As Rushdie says, the dream "is part of our very presence. Given the gift of self-consciousness, we can dream versions of ourselves, new selves for old" (Rushdie: 1991: 377–78).

It is also in dreams that Freud finds interpretations of reality. He defines the dream-work (*Traumarbeit*) as consisting of two processes, dream-condensation and dream-displacement, which transforms latent content into manifest content. Thus, Freud defines displacement as a psychic process and associates the concept with change and transvaluation.[11] In the Freudian context, displacement is central to the operation of the dream-work: the process by which uncomfortable thoughts and feelings (latent dream-thoughts) are pushed aside to the safer manifest dream-content. Displacement here is not only replacement but it is also translation, for "[d]reams, just like literature, do not usually make explicit statements" (Barry : 2002:98). Literary critics and cultural theorists are therefore interested in Freudian methods of interpretation because dreams and displacements do not say things, but rather they show things. Hence, literature is capable of telling us how the unconscious works; just as in the interpretations of dreams, one must dig beneath the manifest content to understand and find its symbolic core: its latent dream-content.

Furthermore, Deleuze and Guattari's *Anti-Oedipus: Capitalism and Schizophrenia* radically critiques Freud's theory of displacement through a reversal: they reject the notion that it is the unconscious that pressures the conscious; on the contrary, they believe that it is the conscious that pressures the unconscious. For Deleuze and Guattari, the "talking cure" for obstructions to the healthy resolution of the

Oedipus complex and the bringing to consciousness of repressed desires is the problem itself; for this activity is founded upon and perpetuates such Oedipalized territorialities such as church, family, school, nation (and any other institutions and boundaries outside the family), and especially the enlightenment concept of the individualized coherent subject. In other words, the talking cure maintains the status quo in its so-called healing, which is to countenance and promote, like fascism, the repressive forces of the cultural superego. That is why Deleuze and Guattari's Anti-Oedipus theory is considered, for example, as a fight against fascism: because it deterritorializes fascism and moves authority away from between place (boundary) and self.

Deleuze and Guattari's work on Freud's theory of displacement is indeed revamping for its rejection of Freud's belief that the conscious mind is always overwhelmed by the constant pressure of repressed (libidinal) desires, fantasies, and subliminal feelings and/or perceptions. Such feelings and perceptions derive their energy from primary physical instincts seeking immediate satisfaction and run counter to elements of the mind that is concerned with adaption to an external reality and avoidance of external danger. While Freud sees the unconscious as the repository of repressed, primarily sexual desires and wishes, Deleuze and Guattari do not see the unconscious as such a reservoir, but as a productive process itself.[12]

What Deleuze and Guattari propose as more appropriate for the new world order is "schizoanalysis," which follows the lines of flight of desire as it moves between extremes from the zero point of selfless mechanization to an all-powerful megalomania. Schizoanalysis is put in oppositional and revolutionary contrast to psychoanalysis such that,

> the task of schizoanalysis is that of ultimately discovering for every case the nature of the libidinal investments of the social field, their possible internal conflicts, their relationships with the preconscious investments of the same field, their possible conflicts with these—in short the entire interplay of the desiring-machines and the repression of desire. Completing the process and not arresting it, not making it turn about in the void, not assigning it a goal.
> (Deleuze and Guattari: 1983: 382)

This rethinking of the Oedipus complex and hence the role of displacement in the context of a "global field of coexistence" (Deleuze and Guattari: 274) in order to discover the lines of flight and escape of desire has been very useful in broadening the scope of a number of different disciplines such as sociology, literary and cultural studies, linguistics, and geography.

Placing Displacement: An Introduction 15

In contrast to both Freud and Deleuze and Guattari, however, this book argues between their positions: although the idea of maintaining "familial pseudo etiologies" (Deleuze and Guattari: 1983: 278) as with Freud is critiqued here, what is also critiqued is the notion that one might flout etiology altogether so as to create "a domain of indifference between the microphysical and the biological" such that "there are as many living beings in the machine as there are machines in the living" (Deleuze and Guattari: 1983: 286). The contention here is that whatever is repressed and, in Freud's terms, "pushed aside," nevertheless remains psychologically imprinted perpetually causing trouble and restlessness. Displacement, when cast in geographical, cultural, and psychological contexts,[13] becomes something more material, though no less uncanny. When displacement is understood as a material condition, as it is in the literary texts analyzed in Chapters 3 and 4, the past and history become real issues that continually haunt and leak into the present. This condition can be equated with what Bammer calls "the shifting ground of signification that makes meaning tremble" (Bammer: 1994: xiii). Meaning is therefore neither in the past nor in the present alone. It is rather recognized and acknowledged in and through a dialogic translation between both. Displacement here is material, psychological, and intimately bound to the formulation and interpretation of the self. "For there is always going on within us a process of formulation and interpretation whose subject matter is our own self" (Auerbach: 1993: 549). Material and psychological displacements are linked therefore with the ongoing activity of making meaning in relation to the complex emotional states that this produces—melancholia, desolation, isolation, and suffocation—and in relation to memories and nostalgia. This often entails a change in the politics of identity, the representations of home, and the conceptualizations of belonging and affiliation, through the figurative and physical journeying, in time and across space.

Chapter 1

Writing Displacement

Section 1: Debunking the Nomadic Rhizome

In 1980, Deleuze and Guattari coined important concepts in philosophical studies, namely nomadology, the rhizome, or nomadic rhizome, and deterritorialization. These concepts primarily deal with geographical as well as psychological displacements and are concerned with the nomad's identity, boundaries, and environment that surround the self, continuity, and points of departure and arrival. Celebrating the removal of power and authority over a territory by its inhabitants, the deployment of these concepts weakens the ties between the displaced and land, between culture and place. These concepts embrace uprootedness and reject points of origin in particular as Oedipalized territorialities. Revisiting displacement does not totally reject Deleuze and Guattari's concept of a nomadic rhizome; however, it does reject what might be considered its inhuman and unethical character. For the rhizome

> has no beginning or end; it is always in the middle, between things, interbeing, intermezzo. The tree is filiation, but the rhizome is alliance, uniquely alliance. The tree imposes the verb "to be," but the fabric of the rhizomes the conjunction. "and...and...and." This conjunction carries enough force to shake and uproot the verb "to be." Where are you going? Where are you coming from? What are you heading for? These are totally useless questions. Making a clean slate, starting or beginning again from ground zero, seeking a beginning or a foundation—all imply a false conception of voyage and movement.
>
> (Deleuze and Guattari: 1992: 25)

Deleuze and Guattari's concept of the nomadic rhizome, and subsequently of its applicant the nomad, promotes "short-term memory, or antimemory," rootlessness, and no history; both nomadology and the rhizome "overthrow ontology, *do away with foundations*, nullify endings *and* beginnings" (Ibid: 25; my italics). Furthermore, "nomads have no points, paths, or land" (Ibid: 381). They are directionless, without history, memory free, without homeland or territory, without beginnings and/or starting points, detached and rootless, deterritorialized, and forgetful.

By contrast, this study argues that while the nomadic rhizome resists the organizational structure of the tree-root system which looks for the original source of things, and while multiple identities may seem to be directionless, identities are not without beginnings, nor are they forgetful or without history. This can be illustrated through the voices of black and Asian displaced writers who reflect on their past through memory and whose displacement intensifies and transforms through memory. These displaced writers, unhomely and hyphenated, made it to the metropolitan city of London and brought with them a concept of not only "writing back with vengeance" but also bringing the margin into the center. By doing so, they initiated a process by which the metaphor of "center and periphery" becomes obsolete. Black British writers occupy both center and periphery simultaneously. The displaced black (non-white) British,[1] formerly colonized, intellectual writers discussed here are migrants through whose life London has become a transient location which offers a fertile soil for aesthetic expression, interracial and intercultural mingling, allowing for critical distance; they are the "decentred sons and daughters of the black diaspora ... the offspring of Britain's colonial history" (Bammer: 1994: 156). They are minor, marginalized, displaced writers as exiles: the Caribbean/the West Indian, East African, Middle Eastern, Asian, Indian, and Pakistani. Bhabha calls them the "army of metaphors," those "wandering peoples who will not be contained within the Heim of the national culture and its unisonant discourse, but are themselves the marks of a shifting boundary that alienates the frontiers of the modern nation" (Bhabha: 2005: 237). Young calls them "tricontinental," by which he means those who as well as marking a shifting boundary also "suggest an alternative culture, an alternative 'epistemology', or system of knowledge." The Caribbean, Asian, and African (tricontinental) form a postcolonial "global alliance resisting the continuing imperialism of the west." In fact Young's alternative term for postcolonialism is tricontinentalism where he emphasizes that the term "postcolonial" involves only those formerly colonized (Young: 2003: 17–18). In *Re-routing the Postcolonial*, furthermore, there are attempts to expand the subject to involve all those living within the postcolonial era, namely Eastern Europe and China, from Poland to South Africa and Canada in order to take a new route of inquiry. *Re-routing the Postcolonial* also suggests that to be global is to be postcolonial and to be postcolonial is always already to be global. For "[l]ocality itself has been globalized, its boundaries dilated by the mass migrants" (Wilson *et al*: 2010: 32). Either term however implies that the new emerging knowledge and the new (hi)story is being written not by the winners in history but those who are dispossessed and marginalized. Those "tricontinental" subjects are here to make sure that we "are looking at the world not from above, but from below" (Young: 2003: 17–20).

Although the displaced writer as migrant to a certain extent escapes the Heim(at)[2] of the national culture, like Foster in Selvon's *An Island Is A World*, or that of Khayyam in Rushdie's *Shame*, or even Karim in Kureishi's *The Buddha of Suburbia*, the displaced as migrant or exile is not a nomad. For in what Aciman calls the "bipolar mentality" of the displaced person "the idea of home may become too dramatized or sentimentalized," whereas in the "'nomadic' configuration, exile loses its charge" (Aciman: 1999: 58) for the nomad is not expelled *from* a place and thus the seductive power of the concept of home is nonexistent.

As indicated in *The Empire Writes Back*, displacement and place have been major features of postcolonial literature. What is argued here, however, is that displacement always registers a starting point, a beginning; it strongly promotes the importance of a writer's coming from and gravitating to "somewhere"; in a nutshell, it promotes a writer's beginning. Edward Said criticizes V. S. Naipaul, for example, for the total absence of belonging and of falling back to no starting points. For Said, Naipaul "begins to suspect that those roots in 'the beginning' were little more than 'a fabrication, a cause for yearning, something for the tomb'" (Said: 2001a: 100). This book argues against what Said dispassionately labels as the "free-floating intellectual" (Said: 1994b: 47), the traveler as cynical judge as opposed to guest. "No one is free of attachments and sentiments of course," Said confirms (Said: 1994b: 47). Rushdie's criticism of V. S. Naipaul emanates from the same analogy; for Rushdie sees Naipaul an ontologically rootless writer, "an artist from nowhere and everywhere" (Rushdie: 2002: 159).

The concept of the rhizome is also too flexible and too adaptable in terms of land and movement. Displacement thus translates and is placed between closed, rigid territories, segregation or what Rushdie calls mental and cultural ghettoization[3] and Deleuze and

Guattari's concept of the nomadic rhizome. Although displacement as it is understood here shares with the nomadic rhizome its conjunctions (and... and... and...), and thus its discontinuous yet collective currents, botanic multiplicity (becomings), no endings, metamorphosis, and "collective assemblage of enunciation," the displaced celebrates a beginning which adds to and fertilizes further multiple points of other displacements. The experience of displacement is ambivalent and inconsistent which is why the assertion of beginnings is so vital. The displaced can learn to utilize and thus celebrate the multiplicity of answers and the complicatedness of such questions as "Where are you going? Where are you coming from? What are you heading for?" which for Deleuze and Guattari "are totally useless questions": for them "[m]aking a clean slate, starting or beginning again from ground zero, seeking a beginning or a foundation—all imply a false conception of voyage and movement" (Deleuze and Guattari: 1992: 23).

In contrast to Deleuze and Guattari's nomadism and concept of the rhizome, the argument here is that metamorphosis and translation always require two points: the point of departure and the moment of transition. In order for identity and the cultural understanding of what it means to be "at home" to take a conceptual turn, it has to be located historically and geographically, it has to "begin" some "where." Going back to the case of the Palestinians, as Edward Said states in his aforementioned conversation with Salman Rushdie, "[t]he further we get away from the Palestine of our past, the more precarious our status, the more disrupted our being, the more intermittent our presence" (Rushdie: 1991: 167).

Deleuze and Guattari state, however, that the "nomad has a territory; he follows customary paths; he goes from one point to another; he is not ignorant of points (water points, dwelling points, assembly points, etc.). But the question is what in nomad life is a principle and what is only a consequence" (Deleuze and Guattari: 1992: 380). Displacement as it is used here considers all units and points of identification as principles as it translates between the here and there without central authority or concluding choices.

For example, in her Euro-American study, *Questions of Travel: Postmodern Discourses of Displacement* (1996), Kaplan compares travel and displacement and examines how notions of home and away, location and dislocation, place and displacement came to play a role in contemporary literary and cultural criticism in Europe and the United States. Unlike traveling where journeying from one point leads to arriving at another, displacement starts somewhere and ends nowhere:

thus, it shares with Deleuze and Guattari's nomadic rhizome its multiplicity and its continually shifting and turning nature. Displacement therefore starts somewhere and takes on a turn, as opposed to an ending. It is a present that is interrupted by a continuously seductive nostalgia but is not romantically allured by it for it is also an independent present, the time of now and here, that has taken a deflection in a new itinerary. Displacement here is a "'postmodern' manifestation of existential homelessness" through which the displaced writer gains "access to a universalised 'experience'" (Kaplan: 2005: 140).

"I do not believe," Kaplan states, "that we are all rootless, existentially adrift, and limitlessly mobile...Nor do I believe that we are all at home, fixed into neat identities, enjoying stable similarities" (Kaplan: 2005; 1994: 26). This point is avidly supported throughout this project. Sam Selvon's Foster, for example, the protagonist of his most philosophical and Joycean-styled work *An Island Is a World* (1955), reinforces this idea and states that "[a]n island is a world and everywhere that people live, they create their own worlds." "But sometimes that world is small," Foster adds. "Sometimes you feel as if you are at the top of it, and you want more. Your mind is cramped" (Selvon: 1993: 73). Near the end of the novel, Foster realizes, however, that "you can't belong to the world, because the world won't have you. The world is made up of different nations, and you've got to belong to one of them, and to hell with the others" (Ibid: 107). Selvon's novel emphasizes the fact that one has to represent a particular experience of a particular place while reflecting on the world—hence the novel's title. This can be demonstrated through Foster's imagining of Trinidad as a dot on the globe; Foster transmits thoughts into the universe the way an RKO Radio radiates from a single place while simultaneously broadcasting to the universe. One, according to Selvon's narrative, cannot free-float or claim no historical specificity and be nomadic and thus claim to be a "citizen of the world." One is not only and merely a human being who does not belong, or belongs everywhere by virtue of belonging nowhere, because

when you leave the country of your birth, it isn't like that at all. Other people belong. They are not human beings, they are Englishmen and Frenchmen and Americans, and you've got to have something to fall back on too, you can't just go up and say, "Hello fellow being, I'm new here, and I'm looking for a job." Or you can't go to the United Nations and say, "Look, I don't belong to any country, I have no ties of any sort to any particular nation. Maybe I could help you sort out some of your problems."

(Selvon: 1993: 106)

The concept of displacement in particular "appears to some critics to be neutral" (Kaplan: 2005: 3), but it is important not to let it slide toward nomadology for this concept promotes a floating belonging to everywhere, to the world, by virtue of belonging nowhere. This is because, as Kaplan points out, belonging everywhere is "another manifestation of imperialism" and so "no one can be fully belonging everywhere because the world is not equally available to be occupied or represented or identified by any subject" (Ibid: 127). Nomadology is thus set against history (Kaplan: 2005; 1994: 89). The nomad's movement therefore cannot be tracked or linked to a starting point.

Among different states of displacement (exile, homelessness, expatriation, immigration, emigration, travel, tourism, refugees, and émigrés), Kaplan concludes that "[n]omadism is the most attenuated concept in relation to location" (Ibid: 143). It is therefore a loose concept that almost erases the concept of home, of the gravitation to a starting point, a beginning. Displacement is understood here more rigorously; it is more closely related to the concrete reality of the state of exile brought about by the material and physical movement in the crossing of frontiers and borders. Equally, displacement can be a benefit aesthetically, as the writers here testify, not to mention that it creates conditions for critical distance. Exilic experience can undergo metamorphosis too, moving from the melancholic to celebratory detachment. Furthermore, the classical definition of exile has nowadays been playfully overturned, to signify a break from the daily routine, to open up restricting boundaries in order to escape what Joyce once called the national and religious "nets" that caused him cultural paralysis (Joyce: 2001), to seek adventure, to hunt for artistic vocation, to seize what critical distance has to offer, and to represent what Rhys calls, in *Wide Sargasso Sea*, the "other side": because "[t]there is always the other side, always" (Rhys: 1966: 82).

This notion of displacement therefore stands in contrast to what, for example, Naipaul celebrates, via his protagonist in *The Mimic Men* (1969), in belonging to a community or belonging to a past: he sees it an excessive sense of responsibility. In being rootless or free-floating, R. Singh, Naipaul's protagonist, celebrates "the absence of responsibility" (Naipaul: 1969: 11). In response, it is best to quote Said on geography and power: "none of us is outside or beyond geography, none of us is completely free from the struggle over geography" (Said: 1994a: 6). Mahmoud Darwish, the Palestinian national poet and exile, reinforces such ideas by reminding us that we, as human beings, are desperately and naturally nostalgic, and that "we are sick with hope, and sentimental!" (Darwish: 2010: 85). To be rootless and not to belong is to an extent being unsentimental, unemotional, and less human. A displaced person therefore is sickly hopeful and sentimentally nostalgic. To be displaced is not to celebrate the absence of responsibility, but to celebrate responsibility toward a beginning, without being locked in its attic.

Section 2: What Is Displacement? Answering by the Example of *Nuzooh*

I

An access to historic memory is always significantly important because it provides the context for politically fruitful invention. My understanding of displacement therefore has emerged and emanated from my own experience of exile and familial Palestinian experience of multiple exilic displacements. The Colonized Territories of Palestine, particularly as represented in the works of Edward Said and Mahmoud Darwish, are flagged up in this section as exemplary for the current and ongoing struggle for self-determination under Israeli colonialism, the enduring struggle in preserving memory and thus the nation, and a historical association with the semantic as well as the alienating and dislocating nature of the concept of displacement.

Although the majority of the Palestinians' historic circumstance and color of skin are different compared to those of the Indians and Pakistanis, the Indians of the Afro-Caribbean Diaspora and the West Indians, they all share a history of oppression as postcolonial subjects whose homes have become imaginary constructs and whose identities are still burdened with a British colonial history.

The concept of displacement is in part defined here therefore within the context of the Palestinian displaced narrative and exilic experience of scatterings. The Arabic translation of the word displacement is *Nuzooh*, a noun that is derived from the verb Nazaha, which literally means to forcibly (e)migrate, to evacuate. Within the Arab world, this particular concept/verb (to evacuate, to be displaced) has always been particular and exclusive to the Palestinian experience after the *Nakba*, The Catastrophe of 1948, and the *Naksah*, The Six-Day War of 1967, which signaled the return of the Jewish diaspora and consequently triggered mass Palestinian displacements. All Palestinians who were forced out of the historic land of Palestine in 1948 are therefore known and labeled as *Lajie'en*, Refugees; whereas those who were displaced after the 1967 Arab–Israeli war are known and labeled as *Naziheen*, Displacees.[4] The Palestinian narrative also consists of multiple displacements: those who left after the *Nakba* of 1948, those who left after the war of 1967, those who left after the first and second Intifadas (rebellion and resistance) in 1987 and 2000, respectively, those so-called Arab-Israelis who remained within the now Israeli territories and hold Israeli identity cards, stateless Gazans, and lastly those third and fourth generations who remain in refugee camps in the Middle East and elsewhere around the globe. This is to be further illustrated in Section 4 of this chapter, where the Jewish diaspora and return is contrasted with the Palestinian experience of exilic displacements.

The understanding of the concept of displacement here is therefore based on both a personal and familial experience of displacements as well as on the works of Edward Said and Mahmoud Darwish. While Said and Darwish are invoked frequently throughout this chapter as well as elsewhere, Mourid Barghouti is singularly invoked here for his understanding of the experience of displacement as multiple and for his referencing of the Palestinian experience of exile through his particular use of the concept of displacement in his memoir *I Saw Ramallah*. Evidently, Ahdaf Soueif, the translator of the work from its original Arabic to English, finds it linguistically as well as culturally appropriate to translate the title of the seventh section *Ghorba't* (literally meaning *alienations*) as Displacements to fittingly express Barghouti's Palestinian experience of thirty years of exile outside as well as inside of Palestine.

I Saw Ramallah (published first in Arabic in 2000; published in English in Britain in 2004) episodically and passionately narrates Barghouti's homecoming after thirty years of exile. It is a work of world literature, not only because of its subject matter (exile and displacement, return and its irreconcilability, colonialism and postcolonialism, memory and nostalgia) but also because it is written by a Palestinian exile, published by the American University Press in Cairo, and has been translated into English by Ahdaf Soueif, a first-generation Egyptian writer in English. It is also one of the rare occasions where Edward Said has ever written a foreword for a Palestinian work of literature, calling it "one of the finest existential accounts of Palestinian displacement that we now have" (Barghouti: 2004).

Barghouti registers the concept of displacement in the very opening section titled *Displacements* (*Ghorba't*) where he states that

Displacements are always multiple. Displacements that collect around you and close circle. You turn, but the circle surrounds you. When it happens you become a stranger *in* your places and *to* your places at the same time. The displaced person becomes a stranger to his memories and so he tries to cling to them. He places himself above the actual and the passing. He places himself above them without noticing his certain fragility. And so he appears to people fragile and proud at the same time. It is enough for a person to go through the first experience of uprooting, to become uprooted forever. It is like slipping on the first step of a staircase. You stumble down to the end.

(Barghouti: 2000: 131)

Displacement therefore is encompassing, claustrophobic, estranging, ambivalent, multiple, and uprooting. This forces the displaced to cling to history, to hang on to memory; for when one is nostalgic, one remembers; for displacement alienates one from both time and place. And the displaced becomes alienated not only from places but also from himself, thus becoming fragile and disoriented. The *Oxford English Dictionary* registers the word displacement in 1605 as "the removal of someone or something by someone else which takes their place." In other words, substitution. This also echoes the Palestinian experience of displacement whose place has been substituted by the Jewish Diaspora. Furthermore, the dictionary describes the concept as "the enforced departure of people from their homes, typically because of war, persecution, or natural disaster." On the other hand, the *Dictionary's* psychoanalytic conception of displacement is "the unconscious transfer of an intense emotion from one object to another" (*OED:* 2010: 505). Displacement *is* indeed a removal: a removal from a geographical place, or an imaginative space, *from* a precolonial history; a removal *because of* colonial past; and a displacement *in* a postcolonial present. It is also an intense emotional transference that is carried across space and, ultimately, time.

The concept of displacement, however, has been expanded. For example, it is no longer exclusively or merely enforced and/or unconscious as the dictionary defines it. Furthermore, the conventional meaning of the figure of the exile no longer relates simply to the bourgeoisies either, but to the middle-classes too as it is explained below in the case of the Palestinians. Once defined by Victor Hugo as "a place of punishment" (Hugo: 1994: 69), exile had implied political persecution and a particular, central trauma. "There is no beautiful exile," according to Hugo (Ibid). Now, however, exile is no longer primarily agonizingly paranoiac; nor is it necessarily a radical displacement. Exile can indeed be a cry over a lost home, over the past, but it is also a state within and through which a home and an identity can be reconstructed anew. Exile can be pleasurable. It becomes home through the very experiences and attempts of trying to belong. Or, as the narrator(s) of Rushdie's controversial *The Satanic Verses* say: "the journeying itself was home" (Rushdie: 2006a: 94).

In his *Step Across This Line* (2002), Rushdie describes how a transformed crossing migrant is stripped down in the journeying by the frontier, and "then you are what you are, and you do what you do. This is how it is. What does it matter what you say about people?" (Ibid: 418). "The journey creates us," he adds. "We become the frontiers we cross" (Rushdie: 2002: 410). The melancholic problematics of displacement can therefore be playfully celebratory. In this sense, "[w]hat was initially felt to be a curse—the curse of homelessness or the curse of enforced exile—gets repossessed. It becomes affirmed and is reconstructed as the basis of a privileged standpoint from which certain useful and critical perceptions about the modern world become more likely" (Gilroy: 1993: 111).

Displacement therefore is not merely substitution. Primarily it is multiplicity. Like Said's model of exile, it "promotes innovation and experiment as opposed to [the] authoritatively status quo" (Said: 1994b: 47). As the exile of the soul—displacement is spiritual and abstract as well as physical and concrete. It is the schizophrenic paranoia that grants its beholder a double insight. Here there is no arrival: one might return, but never arrive. The difference between displacement and traveling, for example, is that in traveling one leaves, arrives, and might have to eventually return. Displacement is not merely a journey either: it is an ongoing, continuous, and perpetual eventful odyssey. It becomes a recreational experience through which the displaced is privileged with a creative insight, a vantage point into both the so-called center and the periphery. This kind of insight provides what might be called a thinly universal experience, not exactly a view from nowhere, but greater comparative access to what Appadurai calls "ethnoscapes," "mediascapes," "technoscapes," "financescapes," and "ideoscapes" which are the building blocks of "imagined worlds," or "the multiple worlds" that are constituted by the historically situated imaginations of persons and groups spread around the globe (Appadurai: 1996: 33). In other words, with displacement, the veil of racial, ethnic, and national consciousness is critically reconstructed and a more self-conscious identity and image of the world becomes available. Displacement in this sense opens doors to aesthetic creativity via critical distance.

Displacement is not replacement or substitution, but it does involve ambivalence: estrangement and loss but also creativity and gain; here and now and there and then; tradition and newness, old and new. Moreover, what characterizes the concept of displacement in the end is multiplicity not singularity, achievement not regret or compunction, flexibility not rigidity, continuity not completion, eventual celebration not persistent melancholy. With displacement there is duality; this means that cultural engagement can be antagonistic and/or affiliative; exile can be prosperous and daunting, tragic and comic, consensual and conflictual; and migration can be passive and/or active. Displacement allows for, in Bhabha's words, hybridity; in Gilroy's words, syncreticism. For hybridity/syncreticism means doubleness and not homelessness. It means addition not division.

Displacement (displacement as displacements, since displacement leads only to further displacements) consists of a chain and a series of continuities and ruptures which accentuate and register a beginning, a starting point as opposed to nomadic, free-floating mobility. What this study adds and contributes to knowledge is a revisited concept of displacement in a particular postcolonial time frame pertaining to a particular literary context, with new subject matter that keeps the specificity of identity alive without being caught up in the dangerous nets of nationalism, racism, and/or what Rushdie calls mental ghettoization. It covers two generations of displaced writers, and hence a multiplicity of locations and displacements; in doing so, this revisiting focalizes certain specific characterizations of a body of postcolonial metropolitan literature written in English which are engendered by this very multiplicity of displacements. Displacement is also depicted as a multiple complex of rerouting and rerooting experiences: since displacement rejects the myth of return, settlement, and arrival, and since "once displaced forever displaced," the displaced starts somewhere and reroots him/herself in another place, another experience, forming within him/her an identity that is articulated in the negotiation of these multiple experiences.

Hence, displacement does not glorify or romanticize a home or a return to a home, wherever and whatever it may be; rather it celebrates a beginning, a starting point. It embraces the need to have, in Samuel Selvon's words, "something to fall back on" (Selvon: 1993: 106); what Lamming calls "an acre of ground in the New World" (Lamming: 1960: 50). Displacement celebrates therefore an identity's history, its gravitating "somewhere," as well as its simultaneous undergoing of transformation, its multiple metamorphoses.

For the exilicly displaced, home and identity resemble the metaphoricity of the postcolonial age; that is, the turning from a melancholic paranoia to a schizophrenic celebration, from a finished project to an actively shifting process, from selection to interaction, and from representation-through-opposition to representation-through-negotiation. Identity is no longer a fixed entity or a destination that is finalized or gravitated to a past or a fixed position. Home is no longer a promise or a place that is God-given. Displacement is

> that moment of the scattering of the people that in other times and other places, in the nations of others, becomes a time of gathering. Gatherings of exiles and émigrés and refugees; gathering on the edge of "foreign" cultures; gathering at the frontiers; gathering in the ghettos or cafes of city centres; gathering in the half-life, half light of foreign tongues, or in the uncanny fluency of another's language; gathering the signs of approval and acceptance, degrees, discourses, disciplines; gathering the memories of underdevelopment, of other worlds lived retroactively; gathering the past in a ritual of revival; gathering the present. Also the gathering of people in the diaspora: indentured, migrant, interned; the gathering of incriminatory statistics, educational performance, legal statutes, immigration status.
> (Bhabha: 2005: 199)

Because displacement is characteristically about temporariness, it also demands improvisation on everyday's new beginnings. Favoring flexibility over stability, multiplicity over singularity, displacement becomes a state of mind that neither places or passports, nor returns or homelands can ever contain. The status of the displaced is always complicated. And the Diaspora becomes the meeting space of these intellectuals. Diaspora and Creolite have in common a mutual operational system; they both construct identities from the debris of historical and future possibilities.[5]

Displacements therefore are the "recreational travel experiences [which had been restricted] only to whites while viewing black peoples' experiences of displacement and relocation through different types of travelling...refugees, migrants and slaves" (Gilroy: 1993: 133). In displacement, the veil (of race and ethnicity), a metaphor for the specter of segregation and isolation in the discussion of black culture, is lifted and a second insight, a vantage, privileged standpoint, is being gifted through which new self-consciousness is articulated and expressed. For displacement is the decoding of racial and national consciousness that is most likely to be centrally anti- and countercolonial; it can be the self-discovery of a new consciousness that is experienced outside the closed and restricting codes of the original environment, the so-called Oedipal territory.

Finally, facilitated by low-cost international transportation, or the so-called budget airlines, the Second World War, and advanced modern technology, displacements and other forms of cosmopolitan dispersals, i.e., immigration, exile, and Diaspora, have interrupted "the point at which the West began to universalise itself" and at the same time have become, from inside the metropolis, a part of its "attempt to construct the world as a single place, with the world market, with globalisation and with that moment when Western Europe tried to convert the rest of the world into a province of its own forms of life" (Hall: 2001: 18). This emphasizes unclosed cultural translation between here and there in which cultural languages learn from one another too. In this process, the inside is translated from the outside and vice versa. "Easterns and Others" are in here "in the cosmopolitan metropolis, trying to become like you, but also making you different" (Ibid: 19). Thus the very physical existence of the formerly colonized and colored Other within the metropolitan center displaces the paradigm of centrality and peripherality. The world, thanks to displacements and migrations, should no longer be thought of culturally or politically in terms of center and periphery; "it has to be defined in terms of a set of interesting centres, which are both different from and related to one another" (Ibid: 21).

Displacement as it is used in this project refers primarily to the diasporic masses engendered after the Second World War in London and the consequent "McDonaldization of the world" (Hall: 2001: 21), something that Rushdie refers to as "the Pepsi-Cocacolization of the planet" (Rushdie: 2006a: 406), both referring to the global capitalist system in which the postcolonial displaced migrant is prospering whilst residing in what Hall calls "the belly of the beast" (Hall: 1994: 392). This is the metropolitan capitalist center, London, and it is undoubtedly the case that the "economic horizon of capitalist internationalization remains crucial to any understanding of how sensibilities of identity are dislocated between cultures and territories" (Lavie and Swedenburg: 2001: 6). Deterritorialization offers a good example here as it stands for the dislocation of the authority over culture and territory, self and place. It therefore promotes nomadic existence in the sense that it deals with the whole world and narrows the gap between cultures, territories, selves, and places. The Internet, for example, deterritorializes all communities that have access to the Internet and forces it to engage with a global culture. The mass media comes in to do the reterritorialization: the restructuring of the deterritorialized territory so that it starts producing global culture itself.

The so-called Eurocentric powers control the underdeveloped world through such globally capitalist political economy. "The Eurocentre's multinational and transnational corporations take advantage of their global organization of production to increase their hegemony" (Ibid). Consequently, very crucial to the "globalization of production processes has been the multinationals' exploitation of female labor at extremely low rates. And also by undocumented migrants in low-paying sweatshop conditions" (Ibid). Globalization clearly can be negative when associated with globalized capital and its "inequitable distribution of global resources" (Rushdie: 2002: 298). Globalization is negative when it creates "global defensiveness" that leads "towards apartheid, towards ethnic cleansing, towards the gas chamber" (Ibid). This kind of globalization also leads to the conflation of cultures. In this context, displacement acts as a critique of homogenizing processes endemic to globalization because it promotes the open, fluid, and constantly changing. After all, "[i]s not melange, adulteration, impurity, pick'n'mix at the heart of the idea of the modern, and hasn't it been that way for most of this all-shook-up century?" (Rushdie: 2002: 298).

II

Displacement can be divided into shifting orders (geographical, psychological, and cultural, the latter being subcategorized into linguistic displacement), which influence the experiences of self, space, and time. What lies at the heart of the four orientations of displacement generally, and geographical (colonial) displacement in particular, is a displacement from history, or what one can call a historical displacement. To start an elaboration of the latter is to give the other subcategories a sort of historic background and platform; it is also to demonstrate the interrelationship between history, psychology, geography, culture, and language. Colonial presence first intervenes between the native and his/her land/place to which he/she belongs and connects historically. A place on the map is ultimately a place in history. It also disrupts the colonized's self/identity, let alone other subsequent disruptions such as linguistic displacement and internal exile. Second, when colonizing forces withdraw new waves of migration and displacement are initiated.

For example, the Pakistani before the partition of India and Pakistan experiences displacement in colonialized India, which is complicated and carried forward in decolonized India and then partitioned Pakistan, and continues in the promised land of England. In the case of the Palestinian exile, exilic displacements start in the decolonized Arab Peninsula, are carried forward and complicated in the partition between Transjordan and Palestine, the return of the Jewish Diaspora, the beginning of the Palestinians', once in 1948 and again in 1967, the return of a few of its refugees to the Colonized Territories of Palestine, and/or indeed their exilic displacement around the world. For the West Indian or Caribbean, historical displacement starts in colonized Africa to which the displaced now returns through "a spiritual journey of discovery" since the "original" Africa is no longer there. What remains is the Africa "as we re-tell it through politics, memory and desire" (Williams *et al*: 1994: 398). The journey continues across the Atlantic to the decolonized West Indies, and eventually ends in the so-called mother country, England. Exceptionally, Naipaul's journey from Trinidad to his ancestral home in India passes through an English experience to which he is indebted. Naipaul's "aloofness and seemingly ontological rootlessness," however, leads him to be portrayed as "an eternal migrant" who keeps on "asserting his homelessness, while considerable numbers of genuinely disowned people battle to be acknowledged as legitimate members of the society he is at liberty to reject rhetorically although he depends upon it in every way" (Kaplan: 1996; 2005: 125).

The first order of displacement is the geographical and territorial that is concerned with place/space. It refers to familiar or familial places, countries of exile and refuge, or adventurous relocations. It is partly concerned with the leaving from and arriving in geopolitical places, homelands, physical, and spatial here and there. The geographical is concerned with both real, concrete places and metaphorical, abstract, imaginary spaces. Admittedly, however, an imaginary place is not completely fictional and fantasized because it is anchored in reality. It "is assumed to be *there*: a substance that is relatively immune to the workings of time" through memory (Kaplan: 1996; 2005: 147). Space is therefore an abstract, imaginative idea based on a concretely constructed place. In other words, imaginary homelands are in essence homelands; they are an "imaginative *truth* [that are] simultaneously honorable and suspect" (Rushdie: 1991: 10; my italics). They are a creation that is built on the remains of memories and to which one can feel that one belongs. Their metaphoric designation for and of a place is in itself based on a place that exists even though figuratively, even as an absent presence. "Daily life in the real world," Rushdie writes eleven years after his publication of *Imaginary Homelands* (1991), "is also an imagined life. The creatures of our imagination crawl out from our heads, cross the frontier between dream and reality, between shadow and act, and become actual" (Rushdie: 2002: 436).

With the emergence of imaginative homelands and spatial metaphors, "space is in the midst of a renaissance. It finds a new reassertion in the postmodern critical practices" (Rushdie 2002: 147); displacement has significantly contributed to such critical practices with all its modes: immigration, exile, diaspora, and expatriation. In fiction, one can indeed find examples of geographical displacements in works where the protagonist, his double or alter-ego, emigrates from or immigrates to a place different in language and culture than the natal one. What is important, however, is the multiplicity of places within one narrative of a novel which implies the multiplicity and diversity of the age during which it is written: global, displaced, hybrid, multiple, mobile, unstable, plural, and syncretic. Examples of this multiplicity and diversity can be found in the representation of Bangladesh and England in *Brick Lane*; suburban and cosmopolitan England, India, Pakistan, and America in *The Buddha of Suburbia*; Trinidad, London, and Jamaica in *The Lonely Londoners*; England and Dominica in *Wide Sargasso Sea*; Libya, Egypt, and England in *Season of Migration to the North*; and the Congo, Belgium, and England in *Heart of Darkness*.

The second category of displacement is cultural which is concerned with natural and cultural identities, filiative (philological) and affiliative (philosophical) identities, past and present, cultural change, alienation, resistance, integration, mimicry, and/or assimilation. Cultural displacement is concerned with the cultural environment and of the cultural space and background in which one resides or is born. It is also concerned with language as an identity; this will be further discussed below as linguistic displacement is subcategorized under cultural displacement. To be removed from an imagined regular, habitual cultural and familiar environment is to be culturally displaced. To be dispossessed from the authorization and legitimatizing of one's natal culture and its judicial power is to be culturally displaced.

The cultural can be represented and registered in fiction in the changes of costumes and colors, weather and climate change, food and cuisines, customs and traditions, rituals and religion. It is also concerned with what could be termed racial displacement which will be discussed thoroughly in Chapter 2. Upon their arrival in London, the Windrush Generation, for example, was explicitly exposed to racial abuse and exclusion, and cultural differences, or what is usually referred to as the unwritten rules of the city. "Caribbean people's ignorance of customs such as lining up in an orderly manner at a bus stop; their insistence on wearing loudly coloured shirts and ties: complaints such as these are commonly directed towards new groups of immigrants in any place at any time" (Phillips: 2001: 271). Cultural displacement can be seen in the bitterness expressed toward and affected by the unwritten rules of the metropolitan city.

These practices, values, and changes/contrasts within the national frontiers or geographical borders are what differentiate one place from another and one culture from another. But being outside this community, this society and culture provides one with a critical distance. "Distance," Kaplan states, "forges new affiliation between past and present, home and away that are no longer based on religion or family." She summons Said's traveling theories and emphasizes his usage of the term and figure of the exile to construct a worldly, cosmopolitan set of linked affiliations that can destabilize nationalist or religious identities. Said's traveling theory in essence is about the fact that a theory comes from somewhere and is marked by places of origin. Theory (looking and viewing in Greek) is a product of displacement and of exile and comparison. For Said, theory consists of four stages of travel: an origin; a distance traversed; acceptance or rejection; and finally a transformed idea occupying a new position in a new time and place. A traveling theory therefore exemplifies the stages through which the exilic displaced migrant goes. From an origin, through and across time and place, and depending on a subsequent acceptance or rejection, the displaced becomes either passive or active, translated or not, transformed or not. A traveling theorist, or the exilic displaced intellectual, is not exiled but rather changed and translated by the traveling, simultaneously marked by his/her origin. Said's work therefore travels between the so-called First and Third World.

To be distanced from and to be outside the dominant culture is to have a reborn consciousness; it is to have an aesthetic distance which gifts one with a critical and a distinctive point of the filiative and naturally registered. To be outside is then to have the familiar and acceptable questioned, to question what otherwise would have remained unquestioned, and to destabilize the seemingly fixed. Thus, distance brings and opens up doors for criticism. Displacement is not only a distance, it is also an aesthetic distance. "Through this painterly distance a vivid strangeness emerges; a partial or double 'self' is framed" (Bhabha: 2005: 20). In and through distance, a new consciousness is born. The filiative, natal culture devolves and transforms into becoming affiliative *because of* cultural displacement and geographical distance.

Observations about architectural designs can be seen as marking cultural differences between two places; architectural differences within the lived environment shape and nurture nostalgia for a real or imagined home and indeed mark a place's cultural difference. Once such difference is marked and recognized, the displaced compares and turns the reflection of difference inward toward the self; hence, nostalgia overwhelms its beholder or subject and translates into homesickness. Other aspects of cultural change extend to involve language, clothes and fashion, food and cuisine, weather, and politics.

The subcategory of cultural displacement is linguistic displacement that is concerned with acquired and required languages and tongues. In fiction, this can be seen in the new english language appropriated to carry the burden of a colonial experience and carry a postcolonial voice. Displacement is a passage that involves a crossing of language frontiers so that "[a]nyone who has crossed a language frontier will readily understand that such a journey involves a form of shape-shifting or self-translation. The change of language changes us. All languages permit slightly varying forms of thought, imagination and play" (Rushdie: 2002: 434).

Writing in the language of the former colonizer, however, is in itself troubling. In contemporary english fiction, this can be seen among generational division of immigrants (for example, the correction of grammatical mistakes between daughter (third generation) and father (first generation) in *Brick Lane*); or the creolizing of English (the language of the Boys in *The Lonely Londoners*). "In each case a condition of alienation is inevitable until the colonising language has been replaced or appropriated as english" (Ashcroft *et al*: 2002: 8–9). To speak in english instead of English, to narrow the gap of linguistic displacement imposed upon the (formerly) colonized, and to contextualize it is to become postcolonial. To be postcolonial is to write in English and vice versa. The formerly colonized takes English and makes it his/her own. To create new vocabularies, codes, and "language" requires one to develop a new sense of "place" and subsequently another of "self," that is a new consciousness and thus anew perceived reality. One needs to "interrogate and subvert the imperial cultural formations" in order to develop a "conscious de-colonising stance, the experience of a new place" which also demands a new language for expression and articulation (Ashcroft *et al*: 2002: 11).

Language, Ngugi wa Thiong'o tells us, "has a dual character: it is both a means of communication and a carrier of culture" (Williams *et al*: 1994: 439). Ngugi, however, believes that a writer should abandon the colonizer's language and revive the tribal and national tongue of his/her own people. On the other hand, Nigerian writer Chinua Achebe argues that the postcolonial writer "should aim at fashioning out an English which is at once universal and able to carry his peculiar experience" (Williams *et al*: 1994: 431). Achebe encourages fashioning a new English that carries the African experience of writers such as Ngugi and Achebe himself within it. Ngugi sees in language a linguistic and a cultural side: the linguistic one is the communicative speech and written word of a language in use; the cultural, on the other hand, is the experience carried within this linguistic expression. He asks why "should an African writer, or any writer, become so obsessed by taking from his mother-tongue to enrich other tongues?" He adds, "[w]e never asked ourselves: how can we enrich our language?" (Ibid: 435).

English has become the world's language. Alternating between the languages of the formerly colonized writer shows an alternation and a reconfiguration of the language and the decolonizing of the mind in which it thinks. To write in english is therefore decolonizing, freeing. It is an opportunity to reach a wider audience and cross borders to make the African experience and literature more international. Those African writers, Achebe writes, "who have chosen to write in english or French are not unpatriotic smart alecks with an eye on the main chance—outside their own countries. They are by-products of the same process that made the new nation-state of Africa" (Ibid: 430).

Language after all is not only a mere linguistic sign that expresses a human experience and shares among its participants a commonality of existence and intercourse with nature as well as with each other. It is also and primarily a cultural reference to a historical experience.

An example here would be Creole English used by West Indians of African descent, born and naturalized in the Caribbean. This language is characterized by exaggerated grammatical errors and its mixing of English and another language. The broken language used in the West Indian novels reflects the broken identity of its speakers. Selvon uses such language in *The Lonely Londoners*: "Jackson is a bitch," Moses says, "he know that I seeing hell myself" (Selvon: 2006: 3). english conveys and delivers the sound of the immigrant/emigrant in the early 1950s and 1960s emphatically. Another feature is the injection of foreign languages within the english text. Examples can be found in Achebe's Igbo idioms and other phrases in *Things Fall Apart* and the introduction of Urdu in Rushdie's work.

Linguistic appropriation in this case is an example of how histories are indeed interdependent—contrapuntal. As slavery, however dehumanizing, was positively influential in facilitating the creation of transnational Black identities (by its urging Black folks toward group consciousness and their ability to easily mingle and adapt to other ethnicities and cultures), colonization had left India and its peoples and tribes sharing a language. Language is a crucial aspect of one's identity and of one's cultural consciousness and social awareness and is one of the first attributes one acquires when one is born into a new world. Language therefore does not only become a tool or a means of communication and self-expression but also primarily a way of understanding and seeing. Different experiences therefore speak different languages: english becomes the language of the cosmopolitan exilicly displaced migrant.

Language offers access to meaning, to enunciation, to the significance of things that are lived across time and space. Its codes signify from the places they are learnt; ultimately, they signify from the world around us. The language and words of the displaced, their narratives and stories debunk representations and other stereotypical images; they debunk, in Said's words, the "Orientalist vision," the vision that is "fixed, laid out, boxed in, imprisoned." In other words, the immigrant and displaced writer dissembles the "western imaginative geography" that is based on the Orientalist vision whose "self-containing, self-reinforcing character [is] of a closed system" (Said: 2003b: 68–70). Displacement therefore dismantles such system by presenting (hi)stories in a new language. In the course of discussing displacement, language is paramount because it "becomes the medium through which a hierarchal structure of power is perpetuated, and the medium through which conceptions of 'truth', 'order', and 'reality' become established" (Ashcroft *et al*: 2002: 7). english becomes therefore a postcolonial voice.

Between the strange and unfamiliar and its opposite (familiar culture, language, place, and history), the displaced is caught between the melancholy of loss, nostalgia, homesickness, loneliness, estrangement, change, and instability and the celebration of creativity, newness, openness, and flight from national and religious nets. The displaced is located in-between the poetics and the problematics of displacement. Thus the four aforementioned categories of displacement all imply and produce negative as well as positive side effects. What the next section suggests is that a disorienting and melancholic condition such as exilic displacement can be pleasurable and poetic through its very problematics: "gain through pain."

Displacement is fundamentally concerned with self: its depths and consciousness, its dreams and complexities, its identity, and experiences of restlessness, desolation, isolation and suffocation, memories, uncertainty, and nostalgia. In contemporary metropolitan postcolonial english fiction, symptoms of psychological anxiety and psychic splitting are exemplified in symptoms such as hallucinations and deliriums, insomnia, amnesia and seclusion, dreams and nightmares (for example, Nazneen's mother's lecturing her while asleep in *Brick Lane*; Gibreel Farishta's phantoms and dreams in *The Satanic Verses*). They can also be associated with other redemptive and/or fulfilling actions such as burning and demolishing places (for example, Antoinette's burning of Mr Rochester's mansion in *Wide Sargasso Sea*); or building and constructing places (for example, R. Singh's buying land and building on it in *The Mimic Men*; or the demolishing of cottages and the building of a new house in *The Enigma of Arrival*). They can also be studied through narrative devices and techniques such as (semi-)autobiographical narrative, nonlinear narrative, and unreliable narrators (for example, Karim in *The Buddha of Suburbia*; Saleem Sinai in *Midnight's Children*). Along with nonlinear narratives, the structures of which mimic the human memory in its disjointed assimilation and marshaling of past and present, unreliable narrators are often used so that "[w]hen attacked for his views, the writer can then claim to have written a work of the imagination which he never intended to be read as fact" (Alexander: 1990: 143).

Sexual metaphors are also another important device used in the depiction of the process of psychological displacement, that is, in the depiction of the displaced's desire to escape through sexual empowerment. Part of the compensation for exilic displacement can indeed be expressed in sexual metaphors. Examples are those of "the boys" in Selvon's *The Lonely Londoners* and Karim in *The Buddha of Suburbia*. In the latter, Kureishi uses sexuality as a journey from repression to liberty as Karim's identity develops.

Other features of psychological displacement include suicide, seeing ghosts and spirits, changes of names and nicknames which is seen as a psychic fission (for example, the black Briton Ali Abdulrahman also known in *Bombay Duck* as Gerald Blossom); and more recently, body transplantation and metamorphosis as in Adam's operation where his mind is transferred into a younger body in Kureishi's *The Body* (2002). In the latter, the story affirms how the mental and the physical, concrete and abstract (that is, mind and body; identity and homeland) cannot be separated. "A man's body and his mind, with the utmost reverence to both I speak it, are exactly like a jerkin, and a jerkin's lining;—rumple the one,—you rumble the other" (Sterne: 2009: 107). Kureishi's novel also confirms Auerbach's view that "mind and body must not be separated" (Auerbach: 1993: 303) as he eschews realism in order to depict the idea that people and their identities can be caught or dehumanized in the physical body and natural world. Adam has a narcissistic and/or masochistic desire to be objectified and commodified. This desire has to do with sexuality as he wishes to turn his body into meat or pornography. It is an escape through sexual empowerment.

The constant internal and external changes the displaced figure is subjected to, the inner impulses that provoke imagination, memory, and nostalgia, the splitting of the psyche in what Du Bois calls double consciousness,[6] and what Freud called psychic fission and the multiplicity inherent in resistance and adaptation, is referred to here as psychological displacement. In such displacement, the displaced suffers from what Aciman calls a "'compulsive retrospection': memories perpetually on overload, seeing, feeling, being doubled in exile. When exiles see one place they're also seeing—or looking for another behind it. Everything bears two faces, everything is shifty because everything is mobile" (Aciman: 1999: 13). One could argue that with psychological displacement whatever is lost is always reconstituted in its displacement since displacement is a process entailing perpetual series of "becomings."[7]

There is always a constant fear, however, of permanent exile, permanent alienation, against which the exile keeps the hope of a return alive. But the exile's return remains hypothetical and mythical. Exile itself becomes home, a spiritual circumstance in which a transnational and transregional cultural diversity and healthier adversity becomes available. It "becomes a condition of the soul, unrelated to facts of material life" (Ahmad: 2008: 86).

A human identity therefore is acquired in a space, across a multiplicity of cultural experiences, whether it is the geopolitical or the imaginary/recreational. These psychological aspects of one's identity, the self, and its interaction with a physical space, a home, are strongly interrelated. What exilic displacement does to this interaction is to deframe it, debunk its origins, and decode its instigating elements. It provides one with new ways of observing and raises questions that otherwise would have been unasked.

Section 3: Nostalgia and Memory between Melancholy and Celebration

In this section, an interrelated connectedness between place, nostalgia, and memory is established to demonstrate the contrapuntal effect between place and the displaced self, its identity and sense of belonging. Memory and nostalgia are particularly addressed here for they accentuate the importance and influence of the past and especially of starting points and the perpetual longing for a return to homely beginnings in the course of displacement. "The malady of homesickness," Kaplan writes,

> that can never be cured without a return home is akin to melancholia. Freud's distinction between mourning and melancholia, between a "normal" period of grieving and a continuing, debilitating fixation on loss, proposes a useful model for the study of modernist exile poetics and politics. This psychoanalytic model located the source of melancholia in unresolved anger toward one who has died or been irrecoverably removed; unable to resolve the conflict or express this anger openly without guilt, the melancholic subject remains in a state of acute loss. When this particular kind of aggression is turned inward, against the self, melancholia becomes a preoccupying state that replaces or fills the space left by death or separation.
>
> (Kaplan: 1996; 2005: 33)

The distinction made by Freud between mourning and melancholia is useful for understanding the persistent sense of loss experienced by the displaced. Melancholia, as a continuing, debilitating fixation on loss is associated with anger: if given expression, this is linked with guilt; if turned inward, it is linked with aggression. This melancholic state thus perpetuates the sense of loss. Only through memories can this sense of loss be stemmed.

Some postcolonial writers have romanticized displacement as a melancholic condition of a desolated self and linked it with the postmodern condition of existential anxiety. For Ahmad, for example,

> [in] an earlier time, right into the heart of modernism, such desolations of the self were still experienced quite frequently as a loss; what postmodernism has done is to validate precisely the pleasures of such unbelonging, which is rehearsed now as a *utopia*, so that belonging *nowhere* is nevertheless construed as the perennial pleasure of belonging everywhere.
>
> (Ahmad: 2008: 157)

Ahmad explains that this metamorphosis and shift of focus from melancholy toward celebration "is by no means new; what *is* new, and decidedly postmodernist, is the emphasis...on the productivity, rather than the pain, of dislocating oneself from one's original community, as well as the idea...of multiple belongings" (Ahmad: 2008: 134).

It seems like the melancholic paranoia of the displaced colonial and modernist has become triumphantly celebrated and replaced with a schizophrenic character. While the colonial, for example, "tries to breathe life into an exhausted stereotype where 'third world' is always located in a clearly defined periphery," the postcolonial writer "addresses the complex, transnational effects of postmodern cultures on a global scale" (Kaplan: 1996; 2005: 84). The modernist melancholic paranoia is now displaced by a postcolonial celebratory schizophrenia. It is schizophrenic for it simultaneously splits the psyche of the displaced and gifts him/her with a double consciousness through which a new system/self is born. It is also schizophrenic for schizophrenia resembles in its doubly splitting and changing nature the hybrid and syncretic identity and double insight the displaced is gifted with.

Contradictory to the paranoid colonial, postcolonial intellectuals voyaged in, they stood outside the Western cultural tradition while they "had a good command of European critical thought inside" (Ahmad: 2008: 207). Moving from the antagonistic toward the affiliative and from the conflictual toward the dialogic turns the displaced postcolonial figure from melancholia to celebration because he/she becomes aware of both worlds at the same time. To go beyond grand narratives assumed and imposed by history "opens up the possibility of cultural hybridity that entertains difference without an assumed or imposed hierarchy" (Bhabha: 2005: 5). Thus, we today live in a world where irrationality and placelessness, melancholy and chaos are becoming more playfully celebrated and where displacement is privileged and no longer considered severely disorienting. Postcolonial British fiction, for example, does not focus exclusively on fragmented identities and paradoxical and unreliable narrators. It departs from a self-asserting national consciousness that is founded on national traditions, literatures, and other comparative studies. It emerges as a parody of the writer's quest for meaning in a chaotic world. As Gilroy says of the Afro-Caribbean and Asian Blacks of the diaspora, it is "displacement, migrations, and journeys (forced and otherwise) which have come to constitute these black cultures' special conditions and existence." It is therefore within the context of these conditions that "the appeal to and for roots and rootedness [is] to be understood" (Gilroy: 1993: 111). The poetics of displacement are to be found in the "in-between spaces [that] provide...new signs of identity" (Bhabha: 2005: 2) and in "restaging the past [which] introduces other...invention[s] of tradition. This process precludes any immediate access to an originary identity or a received tradition" (Bhabha: 2005: 3). This also allows for resourcefulness and creativity which are the essence of the poetics of displacement.

Being displaced is to be dislocated in endless circles without central authority of either the natal cultural identity or the adopted one. Being in-between spaces is to live in the shadow of borders and borderlines; it is to be between passing locations, in transit. In-betweenness, then, provides the displaced with a "fluidity, a movement back and forth, not making any claims to any specific or essential way of being" (Bhabha: 2005: 4). Fluidity is therefore an aspect of the poetics of displacement where in-betweenness, like Bhabha's hybridity, "entertains difference without an assumed or imposed hierarchy" (Bhabha: 2005: 5). Poetics of displacement provide the displaced with (a) a "double vision" (Ibid: 8), (b) an "insider's outsideness...[which] defines a boundary that is at once inside and outside" (Ibid: 20); (c) an "ethical and aesthetic project of 'seeing inwardness from the outside'" (Ibid: 23). Living such double lives (d) "affirm[s] the borders of culture's insurgent and interstitial existence." Living what Bhabha calls "'otherwise' than modernity but not outside it, the Utopian moment is not the necessary horizon of hope"; it is rather a "second coming" (Bhabha: 2005: 26).

The present is then neither a break nor a bonding with the past; the past is no longer "factual" but "constructed through memory, fantasy, narrative and myth." The present hence is what comes "after the break" (Hall: 1994: 395); it is a second coming. Oscillating between melancholy and celebration, between constant mourning and resolved conflict resembles therefore the dialogic negotiation between past and present. They are not separated but coexistent, one feeds the other.

On the other hand, nostalgia accentuates the importance of place, of locality, and the acute loss caused by the removal from it. Nostalgia is derived from the Greek *nostos*, a return home, and *algos*, a painful condition. Synonyms of the word nostalgia also indicate much about its nature: homesickness, longing, reminiscence, and melancholy. It is not only a syndrome of homesickness or of physical detachment from a place. When exiled or displaced, we are "announcing the end of Time, the hour that is beyond measuring, the hour of the exile's return" (Rushdie: 2006a: 215). Such return, however, is impossible, for the home the displaced misses is not geographical anymore; it is a state of mind, imaginary, or a simulated location. Nostalgia becomes a retreat to a personal life and private past since one no longer feels part of public history for it becomes rapidly changing, foreign, and remote.

According to Darwish, nostalgia is

> the excuse for being unable to keep up with the train's passengers, who know their address well... It is an evening visitor, when you look for signs of yourself in your surroundings and do not find them, when a sparrow drops onto the balcony which seems to be a letter from a land you did not love, a land

when you were there, as you love it now, when it is within you. It was a given thing, a tree, a rock; it became the tokens of spirit and thought, a live coal in language. It was air and earth and water, and it turned into a poem... It is the swallowing up of nature by consciousness and unconsciousness, and the complaints of time lost from the sadism of the present.

(Darwish: 2010: 85)

Seeing in nostalgia a passing, uncatchable train, Darwish, the Palestinian exile, experiences home through the eye of the mind: imagination. It is no longer the concrete land. A rock metamorphoses into a poem: the given concrete becomes a poetic formation. Nostalgia is transformative: between the filiative, the given concrete, and the affiliative, the poem. Darwish romanticizes the lost and debris of a so-called home. Rushdie also views nostalgia as a "broken glass"; however, for him "it is not merely a mirror of nostalgia. It is also a useful tool with which to work in the present" (Rushdie: 1991: 12). The perception of the displaced of place becomes confused with perplexed feelings toward the lost past which disrupts one's moment in the current moment. The lost physical place becomes therefore metamorphosed into a nonverbal past and an unwritten history. Place becomes an embodiment of history and a reflection on colonial experience—a mirror of the postcolonial present. The naming of various places in postcolonial fiction can thus be seen as a representation of multiple belongings to multiple moments.

In *Parallels and Paradoxes*, Daniel Barenboim, the Israeli musician, in conversation with Edward Said, the Palestinian musician, avers that he feels "at home" whenever he plays the piano or whenever he travels with his orchestra. "I feel at home in a certain way in Jerusalem, but I think this is a little bit unreal, a *poetic idea with which I grew up.*" He continues:

I feel at home *in the idea* of Jerusalem... I am not a person who cares very much for possessions... or reminisces from the past... my feeling of being at home somewhere is really a feeling of *transition*, as everything is in life. Music is transition, too. I am happiest when I can be at peace with the idea of fluidity. And I'm unhappy when I cannot really let myself go and give myself over completely to the idea that things change, evolve, and not necessarily for the best.

(Said and Barenboim: 2002: 3–4; italics added)

Barenboim finds solace in the homely *idea* of Jerusalem. But this could largely stem from the fact he is a member of the Jewish Diaspora to which Jerusalem had always been the "promise land" of repatriation, the end of the very Jewish Diaspora. He is also a musician: an artist whose words are melodic cries of his exilic soul. Born in Argentina to Russian Jewish parents, a traveler between Germany, Israel, and Russia, a home was never a stable or a fixed concept for Barenboim. Thus he carried home within him, just as Said did, in the idea of Jerusalem which was also nurtured through nostalgia. It is naïve, however, to compare Barenboim's experience to that of Said's. After all, Barenboim is a member of the Jewish Diaspora whose end is ultimately reconciled by the physical return and (re)settlement in Jerusalem. Barenboim's return becomes, then, Said's sending to exile, so to speak, so the nostalgia for homeland is configured very differently in their respective imaginations.

Said's nostalgia functioned more profoundly in his experience as a second-generation Palestinian exile after the Arab–Israeli war in 1967. He is always out of place as a member of a Palestinian exodus, an Arab exile, and an American academic. The overly emotionally charged concept of a home with its nostalgic ties is therefore one Said comes to resent at later stages of his career.

> One of my earliest memories is of homesickness, of wishing that I was somewhere else. But over time, I've come to view the idea of home as being overrated. There's a lot of sentimentality about "homelands" that I don't really care for. And wandering around is really what I like to do most... I ended my memoir *Out of Place* with a similar thought, which I think is quite important- the sense that identity is a set of current, flowing currents, rather than a fixed place or a stable set of objects.
>
> (Said and Barenboim: 2002: 5)

Said might seem overly cosmopolitan or a member of the elites who are detached from the national struggle of the lower classes; he is after all more metropolitan than local, more exilic and hence multiply located as opposed to those Palestinian nationals, for whom he spoke effortlessly and who remain internally exiled in the Colonized Territories of Palestine, fighting for a still colonized land. However, Said's first unofficial memoir, prior to *Out of Place*, is *After the Last Sky*. In the latter, he comments on the lives of scattered masses of Palestinian families in the Middle East and its refugee camps. In this book he presents himself as part of a Palestinian society as opposed to presenting his personal and individual accounts of being displaced as he does in *Out of Place*. Said himself confesses in a conversation with Salman Rushdie that "I found myself writing [*After the Last Sky*] from the point of view of someone who had at last managed to connect the part that was professor of English and the part that lived, in a small way, the life of Palestine" (Rushdie: 1991: 184). Said also seems to personally identify with the discontinuity of Palestinians across the Middle East in those pictures. In *After the Last Sky*, Said's private and public stories intersect: that is, his larger public image as a professor and his small private life and memories as a Palestinian. Nostalgia, it seems, reconfirms the idea that home is never dead; the past cannot be erased, and the idea of home will never be overrated. Ultimately, the sentimentality which Darwish reminds us of is about what it means to be human. And as humans, we belong to and long for places in which we started to acquire meaning of the world we live in.

Memories of different moments are usually registered through senses: smell, touch, sight, sound, and taste. Memory itself can in fact act as the displaced's sixth sense. Darwish too evokes smell in his remembrance of cities. He defines memory as a "personal museum" (Darwish: 2010: 60). At first, Darwish emphasizes the metaphoric designations and synonymy of displacement: migration, traveling, and journeying. Then he accentuates the importance of space and place from which one writes and with which the exile identifies. Eventually, he admits that place exists in other places, contrapuntally; that one occurrence of displacement leads to another; that once displaced, forever displaced: the smell of one city/place reminds him of other cities/places. Memory consists therefore of a chain of disrupted images: memories as channels of displacements. The cities in which Darwish lived and through which he traveled are spaces that are remembered not for what they are but for something else. They are born in his imagination, "not in a suitcase. Only words are qualified in this sunset to repair the breakage of Time and place." He also stresses writing as an avenue to cultural and psychic survival. "Words are the raw materials for building a house," he says. "Words are a country" (Darwish: 2010: 61). The exile converses through writing with his country, through his memory of it.

Darwish fashions a voice that emerges through memories but one that is not entrapped by or in them. He gathers pieces from the past. His rapport with past memories is not an overwhelming romanticism of the lost and left behind. The present had to be narrated and written through and despite the gloominess of a lost past and a vanishing homeland. Now and here, the present is familiarized and appropriated while ironically the past becomes the territory of the imaginary collected memories of shops, smells, corners, and pictures. For nostalgia is not a memory; "rather, it is what has been selected from the museum of memory. Nostalgia is a selector, like an expert gardener; it is the repetition of a memory which has been cleansed of impurities" (Darwish: 2010: 84).

Memory and remembrance, recollection and forgetting can be seen in fiction through flashback literary techniques (analepsis) while the epistolary style exposes the reader into the narrative's stream of consciousness and the character's/writer's psyche. For instance, it is through the nonlinear technique of narratives (the juxtaposition of past and present times and memories, not intertwined but rather in parallel) that the past is summoned and contrasted with the present.

Between the struggle to preserve memory, as in Rushdie's *Midnight's Children*, for example, and the "syntax of forgetting—or being obliged to forget," "the problematic identification of a national people becomes visible." In forgetting, or trying to forget, the displaced is always in agony. To remember is to be reminiscent of the past while living in a different and another time and space. To forget is paradoxically to remember and provoke a historic memory. The more the displaced figure tries to forget, the more he/she remembers. Rushdie favors eclecticism even in his reminiscences. "My bad memory—what my mother would call a 'forgettery'—is probably a blessing. Anyway, I remember what matters" (Rushdie: 2002: 3). It is, however, "this forgetting—a minus in the origin—that constitutes the beginning of the nation's narrative." To keep memory alive then "becomes the basis for remembering the nation, peopling it anew, imagining the possibility of other contending and liberating forms of cultural identification" (Bhabha: 1990: 310–11).

Displacement is always transformed therefore through memory. For memory is a kind of a resurrection from the past, an anthology of snapshots whose arbitrariness has a particular sensation about remembering. Between the original experience and the hallowed remembrance of it, fragments of existence are withdrawn from the time of the past. Salman Rushdie uses memory in *Midnight's Children* as a tool to recover his past in Bombay. He writes:

Memory is truth, because memory has its own special kind. It selects, eliminates, alters, exaggerates, minimizes, glorifies, and vilifies also; but in the end it creates its own reality, its heterogeneous but usually coherent version of events; and no sane human being ever trusts someone else's vision more than his own.

(Rushdie: 2006: 292)

Other displaced writers in this book use memory as a tool for survival too. An example of memory and nostalgia can be found in the very beginning of *The Lonely Londoners* where Moses resents the cold, foggy, and harsh English weather. Selvon begins the story by introducing contrasting sceneries which Moses encounters on the bus on his way to pick Henry Oliver from Waterloo Station as he arrives from the tropical shores of Trinidad. At Waterloo train station, a place of transition, Moses "had feeling of homesickness that he never felt in the nine-ten years he in this country ... this feeling of nostalgia hit him" (Selvon: 2006: 4). To Moses' surprise, Henry arrives wearing "a old grey tropical suit and a pair of watchekong and no overcoat or muffler or gloves or anything for the cold, so Moses sure is some test who living in London a long, long time and accustom to the beast winter" (Ibid: 12). The comparative contrast between the tropical weather of Trinidad is evoked because of the beastly winter of England. The English weather, one of "the most changeable and immanent signs of national difference," serves to revive "memories of its daemonic double: the heat and dust of India; the dark emptiness of Africa; the tropical chaos that was deemed despotic and ungovernable and therefore worthy of the civilizing mission" (Bhabha: 1990: 319).

Section 4: Contrasting Palestinian Exilic Displacements and Jewish Diaspora

I

In an age of rapidly increasing mass migration and displacements, the concept of Diaspora expands and other "global Diaspora[s]" (Cohen: 1997) are formed to incorporate rather larger and wider cultural experiences and ethnic groups. "Airplanes, telephones, tape cassettes, camcorders, and mobile job markets reduce distances and facilitate two-way traffic, legal and illegal, between the world's places" (Clifford: 1994: 304), turning the world into what has been termed a "global village."[8] Diaspora, like displacement, transcends the nation-state, national particularity, and constraints of ethnicity. People move from the national to the transnational. Diaspora then becomes a rhetorically metaphoric label.

The term "Diaspora" no longer retains its conventional significance as an exclusive referent to the Jewish scattering away from the so-called "promised land" but now rather includes larger spheres of cultural and geographical disseminations such as those of the Caribbean, China, Africa, India, Romania, and Palestine. Diaspora now shares meanings with a "larger semantic domain," with other dispersions (Clifford: 1994). This section will go on to stress, on the one hand, the fact that the concept of Diaspora generally carries a strong sense of origination, of territory, and of a national, Oedipal framework, as in the Jewish Diaspora. It is therefore not only dispersal but dispersal *from somewhere*. In this sense, home is not deferred and the diasporic group's consciousness is defined by a strong relationship with it. This also reinforces the importance of keeping the specificity of home and identity alive. On the other, this section will argue that other forms of disseminations register the search for possible cultural turns,[9] like the Palestinians' and, despite differences in historic situations, the South Asian and the Caribbean. Just as much as Selvon's and Lamming's writings and crossing of the Caribbean geographical borders across the Atlantic and to the metropolis of London changed Caribbean consciousness and identity, so did Said's and Darwish's for the Palestinians. In this new consciousness, Palestinian writers celebrate a perpetual multiplicity of exilic displacements. Edward Said uses the term "exilic displacement" with an unsurprising emphasis on the metaphor of "exile" in *Culture and Imperialism* (1993). In the case of the Palestinians, displacement is "perpetual" since, like the nomadic rhizome, it is without ending and always in the state of becoming as opposed to being. Displacement is also "multiple" and pluralized because of the subsequent ongoing disseminations since the Catastrophe of 1948: those who left after the *Nakba* of 1948, those who left after the war of 1967, those who left after the first and second Intifadas (rebellion and resistance) in 1987 and 2000, respectively, those so-called Arab-Israelis who remained within the now Israeli territories and hold Israeli nationalities, stateless Gazans, and lastly those third and fourth generations who remain in refugee camps in the Middle East and elsewhere around the globe. It is furthermore "exilic" since each individual's narrative differs from the other. In this, the individuality of the state of exile is not "tempered by networks of community" nor is it tempered by "collective practices of displaced dwelling" (Clifford: 1994: 329). Reflections on exile nonetheless can apply on experiences of diaspora, but not vice averse.

Throughout such exilic displacements imagination and memories bridge the distance between now and then, between authenticity and allegory. Memory can, as it were, create nations. In the case of the Palestinian exilic displacements, a historic Palestine is preserved in memories but has long been vanished on the political map of the world—once after the accelerated migrations of Israelis during the 1940s and 1950s and thereafter generally, and after the Oslo Accords/Peace Processes particularly (1993–1995).[10] It is for this reason and more that it is difficult to write a Palestinian narrative without being viewed within or against the Israeli one; for both of them are intertwined through a paradoxical interplay as they share many common as well as different things between their sense of identity.

Normally, literature is born out of the womb of a growing sense of national identity. R. Khalidi states

that it is so difficult to perceive the specificity of Palestinian nationalism. This is so partly because of the way in which identity for the Palestinians is and has always been intermingled with a sense of identity on so many levels, whether Islamic or Christian, Ottoman or Arab, local or universal, or family and tribal.

Palestinian narrative therefore "intersects with other powerful narratives, religious and national" (Khalidi: 1997: 6).

In their attempt to articulate a Palestinian national literature, for example, Said stresses the fact that Palestinian literature should not always be written simply as a counternarrative. Rather, Said encourages Palestinians to "force the unitedness of life into a coherent pattern of our own making." For "[w]henever we try to narrate ourselves we appear as dislocations in *their* discourse" (Said: 1986: 140). Palestinian literature therefore should rather represent itself as one of a national significance and experience; such an experience should emanate from and take a turn that forges a new consciousness "where resistance is a necessity, but where there is also sometimes a growing realization of the need for unusual and, to some degree, an unprecedented knowledge." Hence, Palestinian exilic displacements "form a counterpoint (if not a cacophony) of multiple, almost desperate dramas, which each of us is aware of as occurring simultaneously with his or her own" (Said: 1986: 159–69).

Although Palestinian exilic displacements started out just as returning members of the Jewish Diaspora in 1948 signaled the start of Palestinian *Nuzooh*,[11] what the concept of Jewish Diaspora shares with Palestinian exilic displacements is this ongoing activity of inconsistency, of a struggle to articulate an identity (collective, political, historical, national, resistant, etc.), of departure and arrival. Within the current geopolitical circumstances, some Palestinian exiles consider return a Utopia while others consider it a fantasy, a mystic idea. Palestine is no longer a geographical location only, but also a reservoir of memories. What was remembered, however, is now reterritorialized in the imagination. Return here is redundant.

Such return, however, is an essential characteristic of the Jewish Diaspora. Almost half a dozen million refugees and displaced Palestinians around the world have resettled elsewhere outside the

Colonized Territories of Palestine and regenerated and successfully integrated with the host society. Unlike the Jewish Diaspora that is referent to narrow and consecrated frontiers allegedly set for a chosen people, Palestinian exilic displacements share with the Caribbean Diaspora its ability to integrate and its movement from the national to the transnational; for, to draw similarities with the Caribbean experience, it is "through their roots and branches...[that] people themselves make their diasporas. The frontiers of the region are beyond the Caribbean—not only in the consciousness of Caribbean people to be sure, but also in their social conduct, migration patterns and achievements in their places of settlement and sojourn" (Ibid: 153). In *Diasporas*, James Clifford emphasizes Amitav Ghosh's argument (1989) that South Asian Diaspora, for example, "is not so much oriented to roots in a specific place and a desire for return as around an ability to recreate a culture in diverse locations" (Clifford: 1994: 306). In this, Palestinian exilic displacements share with the South Asian Diaspora its ability to reroute identity.[12]

Moreover, Palestinian displacement and Jewish Diaspora mainly differ in the degree of their connection to their real or symbolic homeland since transnational connections linking Diasporas need not be articulated primarily and merely through geography. Displaced Palestinians have imaginatively formed a hominess which has itself become a holder of the temporariness of their exile instead of settlement elsewhere. Here however there is recognition that cultural continuity is disrupted with departure, and thus a point of return is unavoidably lost. "There is no longer any stability," Cohen states, "in the points of origin, no finality in the points of destination and no necessary coincidence between social and national identities" (Cohen: 1997: 175). Such statement reinforces the fact that by virtue of being unstable and displaced the Palestinian, often forcibly rather than voluntarily, opts for articulating homes and identities en-route, selecting mobility over constancy, movement over settlement.

On the one hand, the exilicly displaced Palestinian keeps looking for an alternative home simply because neither is the old one available anymore nor does the new adopted one in any way resemble or bear any relationship to the old; on the other, all returning Israelis are being accommodated in the increasing constructions of settlements in their "promise land" at the expense of the Palestinians. Palestinian exilic displacements and Jewish Diaspora differ mainly in the choice and availability of return as well as their belief in the finality of their points of destinations. They,[13] however, both share an identity that "is centrally defined by collective histories of displacement and violent loss [which] cannot be 'cured' by merging into a new national community. This is especially true when they are the victims of ongoing structural prejudice." In this sense, "[p]ositive articulations of diaspora identity reach outside the normative territory and temporality (myth/history) of the nation-state" (Clifford: 1994: 307). What differs in this sense between the two dispersions, nonetheless, is that while Israelis were subjected to violence and ongoing structural prejudice outside Historic Palestine, Palestinians have been subjected to both violence and structural prejudice by the newly constructed nation-state of Israel within Historic Palestine. Evidently, "Israelis, many of them descended from victims of persecution, pogroms, and concentration camps, have themselves been mistreating another people. We thus find that the sins done to the fathers have morally desensitized the sons to their sins toward others, and have even sometimes been used to justify these sins" (Khalidi: 1997: 5).

Different other types of ethnic and national diasporas (the victimized African, Cultural Caribbean, Trading Lebanese and Chinese, Indian Laboring Diaspora, or even the British colonial Diaspora) also suggest that there is a historical specificity to using the term diaspora. The destruction of Jerusalem was what had presumably sparked the negativeness that surrounded the term diaspora in the first place. After all, diaspora causes its members isolation and insecurity since they will always be alienated by a ruling class. While the Greek diaspora had a positive connotation to it, the Jewish carries connotations of oppression despite its positive "new and exciting way of understanding cultural differences and identity politics" (Clifford: 1994: 307). Diaspora has generally contributed to the understanding of postcolonial politics of home and identity significantly. It also helped the Jewish population particularly, despite a painful and stateless life, to establish a basis of "intellectual and spiritual achievements which simply could not have happened in a narrow tribal society like that of an ancient Judaea" (Ibid). Examples of members of this fruitful Jewish diaspora can be found in Freud, Kafka, Einstein, and Picasso among many others.

Diasporas therefore have their poetics and problematics: celebratory, enriching, and creative factors as well as their fearful, melancholic ones. The poetics are manifest in the open possibilities aesthetic distance and the journeying itself offer, as well as the meeting with other diasporic communities; the problematics are manifest in the agonizing dream of the myth of return and the lack of integration to the host society. Displaced writers of the diaspora can therefore be "service agents filling the cracks and crannies between the great civilisations"

(Cohen: 1997: 102). They also stimulate hybridity which "denote[s] the evolution of new, dynamic, mixed cultures" (Ibid: 131). They have furthermore changed conceptions of home and identity: both are plural, emerging, always in transit, and incoherent as they attempt at "harmonizing old and new without assimilation or total loss of the past"; these are called "cultures of hybridity" (Ibid: 131).

While immigrants and exiles tend to reinvent their past and restage it to synchronize with the present, affiliate with a new language, and integrate into a new cultural system, diasporas tend to maintain rather stronger connections and bonding to their regional place and with traditional cultural values. Stuart Hall stresses that a diasporic experience should be defined, however, by a conception of an identity that "lives with and through, not despite, difference; by hybridity" (Hall: 1994: 401). In this sense, diaspora rejects the "natural" connections to the motherland and transcends them to becoming "cultural" so that natal filiation gives birth to social affiliation. On the one hand, diaspora challenges cultural, ethnic, and national narrowness and Oedipal territorialities. On the other, it opens doors for discovery; that is, to travel "beyond the conventional and the comfortable" (Said: 1994b: 47). It has certainly loosened cultural and national ties but has not broken them. In this sense, a new understanding of diaspora "respects temporal succession, [while it] is not wholly commanded by it. Neither past nor present, any more than any poet or artist, has a complete meaning alone" (Said: 1994a: 2).

Stimulated by critical distance, opened possibilities, and achievements in the places of their sojourn, a network of displaced writers with their traveling theories and shared experiences of exilic displacements can also create an intellectual diaspora whose home is language and intellect. This is evident, for example, in Bhabha's recognition of other displaced writers in the acknowledgment section of his *The Location of Culture*. He draws attention to and thanks Said for his "oeuvre and critical terrain and intellectual project," Spivak for her "excitement," Hall for his "inspiring vision of inclusion," Morrison for her "narrative and historical temporality," Rushdie for "his ideas on migrant and minority space," and Kapoor for his "exploration of sculptural space." Bhabha also acknowledges these "subaltern scholars" for providing and themselves being "examples of historical temporality" (Bhabha: 2005: xxvi). This empathy from Bhabha toward his mutual fellow members of the Diaspora is an acknowledgment of a shared history of marginalization and exclusion. It also indicates a shared and profound understanding of representations of cultural differences and a collective group consciousness based on an exilic experience. All the displaced writers and scholars discussed in this project deal therefore with "fluidity, a movement back and forth, not making any claims to any specific or essential way of being" (Bhabha: 2005: 4). Diaspora can be used here therefore to describe these displaced writers metaphorically, regardless of whether or not they belong to a particular, shared national territory and/or ethnicity. On the contrary, what unite these displaced postcolonial intellectuals are their shared experiences of multiple exilic displacements, their metropolitan position, the colonial experience itself, their nourishing critical consciousness, their reinvention of new forms of reading non-western history and culture, and their creating of new spaces for imagining newness.

The concept of diaspora has been shifted. Stuart Hall for example restructures the definition and uses it "metaphorically, not literally: diaspora does not refer us to those scattered tribes whose identity can only be secured in relation to some sacred homeland to which they must at all costs return, even if it means pushing other people into the sea" (Hall: 1994: 401). Kaplan furthermore describes diaspora as "a postmodern turn in cultural criticism." It is a turn that should encourage racial mixing, hybridity, "cultural creativity," and to "respect the irreducibility and the positive value of cultural differences" (Kaplan: 1996; 2005: 135). Such turn will be further discussed and promoted for in the conclusion of this book.

II

Palestinian exilic displacements are multiple and diverse and therefore cannot be contained in a simple, single narrative. The Palestinian narrative is one of many narratives. It is too various and scattered. The experience of exiled Sunni Palestinians, for example, in Jordan and Syria is different to that of exiled Christian Palestinians in Lebanon. The experience of these two groups is furthermore different to that of the so-called Arab-Israelis living in the current Jewish territories maintaining Palestinian culture and hence pinpointing their existence within Israeli territory and ID cards. Moreover, the experience of those exiles who were dispersed after the *Nakba* (the Catastrophe) in 1948 is different to those dispersed after the Arab–Israeli war in 1967 because the representations and politics of home and identity differ from one generation to another. All the aforementioned differ in their representations and politics from the stateless Gazans, locked up between a hard place and a rock, between Egypt and Israel and who furthermore possess no recognized, legal documentation, or identity to allow them mobility.

This scattering poses the central problem. It is almost impossible to articulate or envisage a single Palestinian narrative. Exilic displacements of Palestinians are therefore too fragmented, too discontinuous, too formless, and too dispersed to be collective and/or communal. What holds the Palestinian experience together, however, is not a single narrative; on the contrary, what holds it together is a multiplicity of narratives inside as well as outside Palestine. What all generations of Palestinians throughout multiple exilic displacements share is an imaginative community based on suffering and exile, on memory, a self-preserving memory without which Palestinians could hardly exist, and a sentimental hope of return.

Although both Salman Rushdie and Edward Said are formed by colonial histories and by peripheral existence within the west, Rushdie uses the term diaspora freely, whereas Said maintains reservations about the term. Said believes Palestinians are always stateless and exilic, even in their own country of birth, the Colonized Territories of Palestine as well as in refugee camps across the Middle East. Palestinians are "out of place" wherever they are, both at home and abroad. Colonial interference inside Palestine has indeed interrupted any possibilities of full identification. Although "identity—who we are, where we are from, what we are—is difficult to maintain in exile" (Said: 1986: 21), Palestinian identity faces a more severe difficulty in maintaining an identity while living inside: an internally eternal exile.

Said differentiates between the Palestinian endless exilic displacements and the conventionally perceived concept of a diaspora. Rushdie sees that Said's viewpoint is distinct in the fact that

> in the West, everyone has come to think of exile as a primarily literary and bourgeois state. Exiles appear to have chosen a middle-class situation in which greater thoughts can be thought. In the case of the Palestinians, however, exile is a mass phenomenon: it is the mass that is exiled and not just the bourgeoisie.
> (Rushdie: 1991: 171)

Diaspora also connotes historically and circumstantially a possibility of an eventual return which has been inevitably lost in the case of the Palestinians. Said points out that The Palestinians' scattering is not a Diaspora because "there is only an apparent symmetry between our exile and theirs [the Jewish]" (Said: 1998: 1949). He emphasizes that the Palestinian, middle- or upper-class, inside or outside of Palestine, continues through multiple displacements while the Jewish always longs for a final return. Ironically enough, the Palestinian displacement has become the result of redemption and return, the primary characters of the Jewish diaspora. The Jewish return, and therefore the end of their diasporic existence, signaled the beginning of Palestinian multiple exilic displacements. Palestinians ironically become "the Jews of the Arab world" (Rushdie: 1991: 173).

A diaspora is normally defined as an involuntary movement of mass population of the same ethnicity—the Jewish and the Armenian, for instance. The question of return, and what Cohen calls "redemption," seems to be a more crucial factor to the mass diaspora compared to the condition of the individual exile. While the exile can be to a certain qualified extent helplessly satisfied with an imaginary constructed homeland abroad and a rerooting series of displacements, the traditional Jewish diasporic figure always longs for a physical return and an ultimate reunion with the Promise Land. The label that describes the state of being diasporic drops once this return is fulfilled. In the case of the Palestinians, however, return is impossible because the cultural distance created has been too disconnecting to bridge, the social gap has been too wide to narrow, and land has gone under many severely damaging cosmetic surgeries. The metaphoric reference to a diasporic identity remains unidentifiable with a past and a land to which the Palestinian can eventually return. Darwish states that upon returning

> [y]ou are distracted from the state you are in by confusion between the curiosity of a tourist, the grief of a visitor and the joy of a returning exile. Three decades of the absence of the self from its place make the place a unique self, make the self a part of a mobile land.
> (Darwish: 2010: 104)

Darwish concludes: "I have come but I have not arrived, I am here but I have not returned!" (Darwish: 2010: 99). Caryl Philips' statement upon arriving back in the Caribbean echoes Darwish's: "I recognise the place, I feel at home here, but I don't belong. I am of, and not of, this place" (Phillips: 2001: 1–5). It is worth mentioning here that although second- and third-generation Caribbeans and South Asians did not emigrate they are still considered a part of the postwar black diaspora discussed in this book.

With the arrival of the West Indians, Pakistanis, and East Indians to the British mother country, a British identity is no longer a purely white one; neither does British fiction take place exclusively in London. It has been broadened and transnationalized by the significant contribution of its immigrants and diasporic communities. Most importantly, one needs to acknowledge that "the movement of ideas or the syncretisation of cultures...are caused by the existence of diasporas" and of its subsequent traveling theories (Cohen:

1997: 175). Diasporas therefore become "capable of bridging the gap between global and local tendencies" (Ibid: 176). Although such a process of bridging the local and the global and bridging cultural differences is never a smooth one, the movement of immigrants and diasporas and the traveling of cultures and theories have made it possible to question again: why cannot we celebrate the resourceful and elevating, celebratory and poetic side of living in Babylon, the radiance of difference? Such a question is promoted throughout the book, but through the next two sections of Chapter 2, such a question is problematized with two burdens: namely color and nationalism.

CHAPTER 2

DISPLACING CULTURAL IDENTITY

Arriving in the western metropolis fresh from a natal environment, the displaced is initially caught between two political, cultural, linguistic, and perhaps religious systems which close upon themselves contradicting each other and prohibiting negotiation and translation. Two main complications arise then: the first is color consciousness and a sense of inferiority which follow from racial discrimination and exclusion; the second is a very strong longing for a familiar culture, religion, and community based on the past and imaginatively configured in the present. The consequence of this conjunction is often the emergence of what Rushdie calls "ghetto mentality" (Rushdie: 1991: 19), which amounts to a self-imposed, diasporic community sanctioned ghettoizing nationalism, walled-in and unable to negotiate an alternative form of existence. This "ghetto mentality" acts as a resistance to racism not to mention the "consumptive" or "consumer" mentality characteristic of western capitalism and endemic in neocolonialism. These two complications impinge profoundly on the struggle to belong and the reformulation of an identity that is neither racially constructed, nor etiologically or nationalistically "locked-in." These complications also explain why, answering the question above, all people cannot live peacefully in Babylon, the radiance of difference.

The following section suggests therefore that the displaced migrant must displace ghettoizing traditional identity politics (filiative, natal, unchangeably fixed, racially coded, closed, absolute, and specific) by articulating a more open (anti-ghettoizing) cultural politics of identity (affiliative, fluid, changing, turning, flexible, and culturally translated). To displace traditional identity politics is to translate between the filiative and affiliative, past and present. To translate is to survive the ghettoizingly nostalgic pulling of the past and the seductive pushing away in the present and finding a way in-between. The word translation, says Rushdie, "comes, etymologically, from the Latin for 'bearing across'. Having been borne across the world, we are translated men. It is normally supposed that something always gets lost in translation." But he remains resolutely optimistic: "I cling obstinately," he avers, "to the notion that something can also be gained" (Rushdie: 1991: 17).

The following section also argues again that a translated cultural identity is one that does not totally break from the past but rather takes on what Hall calls a "cultural turn" (Hall: 2001). The past and its experiences, however, should not accumulate to articulate the migrant's cultural identity[1]; they should rather add *to* the totality of the experiences of the displaced. The literature that came out of such cultural translation and displacement chronicles departures and arrivals, and exposes restlessness and the complexity of being homeless, racially excluded, and self-consciously different.

Section 1: Cultural Identity between Ghettoization and Displacements

I

Cultural identities are normally divided into two kinds: filiative and affiliative. While the former is acquired by birth, the latter is "a method or system acquired affiliatively (by social and political conviction, economic and historical circumstances, voluntary effort and willed deliberation)" (Said: 1983: 25). While one is already in filiation with the natal culture, the other is affiliated by virtue of displacement and distance. The transition between the filiative (that is, natural and natal; biological; by birth; and nationality) and the affiliative becomes the essence of the process of displacement and cultural translation.

All displaced writers look back at their natal places and their pasts through their present identities. This is due to the fact that their natal cultural identity alone becomes insufficient to contain all that is changing and new within the newly adopted cultural environment. The need for a reconstruction, a translation, or a reconfiguration becomes a necessity because melancholy (a persistent mourning) over a lost past keeps the displaced distant from the moment of now and here. Between the host society and the ancestral origins, displaced individuals survive either on memories or on imaginary identifications. This produces an internal, soulful exile and another external traveling: one of thought and within the self; the other is of space and outside the self. Displacement in this sense becomes a "breaking of ties with family, home, class, country, and traditional beliefs [which are seen] as necessary stages in the achievement of spiritual and intellectual freedom" (Said: 1983: 19). Intellectual freedom from the ties of the past therefore cannot be resourceful unless they are negotiated with present ties. For the displaced neither past nor present is efficiently functional or resourceful independently; they must be in negotiation with, as opposed to in exclusion of, one another. In other words, the "transition from a failed idea or possibility of filiation to a kind of compensatory order that, whether it is a party, an institution, a culture, or a set of beliefs, or even a world-vision, provides men and women with a new form of relationship, which I have been calling affiliation but which is also a new system" (Said: 1983: 20).

For Said, the new system of ideas and values "and the systematic totalizing world-view validated by the new affiliative order are all bearers of authority too, with the result that something resembling a cultural system is established" (Ibid: 20). A filiative or an affiliative system could indeed be dangerous when it is independent or set against one another. Affiliation and filiation both establish a new cultural system in a process of dialogic negotiation and translation. Such a new cultural system lies at the heart of the politics of displacement. The interaction and the en-route between filiative and affiliative identities alter bonds or "natural forms of authority— involving obedience, fear, love, respect, and instinctual conflict." After all, the filiative scheme belongs to the realms of nature and of a life from which the displaced departed and because of which remains nostalgic and homesick, whereas affiliation belongs exclusively to culture and society which also "sometimes reproduces filiation" (Ibid). Similar to Said's thoughts on affiliation are Bhabha's. For the latter, there are two "traditions in the discourse of identity: the philosophical tradition of identity as the process of self-reflection in the mirror of (human) nature; and the anthropological view of the difference of human identity as located in the division of Nature/Culture" (Bhabha: 2005: 66). It is, however, in-between "disavowal and designation" that "the very question of identification only emerges" (Bhabha: 2005: 72).

Displacement in this sense becomes a revision, a restaging of the hierarchy and structure of the dominant and authoritative elements and/or values of a cultural identity. In other words, the new system debunks the rigid, imposed, assumed, preconstituted systems. In this, each dominant hierarchy becomes the "single formula, whose power of suggestion imposed solidarity, and which ostracised everything which would not fit in and submit." And dangerously, as Auerbach says, this power of suggestion can produce a temptation that is "so great that, with many people, fascism hardly had to employ force when the time came for it to spread through the countries of old European culture, absorbing the smaller sects" (Auerbach: 1993: 550).

Indeed, Said argues that distance can provoke a nostalgic national consciousness that sends one into a powerful assertion of natal place, a glorified sentimentality of nation and culture, the overrated myth of origin, and thus reaches stages of defensive nationalism or even chauvinism. He states that nationalism "affirms the home created by a community of language, culture, and customs; and by doing so, it fends off exile, fights to prevent its ravages." Furthermore, all nationalisms in their early stages "develop from a condition of estrangement"; and estrangement is at the heart of the state of exile. There is a very thin line, therefore, between nationalism and the rhetoric of belonging. A homeland with its borders and frontiers becomes the landmark of such identity and belonging. "And just beyond the frontier between 'us' and the 'outsiders' is the perilous territory of not-belonging" (Said: 2001a: 176). Distance, alienation, and estrangement may indeed send the displaced into defensive nationalism. The difference between displacement as it is understood in this thesis and nationalism lies in displacement's nature as a "discontinuous state of being."

II

Stuart Hall is strongly influenced by W. E. B. Du Bois, the African-American activist and "the first black sociologist" (Gilroy: 1993: 114), particularly with his concept of double consciousness where Du Bois stresses that one needs a double perspective on race and identity. Hall and Du Bois, however, share an Otherness, coming from the periphery, from a closed world. Such a world is a ghettoized, imposed, rigid, and preconstituted system. What Hall goes on to suggest, however, is that while one is normally bound by virtue of birth to a certain place, the newly adopted place should not be of a lesser importance: "you also have to be true to your own culture of debate and you have to find some way to begin to translate between those two cultures. It is not easy, but it is necessary" (Hall in Adams: 2007). Once this process is negotiated, differences are acknowledged and a cultural identity is balanced without a central, assumed hierarchy. It is then that a cultural dialogue and translation between the past and the present can occur. The new translated system is then founded on "the gathering of experiences so that they add up to memories, from the accumulation of understanding, from placing ourselves squarely where we are and living in a framework shared with others" (Hoffman in Aciman: 1999: 57).

In her essay "The New Nomads," Hoffman draws on personal experience. A Polish immigrant in Vancouver at the age of thirteen, she opted to synthesize the different worlds within her and express an identity that was fluid and at times nomadic. Her concept of identity as an "open square" is a metaphor used to represent how one allows one's living to be shared with, and be open to, other experiences or what Hall calls "cultural turns": "A turn is neither an ending nor a reversal," Hall clarifies. It is rather a

process [that] continues in the direction in which it was travelling before, but with a critical break, a deflection. After the turn, all of terms of a paradigm are not destroyed; instead, the deflection shifts the paradigm in a direction which is different from that which one might have presupposed from the previous moment. It is not an ending, but a break, and the notion of breaks—of ruptures and of turns—begins to provide us with certain broad handles with which to grasp the current crisis of modernity.

(Hall: 2001: 9)

The present is thus continuously interrupted and preoccupied with the past. This interruption and discontinuity allow for "succession, temporal break, a new period (if not a new start)" (Williams *et al*: 1994: 12).

Identity "is not nomadic, endlessly wandering or deferred; on the contrary it recognises that every identity is placed, positioned, in a culture, a language, a history." It rather "insists on specificity, on conjuncture. But it is not necessarily armour-plated against other identities. It is not tied to fixed, permanent, unalterable oppositions. It is not wholly defined by exclusion" (Procter: 2004: 121). No matter how strongly writers try to ditch or escape a past, these pasts remain inevitably remembered and valued.

Some writers of Indian decent (V. S. Naipaul and Bharati Mukherjee, for example) reject the ethnic label of "Indian writers," perhaps in an effort to place themselves in other, better understood contexts. Mukherjee sees herself nowadays as an American writer, while Naipaul would perhaps prefer to be read as an artist from nowhere and everywhere. Indians (and, since the partition of the subcontinent over fifty years ago, one should also say, Pakistanis) have long been migrants, seeking their fortunes in Africa, Australia, Britain, the Caribbean, and America, and this diaspora has produced many writers who lay claim to an excess of roots.[2]

This claim to a multiplicity of roots is an evident characteristic of the postcolonial, displaced writer. It is, however, surely as evident that a writer's distance from his/her past and descent is what enabled such writers to gain a double perspective on the world. Rushdie's Bombay/India/Pakistan, Du Bois's Ghana/Africa, Said's Jerusalem/Palestine, Hall's Jamaica/The Caribbean, Bhabha's Bombay/India, Selvon's The Caribbean/Trinidad, Achebe's Nigeria/Africa, Rhys's The Caribbean/Dominica, and Naipaul's West/East India are all at the very heart of their writings and provide the distance from which their writings are envisaged and critically and imaginatively formulated.

Hall, one of the pioneer Windrush Generation writers, a Jamaican emigrant in Britain since the 1950s, emphasizes the fact that "post" in postcolonialism or post-structuralism or even postmodernism does not merely mean "after" but also "the aftermath and the after-flow of a particular configuration." This highlights the fact that without colonialism, postcolonialism would not have existed; without modernity, postmodernity would not have existed: in both instances "post" signifies not an ending, but rather a break and a continuation. This leads to the conclusion that, without beginnings, there can be no turnings or translations. The past continues in the experience of the new but it is disseminated and displaced to allow what Hall calls an "original impulse" to translate and take on new directions (Hall: 2001: 11). Like the translation between the displacement of filiative and affiliative identities, nature and culture, the philological and the philosophical, Hall defines the cultural turn as that "deflection from history to culture" (Hall: 2001: 11), a deflection that breaks from history but also keeps bringing it through ruptures to the present course.

While Hoffman speaks of "adding up to memories" the gathering experiences of the present, Bhabha, by contrast, emphasizes the "adding to" as opposed to the "adding up." Bhabha states that whatever comes after the organic and the filiative, it all comes "'in addition to' it, gives [it] the supplementary question the advantage of introducing a sense of 'secondariness' or belatedness into the structure of the original demand" (Bhabha: 2005: 222). In other words, it is not the accumulation of experiences but rather the interdependent interaction of all experiences contrapuntally. The concept of an accumulative cultural identity sounds therefore very fragile and vulnerable. Whether there is the adding to or the adding up, however, both possibilities share a common feature. They both "disturb the calculation" of "the preconstituted social contradictions of the past and present." The force this process holds indeed "lies in the renegotiation of those times, terms and traditions through which we turn our uncertain, passing contemporaneity into the signs of history" (Bhabha: 2005: 222).

Adding to, adding up, (re)negotiation, (re)evaluation, translation, syncreticism, and hybridity, despite differences in terminology, all involve resistance and/or acceptance, forgetting and/or remembrance, repetition and/or reoccurrence. That is,

> the subject of the discourse of cultural difference is dialogical or transferential in the style of psychoanalysis. It is constituted through the locus of the Other which suggests both that the object of identification is ambivalent, and, more significantly, that the agency of identification is never pure or historic but always constituted in a process of substitution, displacement or projection.
>
> (Bhabha: 2005: 233)

Our knowledge of our culture and the Others' should be therefore enriched and opened up by the contribution and presence of the migrant and the displaced. By emerging in and challenging the "center," displaced writers not only change their selves but also those of others. As Hall states, "[t]he world is moving outwards and can no longer be constructed in terms of the centre/periphery relation. It has to be defended in terms of a set of interesting centres, which are both different from and related to one another" (Hall: 2001: 21).

Constructing an identity within a culture demands therefore a re-evaluation of tradition and the debunking of generalized stereotypes, a denial of homogenizing cultural experiences, of pre-given boundaries, and acknowledging limitations; such re-evaluations ultimately broaden our cultural horizon and knowledge beyond the national. For example, displaced identity can seem to move between two points of reference, past and present, without a presumed central power or authority, each with its own meaning and particular experience. "A choice...between two realities," Rushdie writes in *The Satanic Verses*,

> this world and another that was also right there, [is] visible but unseen. He felt slow, heavy, distanced from his own consciousness, and realized that he had not the faintest idea which path he would choose, which world he would enter. The doctors had been wrong, he now perceived, to treat him for schizophrenia; the splitting was not him, but in the universe... *My name is Gibreel Farishta*...belonged in both worlds, with a different meaning in each.
>
> (Rushdie: 2006: 351)

The displaced's home and identity is too flexible to be contained and/or identified by passports which are either given due to long-term residency, birth, or descent. Rushdie's hyphenated identity, which resembles that of Gibreel Farishta, as an American-British-Indian-Pakistani writer, as with many others of his contemporaries, cannot be contained in a passport (despite the latter's importance in international traveling and national identification and security for its holder). He explains:

Imagine a novel being eulogized for being "authentically English," or "authentically German." It would seem absurd. Yet such absurdities persist in the ghetto. In my own case, I have constantly been asked whether I am British, or Indian. The formulation "Indian-British writer" has been invented to explain me ... You see the folly of trying to contain writers inside passports.
(Rushdie: 1991: 67)

III

Cultural commingling is not always welcomed since some feel threatened by change and newness. Thus, some acts of emphasizing cultural specificity often cross the thin line between nationalism and racism. Self-assertion therefore could be transformed into chauvinism, making some cultural identities grimly dangerous in the second half of the twentieth century and the beginning of the new millennium. Furthermore, the independence of a rapidly increasing number of countries and states asking to be recognized has given birth to an urgent need for an independent national and cultural identity. The Second World War had also left people wandering about, strangers in and out of their hometowns and countries needy to belong, to be rooted, to be part of a whole (a group) and be whole (individually) at the same time. Clinging to a past can also be viewed as a reaction to western imperialism and liberality which is perceived as a threat. The sense of loss, dispossession, and severe detachment from a history, of not belonging can often be resolved through settlement in a geographical space in which certain cultural and social practices can be performed, languages can be spoken, and histories can be continued to be (re)written. Thus the frontier the emigrant crosses is not a mere geographical border but also a "wake-up call" (Rushdie: 2002: 412). It is a call for change, a new start, a rebirth. To cross a frontier is to be changed. Rushdie defines the migrant as "the man without frontiers, [he] is the archetypal figure of our age" (Ibid: 415). Distance from a place, it would seem, provides one with a privileged standpoint. It is this distance that "forges new affiliations between past and present, home and away, that are no longer based on Western organic categories of religion and family ties" (Kaplan: 1996; 2005: 119).

Nevertheless, this forging of new affiliations does not preclude political identifications that supersede or go beyond mere affiliations. For example, Edward Said has always identified politically as a Palestinian[3] and has written on the Palestinian–Israeli, or the Arab–Israeli conflict, on many occasions. This political identification, however, should not be conflated with a sense of home: although having written more than twenty different books and many articles, not in one, except when he is quoted in conversation with Barenboim above, does Said express a sense of home.

For a writer like Naipaul, on the other hand, the concept of home seems to slip away and almost become completely erased. In his *The Mimic Men* (1969), and in a celebratory tone, Naipaul frees himself from the "small community which in this part of the world was doomed." He says, "[w]e were an intermediate race, the genes passive, capable of disappearing in two generations into any of the three races of men" (Naipaul: 1969: 57). R. Singh, Naipaul's protagonist and thinly disguised self, admits that Asiatic emigrants "have withdrawn from unnecessary responsibility and attachment. We have simplified our lives" (Ibid: 247). Furthermore, he declares: "I felt I had no past...I do not wish to be re-engaged in that cycle from which I have freed myself" (Ibid: 250–251), suggesting that the self can be totally autotelic, that is entirely disengaged from historical contingencies. Hall, on the other hand, affirms that identity "is something—not a mere trick of the imagination. It has its histories— and histories have their real, material and symbolic effects" (Hall in Williams *et al*: 1994: 395).

To be mentally ghettoized is to "forget that there is a world beyond the community to which we belong, to confine ourselves within narrowly defined cultural frontiers"; for doing so "would be, I believe, to go voluntarily into that form of internal exile which in South Africa is called the 'homeland' " (Rushdie: 1991: 19). Although belonging to a beginning, to "somewhere," and to a starting point as opposed to being ontologically rootless and nomadic is stressed throughout this book, it is also of an equal importance to emphasize the dangers of an excessive focus on beginnings. That is, the danger of crossing the very thin line that separates belonging to a past and reflecting on a beginning every now and then, and a constant oscillation with the past that might result in national extremism or extreme nationalism.

Rushdie sees a strong interlinked relationship between the development of the nation-state and that of the novel. He warns us, nevertheless, of "the writer who sets himself or herself up as the voice of a nation. This includes nations of race, gender, sexual orientation, elective affinity." He stresses that good literature is, as the nation itself should be, "frontierless." To view literature as "inescapably political" is to substitute "political values for literary ones." "[I]t is the murder of thought. Beware!" he warns and concludes that in the best of writing "a map of a nation will also turn to be a map of the world" (Rushdie: 2002: 66).

Said always emphasizes that "none of us is outside or beyond geography, none of us is completely free from the struggle over geography" (Said: 1994a: 6). As mentioned elsewhere, identity can be affiliative and required (in the present, now, mature, invented, by profession and nationality, by cultural acquisition, figurative) and/or filiative and acquired (derived out of a past, then, immature, given, by birth or residence, by natural acquisition, reality). Identity changes and shifts; it is positional and varies in its reference and reality from one generation to another and from one place and time to another. Identity is a flexible entity, an open production that is shaped by continuous experiences and perpetual displacements; it is fluid and never "is," but rather "is in the state of becoming." However, in all cases, its continuity begins "somewhere." "Identity is at once plural and partial. Sometimes we feel that we straddle two cultures; at other times, that we fall between stools. But however ambiguous and shifting this ground may be, it is not an infertile territory for a writer to occupy" (Rushdie: 1991: 15). Identity after all is not given but constructed. To recognize limitations in the construction of the self and focus on the strengthening links drawn between past and present seems more viable. Said states that

> the development and maintenance of every culture require the existence of another different and competing alter ego. The construction of identity—for identity, whether of Orient or Occident, France or Britain, while obviously a repository of distinct collective experiences, is finally a construction—involves establishing opposites and "others" whose actuality is always subject to the continuous interpretation and re-interpretation of their differences from "us."
> (Said: 2003: 332)

Belonging to one place and always having a geographical, historical, or cultural reference point related exclusively to one place can lead to nationalism. Ahmad believes that nationalism "can become an anti-imperialism" (Ahmad: 2008: 317); nationalism can be a form of, not only resistance but also self-affirmation. But the line between imperialism and nationalism is very thin: nationalism can be a form of resistance but also a type of imperialism. As argued previously, nationalism can be a mental ghettoization. It can operate within a totalitarian system. In other words, with nationalism, identity and belonging are almost entirely "natural" and stable allowing no room for displacement, no room for destabilization or revisions, self-criticism or translation, and no space for openness. Metropolitan displaced writers therefore are sometimes seen as dissidents and outlaws who question and doubt the culture's values and credentials. They are sometimes considered traitors. Vulgar nationalism creates identities that bear to an extent negative or hostile attitudes and views toward other nationalities, races, or ethnicities in the countenance of monoethnic communities. But most importantly, nationalism, as Rushdie argues, can restrict creativity and openness. For nationalism

corrupts writers, too. In a time of ever more narrowly defined nationalisms, of walled-in tribalisms, writers will be found uttering the war-cries of their tribes. Closed systems have always appealed to writers. This is why so much writing deals with prisons, police forces, hospitals, schools. Is the nation a closed system? In this internationalised moment, can any system remain closed? Nationalism is... [t]o force in what should be frontierless. Good writing assumes a frontierless nation. Writers who serve frontiers have become border guards.

(Rushdie: 2002: 67)

Displacement proves that in such an internationalized moment, systems cannot remain closed, or ghettoized. Displacement in this sense opens doors for creativity, debunks the status quo, promotes for criticism, and allows for revisions. Displacement certainly appeals to writers because it is frontierless, liberating, and transcends nation, religion, and indeed race.

Section 2: Racism and Immigration

For W. E. B. Du Bois,[4] the Color Line (referring to the Afro-American experience of double consciousness and inequality based on race, or what is known as institutionalized racism) and the Color Bar (referring to the British and its former colonial subjects of the same experience) are terms that highlight racial discrimination, marginalization and inferiority, elimination and exclusion. Caryl Phillips sees in Du Bois' *The Souls of the Black Folk* (1903), the first sociological account of black identity, an overwhelming dilemma that is unbelonging: "Feeling both of, and not of, the nation is a cripplingly anxious condition" (Phillips: 2001: 11). The black British migrant shares with the American Negro a "strife,—this longing to attain self-consciousness manhood, to emerge his double self into a better and truer self. In this merging he wishes neither of the older selves to be lost" (Du Bois: 1994: 3).

The American Negro example,[5] within the context of Du Bois' perspective on double consciousness, is drawn upon here to indicate two intersections. First, both the African-American and the black British share the "confusion and doubt in the soul of the black artist" as well as their "seeking to satisfy two unreconciled ideals," past and present, self and Other, old and new; second, they both exemplify how "[t]he battle against South African Apartheid and the rekindling of US civil rights struggles would prove to be inspirational far from their immediate places of origin. The struggles that black Britain conducted for rights, dignity and recognition would be influenced, if not exactly guided, by those examples" (Gilroy: 2007: 114). In other words, what was happening in Georgia and Arizona affected and influenced what was going on in London, Brixton, and Notting Hill.

Across the Atlantic, the story was not much different. "The 1960s saw racism become a much more pervasive, institutionalised feature of British culture. In 1962, 1968 and 1971 a series of Immigration Acts were introduced specifically designed to reduce the influx of black settlers. Rising racial intolerance was registered at the level of popular politics in this decade, reaching its pinnacle in the anti-immigration speeches of Enoch Powell" (Procter: 2004: 83). Powell's ideology saw "racial politics as a significant element in the formation and reproduction of English national identities" (Gilroy: 1993: 4). Racial exclusion of Commonwealth immigrants (physical and political unaccommodation) and Powell's 1968-River-of-Blood Speech were followed by Thatcher's "One Nation" and its subsequent limited inclusion of black political figures against which Britain's diverse ethnic communities raised their voices. It is suggested, however, that "Powellism is about much more than 'racism'. It is about how the 'crisis' of authority post-1968 became condensed around the imagery of race." This Hall calls "racism as displacement" (Procter: 2004: 84). In other words, justifications for not wanting foreigners/outsiders in Britain—lack of accommodation, increase in diseases, famine, and other problems—were in reality excuses that served to displace the real reason which was prejudice against outsiders. Thus internal problems were projected as being the result of external factors.

Bruce King argues, however, that the institutionalized beginning of England's transformation into a multicultural society began with such immigration acts as that of 1971 which tried to police immigration into Britain except for the reunion of families, and the 1981 Citizenship Act which depended on citizenship of parents as opposed to the place of birth. The new multicultural England was also marked culturally with the 1975 Notting Hill Carnival,[6] when the School of English at Leeds University promoted Commonwealth Literature, and the University of Kent offered an African and Caribbean studies degree. It was also marked in 1978 by Margaret Thatcher's proclamation that immigration should stop before England was "swamped" by other cultures (King: 2004: 79). The beginning of second-generation Masala Fish writers began therefore after the 1970s and with it, England, its politics, and literature had undergone significant transformation. There was also an evident presence of writers from East Africa and the Arab world too: Ahdaf Soueif, Abdulrazak Gurnah, Leila Aboulela, and Jamal Mahjoub. This indicated and reflected diversity.

Procter argues, however, racism as displacement also works through the mediums of "profound historical forgetfulness," "'a kind of historical amnesia, a decisive mental repression'... involving the displacement of its colonial history" (Procter: 2004: 82). In this, amnesia is used as a defense mechanism. In other words, the British were "[h]eld hostage by the idea that they too are immigrants" and the new "incomers may be unwanted and feared precisely because they are the unwitting triggers for the pain produced by the memories of that vanished imperial and colonial past" (Gilroy: 2004). It is this very amnesia, Hall states, "which has overtaken the British popular memory of its long imperial past... as if it all only began the day before yesterday" (Hall in Gilroy: 2007: 5).

Although Thatcherism[7] had its basis in Powellism (Procter: 2004: 95), post the 1980s a significant cultural change occurred. Pioneered by publishing houses such as Routledge, for example, literary and cultural studies focused on "discussions of 'race', beauty, ethnicity, and culture [that] have contributed to the critical thinking" (Gilroy: 1993: 7). The role of migration and displacement in this change cannot be underestimated. Equally, as postcolonial and racial conflicts and ethnic revolutions accelerated, celebratory multicultural expressions in music, film, media, politics, sports, and literature and a New England were in the making.

Music for example "offers an inventory of queries about the ideas of ethnic authenticity... the gender identities it celebrates, and the images of 'race' as family that have become an important part of both producing and interpreting it" (Gilroy: 1993: x), starting with Jimi Hendrix's *Purple Haze* in 1967, Bob Marley's *Get Up, Stand Up* in

1973 to Soul II Soul who sang *Keep on Moving* in 1996, and *Back to Life* in 1989 or *Get a Life* in 1989.

The lyrics here and sometimes the bands' names offer newly hybridized identities and a move, not toward the past or tradition, but forward, that is, after the break with the past. The songs and their lyrics form an articulate message first to the black man and second to the world. The lyrics express and confess "restlessness of spirit which makes that [playful diasporic] culture vital" (Gilroy: 1993: 16). Themes of these songs and other cultural performances varied from emancipation, autonomy to citizenship. Music and songs were melodic human expressions of various experiences, particularly for the oppressed. For a melody becomes a word and a rhythm becomes a howl and both mix together to become an unwritten, oral history and heritage of the Black folks. For "music is far more ancient than the words, and in it we can trace here and there signs of development" (Du Bois: 1994: 157). Music can be "the voice of exile" (Ibid: 158). Such cultural interventions "provide a means to re-examine the problems of nationality, location, identity and historical memory" (Ibid). One can find in Bhangra, for example, a genre that has become internationalized and has been changed as it crossed frontiers and transcended Oedipal territoriality. With an increasing Asian population in England, with the emergence of third and fourth generations in the meantime too, a fusion of the past and present, of the old and new, of a folk music of rural India and Pop music gave voice to Bhangra as it is today.

The Punjabi migrants who came to this corner of west London did so in search for jobs and prosperity, but Bhangra also became an important part of community life, particularly at weddings and family parties where the first Bhangra bands started to play. "Some of the most famous British Bhangra groups, such as Alaap, Heera and Premi, first started playing at weddings and rapidly established a reputation for themselves within both Britain and India, often selling hundreds of thousands of records but barely getting noticed by the mainstream music industry." As immigration increased, Bhangra's language, Indian/Punjabi, was not understood by all those who listened to it. However, the richness of the rhythm emanates from its mixing traditional Asian music with soul, hip-hop, and R&B. This genre of music can be a cultural tool that transcends cultural conflicts by bringing a wider audience into its scenery. It is an Indian folk music and the traditional music of Punjab, northern India, where displacement has always been a predominant characteristic. *The Guardian* (August 15, 2003) writes that "For over a decade now, Bhangra music has been the vanguard for Asian culture's crossover into the mainstream." Not only has Bhangra been used by the Asian community to maintain cultural links, but it has also featured as an established phenomenon of the British Asian music scene for the last half a century or so, reflecting the conforming nature of its people as well as the society from which it has emerged.

The existence of the migrant in the metropolis significantly contributed to the rapid change of its cultural landscape in the second half of the twentieth century. For example, Salman Rushdie who won the Booker Prize (formerly known as the Man Booker Prize) for his 1981 debut novel, *Midnight's Children*, and was sent into exile for his 1988 *The Satanic Verses*; *Aswad* (*Black* in Arabic) sang their *Chasing for the Breeze* (I walk my feet to the phone/Cannot get work nowhere) in 1984, introducing Reggae to the British musical scenery that was already injected with African soulful jazz; Ian Wright joined Crystal Palace, the South London football club, making his name one of the first Black British footballers to join the English national football team in 1991[8]; Ben Okri injected a new African narrative to the British literary scene writing his first novel, *Flowers and Shadows* (1980), joining Rushdie in his dream-logic narrative, or what is known as magic realism, winning his first literary prize for his first collection of short stories, *Incidents at the Shrine*, 1987. Furthermore, there were those contributions of the pioneer emigrants to the BBC Radio Broadcasting (e.g., Tayeb Salih for the BBC Arabic Service and Sam Selvon for the BBC Caribbean Voices) to the contribution of later immigrants to Black British cinema (e.g., Sam Selvon, James Baldwin, and Horace Ove in their screenplays for *Baldwin's Nigger* (1969) and *Pressure* (1970) to Kureishi's *My Beautiful Launderette* (1985), Ishiguro's Academy Award winning *The Remains of the Day* (1989), and Caryl Philips's screenplay of V. S. Naipaul's first novel *The Mystic Masseur* (2001)).

Britain was going through some significant transformations in social, cultural, and political lives. It was a fertile soil on which interactions between African, Asian, and Caribbean diasporas and British natives, between the formerly colonized and the former colonizer, were rapidly shaping. While the earlier revolutionary voices were observant of the cultures they arrived at and more concerned with lost homelands, later evolutions of migratory narratives proved interpretative and more openly transnational in perspective.

The presence of migrant communities had not, however, been all rosy and peaceful. Stuart Hall asks: "When do black communities emerge and why do they awaken such hostility? How does a visible, identifiable and distinctive black identity arise?" (Hall in Gilroy: 2007: 9). Earlier generations of emigrants during the fifties, sixties, and seventies struggled and paved the way for later generations to flourish during the eighties and nineties. Violence, ethnic discrimination, and racial exclusion were always based on a color bar: the inferiority of earlier black Jamaicans and Trinidadians to the superiority of the purely Anglo-Saxon. What is evident is that chains of migrants were becoming an unavoidable part of a politically and ethnically changing British society. Migrations

> of the fifties and sixties happened. "We are. We are here." And we are not willing to be excluded from any part of our heritage; which heritage includes both a Bradford-born Indian kid's right to be treated as a full member of British society, and also the right of any member of this post-diaspora community to draw on its roots for its art, just as all the world's community of displaced writers has always done.
>
> (Rushdie: 1991: 15)

Decolonizations in two different continents and America's Civil Rights Movement (dominated between 1955 and 1969 by renowned figures such as Martin Luther King, Malcolm X, Muhammad Ali,[9] and Du Bois) influenced later Black political movements and awoke its consciousness within Britain. Black meant difference and empowerment. Black also brought Caribbean, East and South Indians, and Africans together in the face of racism. Black meant an identity through which a displaced migrant could translate an experience of elimination, of racism. In Lamming's *In the Castle of My Skin*, the narrator states that "we all used the colour as a weapon against interference" (Lamming: 1953: 127). Feeling inferior and excluded, ashamed and fearful, racism and Britain provoked the displaced to organize and turn racism on its head by recuperating the very tool of oppression—racism—and using it proudly as a mark of identity. Du Bois's two-ness was easily resolved, for example, "by viewing himself as black, which for him meant being wedded to a distinct experience which cherished discipline, eloquence, grace and good manners. However, he also knew himself to be intrinsically a part of the larger [American] culture" (Phillips: 2001: 15–16).

Contrastingly, to be black and British was no option. A black subject either assimilated to be fully British or remained an uncivilized outsider in the eyes of the native. For in the land of the foreign, "they won't know you. They won't know the you that's hidden somewhere in the castle of your skin" (Lamming: 1953: 261). A few generations after the Windrush Generation, first and second generations of migrants had by the mid-eighties bred third and fourth generations of British blacks. Thus the periphery has not only entered the center but also occupied both, center and periphery simultaneously. The outsider is now inside, thinking effectively inside-out.

Racism, nevertheless, continues virulently even today in Britain and its institutions. It is an imperial ideology: slavery of the modern age. There is no doubt then that "anti-imperialism and anti-racism might seem to interact but not fuse" (Gilroy: 1993: 4). Racism works provocatively through violence and rioting. Racism is therefore an act that involves and changes both, the colonizer and the colonized, the native and settler. Racism is a colonization of the Others' free will: the sheer physical restriction from being and becoming. It restricts dreaming. Racism can become an extension of nationalism, too. The overwhelming pride of belonging to a particular race can lead to an aggressive antagonism toward other races. "From nationalism we have passed to ultra-nationalism, to chauvinism, and finally to racism" (Fanon: 2001: 125). Racism furthermore "is not a side-crisis in contemporary Britain." Rather, it is "a crisis of the whole culture, of the society's entire sense of itself. And racism is only the most clearly visible part of the crisis, the tip of the kind of iceberg that sinks ships" (Rushdie: 1991: 129).

From inside the metropolis of London, the migrant speaks his former colonizer's language and develops a consciousness of a cultural identity and of an ethnic belonging, seeking a place which resembles Du Bois's attempts to reconcile himself and other comrades to being a Negro and an American at the same time. For racism, or, in other words, the problem of the color line/bar, caused the displaced a depersonalization problem: "No black boy wanted to be white, but it was also true that no black boy liked the idea of being black" (Lamming: 1953: 127). The former colonial subject, now inside the metropolis of the former colonizer, must, nevertheless, reconcile place, home, self, and identity with the imperative to be black *and* British, a double cultural and intermixed identity. As Rushdie says, "they, we, are at one and at the same time insiders and outsiders in this [British] society" (Rushdie: 1991: 19).

Arriving with the impression that they were needed, most emigrants arrived with British passports and thought of themselves as citizens. Instead, they came to realize their presence was unwanted. Thus the migrant is made an alien twice: once from his own "motherland" by the act of colonization, and second in the "mother country," the allegedly "promise land," by virtue of migration and racism.[10] The migrant therefore has a double identity, a dual belonging to the mother land and to the mother country. In other words, "to be both European and Black requires some specific forms of double consciousness" (Gilroy: 1993: 1). This double and dual identity is a parallel, asymmetric existence which requires in Du Bois's words, two-ness.

Two-ness, however, still wrangles with the question of beginnings. Du Bois, after all, gave up his American citizenship in favor for his ancestral Ghana at the age of ninety-four. His first visit to Ghana was in 1961. "Surely he loved it on sight, which is why he renounced his American citizenship and took a Ghanaian passport?" (Phillips: 2001: 9). This demonstrates a strong concrete attachment to a historical and ancestral past. The Negro, says Du Bois, is

born with a veil, and gifted with second-sight in this American world, – a world which yields him no true self-consciousness, but only lets him see himself thorough the revelation of the other world. It is a peculiar sensation, this double consciousness, this sense of always looking at one's self through the eyes of others, of measuring one's soul by the tape of a world that looks on in amused contempt and pity. One ever feels his two-ness,—an American, a Negro; two souls, two thoughts, two unreconciled strivings; two warning ideals in one dark body, whose dogged strength alone keeps it from being torn asunder.

(Du Bois: 1994: 2)

Du Bois's description almost equates the dark body with its dark and struggling soul in their desperate attempts to reconcile. The body is described as almost torn because of the burden of wholeness, the struggle for oneness. Said, on the other hand, in *No Reconciliation Allowed*, is of the opinion that "[i]dentity as such is about as boring a subject as one can imagine. Nothing seems less interesting than the narcissistic self-study that today passes in many places for identity politics, or ethnic studies, or affirmation of roots, cultural pride, drumbeating nationalism, and so on" (Said in Aciman: 1999: 111–12). He instead invites one to "transform oneself into something different than it is to keep insisting on the virtues of being American in the ideological sense." Despite gaps of differences between Said the Palestinian exile and Du Bois the black civil rights activist, they are similar on two counts: First, both are colonial as well as postcolonial subjects; second, both are doubly conscious of being more than one thing. Ultimately, once out of place, not even writing can offer an alternative construction of reality nor a fully powerful representation of oneself. One's identity never "achieves at most [but] a provisional satisfaction, which is quickly ambushed by doubt, and a need to rewrite and redo that renders the text uninhabitable. Better that, however, than the sleep of self-satisfaction and the finality of death" (Ibid: 114).

The story of Du Bois,[11] a black Atlantic thinker and traveler, is slightly different, nevertheless. He was a sociologist, a Pan-Africanist who was born in America, and was educated in its universities to ultimately becoming the first African-American to achieve a PhD from Harvard University, a university that subsequently named its institute of African and African-American Research after him. Du Bois's travels certainly played a major role in his understanding and interpretation anew of race and ethnicity. "The problems of racialised ontology," Gilroy reminds us, "and identity—the tension between being and becoming black—are therefore deeply inscribed in Du Bois's own life" (Gilroy: 1993: 115).

Out of this learning and striving for knowledge and "longing to know," "a new vision began gradually to replace the dream of political power." Book-learning, as Du Bois puts it, sent the black man through a journey which minimally "gave leisure for reflection and self-examination; it changed the child of Emancipation to the youth with dawning self-consciousness, self-realization, self-respect." The evolving self-conscious youth "began to have a dim feeling that, to attain his place in the world, he must be himself, and not another" (Du Bois: 1994: 5). A truer self was now in the process of becoming; a new enunciation was in the process of articulation. Black was then considered as a positive, celebratory example of racial pride. Du Bois describes this new attitude when he says, "we black men seem the sole oasis of simple faith and reverence in a dusty desert of dollars and smartness" (Ibid: 7).

Rushdie describes a somewhat more colorful oasis in *The Satanic Verses* as "Gibreel enumerated the benefits of the proposed metamorphosis of London into a tropical city":

increased moral definition, institution of a national siesta, development of vivid and expansive patterns of behavior among the populace, higher quality popular music, new birds in the streets (macaws, peacocks, cockatoos), new trees under the birds (coco-palms, tamarind, banyans with hanging beards)... Emergence of new social values: friends to commence dropping in on one another without making appointments, closure of old folks' homes, emphasis on the extended family. Spicier food; the use of water as well as paper in English toilets.

(Rushdie: 2006: 354–55)

Immigration did not only alter social behaviors and cultural life, it also changed the infrastructure of British identity, i.e., what it means to be British in the midst of this wave of the formerly colonized migrants. Thus, Britain had to be thought of in terms of India and vice versa. The "transformational process" and "cultural excess" Rushdie mentions after this paragraph are two critical features of how newness has entered the world of England. "Once," he writes, "the new was shocking not because it set out to shock but because it set out to be new. Now, all too often, the shock is the new" (Rushdie: 2002: 440). New to the nationally and racially (white) constructed nation of Britain, immigration shook London's sense of itself, the sense of racial and ethnic homogeneity: immigration was an interruption to its sense of imperial continuity. This cultural excess of the migrants was not all rosy, nonetheless. Displaced writers of the 1980s balanced their narratives between positives and negatives of the communities to which they belonged. Rushdie follows the above descriptive paragraph with the fact that immigration brought with it disadvantages too, such as "cholera, typhoid, legionnaires' disease, cockroaches, dust, noise" (Rushdie: 2006: 355).

What is of no doubt, however, is that "immigration became the substance and the limit of Britain's racial politics" (Gilroy: 2007: 168). Du Bois raised the same question and concerns as he tackles the problem of the twentieth century: "What shall be done with Negroes? Peremptory military commands, this way and that, could not answer the query; the Emancipation Proclamation seemed but to broaden and intensify the difficulties; and the War Amendments made the Negro problems of to-day" (Du Bois: 1994; 1903: 9). The same case scenario was happening in Britain.

After the early slogans and demands of "Keeping Britain White," such abstractions (such as KBW; or no coloreds allowed) "were succeeded by a crudely concrete concern: what are we going to do about *them*? The inducements to leave these shores were murderous and informal as well as polite and political" (Gilroy: 2007: 206). The emergence of these "ultra-nationalists and neo-fascist grouplets" resulted in the formation of "a common political identity centred on the idea of blackness, which was opened up to accommodate diverse experiences and postcolonial histories" (Ibid: 209). Both histories of British postcolonial immigrants and the emancipatory American slaves share a history of racism and discrimination. While the American model was based on what Du Bois called the Color Line, Gilroy defines the Color Bar specifically and in details as one that "help[s] to define the painful period in which Britain's blacks enjoyed extensive but empty rights of citizenship that could be easily overridden by informal patterns of exclusion in public and in private...through a racialised division of labour...in the use of racial quotas and the patterning of shiftwork" (Gilroy: 2007: 85). The Color Bar simply meant "the tragedy of a black presence that appears stubbornly out of place—homelessness in its new home" (Ibid: 81). Selvon's Moses, for instance, draws attention to the treatment of blacks in both Britain and America pointing out a slight difference in *The Lonely Londoners*. In America, he states, "you see a sign telling you to keep off," however, in Britain, "you do not see any, but when you in the hotel or restaurant they will politely tell you to haul—or else give you the cold treatment" (Selvon: 2006: 63).

In time, the problem of the color bar, however, shifted focus from the biological to the behavioral: from the racial to the cultural. Resistance to black presence gradually changed to include not only arguments about racial inferiority based on the development of the species, but also sociological arguments such as blacks are submissive and poor, dirty and ill-cultured. To Keep Britain White (slogans and mottos pleaded then by The White Defence League and the Teddy Boys) meant that the migrant was not welcomed to be accommodated, socially, culturally, or physically. It meant the migrant became homeless yet once again. And still, Phillips sees in British cultural life a rather rich amalgamation. "So how should Britain define itself as a nation?" he asks, considering the accelerating growth of migrant communities within Britain. "A synthesis of Indian takeaways, baked beans, soccer, Jamaican patties, St Patrick's Day, pub on Saturday, Notting Hill Carnival, church on Sunday, mosque on Friday and fish and chips? I say emphatically, yes" (Phillips: 2001: 281).

Migration continued nonetheless "to repudiate the dangerous obsessions with 'racial' purity" despite its ideological system (Gilroy: 1993: xi). Migration and Britain's black settlers debunked what Gilroy calls "cultural insiderism" which "construct[s] the nation as an ethnically homogeneous object and invoke[s] ethnicity a second time... to make sense of its distinctive cultural content" (Gilroy: 1993: 3). Their seeking for a place in what Gilroy calls "the cosmopolitan hub of the Commonwealth family of nations" (Ibid: 140) was yet to be capitalized upon and aesthetically articulated by the appearance of "that unthinkable, impossible character: a 'negro' intellectual" (Ibid: 144). Selvon portrays his Boys in *The Lonely Londoners* practicing reading and writing, debate and discussion. In the lounge of a hostel, "the genuine fellars with text-books in they hand, and some fellars with the *Worker*, and big discussion on politics and thing would start up" (Selvon: 2006: 30). The displaced migrant's identity becomes bound by racial discriminations, by the very color bar; it becomes bound to

urgent social contests involving such concrete political issues as immigration laws, the legislation of personal conduct, the constitution of orthodoxy, the legitimization of violence and/or insurrection, the character and content of education, and the direction of foreign policy, which very often has to do with the designation of official enemies. In short, the construction of identity is bound up with the disposition of power and powerless in each society.

(Said: 2003: 332)

The perception of black migrants "as agents, as people with cognitive capacities and even with an independent history" are indeed "attributes denied by modern racism" (Gilroy: 1993: 6) and its Color Bar which the black displaced writer lifts by writing back, translating between, resisting injustice, and debunking color-coded cultures.

The next two chapters discuss the remarkable transformation which such writing, the new english literature, has undergone. The word "new" refers here to the new era of English literature: its new concerns and subject matters, its increasingly international audience, and its new postcolonial english language which is re-appropriated to contain the new emigrants' experience and serve its purposes. During the second half of the twentieth century, literature of England has gone through a major change: a change in the subject matter based on and altered by a large influx of migrants from elsewhere, mainly the Caribbean, the West Indies, East Africa, India, and Pakistan. The cultural, economic, political, and national impact of these migrants among the natives in cosmopolitan cities such as London questions what it means to be British after the collapse of its empire, and indeed the literary nature of its market.

After the vanishing of Empire, and its last glimpse overseas of colonial land of the Suez in 1956 and of Hong Kong in 1997, the once-colonized started to flee to what was considered the Mother Country. A few had taken England as a permanent residence. Others stayed over to profit economically, establish a business, and reunite with family members or for literary publication and a career as writers-in-exile; fewer numbers were invited on studentships. Many returned home while others kept the "myth" of return at bay. Many more felt compelled to write from within England and reflect on their countries outwardly and contrastingly from within the so-called belly of the beast. Hence, the Windrush Generation was born and remained to breed a chain of following generations.

Chapter 3

The Windrush Generation: Remapping England and Its Literature

I

Due to the large and accumulative number of emigrants and the subsequent emergent fiction, where roughly a hundred British novels are released weekly and with more than three quarters of the people living in the world today having had their lives shaped by the experience of colonialism, neither of the following chapters are or can be entirely representative. The chapters are divided, however, according to subject matter across a chronological sequence. The division and structure of generational division should trace therefore different shifts in identity politics and their relational conceptions of home. This discourse of displacement and migration through literary and cultural interlocution should demonstrate how variable and shifting pre-given, pre-assumed, and fixed ideas can be, and how they are altered, or restaged, once taken out of their originary places, out of their Oedipalized territories, that is, once they are displaced. In this context, then, England can be considered a fertile soil and an open site upon which postcolonial black and Asian cultures developed creatively in relation to their colonial history. The empire, Rushdie tells us, writes back to the center. The very historically and colonially scarred relationship between the migrants' colonial past and the current postcolonial present brings a rather interesting cultural dimension and challenge to the displaced intellectual's writing. Writing back to the center also connotes not only being part of the center marching from the margins; it is also a turning look forward, a look that is not restricted by a colonial past but a rather optimistic look toward an open future.

George Lamming, a Windrush pioneer, states that being in the "headquarters," i.e., England/London, "the West Indian is already familiar with the Englishman." Had elsewhere been the residence for the West Indian,

> his development would probably be different, indeed, of an opposed order to that of a man who matured in England... his reservation, his psychology, his whole sense of cultural expectation have not greatly changed. He arrives and travels with memory, the habitual weight of a colonial relation... it would have been better, perhaps, if he had gone to study in France or Germany, to mention countries of a different language; any place where his adjustments would have to take the form of understanding the inhabitants from scratch.
> (Lamming: 1960: 24–5)

The above quotation highlights the importance of this rhetorically historical colonial–colonized relationship which not only shaped and stimulated most of their earlier writings but also shaped their very national West Indian identities. It emphasizes various impacts on displaced figures: the historically colonial, geographical, cultural, social, and psychological and foremost the linguistic. Caryl Phillips, a second-generation immigrant, highlights a rather crucial aspect of this rhetorical relationship. For him, Caribbeans were the most threatening group to an essentially racial and ethnic British national identity. "They were," he writes, "English-speaking Christians, who had studied their Shakespeare and Wordsworth at school, and while they might like saltfish and ackee, or curried goat and jerk chicken, they seemed able to synthesise these peculiar ethnic aberrations with a broad understanding of the ways of the British" (Phillips: 2001: 273).

Lamming, however, emphasizes how displacement and distance brought upon the West Indian not only a different cultural experience but also made him[1] a more aware and self-conscious individual of his precolonial past and colonial history. He states that "[n]o black West Indian, in his own native environment, would have this highly oppressive sense of being Negro" (Ibid: 33). In his masterpiece, *The Emigrants* (1954), Lamming emphasizes the physicality of displacement and its psychological effect embodied in the act of remembrance and memory. Describing a group of West Indian emigrants carried on the deck of a ship, thinly disguised as *The SS Empire Windrush*, traveling across the Atlantic, the unnamed narrator's commentary confirms:

When them stay back home in they little island them forget a little an' them remain vomit; just as them was vomit up, but when them go "broad, them remember, or them provin" a name. A good name. Them is West Indians. Not Jamaicans or Trinidadians. Cause the bigger the better.
(Lamming: 1954: 68)

The emergence of the Windrush Generation was subsequent to the end of imperial England and signaled the beginning and rise of multiracial and multicultural Britain. Subsequently, Commonwealth Literature started to be taught at universities, with Leeds University starting it in 1964 (King: 2004: 68). The (Man) Booker Prize was also established in 1969 manifestly coinciding with the rapid and unavoidable emergence and presence of the displaced postcolonial migrant intellectual within the metropolis. After the expiry of the British mandate in Palestine in May 1948, the failure of taking over the Suez Canal in 1956 and the decolonization of India, Ghana, and Nigeria among others, the sun had almost set upon the British Empire. Civil rights, on the other hand, were moving in America and influencing those in England. Other symptoms of cultural expression and self-assertion were becoming more evident too: Jazz and Calypso music, the publication of the West Indian Gazette following the Notting Hill riots in 1958, and the establishment of the London-based BBC Caribbean Voices on radio.

Characteristics of this generation's style of writing revolved around the psychological anxiety implied in the emigrant's disappointments and dissatisfactions with the Mother Country. Although recurrent in the writings of later generations, racial discrimination and emphasis on cultural differences are more evident and central to the writings of the Windrush Generation. The racist's nightmare is always manifested through problems of not being physically or socially accommodated. The emigrant was also trying to form a bigger picture of the world while still defining a Caribbean consciousness within a British context. From within this context, moreover, emerged "a dozen or so novelists in the British Caribbean with some fifty books to their credit or disgrace, and all published between 1948 and 1958." Literary publications of that period were predominantly written by West Indians/Caribbeans. And hence, "[t]here has been no comparable event in culture anywhere in the British Commonwealth during the same period" (Lamming: 1960: 29). The West Indian novel did investigate not only the inner experiences of West Indian communities but also the inner experiences of the British, with the emergent migrant in its midst. "The West Indian contribution to English reading,"

Lamming observes, "has been made possible by their relation to their themes which are peasant. This is the great difference between the West Indian novelist and the contemporary English novelist" (Lamming: 1960: 44). The peasantry narrative added a new reading of the cosmopolitan city of London and its geography. The peasant-orientated writings were in a sense an attempt at claiming authenticity in the face of the modern and changing.

Across writings of this time, a celebratory romance of the past prevailed alongside the assimilationist dream and cultural mimicry. The latter is considered to be a mask behind which the emigrant possessed no identity.[2] Mimicry was a copying of the White man's action without understanding its meaning, culture, or context. Nostalgic dreams of an idealized past and a possible return to the motherland were evident. Attia Hosain, an Indian emigrant writer, describes how, after the partition of India and the "cutting apart of human beings," Britain became a third choice for flight. Being a first-generation emigrant who has deep roots in Indian culture and belongs to "the blood of my ancestors for eight hundred years in another country," Hosain

> could never have written so truthfully about Britain and the British as I did about India. I see that as a limitation. Perhaps it was because I was always an observer, watching through glass, never really made to feel at home as in the Eastern tradition. I could have described what I saw, but I could not penetrate that invisible barrier to enter into a "self" other than the polite exterior.
> (Hosain in Dennis and Khan: 2000: 27)

Hosain compares herself to a later generation of writers who were of a different time and belonged in a different place. She recognizes her limitation of being no inventor, interventionist, or cultural translator. She is a mere observer and of a nationality that is purely East Indian. "The second and third generations, perhaps because of the seamless nature of the crossover, have created their own transliterations of influences. The vitality of writers like Salman Rushdie," she adds, "is markedly due to the fusion of so many voices and influences" (Hosain in Dennis and Khan: 2000: 26–7).

In contrast to the fusion of so many voices in the following generation, the Windrush writers share to an extent "a great silent gap … beyond which the two cultures [British and Other] can neither clash nor merge nor come to terms with each other" (Ibid: 24). In this sense, the inability to integrate or assimilate pushes the emigrant to a state of limbo. Creating new systems, or the route from filiation to affiliation, remains incomplete. In other words, mobility and habitation could not be maintained simultaneously. To be West Indian or Indian *and* British was not possible despite the formerly colonized's right to a British citizenship. Hosain, however, helplessly and hopelessly seeks refuge in "belonging to the whole world" through which "one seeks to balance consciousness of one's roots" (Ibid: 27).

What Selvon's Foster contrarily states, however, in his most philosophical work *An Island Is a World* (1955) is that "[a]n island is a world, and everywhere that people live, they create their own worlds. 'But sometimes that world is small,'" Foster said. "Sometimes you feel as if you are at the top of it, and you want more. Your mind is cramped" (Selvon: 1993: 73). Near the end of the novel, Foster realizes that "you can't belong to the world, because the world won't have you. The world is made up of different nations, and you've got to belong to one of them, and to hell with the others" (Ibid: 107). Despite Foster's blunt and to an extent nationalist viewpoint, Selvon's novel stresses the fact that one has to represent a particular experience of a particular place while, however, reflecting on the world—hence the title, *An Island Is a World*. This can be demonstrated through Foster's imagining of Trinidad as a dot on the globe; he transmits thoughts into the universe the way an RKO Radio radiated from a single place broadcasting to the universe. One, according to Selvon's narrative, cannot free-float and claim no historical specificity or locality. One is not only and merely a human being who does not belong, or else belongs to the whole world by virtue of belonging to none. No single human being can belong to the whole world.

> When you leave the country of your birth, it isn't like that at all. Other people belong. They are not human beings, they are Englishmen and Frenchmen and Americans, and you've got to have something to fall back on too, you can't just go up and say, "Hello fellow being, I'm new here, and I'm looking for a job." Or you can't go to the United Nations and say, "Look, I don't belong to any country, I have no ties of any sort to any particular nation. Maybe I could help you sort out some of your problems."
>
> (Ibid: 106)

Lamming shares a similar sense of specificity and rootedness with Selvon. He states that the "pleasure and paradox of my own exile is that I belong wherever I am." And yet, Lamming, being a first-generation emigrant writer, could not stop there. He adds: "and yet there is always an acre of ground in the New World keeps growing in my head. I can only hope that these echoes do not die before my work comes to an end" (Lamming: 1960: 50). V. S. Naipaul, on the other hand, is "a colonial who is nervous both in and away from his native country"; he is a writer whose "books can't move beyond a castrated satire." "When such a writer is colonial," explains Lamming, "ashamed of his cultural background and striving like mad to prove himself through promotion to the peaks of a 'superior' culture whose values are gravely in doubt, then satire, like the charge of philistinism, is for me nothing more than a refuge. And it is too small a refuge for a writer who wishes to be taken seriously" (Lamming: 1960: 225).

Lamming's defensive attitude toward Naipaul, one of his contemporaries, emanates from the fact that Naipaul does not wish to relate to

a common background of social history which can be called West Indian: a background whose basic feature is the peasant sensibility. Neither Sam [Selvon] nor I could feel the slightest embarrassment about this; whereas Naipaul, with the diabolical help of Oxford University, has done a thorough job of wiping this out of his guts.

(Ibid: 225)

Naipaul, according to Lamming's comparative description, is a traitor to his own native culture and country. "To me," admits Naipaul, on the other hand, "situations and people are always specific, always of themselves. That is why one travels and writes: to find out" (Naipaul: 2002: 503).

West Indian writers and their literature emerged as a phenomenon during the first ten or so years after the Second World War because of that kind of explorative traveling. Admitting that he comes from "an agricultural immigrant community from India," Naipaul adds that "it couldn't be said that we were literary people." He believes it was necessary to leave Trinidad to become a writer for that very reason: it was impossible to write from within the culturally barren Trinidad. Moreover, he plays tribute to a universal civilization and an outer world for the artistic and literary vocation with which he had been gifted. The center, and that is particularly England for Naipaul, is that fertile soil that opened spaces for him to becoming a writer. "I couldn't have become a writer in the Mohammedan world; in China; in Japan...in Eastern Europe or the Soviet Union or black Africa. I don't think I could have taken my gifts even to India" (Ibid: 2002: 507). Selvon and Lamming do share these aspects of becoming writers and escaping national ties with Naipaul. What they do not share with him, however, is his triumphant celebration of an ontologically free-floating identity and his judgmentally satirical and cynical writings.

II

The generation of emigrants that arrived at Tilbury in 1948 docked by the *Empire Windrush* was primarily fleeing the increasing unemployment in their homeland. "One hundred and twenty-five thousand people came from the Caribbean to Britain between the years 1948 and 1958," says Caryl Phillips:

> Between 1959 and 1962 approximately another 125,000 arrived, making a grand total of about 250,000. With the passing of the 1962 Commonwealth Immigration Act, this flow slowed to a trickle. Further legislation in 1968 made immigration from the Caribbean virtually impossible. A great number of the pre-1962 migrants were actively recruited by British companies such as London Transport, or Wall's Ice Cream, which, like countless other companies in the immediate postwar years, were in desperate need of labor. Some migrants arrived with the altruistic purpose of helping the "mother country," but everybody wanted to better themselves, both financially and in terms of their experience of the world.
>
> (Phillips: 2001: 268)

This analysis of the character of the emigrant within the context of the immediate timescale after the Second World War underpins the kind of fiction written in english between 1948 and the late 1960s too. Emigrants of this period were primarily working-class, adult workers as part of pioneer literary antecedents of a growing body of world and postcolonial literature. They were reporters of and commentators on two worlds, the colonizer's and the formerly colonized. Furthermore, the Windrush Generation was looking and aiming for a group consciousness while still drawn into colonial traditions and being caught in a new cultural and political environment. Later generations, on the other hand, facilitated social change and promoted entertaining differences.

What Lamming, Rhys, Naipaul, and Selvon share among themselves, despite differences of their exilic experiences and proscriptions, is their articulation of a desire to escape the restrictions of ethnicity, national identification, and perhaps race itself. They share the journey from the periphery to the center of London, their metropolitan locus, and its influence on their literary production and career. How they differ is in their outlooks toward their cultural backgrounds and in the representations of home and identity in their writings. Naipaul, for example, is usually associated with Conrad and his ruthless truths. He sees in Conrad "a traveler to render exactly what he saw, [and] was able at a time of high imperialism to go far beyond the imperialistic, surface ways of writing about the East and native people." Conrad did not treat the foreign reality of the Far East as a joke or an imaginative geography. He described them seriously and gave them philosophical implications (Phillips: 2001: 513). Naipaul shares with Conrad this bleakly realistic view. Accordingly, Naipaul sees in India, the country of his ancestors, "a word, a mystical idea that embraces all those vast plains as the train moves, all those anonymous figures asleep on railway platforms and the footpaths of Bombay, all those poor fields and stunted animals, all this exhausted plundered land." Naipaul's India "is an ache, for which one has a great tenderness, but from which at length one always wishes to separate oneself" (Naipaul: 2002: 7).

In contrast to Naipaul's momentary tenderness and eternal aloofness, Sam Selvon is considered "the least political of us [West Indian writers] all." Selvon furthermore "made the fundamental point that what he needed was a little rent money, and the chance to change the monotonous half a pint of bitter for a little shot o' whisky from time to time" (Lamming: 1960: 43). Selvon, similar to Lamming and Rhys, "never really left the land that once claimed their ancestors like trees" (Ibid: 45). As a West Indian of East Indian descent, Selvon's language differs from that of Naipaul's. His style is the most humorous among all other Windrush writers and it is humor that makes his narratives more insightful and lively. While some of his earlier writings are national and focus on the protagonist's individual course of life such as *A Brighter Sun* and *An Island Is A World*, his later writings, although highlighting the protagonist's voice, attend more to the impressions of the collectivity. In *The Lonely Londoners*, for example, we know more about Moses through the other Boys.

Selvon tackles issues such as the limitations of the colonial subject, the psychological effects of the metropolitan city of London on the West Indian emigrant, and cultural nationalism. Although most of the time Selvon is a cultural nationalist urging his protagonists to take action, or satirizing their limitations of taking action, he explores the very beginning of the West Indian romance with London which was simultaneously a nightmare as well as a fertile experience. He tries to reflect the city's effect on his emigrant "boys" through their everyday life, but this is also a reflection on Selvon's own dwelling in postcolonial England. He focuses on the role of London as a metropolitan city turning people and groups into individuals and lonely Londoners. In *The Lonely Londoners* the city leaves one always in the same spot. Despite the West Indian's metropolitanism, that is, the fluidity of West Indian identities, there were many difficulties, such as racism and cultural nationalism which encourage the Caribbeans to maintain solidarity and discourage them from feeling as part of the British experience and nation.

Selvon started as a short story writer. In *The Oxford Book of Caribbean Short Stories* (1999), a Pan-Caribbean anthology of short stories, Selvon's *The Cricket Match* is listed in one group along with Jean Rhys, C. L. R. James, Andrew Salkey, and V. S. Naipaul. Selvon is described as the master storyteller of the Anglophone Caribbean tradition. The collection is divided, however, into four generations: the Pioneers who were born before the First World War; the Nationalist generation born before the mid-1930s, the Independence generation born through the 1940s and who established their careers in the 1960s and after the independence period; and finally the Contemporary flowering period of postcolonial writers. *The Oxford Book* is divided according to the time of the writers' births as opposed to subject matter. It is also a book of short stories as opposed to other forms of fiction. The four generations are therefore divided accordingly to a pre- and post-Second World War times. Jean Rhys stands out in the book as a pioneer because she spent most of her pre-Second World War years in Paris, and the rest of her post-Second World War years in England and the Caribbean. Her subject matter is also very relevant to the other contemporary writers in this chapter as her melancholic writing is illustrative as explained below. According to the Oxford Book, Selvon, Naipaul, and Lamming are all nationalist pioneers who were born in the in-between war times and for whom England played a significant role. They were also carried on the SS Empire Windrush Ship. Rhys, Selvon, Lamming, and Naipaul are therefore postcolonial writers whose language, identity, and writings were most affected and shaped by their multiple displacements of which London was a primary site.

The pioneer generation also includes the writer C. L. R. James among others. All such writers are emigrants who are characterized as being preoccupied with economic, psychological, and emotional costs, as well as the possibilities and frustrations which migration itself causes. Selvon's *The Cricket Match* is listed in this section as "a story of West Indian bold-face boast and bluff meeting English stereotyping and reserve." As most of Selvon's writings, this piece of writing is a comic story "beneath [whose] laughter is the most insightful commentary on the psychological nuances of that immigrant experience to be found anywhere in the literature" (Brown *et al*: 1999: xxiv). Algernon, Selvon's protagonist in the short story, plays cricket on the streets of the West Indies "with a bat made of coconut branch, a dry mango seed for ball, and a pitchoil tin for wicket" (Ibid: 92).

The Boys, predominantly factory workers who know nothing but the basics about cricket, rally against a professional English cricket team in London. The match is ironically interrupted by the typical English weather, saving the Boys' embarrassment. This story depicts how little the English and the West Indies understood one another; nevertheless, what they did share was a passion for cricket.

Farrukh Dhondy, himself a second-generation immigrant from India, a graduate from Cambridge, and the commissioning editor for multicultural programs for the BBC at the time, wrote a biography of C. L. R. James, an intellectual of the Black diaspora, a first-generation emigrant, essayist, and cricket player, in which he emphasizes the importance of cricket. "The task James set himself was to tell the story of cricket and in so doing to comment on the role of games of mass popularity in social evolution. James compared cricket, its organization and its popularity, to the Olympic Games of ancient Greece" (Dhondy: 2001a: 172). He saw in cricket a vehicle through which black people could instigate a social evolution by forging an anti-imperialist consciousness, a black consciousness, and a national pride. He also saw in cricket a means of uniting a set of separate islands of the West Indies into one national team: the West Indian national team of cricket.

The early focus on nostalgia, memories of the idealized past, and the struggle to assert one's (national or ethnic) identity and self was far and wide based on being part of a history: a history that happened to be, and scarred predominantly, by the British presence. Many of those emigrants wrote of their places nostalgically while living the coldness of England.

Lamming's *The Emigrants* stands as one of the pioneer pieces of fiction written by an emigrant writer after the Second World War. Its structure and form, language and subject matter grant it a place in West Indian literature as one of the classic pieces of literature alongside his first novel *In The Castle of My Skin* (1953) whose title incidentally is derived from a poem by the West Indian poet, Derek Walcott. It is worth noting here that most emigrant writings before the emergence of the Windrush Generation were predominantly of poetry—Derek Walcott, Aime Cesaire, Wilson Harris, and Richard Wright, for example—as opposed to the accelerated increase of novel writing that dominated afterward.

It is perfectly appropriate to start with Lamming's *The Emigrants* (*TE* from now on) for it is about a group of West Indians who emigrate to Britain crossing the Atlantic on a ship resembling or thinly disguised as the Windrush Generation's experience. The ship carries

Jamaicans, Trinidadians, Barbadians among many others from the "little islands"; they are picked from Port-of-Spain and the tropicals, "taking ship with their last resources and sailing into unknown lands in search of adventure and fortune and mystery" (Lamming: 1954: 107). The voyage to the unknown was an escape from the cage of reality into freedom: the freedom of recently emancipated colonials. To escape the Oedipal Territory, the cage, was "to inhabit what was beyond." To stay at home "within the cage where they were born and would die, the only tolerable climate of experience was reality which was simply an irreversible instinct to make things matter" (*TE*: 105).

The emigrants on the ship exchange banter and gossip, calypso music, rum and ambitions, expectations and optimisms. Dickson, for example, is an ambitious schoolteacher whose objectives are undermined sexually and racially by white women on his arrival. Higgins is another emigrant whose ambition and goal is to arrive at Liverpool and study to become a qualified cook. Both Higgins and Dickson among many others are confronted with absolute failure. "Men like Higgins," Lamming writes, "they come expectin' to find some kind o' chance, an' they find out that the same kind o' misfortune is in the place ... There ain't nothin' they can do but finish the study as quick as they can an' get back" (*TE*: 189). Thus the theme of eventual return is a characteristic of Windrush Generation writings. The "better break" the emigrant looks for proves after all to be a "primitive curiosity: a vague perception of a better break" (*TE*: 96). London turns out to be another cage, another ghetto of another kind of reality.

The novel's structure and form is divided into three parts. The parts in themselves resemble the emigrant's journey: Voyage, Rooms and Residents, and Another Time. The first part, Voyage, is about the rituals of departure. Men were "in transit...a lucky limitation," Lamming writes (*TE*: 10). Highlighting West Indian cultural life— the importance of calypso music, telling stories and gossiping (oral tradition/oratory), drinking rum amongst other things—the chapter goes on, however, to focus on the West Indian's flight and group consciousness. "Now I see more clearly in what way I belong to this group which has one thing certain. Flight! We're all in flight" (*TE*: 52).

In the context of first-generation emigrants, to emigrate meant to aimlessly cross the Atlantic for a better break which eventually turns to be a mere curiosity. The "flight was always a conscious choice, a choice even to suffer" (*TE*: 52–3). A flight is a way out, a way far from the traditional and religious, from the familial, the accustomed to, the familiar. But with every flight comes a fight. For example, a Barbadian emigrant questions his future had he stayed at home; in

Barbados, "I see my life map out clear in front o' me an' I say to myself I doan' want that." In Barbados, "there wasn't no chance to sort o' educate yuself" (*TE*: 60). Here displacement produces education: to leave the familiar and familial is to discover and to enter into a new education, which profoundly questions and transforms the nature of the self. To leave home for the West Indian nonetheless included a slightly different dimension: adventuring out of the formerly colonized islands was "to prove that them [West Indians] is themselves" (*TE*: 66). Going away therefore was to reinforce the emigrant's identity and the emigrants' group consciousness: not as British but as black, Caribbean identity.

Through various conversations among the lodging islanders, the Voyage from Port-of-Spain to the port of Southampton or Tilbury indicates repeatedly the West Indians' group consciousness and sense of national belonging. West Indians, in Lamming's words, are a "vomit" thrown up by the great nations that colonized the West Indies, namely England, France, Portugal, and Spain. These great nations vomited the peripheral Chinese, Indians, and Africans from around the world "'an' vomit settle there in the Caribbean Sea." Historical displacement here is emphasized from the point of view of the Caribbean/West Indian emigrant. After the Second World War and decolonization, the vomit is "'explodin' bit by bit. It beginnin' gradjally to stir itself, an' you can understan' what hapennin' if you imagine yuh vomit take on life an' start to find out where yuh stomach is" (*TE*: 67).

Despite the fact that the Caribbean stir of vomit emigrates to the stomach of England, the belly of the beast, the West Indian has always been exposed to displacement and migration. Accordingly, the West Indian community is an organically multiethnic one. "'It stirring' itself but there ain't no pot" (*TE*: 67). Geographical displacement and its subsequent change acted as a reminder of the peoples' historical ties which were connected through the very Caribbean island they left. In the away, Lamming writes in his *The Pleasures of Exile*, that "the land begins to take a human shape" (Lamming: 1960: 19). Colonialism thus also acts as an identity shaper, a helper in the articulation of the West Indians' unity. The "Strange Man represent de kind o' confusion dat is West Indies people" (*TE*: 68).

Just as every other novel written around the same time as Lamming's *The Emigrants*, this novel draws on the difficulties of living and dwelling in the host society that is England. The weather is one manifesting feature of change and difference throughout too. Lamming's form and structure of the boys' conversation on the train as they arrive at the shores of England breaks with the conventional style of narrating. Pushing the boys' expression of dissatisfaction and discomfort in the midst of the steaming smoke and fog to the far end of the page, Lamming differentiates between the boys' talking and the interrupting train conductor's announcement and others:

Paddington.

They said it wouldn't be so cold. So cold...so frightened...so frightened...home...go...to go back ... home...only because...this like...no...home...other reason...because... like this...frightened ...alone...the whole place...goes up up up and over over up and over curling falling ... up...over to heaven...down to...hell up an' over ....
(Lamming: 1954: 123)

The most repeated words in the above quotation are "cold" and "home" while the most expressive tone and feeling is fright. What is most important is the discontinuous and broken voice of the freezing emigrant. The weather, Bhabha reminds us, is the most evident of national differences. It is one of

the most changeable and immanent signs of national difference. It encourages memories of the "deep" nation crafted in chalk and limestone; the quilted downs; the moors menaced by the wind; the quiet cathedral towns; that corner of a foreign field that is forever England. The English weather also revives memories of its daemonic double: the heat and dust of India; the dark emptiness of Africa; the tropical chaos that was deemed despotic and ungovernable and therefore worthy of the civilizing mission. These imaginative geographies that spanned countries and empires are changing, those imagined communities that played on the unisonant boundaries of the nation are singing with different voices... the scattering of the people across countries... end[s] with their gathering in the city. The return of the diasporic; the postcolonial.
(Bhabha: 2005: 243)

For Bhabha, dissatisfaction with the English weather and climate evokes a continuing distress in a new land, but it is also evocative of the opposite: the clear sky and sun of the tropicals. This is also a characteristic of literature written by the Windrush Generation, not to mention the following generations. The English weather had a major impact on all writers and particularly the first arrivals for which the tropical weather was part of their very lively home memories. Having been exposed to the tropical warmth through a lifetime of experience back with their families and on a land where they established and acquired their first language and traditional cultural identity, the weather indeed had a psychological effect. Selvon describes how weather can be a very effective self-changing factor as part of the English culture. In summer, "the sun burn away all the tightness and strain that was in their faces for the winter." The wintery force ripe orange in the sky gives "no heat at all" and makes the atmosphere "like a sullen twilight hanging over the big city." In summer, "you forget what it like to see blue skies like back home" (Selvon: 2006: 56). The psychological impact the English weather left on the emigrants is pervasive in the melancholic, expressive images represented in their contrasts and descriptions and is vividly reflected in the gloomy images of their identities and narratives.

Other problems of housing and accommodation, loneliness and individualism are also persistent. The architectural differences are also highlighted throughout. "The way the houses build was that people doan' have nothing to do with one another. Yuh can live an' die in yuh room an' the people next door never say boo to you no matter how long you inhabit that place... What they call a house in London is what we see on the wharf in Port-of-Spain. Just a big place where you throw things like sugar and rum inside" (Lamming: 1954: 76). Despite the difficulties England presented the emigrants with, they remain determined to demonstrating themselves capable of proving the former colonizer wrong, that there was nothing that the West Indian could not do. To fail abroad would be shameful and would indicate to the English man that the West Indian was nothing but a failure. The voice of Lamming's boys echoes Fanon's theory of depersonalization and the psychological factors of shame and fear imparted through colonialism:

When other people say that them is neither one thing nor the other, but just different from every other complete thing, them get frightened, sometimes shamed, till them get together an' make up they minds that them goin' prove what them is. Them all provin' something. When they stay back home in they little island them forget a little an' them remain vomit; just as them wus vomit up, but when them go 'broad, them remember.

(Lamming: 1954: 68)

In the course of this process of discovery, of displacement, in meeting with the White Man, the emigrant also rediscovers his own connection with his native history and his black/Negro identity. Memory once again proves to be critical and essential in the course of identity configuration. Psychological displacement furthermore is generated from the very process of his thinking of his own being and existence. "It was here in the room of garlic, onions and mist that each became aware, gradually, anxiously, of the level and scope of his private existence. Each tried to think, for that too was a kind of action" (*TE*: 187). To provoke thinking of one's identity and of one's existence is evidently inherent in the experience of displacement.

The second chapter of *The Emigrants*, Rooms and Residence, tackles the social formation of the English society and exposes the emigrants' meeting places as well as the English reception of them and their imaginative geographies of the far away and distant. Realizing that the Occident is dependent on the formation of the image of the Other through fictional or mythical representation, one of the Boys says that it "[s]eems to me the people here see things from their side. They know that England got colonies an' all that, an' they hear 'bout the people in these far away places a thought it wus all a story in a book, but they never seem to understan' that these people in these places got an affection for them that is greater than that of any allies in war-time" (*TE*: 186). Lamming establishes a reconnection between the emigrant and his colonial history, and between the colonial and the colonizer because a colonial memory burdens the emigrant and his traveling; and so there are always complexities and reservations that bewilder him/her. Lamming emphasizes that this kind of imaginative landscape or "imagescape" of the colonized Other carried in the minds of English people is being debunked and displaced by the arrival of the emigrant intellectual.

The colonial white man acknowledged the Other from their own Occidental viewpoint; "their whole introduction to something called culture, all of it, in the form of words, came from outside: Dickens, Jane Austen, Kipling and that sacred gang" (Lamming: 1960: 27). Only ten or so years after the decolonization of the majority of the Commonwealth countries was there witness to the birth of the West Indian writer.

Lamming insists, however, that the West Indies form the abstract and principal material of West Indian writings. He also emphasizes the psychological displacement subsequent to the historical one caused by colonial occupation:

The exile is always colonial by circumstances: a man colonized by his incestuous love of a past whose glory is not worth our total human suicide; colonized by a popular whoredom of talents whose dividends he knows he does not deserve; colonized by the barely liveable acceptance of domestic complaint; colonized, if black in skin, by the agonizing assault of the other's eye whose meanings are based on a way of seeing he vainly tries to alter; and ultimately colonized by some absent vision which, for want of another faith, he hopefully calls the Future.

(Lamming: 1960: 229)

The emigrants of the Windrush Generation were in this sense colonial. Some of these early emigrants thought of themselves as minorities and fought to march from the margins to the center. They tried to construct a sense of self by going back in memories, looking for a national identity different to the mainstream in a lost land and a colonial history which alienated their present. First-generation emigrants were looking and aiming for group consciousness and focused on a touristic London, while later generations shifted to other cities, places, and/or suburbs. Earlier writings focused on the dark, gloomy abandonment of home and the subsequent problematics that emerged thereafter; these were all predominantly affected by the ontological condition of homelessness linked with a more recent experience of colonialism. Earlier writings of the 1950s and 1960s had also expressed severe cultural conflicts, racial discriminations, cultural antagonism, mimicry and imitation, and a reactionary cultural nationalism. These all were very central to the narrative of the Windrush Generation. The newly arrived and newly born emigrant was portrayed bemoaning racism constantly, dreaming of assimilation, haunted by nostalgic dreams, waiting for a physical return, idealizing a national image, and instinctively identifying with and focusing on the natal and inherited. The emigrant is also usually portrayed as a peasant-oriented individual who is desperate to claim authenticity and yet burdened by a colonial history and a past which keeps finding its way to their present imagination. Mimetic imperatives, sentimentality, loneliness, and alienation overwhelmed writings of that early period.

Although the crossing of the Atlantic and the arrival of the *SS Empire Windrush* on the shores of England brought mainly West Indians and Caribbeans, there was a lack of geographical and cultural awareness of the former British colonies which also resulted in stereotypical images of the emigrant at the time: all black people were considered African. "English people believe that everybody who come from the West Indies come from Jamaica" (Selvon: 2006: 7). This also gave birth to a revolution in the emigrants' politics of their own identity (how they saw themselves and how they were seen by others) within Britain. Hence, an articulation of double or multiple consciousness was in the making: black identity, Pan-Caribbean identity, and/or an Indo-Caribbean identity. Some were even thinking of themselves as South Americans. "Especially with them who come from British

Guiana and don't want federation in the West Indies, saying that they belong to the continent of South America" (Ibid: 30).

Group consciousness can be illustrated through Selvon's Boys who did not think for instance of returning home to a regional or a particular island. On the contrary, they thought of returning to the greater area of the Caribbean. They also did not identify within Britain as Trinidadians, Jamaicans, or Barbadians. They were all "seen" and hence identified as black. "Them is West Indians. Not Jamaicans or Trinidadians. Cause the bigger the better" (Lamming: 1954: 68). While the English cultural identity was articulated through a sense of nativeness and ethnic exclusiveness to a white race, the West Indians' cultural identity was marked by displacement: a sense of an agonizing distance and exile from their homeland, the country of their birth and residence, and a colonial burden and a psychologically traumatic racial inferiority. Jean Rhys was exceptionally triply displaced: a female, Creole, and a displaced exile.

Rhys can be read as a colonial and/or postcolonial or a modernist feminist. She can be viewed furthermore as a forerunner of the postmodernist way of looking at the politics of home and identity, having spent most of her life being on the run, displaced from Dominica, to England and France. Although she had always been writing nostalgically about Paris and Dominica, she never wrote with the same emotional attachment about England. Her first book, *The Left Bank* (1927), for example, has the Caribbean at its heart. France, however, is as important a point of reference as is the Caribbean in her first book. Melancholic as she was, *Smile Please* (1979), her unfinished autobiography, pessimistically depicts her own life of trouble of which England is a major traumatizing experience. *Smile Please* is divided into two parts, both of which were left unfinished, a testament to Rhys's own identity and being. The first part describes her early years and childhood in Bona Vista in Dominica and is entitled "Smile Please." In the second, "It Began to Grow Cold," she describes her journey to Devon and her high expectations as well as disappointments about England.

Rhys's *Wide Sargasso Sea*, furthermore, is a masterpiece which followed during the seventies on preceding intertextual texts, which borrowed, transformed, and challenged previous texts written by white writers (such as *Things Fall Apart* and *Seasons of Migration to the North*), "writing back" to colonial literary narratives. Not only is Rhys's "mad woman in the attic"—with her dreams, the fire destruction of the house, and the mirror imagery—drawn on from Bronte's *Jane Eyre* but Rhys also indicates that her English male protagonist is incapable of passionate love, by virtue of being English. Mr Rochester is portrayed as an upper-middle-class Englishman who is emotionally reserved and materialistic; he is an Englishman whose colonial mentality stands between him and the Caribbean culture in which he now lives. The ends of power and domination are achieved through his long narrative which interrupts Antoinette's own and whose following dream provokes her to set fire to the house, closing down the narrative with discontent and destruction. Rochester's violent sex with Antoinette also signals the battle of power and domination over weakness and limitation, but he is frightened by the lack of control and seeks sexual experience with Amelie to reassure himself of his own centrality and authority.

The desire for control also involves the process of naming: we are not even familiar with Antoinette's name until the end of the first quarter of the novel. She is furthermore being renamed by Rochester as Bertha in order to distance her from her presumably mad mother. This narrative of renaming replicates Rhys's own renaming of herself as writer: Jean Rhys is not her original name. Born Ella Rees Williams, Rhys opted to write under the name of Jean (presumably a possible masculine French name too) Rhys (which rhymes with Rees). As explained in Chapter 1, naming and renaming are one means of inducing psychological displacement and splitting.

Rhys indicates skepticism over the ability of Rochester to understand the "other side of the story" and succeed in adapting to the new Caribbean culture. Equally, through her female protagonist, Rhys seems skeptical of her own ability to integrate into the English culture and community with such obstacles as racism and in her case sexism in Britain at the time. She portrays migrants generally, and female migrants particularly, as always "out of place" as they are faced with such complexities as racism and/or distance. Such difficulties and complexities not only complicate but also make the migrant aware and conscious of his/her sense of place and self, home and identity. With pale skin, blue eyes, and light hair, Rhys was neither one thing nor another: neither Caribbean, nor black or English. As a writer, she continuously makes attempts at reinventing her self, always motivated by her contradictions and complexities, always seeking hominess in her imaginatively constructed spaces. Burdened by a complex sense of self, she had to reinvent herself all the time and rewrite her own displacements.

Rhys's own contradictions and complexities become apparent through her female protagonists who are marginalized by dominant male characters, eventually being left behind, divorced, and/or psychically traumatized, facing death in the heart of foreign soil. Her semi-autobiographical fiction (particularly *Wide Sargasso Sea* and *Voyage in the Dark*) is generated from the very intimately emotional and close, yet distant, relationship with her homeland. Intervening in and interrupting her present, the past constantly darkened her future possibilities, with memories haunting the time and space of her now and here. Desolation and alienation were even further deepened by the treatment she received from male characters in her life and the many divorces she had been through.

As a displaced artist and an exile, Rhys's fiction portrays a resentment of patriarchal societies, disorientation, and nostalgia in Paris, England, and eventually back in Dominica. Her attempts to create a bridge between home and away, writing, although therapeutic at times, intensifies her traumatic psychological displacement and melancholia. Be it the cold weather, solitariness at convents with nuns, or men and alcohol, Rhys's unhappiness dominates most of her writings; it reflects her alienation and triple displacements: as a female scarred by her male relations, as a Creole, and as a displaced individual in foreign places and languages. Rhys found peace and survival only in "death" (Rhys: 1979: 133).

If Selvon is the most humorous of this generation, Rhys is introduced here as the most melancholically devastated character of the Windrush Generation, a writer whose memory and writings failed to shape her sense of self and belonging. She was skeptical of the migrant's ability to integrate with a new culture and remained an outsider throughout her life. In *Smile Please*, words such as "remember," "death," "change," and "strange" echo repeatedly her earlier experiences in Bona Vista. While in England feeling lonely and remote, "[i]t's to Bona Vista that I have any first clear connected memory" (Rhys: 1979: 16). Memory was all that Rhys possessed when she left as well as upon her return to the Caribbean. And even memory started to fade away as she aged.

When Rhys returned many years later to visit home, she is told that she "must have a guide to visit" (Ibid: 28). A native stranger, the house where she used to stay in Geneva was burnt, and no place that she revisited was the same anymore. The so-called home was "very dirty, not like you remember it" (Ibid: 29). Her high expectations of England also played a major role in her later disappointment and dissatisfaction. "I always felt that life was glorious and would certainly become more so later on (England, England!)" (Ibid: 52).

While England did not offer Rhys the promising land she once hoped for, like the paradise Antoinette imagined in *Wide Sargasso Sea*, the most Rhys felt at home was in Morgan's Rest. "It was there, not in wild beautiful Bona Vista, that I began to feel I loved the land and to know that I would never forget it...I wanted to identify myself with it, to lose myself in it. '(But it turned its head away indifferent...)'" (Rhys: 1979: 66). Rhys always desired and longed for an "inhabitation or annihilation" (Ibid: 67). She wished to belong, to fall onto a foundation according to which she could shape herself and with which she could gather her fragmented self. Failure to do so, constant occurrences of nightmares, death, burnt places, and violent memories had always haunted Rhys throughout her actual as well as fictional characters.

Compared to other writers of her generation, Rhys's psychological displacement is the most severely melancholic. She laments: "I would never be part of anything. I would never really belong anywhere, and I knew it, and all my life would be the same, trying to belong, and failing. Always something would go wrong. I am a stranger and I will always be, and after all I didn't really care" (Rhys: 1979: 100). However, in this sense of eternal directionlessness and fragmentation of self, one finds that Rhys, being postcolonial and modernist, is one of the forerunners in recognizing the inevitable instability of identity: that it is fluid, always turning, and never one thing or another, but multiple. She also recognized that home is not one idealized place and a stable essence: it is a reservoir of memories, imaginative, mobile, and incoherent. What Rhys failed to accomplish, however, because of the inwardly turned sense of melancholia and carelessness, is turning and shifting the focus from melancholia toward celebration.

A haunting colonial past, a nostalgic and sentimental distance, and a melancholic paranoia with regard to belonging anywhere were always overwhelming characteristics of the writing of this generation, though the way each writer dealt with these differs. For example, such experiences are to an extent celebrated and humorously developed in the case of Selvon. It is what he calls the "ha-ha" factor that made his Boys' stories, in contrast to Rhys's female characters for example, more palatable (Selvon: 2009: 28). Selvon's sense of humor is also conveyed through "the nation language" that is more emphatic and buys the readers' sympathy for the Boys' struggle in the metropolis (Ibid: 26). Unlike Rhys, humor and jokes seem to be, among other techniques, a means of survival for Selvon.

A good, representative example of this generation's writings is Selvon's acclaimed London trilogy: *The Lonely Londoners* (1956), *Moses Ascending* (1975), and *Moses Migrating* (1983). His narratives are an exilic, chronicle of black emigrant city life. Selvon's distinct "ballads" are also distinguished from later generations' writings. His oral strategies of the Caribbean calypso, his fantastic transcription of the Caribbean idiom into written English, and his anecdotal style in Trinidadian and its accessibility to readers worldwide are all characteristics that make Selvon an unprecedented phenomenon in the world of contemporary, postcolonial literature generally and the West Indian particularly.

The trilogy can be studied as a single, yet episodic, narrative which portrays the devolving and developing course of the life and identity of the first-generation emigrant as well as a changing England over almost twenty years. The beginning, middle, and end of Selvon's trilogy and its main veteran and protagonist, Moses Aloetta, are predominantly preoccupied with themes of migrant displacement, identification, being caught in-between cultural worlds, racial discrimination, mimicry, assimilation, nostalgia, and exile. The story of Moses poignantly portrays a journey of a first-generation migrant. In *The Lonely Londoners*, living in a basement, Moses struggles in the gray city of London while he tries to form a Caribbean identity while adapting to an English lifestyle and culture; in *Moses Ascending*, he becomes a landlord served by a white butler, Bob, and caught in a Black Power Movement where he eventually ends living in the basement and caught between his own black community and the hosting white one. Thus, Moses eventually descends as opposed to what the title ironically implies; he is forced to give way to his white butler to live in the upper story of the house while he himself descends to live in the basement once again. Selvon's narrative here reemphasizes the fact that the migrant will always be, regardless of his physical ownership of household, marginalized, racially inferior, and melancholically caught and entrapped in-between two cultures. The migrant's life circle ends with Moses's physical return to his motherland and country of birth Trinidad in *Moses Migrating*. It is also worth mentioning here that Selvon himself wrote *Moses Migrating* in Canada where he resided as a Canadian citizen after leaving England in the late seventies. He also eventually returned to his native land Trinidad where he died in 1994. As mentioned previously, first-generation writers tend to be physically attached to a homeland, to a concrete beginning as opposed to constructing what Rushdie calls an imaginary homeland.

In his *An Island Is a World*, Selvon, speaking through the protagonist Foster, declares that one has to belong, for to feel that one has no country is a lonely feeling: it is also a feeling of lacking something, of loss. Therefore, there is always in Selvon's work "a stream of consciousness [which] chant[s] celebrating the regeneration of a deep ancestral awareness of a shared Caribbean identity" (Selvon: 2009:

17). Unlike others in Trinidad who felt the need of a return to India after the independence, Foster expresses despair as he sees "men who had forgotten their nationality in the cosmopolitan population [and] became aware of themselves as Indian. A flame of nostalgia began to spread. Men who had forgotten who they were dusted their memories and began to talk about going back home" (Ibid: 161).

Selvon himself was a mixed-race writer. His father was a first-generation East Indian and his mother was an Anglo-Scottish. He was West Indian by birth, East Indian by descent, English by virtue of a colonial and postcolonial history, and with a nostalgically, displaced identity. He, however, reminds his reader that all that remains from and connects him with the past is historical memory, that "[t]he separation was not only of time and distance. It was in everything but memory, and what was memory but reflection on a past which could never be recaptured?" (Ibid: 142).

First-generation emigrants were predominantly occupied with, and sentimentally attached to, a geographical space, a fixed origin; their agonizing distance from it caused them insecurity, loneliness, and desolation among other effects. Thus such geographical displacement caused much psychological displacement for this generation. These first-generation emigrants were the ones who literally physically and psychologically crossed the wide Atlantic and voyaged through the so-called Middle Passage for days on a ship. Psychological displacement for this generation can also be evidenced in mimicry. That is, failing to consolidate an independent identity, some of the pioneer emigrants became mimic men, or what Selvon called "whitewashed black men" (Selvon: 2009: 9).

Exemplifying this tendency, Naipaul's *The Mimic Men* is about the failure of the formerly colonized to govern and reestablish their own newly independent country. The English were the superior ruling class; the native tried therefore to identify with this culture's codes and values. Their geographical displacement, however, makes it now even more difficult to identify with the former colonizer. They become mimic men who imitate the colonizer's lifestyle and culture, behavior, and thought without understanding its meaning or value. This was not to say, on the other hand, that there was not the opportunity for freedom of choice, for creativity, and for articulating an identity totally anew. "In London I had no guide," says Naipaul's Singh. "There was no one to link my present with my past, no one to note my consistencies or inconsistencies. It was up to me to choose my character" (Naipaul: 1969: 20). Most mimic men, however, could not choose their character as Naipaul's protagonist Singh affirms.

This protagonist, who could be a thinly disguised Naipaul himself, is distinguished from his contemporaries as an odd exception. He

> no longer dream of ideal landscapes or seek to attach myself to them. All landscapes eventually turn to land, the gold of the imagination to the lead of the reality. I could not, like so many of my fellow exiles, live in a suburban semi-detached house; I could not pretend even to myself to be part of a community or to be putting down roots. I prefer the freedom of my far-out suburban hotel, the absence of responsibility.
>
> (Ibid: 11)

While R. Singh feels that being rooted or belonging to a community or a homeland is an excessive responsibility, he is, nevertheless, a representative of the displaced and disillusioned colonial whose sense of home and identity is taunted by melancholic displacement and deeply affected by, and infected with, colonization. Some of Selvon's Boys are also mimic men; one particular boy is Harris:

> a fellar who like to play ladeda, and he like English customs and thing, he does be polite and say thank you and he does get up in the bus and the tube to let woman sit down, which is a thing even them Englishmen don't do. And when he dress, you think is some Englishman going to work in the city, bowler and umbrella, and briefcase tuck under the arm, with *The Times* fold up in the pocket so the name would show, and he walking upright like if he alone who live in the world. Only thin, Harris face Black.
>
> (Selvon: 2006: 103)

Susheila Nasta, a frequent writer on Selvon, sees in Selvon's second novel, his first work written in exile, a work that "translated the humorous dynamics of the Caribbean street talk that they [the Boys] brought with them into an international context. In style and content therefore it represented a major step forward in the process of linguistic and cultural decolonization." Selvon's *The Lonely Londoners* (1956) "has been the most enduring and emblematic" novel that drew a "picture of the world back home whilst defining a Caribbean consciousness within British context" (Nasta in Selvon: 2006: x). The title of the novel suggests the paradoxical formula of the early migrant who struggles to become a Londoner, a part of the British society and the landscape of the city of London; his loneliness keeps him at bay, nevertheless. Such loneliness is caused by nostalgia; haunting memories of a romanticized and idealized past; an identity in limbo, racism, and a hostile reception of the city; and its most changeable, evocative, and provocative climate. In the winter time, you would never think that grass would ever come green again but if you don't keep your eyes open it look like one day the trees naked and the next day they have clothes on sometimes walking up to the Bayswater Road from Queensway you could look on a winter day and see how grim the trees looking and a sort of fog in the distance though right near to you you ain't have no fog but that is only deceiving because if somebody down the other side look up by where you are it would look to them as if it have fog by where you are and this time so the sun in the sky like a force ripe orange and it giving no heat at all and the atmosphere like a sullen twilight hanging over the big city but it different too bad when is summer for then the sun shine for true.

(Nasta in Selvon: 2006: x)

London provokes its double, "and you forget what it like to see blue skies like back home where blue sky so common people don't look up in the air and you feeling miserable and cold" (Ibid: 93).

The cost of Selvon's Boys to becoming "Londoners" is their loneliness in a foggy, unreal, and restless city away from images that always haunt them, their tropical home, and its clear sky. It is so cold in London that "the words freeze and you have to melt it to hear the talk" (Selvon: 2006: 15). The talk about the weather is very frequent throughout the novel that emphasizes, by virtue of contrast, struggle, severity, difference, and change. Moses wishes he could be "back home." The land he expected with his contemporaries to be "paved with gold" fills him now with sorrow and regret, homesickness, and nostalgia. Talking to his Double character, Galahad, Moses says: "Boy, you know what I want to do? I want to go back to Trinidad and lay down in the sun and dig my toes, and eat a fish ... you know where paradise is? Is somewhere between St Joseph and Tacarigua" (125). Selvon, through the voice of his veteran Moses, eulogizes rural and peasant life, which exists in happy opposition to the urban life of the western capital city of London. In what he calls paradise, Moses would "get a old house and have some cattle and goat ... no ballet and opera and symphony" (Ibid: 125). In contrast to Moses, Henry Oliver, nicknamed as Galahad, adjusts to the new unwritten rules of London: he is excited to live by such unwritten rules, coming from the formerly colonized territories of the West Indies. Such rules make him feel like a new man and he is astonished by the cosmopolitan places and touristic sites such as Piccadilly Circus, Waterloo Station, and The Thames.

To be displaced is to become used to temporariness and improvisation. What this means is that you

work things out in your own mind to a kind of pattern, in a sort of sequence, and one day bam! Something happen to throw everything out of gear, what you expect to happen never happen, what you don't expect to happen always happen, and you have to start thinking all over again.

(Selvon: 2006: 40)

Selvon's writings stress the element of surprise and the temporal contingency of migrant and exilic displaced experience: the emigrant is compelled to improvise to accommodate constant and unpredictable change.

The Lonely Londoners also emphasizes emigrant generational differences and the circle of migration that started developing from the early 1950s. Cap, a West Indian emigrant, marries Daniel, a Nigerian-French migrant; another is Joseph.

He married to a English girl and they have four children, and they living in two rooms in Paddington. He apply to the LCC for a flat, but it look like he would never get one. Now the children big enough to go to school, and what you think? Is big fight every day because the other children calling them darkie. (126)

Tolroy, a Trinidadian, is followed by his grandmother, Tanty: "'Old people like you, you only come here to make life miserable,' Tolroy say" (Selvon: 2006: 57). Women and female characters are not part of Selvon's Boys, who are all wandering male characters. Female characters are, on the other hand, portrayed as followers to the city of London, although they still share part of the social and everyday commentary with the Boys. Tanty, arriving at London to join her son, is being asked by a journalist for a photo. She is committed to unity, group consciousness, and a communal identity, and she makes this clear: "you can't take me alone. You have to take the whole family" (11).

Furthermore, the Boys' sense of national and group consciousness starts also within unreal London. In the midst of the city's loneliness, solitude, and racial hostility, the Boys find salvation and consolation in their past.

Looking at things in general life really hard for the boys in London. This is a lonely miserable city, if it was that we didn't get together now and then to talk about things back home, we would suffer like hell. Here is not like home where you have friends all about... Nobody in London does really accept you, they tolerate you, yes, but you can't go in their house and eat and sit down and talk. (126)

Selvon highlights the importance of oratory through gossiping during everyday life for the Caribbean emigrant. He also emphasizes the differences, the variable proscriptions experienced, and the luxuries between the working-class emigrant hustling in the metropolitan city and the student who "spend a few years here, learn a profession, then go back home stupider than they come" (129).

Selvon's Boys are working-class inhabitants of London's undergrounds and bus routes, cafes and factories, restaurants and confined basements. The Boys' attempts to confront the city's harsh weather and its color bar help them to reinvent new ways to survive, and their survival becomes a story and a chronicle of everyday life in the metropolis as well as reminiscent of the tropical days of their past. Home and away are not narrated or recalled in juxtaposition; on the contrary, they are oppositional. The very tangible color bar is an insurmountable difficulty, which makes their integration into the adopted English society harder and sends them summoning memories of the far-off homeland, stimulating rioting and racial violence, and often urging a sense of nationalism. "It was big ballad in all the papers, they put it under a big headline, saying how the colour bar was causing trouble" (Selvon: 2006: 8). Their story is an exilic narrative of formerly unvoiced peripherals that are now, with the might of Selvon's language, given a voice from within the headquarters. As a precursory migrant narrative, Selvon's stories expose London's unreality and debunk conventional perspectives with regard to its Englishness.

The Boys (the nationally patriotic Galahad, Cap the Casanova, Moses the veteran, the lost-in-translation Big City, and the Englishman-want-to-be Harris) are Selvon's chroniclers and practitioners of everyday life in London, inventing ways of living and getting on as they see the English life through a West Indian vernacular. Nevertheless, the Boys, as all other Windrush emigrants of the time, are portrayed as being a constitutive part of London's life. Despite their scattered fates and destinations within the little cities of London, Selvon manages to bring all of them into a single narrative; such a narrative is being held together through the Boys' attempts to try to articulate a West Indian, black identity while living in the former colonizer's headquarters. The Boys hold together through a network of kinship and friendship, gossip and storytelling. Selvon manages in his narrative to ironically portray the racial stereotypes and depictions of blacks from a White viewpoint. By doing so, he effectively recuperates the white reader's sympathy with Selvon's emigrant Boys. First-generation emigrants share "great aimlessness, a great restless, swaying movement that leaving you standing in the same spot... black faces... strained faces... bewildered, hopeless... laughing, but they only laughing because they fraid to cry" (139). With Selvon's "ha-ha" factor, *The Lonely Londoners* addresses what Said calls contrapuntal (i.e., interdependent and interwoven) histories: African, Indian, Caribbean, and British; what Bhabha calls the "starting points" of other national and international histories and geographies (Bhabha: 2005). "People in this world don't know how other people does affect their lives" (Selvon: 2006: 62). Selvon's story shows what happens when East meets West: the former changes and consequently the latter is changed too.

Selvon's second novel of his trilogy, *Moses Ascending*, however, is the anti- or counternarrative to the earlier novel, and can be likened to a rewriting of *Robinson Crusoe* for a modern context, without the inbuilt innocence. Moses, now a landlord with a Whiteman servant/friend, tells a story that supposedly interrogates and destabilizes the canon of English literature while evidently still being affected by its classical pieces of literature, and hence its colonial history. *Heart of Darkness*,[3] *Jane Eyre*, *Robinson Crusoe*, *The Tempest*,[4] and many others are being retold from the Black man's viewpoint from within England.

Not among or one of the Boys anymore, Moses is content with his relationship with Bob, a Whiteman butler. Moses introduces Bob, his Whiteman Friday, as his friend and ally. Moses offers his guests tea, drinks whiskey, and is also writing his own memoir, a Western form, in Standard English. Culturally he is adapted. Moses, however, fails as a landlord and *descends* to live *downstairs* in the basement, while Bob, his Friday, *ascends* to live *upstairs* in the attic. Moses, like Caliban when he loses his land in *The Tempest*, loses his apartment and rights as a landlord and cannot escape his destiny and identity as a mentally colonialized black man. The irony of *Moses Ascending*, of course, is that Moses has been diminished and is now forced to live as a tenant in a lower story in his own house.

In the final novel of the trilogy, *Moses Migrating*, the dream of ascendance is recognized for what it is as Moses returns, or perhaps escapes, back to Trinidad. Hari Kunzru, a second-generation immigrant of mixed race, describes *Moses Migrating* as a novel with "a carnivalesque atmosphere and an underlying tone of cynicism. It's a book full of mockery and dirty jokes, shot through with disappointment and anger" (Selvon: 2008: viii).

Moses Ascending, however, introduces the hostel Moses owns and runs with the help of Bob as a multiracial entity whose residents/tenants form a part of a reformed England: emigrant communities redefine Englishness. The hostel introduces an England with a second generation of emigrants as well as an accelerating speed of migration. Subsequently, the materialization of black political movements such as the Black Power Movement emerges. The hostel itself also dramatizes the introduction of more social security, especially financial resources. "[I]f you are a landlord, it is a horse of a different colour," says Moses. His highlighting of color emphasizes that ownership was exclusive to whites. This is reminiscent of Fanon's "you are rich because you are white, you are white because you are rich." Moses' status as "master of the house" echoes the status of Defoe's Crusoe being lord of the island. Moses, on the contrary, becomes Selvon's black Crusoe who challenges the dominant cultural customs of colonialist narratives. The narrative interrogates the hierarchical structures of Western imperialism through the demonstration of West Indian cultural identity and its impact on Britons. Moses obviously always feels on the periphery of the center. While he seems to be trying to become an Englishman, assimilating food, dress, music, and lifestyle (including writing a memoir and using Standard English), other tenants like Faizul, Paki, and Galahad refuse to accept the culture of the metropolis and retain their traditional and natal cultural forms and lifestyles to resist assimilation. Their realization that they are not being welcomed by the hosting society[5] and that they are on the periphery of the center, the Caribbean emigrant retrieves and reclaims Caribbean identity and resorts to cultural nationalism. Moses tries to affirm that he is "an Englishman with black blood in his veins"; nevertheless, he ends up affirming his identity as a West Indian/Caribbean man.

In *Moses Ascending* the presence of women and of second-generation emigrants is more evident than in the other novels. Brenda, for example, is no West Indian mimic and she is the only second-generation, black Briton character of Selvon's writings, always posing a challenge to Moses/Selvon. In *Moses Ascending*, she criticizes his English, his knowledge of Caribbean literature, and does not feel attracted to him sexually either. Moses is challenged by Brenda; he is intimidated by her confident, rooted self, and worse yet, he is rejected sexually by her. "She didn't sound like some of them women what try to put on English and it don't fit them properly. She sounds like the real thing, and I know without asking that she was a Black Briton" (Selvon: 2008: 22). A "real" black Briton was now evidently emerging and becoming a present part of the British society. Despite her African appearance, Brenda is a palpable example of a narrator who was born and bred English and who cannot "go back home."

The Lonely Londoners is written in a Creole, black English, or what is termed here english: an "appropriated" English. The language, however, suggests that Selvon is a writer who believes that decolonization of the mind does start with language. Writing in Creole, the narrative's language resists and destabilizes the domination of Standard English; but it also and foremost catches the rhythm of the Boys' dialect and describes their everyday life and struggle playfully. It is a "colonization of England in reverse" (Selvon: 2006: v). "During the first six months of the novel's composition, Selvon in fact tried to write the book in Standard English," but it "just would not work." It was not "sufficiently pliable and could not convey the feelings, the moods and the—as yet—'unarticulated' desires of his characters" (Ibid: vi).

Selvon's counternarrative in *Moses Ascending*, his black, broken, and appropriated english in *The Lonely Londoners*, and his final carnivalesque return to Trinidad in *Moses Migrating* together offer the reader a postcolonial, emerging emigrant narrative from a long history of slavery and colonization. They also offer an alternative narrative, a rewriting of constitutional Western views of what is known as canonical literature. In London, Selvon was one of the pioneers to write about what Rushdie called "the new empire within Britain." Rushdie states that

British authorities, no longer capable of exporting governments, have chosen instead to import a new Empire, a new community of subject peoples of whom they think, and with whom they can deal, in very much the same way as their predecessors thought of and dealt with "the flattered folk and wild", the "new-caught, sullen peoples, half-devil and half-child", who made up, for Rudyard Kipling, the White Man's Burden.

(Rushdie: 1991: 130–31)

Since the arrival of the migrant in London, the idea of Britishness as being exclusively white has been challenged and a new multiculturalism has moreover contested and challenged "British racism [which] bears the imprint of the past in many ways." It challenges this exclusive and ethnically white ideology which is "entangled in the history of the idea of culture in the modern West" (Gilroy: 1993: 7).

The writings of pioneer emigrants therefore paved the way to a contemporary multiracial Britain and initiated the beginnings of cultural translation. They also offered very lively and representative readings of the relationship between the colonizer and the colonized, due to the fact that all pioneer emigrant writers were colonials to whom colonialism was a recent, lived experience as opposed to a distant historic memory. Earlier generations were "half natives" presumably because they lived in "a nervous condition introduced and maintained by the settler among colonised people *with their consent*" (Fanon:

2001: 17). Fanon reminds us, however, that the ashamed settler is usually the left-wing at home. The liberals "admit that we were not polite enough to the natives, that it would have been wiser and fairer to allow them certain rights in so far as this was possible" (Ibid). Tayeb Salih, in *Season of Migration to the North*, admits, hiding behind his unnamed narrator, that despite the fact that "there's nothing in the whole world worse than the leftist economists... the same exaggerated emotional energy bears either to the extreme right or to the extreme left" (Salih: 2003: 59).

Windrush emigrant writings were, however, a part of an ongoing process of decolonization, of emigration, and most importantly of articulating a national consciousness. The pioneers offered a dialogue between East and West, but one that was more melancholic than celebratory, for it summoned past memory and produced in its writers a sentimentally haunting nostalgia. Memory for this generation therefore is severely affective, more alive, and fresher: the smell of one place reminds the migrant of another, and the weather of one place invokes memories of another. Memory for pioneer emigrants contributes more negatively to the emigrant's attempts in articulating an identity in exile. It interrupts his/her enunciation of a creative identity since the celebration of a creative aesthetic distance is overwhelmed by loss and melancholic images from the past. Their fashioning a voice is always interrupted by and entrapped in their very memories of the faraway places they left behind. Pioneer emigrants seem to summon memory for resistance more than for survival and/or translation. Romanticization of their past, glorification of their tradition, a lost home, and the debilitation of racism seem to have figuratively kept them "back home." The experience of displacement here is a matter of adding up, of rapid accumulation: the more experiences accumulate, the harder it becomes for the emigrant.

Indeed, the problematics of displacement for pioneer emigrants overbalance the poetics. The gloom of change, of a shifting cultural system, of a linguistic gap, of a racial inferiority, of difference in thought, all stimulated the problematic of a pulling toward the familiar in the face of the new. Acquiring more pain than benefits compared with later generations, pioneer emigrants were more alienated and homesick and consequently talked with a more accentuated tone of national belonging and identity. Most left home at a very mature age, an age when they had already articulated a solidly filiative, natal, philological identity, and hence continued living the imaginary of a factual past from which a turn was not possible because of strong bonds with the country of birth. The majority of the pioneer emigrants were in their mid- to late twenties, working-class emigrants with the exception of few students on scholarship. Nostalgia and the hope for a physical return to a geographical place called home play a major role in the works of such pioneers.

III

In the discussion of the Windrush Generation, emphases are placed on Selvon's so-called London trilogy as well as Rhys's *Smile Please*, Lamming's *The Emigrants*, and Naipaul's *The Mimic Men*. Lamming's work presents one of the first works by an emigrant writer which represents the physical crossing of the Atlantic and the meeting of Caribbean islanders on the deck of the thinly disguised *SS Windrush Empire*. Selvon, father of the folk story, offers a pioneer literary narrative of lonely emigrants and their identity complex as Caribbeans/Other and/or British living in the metropolis. Naipaul's *The Mimic Men* offers a reading of a second-hand, half-made Trinidadian society, but it also seriously investigates a colonial society that is in transition. Although debates and discussions of V. S. Naipaul have been countless, the main concern here has been with the way the works illustrate for what the term displacement does and does not stand.

All writers of this generation have, in one way or another, stressed the rooting of the displaced some "where." As has been argued earlier, however, displacement does not always mean the glorification or romanticization of and yearning for a return to home. Displacement can mean the celebration of a beginning, a starting point, and a locality. Thus "[c]ultural identities come from somewhere, have histories. But, like everything which is historical," as Hall confirms, "they undergo constant transformation" (Hall in Williams *et al*: 1994: 394). Displacement celebrates an identity's history, its gravitating "somewhere" registering its beginning. This new concept of displacement runs against the grain of what Naipaul sees in belonging to a community or belonging to a past: an excessive sense of responsibility, that is. In being rootless or free-floating, Naipaul celebrates, via his protagonist in *The Mimic Men* (1969), "the absence of responsibility" (Naipaul: 1969: 11). The first concern with Naipaul here is therefore the absence of origin, locality, rootedness, and of responsibility toward a gravitating "somewhere," or a historic memory.

Kaplan sees in Naipaul a confusion of dislocation with detachment and the "dehistoricizing" of a writer's connections with diverse national and political identities, which gives him "rhetoric, professional and financial advantage" (Kaplan: 1996; 2005: 125). Between London and New York, Naipaul establishes himself as "an eternal migrant." There is aloofness and an ontological rootlessness about Naipaul that is not in Selvon, Lamming, and certainly not in Achebe or Rhys. Ironically, however, Naipaul's emphasis on his homelessness and his integration into the high culture of metropolitan England very much depends on those half-made, "barbarian" societies in every way. In other words, Naipaul is not only being privileged because of this cosmopolitanism but he is also "hypocritical": that is, he "gains from other people's difficulties" (Ibid: 126).

The early Naipaul is the colonial from the Caribbean island of Trinidad and of an Indian community whose absent sense of inferiority to his native culture developed into becoming the late Naipaul establishing new affiliations and a sense of himself as a cosmopolitan writer in the larger world of literature. His early works are comedies that satirize Trinidadian life and societies which he calls half-society, half-made, and barbarian. Between the "long glance back at one's ancestral societies" and the "illusion-free awakening to the larger world," Naipaul emerges (Naipaul: 2002: xiv). That is, Naipaul transforms in form and perception from his conventionally linear narrative of Mr Biswas's several attempts to build a house in Trinidad, then R. Singh's failure to become a postcolonial politician in *The Mimic Men* (1968) and his society's political failure after decolonization to flourish, to the more adventurously nonlinear narrative of building a new house by demolishing other cottages in *The Enigma of Arrival* (1987), which autobiographically reflects on the growing perception of a self in a new place as he arrives in England from Trinidad. His denial of rootedness and irresponsibility toward a past and his claiming a nomadic identity remain the same, nevertheless. Others believe that Naipaul is too much a part of the center although he sees it constructing the periphery as nothingness. He knows nonetheless that the center is an illusion of reality, truth, and order in itself (Ashcroft *et al*: 2002: 89).

V. S. Naipaul is described by Said as a "scavenger" who "prefers to render the ruins and derelictions of postcolonial history without tenderness; because he taught himself to get used to change" (Said: 2001a: 100). Naipaul is, before and after the formal acceptance of British citizenship, the same expatriate. He transforms from an emigrant to an immigrant. For immigration, Mukherjee believes, "refers to the act of adopting new citizenship, of going the full nine yards of transformation" (Mukherjee in Aciman: 1999: 71). Naipaul's' writing still, however, dealt with cultural conflicts, an uncivilized Third

World and talked about his experiences as an insider and outsider: an Indian in the West Indies, a West Indian in England, and an Afro-Indian British intellectual in a postcolonial world. In his pessimistic and tenderless portrayals of human nature, in his style of "no redemption," Naipaul is usually compared to, and associated with, Conrad's portrayal of the colonial darkness.

Naipaul is, furthermore, accused of being a traitor: he traded his half-made people and naturally inferior culture for a superior one. According to Lamming, Naipaul has a sense of inferiority about his own and the former colonizer's culture. The former colonizer has claimed Naipaul in its own language which he eloquently and insightfully masters. It is a rare moment when he slips into a Caribbean idiom or code in his novels. He is a writer whose

books can't move beyond a castrated satire... When such a writer is colonial, ashamed of his cultural background and striving like mad to prove himself through promotion to the peaks of a "superior" culture whose values are gravely in doubt, then satire, like the charge of philistinism, is for me nothing more than a refuge. And it is too small a refuge for a writer who wishes to be taken seriously.

(Lamming: 1960: 225)

The second problem with Naipaul here concerns his representation as an intellectual who is not traveler-as-guest but traveler-as-judge. Farrukh Dhondy, *the* leading defender of Naipaul against his critics, in an extended article entitled, "The Man and His Mission," writes that Naipaul

[d]oesn't belong to Wiltshire, Trinidad or indeed, in the sense of being circumscribed by its culture and prejudice, to India. He belongs to literature or to writing, the home of his intellect. But that's not the sort of answer you give to *Aap Kahan sey hain, janab?* [Where are you from?] This sense of not belonging has enabled Naipaul, the quintessential writer of our times, to look at the world without the constraints of a mission.

(Dhondy: 2008)

It is well known that Naipaul is colonially Indian in the sense that India was a British colony from which they sent indentured labor to the West Indies where he was born and from which he was sent on a student scholarship to study at Oxford; he is also postcolonial as far as his subject matter and language are concerned, and also for his naturalization as a British citizen and the metropolitan locus of his writings. Dhondy, however, dismisses all this and roots Naipaul in his own writings, defending him in the face of his contemporaries and critics who, like Lamming, accuse him of being a traitor. In Dhondy's opinion, Naipaul always states the obvious and what should have been stated but has been rather ignored or tolerated; in the case of India, for example, Naipaul declares that it suffers of "the defection in public, the total ignorance of social hygiene, the superstition, hypocrisy, double standards, and the comic and malappropriation mimicry of the West." India for Naipaul is, to steal one of his titles, *A Wounded Civilisation*. Naipaul does not flatter. His views of "Caribbean Indian communities expose the cruelty of colonialism and of its greedy transplantation of peasant communities" (Dhondy: 2008). Naipaul sees and discovers. But he also, as Dhondy also triumphantly states, judges. In his discovery and travel books of the Caribbean, India, Africa, Pakistan, Malaysia, and other Muslim countries, Naipaul judges people as half-made, backward, bloodthirsty, and disordered.

Salman Rushdie, for example, makes his own viewpoint in this matter quite clear. In supporting the nationalist movement in India, Naipaul denounces India's Muslims en masse: "By supporting them [the nationalists] V S Naipaul makes himself a fellow-traveller of fascism and disgraces the Noble award" (Rushdie: 2002: 403). In his *Among the Believers*, Naipaul does not talk about "the new Islam" in Iran, its Mujahedeen, or even Shah. "Naipaul sees communism and Islam as 'interchangeable revolutions', both springing from hate and rage" (Rushdie: 1991: 373). On other occasions, there is no discussion of the army in Pakistan. "In my experience of Pakistan," writes Rushdie, "it is not difficult to find people who will talk openly in these terms [of using Islamization as a means of shoring up dictator's unpopular regime]" (Ibid: 374). Overall, Rushdie accuses Naipaul of "simplification" and criticizes *Among the Believers* for being "a rather superficial book" (Ibid: 375). In his writings of people, communities, cultures, and places, Naipaul does seem very judgmental and cynical. His acquired Conradian style in exposing the truths of society in the aftermath of imperialistic colonization and with no vulnerable sympathy seems to have been directed inward, against himself, so that melancholy and misery preoccupy the intellect of Naipaul the person as well as writer.

Rushdie observes that, and despite Naipaul's brilliance in *The Enigma of Arrival*, one word is missing from his Wiltshire narrative and that is of love: "and a life without love, or one in which love has been buried so deep that it can't come out, is very much what this book is about; and what makes it so very, very sad" (Rushdie: 2002: 151). Caryl Phillips admires Naipaul's choice to remain a "double migrant" away from the unreliable and transitory connotation of nationality (Phillips: 2001: 189); he, however, seems to reassert and echo Rushdie's viewpoint. He states that "the region of the heart is a place that Naipaul, more than any writer of his generation, has seemed determined to avoid" (Ibid: 2001: 187). He also thinks that Naipaul is "a writer, unburdened by responsibility to anything beyond the word and himself" (Phillips: 2001: 189). Said moreover criticizes Naipaul for being "a writer who tells the western power what it wants to hear about its former colonies" (Said in Dhondy: 2008).

In his *Representations of the Intellectual: The 1993 Reith Lecturers* (1994), Said writes that

An intellectual is like a shipwrecked person who learns how to live in a certain sense with the land, not on it, not like Robinson Crusoe whose goal is to colonize his little island, but more like Marco Polo, whose sense of the marvellous never fails him, and who is always a traveller, a provisional guest, not a freeloader, conqueror, or raider.

(Said: 1994b: 44)

He goes as far as stating that the "intellectual in exile is necessarily ironic, skeptical, even playful—but not cynical" (Said: 45). For these reasons and more, discussions of Windrush Generation writers are thoroughly illustrated through Sam Selvon's work: a "real" representative whose attachment to his "somewhere" is celebrated because of an agonizing distance from it and a nostalgic memory to it.

Selvon is peasant and humorous, ironic, yet playful, and more celebratory of the gift of displacement and the humor that distinguishes Caribbeans from others. Sam Selvon is historically sensible, humorously painful, sympathetically humane, and politically innocent. Selvon furthermore knew by heart the flora and fauna, the secret shortcuts, hidden allies, and the pages of A to Z of London: "If I were to direct a student," writes Phillips,

towards writing which captures the rhythm, texture and tone of London just as the austere 1950s were about to give way to the swinging 1960s I would not send them to the plays of John Osborne or Arnold Wesker, or to the prose of David Storey or John Braine. For acuity of vision, intellectual rigour and sheer beauty of language they would have to be supplicant at the pages of Selvon and Lamming.

(Phillips: 2001: 237)

On the other hand, Naipaul is painfully sad, politically dense, and historically insensible.

The Calypso flamboyance of a predominantly Caribbean emigrant group could not be entirely frosted by the chilly English weather. Out of this generation, on the contrary, came a group of literary geniuses, the forerunners of postcolonial writing. During the most violent of all phases and postcolonial stages, this generation tasted bitterly and confronted what Phillips calls "a most primitive form of racism"; that is, the "British hostility [that was] rooted in a physical distaste for black people" (Phillips: 2001: 271). Pioneer emigrants, however, challenged and righteously defied the Powellite idea that a black person cannot be admitted "to that [racially] closed, fixed, club called Britain." Caribbean migrants were according to his policy "alien" and "impossible to assimilate, as genetically 'foreign' and should be sent back to where they came from" (Ibid: 274).

In conclusion, the writings of the pioneer emigrants act as their unofficial memoirs. With the exception of the unfinished autobiography of Jean Rhys, none of the members of the Windrush Generation has ever written an official memoir or an autobiography. Most of their writings were nevertheless heavily inspired by their personal experience of displacements. Pioneer emigrants' past, the time of there and then, seems to have had a more authoritative effect in their articulating an identity. There was always an invisible wall between the pioneer emigrant and the new: a wall behind which the emigrant observed but was not able to penetrate and become part.

Geographical displacement for this generation was the most important, the severest, livelier in memories, and more celebrated—however, agonizingly. Cultural displacement was the most assertively celebrated, through music, gossip, costumes, drink, and food. Distance made aspects of cultural displacement become the more available, valuable, and enjoyable. The Windrush simply tried their best to bring home closer. Racism and the English weather stand as the severest problematics of their displacement. Psychological displacement was the most desolating aspect of the pioneer emigrant's identity and exile. Failure to articulate an identity in exile, burdened with racial inferiority, struggling with work and accommodation, directing nostalgia inwardly, suffering the disheartening weather, the emigrants' sense of self is disoriented and is always disrupted. That is why most writings of the pioneer emigrants are (semi-)autobiographical for it was in writing that they found a space to interrogate their given identities, the communities that produced them, and to rewrite their histories and those given realities. Studying the writings of most pioneer emigrants, one finds that their identities are revolutionary as opposed to evolutionary, and this is evident most specifically in the language they used. Linguistic displacement is the most representative and creative of this generation. While writers such as V. S. Naipaul and Rhys mastered and wrote in the Queen's English perhaps as a means to triumph over a colonial supremacy, Lamming and Selvon appropriated the language of the colonizer, creolized it, and fashioned it to serve their own purposes. Other postcolonial writers such as Achebe, for instance, injected the narrative with foreign (Igbo) vocabularies without a glossary to convey a more representative and lively picture of the tribal community.

One more example of this generation's pioneer cultural production is *Pressure* (1975): one of the first leading films of young black Britons in London, which was also cowritten by Sam Selvon. One of the most interesting aspects of the film is its linguistic differentiation and emphasis. While the film portrays differences and solidarities between first and second generations of black Britons, one can easily notice the marker that differentiates the two, and that is language and differences of dialects.

Writers discussed here in this chapter are all familiar to an extent with the flora and fauna of the metropolitan city that is London. Although degrees of familiarization vary, their vantage point as migrant intellectuals allows them to speak volumes for the margins. For Spivak, however, "the question 'Who should speak?' is less important than 'Who will listen?'" (Spivak in Harasym: 1990: 59). Spivak also emphasizes the process of learning how to "speak to" the subaltern as opposed to trying to "listen to" or "speak for" the subaltern. Spivak encourages that we should, as these migrant intellectuals do to a certain qualified extent, "look for a bit at what is being edited out" (Ibid: 21). Studying the subaltern,[6] Spivak complements Said's work on silent and passive voices. She believes, for example, that first world intellectuals use the third world subalterns for, as in Said's Orientalism, self-constitution. They need the image of the Other to constitute a Self. She in this sense feminizes Orientalist discourse and makes it more third worldly. Spivak also compliments Bhabha's work on mimicry and resistance. Whereas Spivak rarely cites Fanon, however, Bhabha extends Said's Oriental discourse as he keeps in dialogue with Fanon. Bhabha furthermore sees in the contemporary metropolitan migrant another version of Spivak's subaltern whose agency not only interrogates but also synthesizes the dominant culture's current narratives of self-representation. Migrants and their literary production therefore rewrite former metropolitan locations (London here), appropriate colonial structures of representation, and underline postcolonial concerns.

Although Spivak's so-called subalterns can speak for themselves, they, Spivak argues, do not have spaces from which they can speak. "You don't give the subaltern voice," says Spivak. "You work for the bloody subaltern, you work against subalternity," the unlearning of privileges and assumptions the otherwise-not-subaltern possesses (Spivak: 1992: 46). Spivak, however, is not fully content with the reduction of postcolonial studies to that which comes out merely from the metropolis by disconnected, disinterested intellectuals of the West because they are exploitive of the subaltern. For Spivak, moreover, these intellectuals (such as the repeatedly invoked in her discussions Deleuze and Guattari and Foucault) do not represent and to an extent do not necessarily work for the rural and indigenous subalterns; this Spivak believes carries the dangers of following on the footsteps of the imperial project. She suggests therefore that the focus should not mainly be on the analysis offered by what she calls the postcolonial "mimic men and women," for they are "as distant from aboriginal subalterns as is Aristotle" (Spivak: 2002: 333).

In keeping with Spivak's insights, all the postcolonial metropolitan displaced writers invoked here represent the pioneer emigrants and literary antecedents who paved the way and offered cultural and literary guidance for succeeding generations. They have offered a reading of history from below, as it were, and have brought back in what has been edited out, interrogated and synthesized the dominant culture's current narratives of self-representation through their agency, and created spaces from which they could speak.

CHAPTER 4

MASALA FISH: CULTURAL
SYNTHESIS AND LITERARY
ADVENTURING

This chapter addresses issues raised by second-generation *im*migrants (with an emphasis on the prefix "im" to emphasize the place they arrived at, as opposed to the place they *em*igrated from, and by which their identities were predominantly influenced and shaped). Emphasis on the prefix also foregrounds the formative years spent in England, which facilitated their integration into British culture. This chapter follows on therefore from the preceding chapter that contextualized the work of the emigrant or pioneer generation in terms of the question of displacement. Thus the Windrush Generation paved the way to what is called here the "Masala Fish" Generation of immigrant. Second-generation writers were no longer mere products of the vanishing Empire but members of a new multicultural British scene.

These immigrant writers were either students (e.g., Farrukh Dhondy and Salman Rushdie), or were brought along with their families at a very early age (e.g., Monica Ali, Timothy Mo, and Caryl Phillips), or were double-caste, born and bred English (e.g., Hanif Kureishi and Zadie Smith). Either they or at least one of their parents' came from metropolitan cities of Mumbai or Hong Kong and resettled in London and/or New York. Although this army of metaphors has had different ways of representing home and identity, they all write about and are stimulated by displacement. Overall, Dhondy wrote about young, second-generation immigrants during the 1970s, Rushdie contrasted East and West and introduced magic realism throughout the 1980s, Mo addressed the Chinese immigrant living in England, Kureishi introduced a new ethnicity during the 1990s, Phillips took and followed on the steps of Selvon, while Smith and Ali injected the scenery with a fresh image of a multigenerational and multicultural London at the end of the twentieth century and post-9/11, respectively.

Moreover, the majority of writers were no longer solely West Indians, but included a multiplicity of Others: Indians, Pakistanis, Japanese, Chinese, Bangladeshis, Egyptians, and Nigerians among others. Memories were not predominantly those of the home left behind, but also of the early years spent in England. Unlike the pioneer immigrants who arrived as adults and whose formative years were predominantly shaped by their homeland, the early age of second-generation writers was a formative phase in their lives and careers. Any memories of the home left behind for the majority of second-generation writers are therefore imaginatively constructed. There was a translating channel of communication between the past (tradition, natal, required, created, philological, inherited, filiative, and closed) and the present (modern, acquired, philosophical, creative, affiliative, and open). In other words, the major focus here shifted from how the emigrant used to see the present in a view that is set against and agonizingly compared to a lost past, to how the immigrant now sees the past in relation to the present, in a dialogic fluctuation. Also, what was remembered is now reterritorialized in the imagined.[1] The Masala Fish is culturally more flexible, synthesized/hybrid, and adventurous.

For example, Lily, a second-generation Chinese immigrant in Mo's *Sour Sweet*, and a multicultural individual whose dealing with food reflects an air of flexibility and adaptation in her identity, is "stuck to the originals where she could and where this was not possible she included something she considered similar (i.e. carrot for rhinoceros horn)" (Mo: 1999: 12). What distinguishes Masala Fish writers from the Windrush Generation is that the "myth of ontological unbelonging is replaced by another, larger myth of excess of belongings: not that he [the displaced] belongs nowhere, but that he belongs to too many places" (Ahmad: 2008: 127). This larger myth of multiple[2] belongings to too many places reflects the multiplicity of displacements and the rerooting of home and identity in many different places and experiences as opposed to a singularly geographical place and exclusive experience. Excessive belonging, however, also risks sliding into becoming a free-floating, ontological rootlessness with no beginning and no end. Ahmad states that "[o]ne did not have to belong, one could simply float, effortlessly, through a supermarket of packaged and commodified cultures, ready to be consumed" (Ibid:

128). A supermarket signifies the availability of all cultures of the world for consumption. "The chief characteristic of the metropolitan supermarket," he adds, "was that entirely diverse products (utensils, fabrics, jewelry, refrigerators, beds) could now be purchased under one roof, while also drawing upon the resources of different countries (Indian textiles alongside Manchester Woollens; Persian carpets alongside French hosiery), making available a wide range of personal consumptions in a wholly impersonal setting" (Ibid). The idea of an individual's identity, home, and belonging being as diverse and metropolitan as a supermarket sounds far too Utopian, consumerist, and, worse yet, nomadic.

The core and essence of the excess of belonging/multiplicity of belonging is that it serves "as a counterpoint against the far less sanguine notion that the fragmented self was the only truly modern self. Ideas of excess and disruption, unity and fragmentation, were held in this imagination in a tense balance" (Ibid: 128). In *The Satanic Verses*, for example, the dreams of Gibreel created another world alongside the visible one which was unseen but visible to his mind's eye. Gibreel nevertheless "belonged in both worlds, with a different meaning in each" (Rushdie: 2006a: 351). Displacements, or the multiplicity of belongings and rerooting of home, promote what Rushdie calls in *The Satanic Verses* a "pluralistic openness of mind" (Ibid: 245). What is interesting about the idea of multiple belongings or what Ahmad calls "the excess of belonging" is not that it cancels the idea of belonging as Ahmad suggests and thus leaves the displaced free-floating, but rather it is that the experience of loss and not belonging is celebrated triumphantly as opposed to being agonizingly bemoaned. The idea of a multiplicity of belonging(s) is about occupying a multiplicity of subject positions: not singular but plural, not tragic but celebratory, not either or but neither nor and both simultaneously, that is, not rigid stability but flexibility.

Second-generation writers therefore are voices that call for pluralistic openness of mind toward other cultures and experiences while simultaneously paying tribute to their parental, natal culture and heritage. This is because granting either past or present a greater authority over one another causes a rather profound psychological displacement and conflict (caused by a sense of loss, imperialist nostalgia, melancholy, and entrapping in-betweenness) rather than inspiring and creative and ongoing translation.

While the previous chapter consisted of an already established group of writers called the Windrush Generation, this chapter envisages a selected group of writers who promote flexibility toward change, a celebratory tone toward integration into other communities, and tolerance toward and entertaining differences. Farrukh Dhondy is selected, for example, as he is the first immigrant writer to write about second-generation young immigrants: their in-betweenness and their upbringing in England among English as well as non-English children and culture. He acts therefore in the context of this project as the connecting link between the first- and second-generation writing and the shift in subject matter. Dhondy, like Selvon, describes Britain through the eyes of its black teenagers with humor, compassion, political naivety, and honesty. Themes across his short stories and novels include generational differences with focus, however, on second-generation black Britons, racial discrimination and violence, in-betweenness, and traditions within the Indian community. *East End at Your Feet*, his first collection of stories, was awarded Children's Rights Workshop Other Award in 1977 and was "the first fiction to use Asian and black British working-class youths as its subject" (King: 2004: 79).

Salman Rushdie, Farrukh Dhondy, Caryl Phillips, and Timothy Mo together emerge from a diversity of immigrant backgrounds themselves as one group writing about bicultural/hybrid diversity and identities (Indo-Pakistani; Japanese and Chinese, respectively). Mo and Rushdie, moreover, use food as a cultural marker and a signifier of hybridity and/or dislocation and difference. They have also injected the English language with Cantonese (yin and yang) and Urdu (the chutnification of English) idioms, respectively. Hanif Kureishi, by contrast, represents a generation born and bred English. He introduces a new ethnicity that breaks the already imposed and rigid ethnicities. He is, however, like his Karim in *The Buddha of Suburbia* (1991), "Creamy": neither white nor black. This chapter focuses on the literary production of the aforementioned writers among others and the politics of home and identity as it evolved and between 1976, marked by Dhondy's *East End at Your Feet*, and 2003, marked by Ali's *Brick Lane*.

In his detailed study across different genres of literature (prose, poetry, and drama), Bruce King, in *The Internationalisation of English Literature* (2004), states:

Immigrant novels of home, social comedy, and cultural conflict were followed during the 1970s by the first books about lives of the children of immigrants, the first fiction written for specific markets, the start of writing in England by an African woman [namely Buchi Emecheta], and other firsts as immigrants began to become part of the British rather than their own national literary scene. The 1980s was characterised by Salman Rushdie's novels, the fatwa against him, various forms of fabulation, the first publications of many writers from Islamic world, an increasing number of books by women, and the first books written by children of immigrants. By the 1990s there was a vital black British literary scene, many authors of mixed race, interest in popular fiction, Indian British novelists, and novelists from many parts of the world settled in England.

(King: 2004: 11)

After the 1970s, writings introduced new subject matters. No longer exclusively about mimic men, physical and cultural unaccommodation, racism, a utopian return, or assimilation (though these were often still addressed), new subject matters included class differences, generational conflicts, multiple and excessive belongings, sexuality, music, and domestic life in England. Examples can be found in *The Satanic Verses* for its adventuring and daringly controversial subject matter; Mo's *Sour Sweet* for its new subject matter, Chinese immigrants in London; and Kureishi's *My Beautiful Laundrette* and *The Buddha of Suburbia* both for their tackling polemical issues in Britain and their adventuring subject matter of music, drugs, and sexuality; Smith's *White Teeth* and Ali's *Brick Lane* for their fresh image of a multigenerational and multicultural London at the end of the twentieth century and post-9/11, respectively.

Furthermore, while earlier writings are, by virtue of the time they were written, revolutionary, later writings were evolutionary. In other words, while earlier writings were about the story of being ("Who am I?"), later writings were about becoming ("What else could I be?"). While earlier writings were predominantly realistic, later writings broke with the realist mode and experimented with the so-called magic realism, which is discussed below. While earlier writings are heavily inspired and also lured by a nostalgic romance with the past, later writings demonstrate the complexity and multiplicity of representations of home and identity and the instability of life. They also indicate the possibility of translating between East and West, past and present, tradition and the modern. This generation furthermore drifted away from the assimilationist dream and the "myth" of a return, to subject matters such as promoting cultural hybridity, racial integration, and social intermingling. Pioneer emigrants were either black *or* British; this later generation was, to a certain qualified extent, black *and* British.

Using food figuratively, as it is in this chapter, to point to something that goes beyond its representational value, however, is not unprecedented. Timothy Mo's *Sour Sweet* (1982) explains, along with

Rushdie's metaphorical handling of food as a celebratory cultural signifier of hybridity, the allegorical title of this chapter's generation: Masala Fish. What most people outside Britain, for example, know about the British is the so-called teatime, or "cuppa." As Procter notes, teatime or the "cuppa" for Stuart Hall is "an extended metaphor [which] allows him to foreground what he terms 'the outside history that is inside the history of the English.'" He adds,

> There is no English history without that other history. Tea and sugar were imported to Britain from colonial plantations in South Asia and the Caribbean respectively. They were commodities that carried with them the burden of slavery, conquest and colonisation and which helped fuel Britain's rise into a dominant and wealthy imperial power. Britain's economy, as well its culture (the British cuppa as "national" institution) were not simply generated from within according to this inside-out history. The sugar and tea of Hall's "British cuppa" were not just metaphors for the trade in the precious commodities of empire, they were also metaphors for the postwar importation of cheap labour from the Caribbean (like sugar) and South Asia (like tea).
>
> (Procter: 2004: 82)

Masala is a South Asian spice. When added to food, it normally changes not only the food's flavor but also its original color—hence, change and metamorphosis. Masala is mildly hot, reflecting the Asian weather; fish, on the other hand, is England's most famous traditional dish. First and second generations of displaced writers alike used fish as a metaphor for Englishness: the English are as cold as (cod) fish, Selvon would say, an image that reflects England's cold weather and "white" culture. On the one hand, "masala," metaphorically speaking, is the Oriental Other/black; on the other, "fish" is the Occident/British. Masala Fish is a synthesized, adventurous, and hybrid dish that brings East and West to one plate. It is also a product of migration, cultural diversity, racial intermingling, and historical displacement. Masala infuses Fish creating a dish that is not only flavorsome but also multicultural; together they synthesize two cultures, two cuisines, two worlds, and the adventuring of a new taste, a new identity that has been added to the English table. This synthesis reflects, resembles, and echoes the hybrid, syncretic literary production of second-generation writers in the aftermath of a long historical displacement involving India and Britain.

Masala Fish is coined here to mark how food acts in the works of many of this generation of writers as a cultural signifier for hybridity and syncreticism, promoting a healthy image of creativity and heterogeneity in contrast to what has earlier been described as a homogeneity producing mental ghettoization and singularity. In Rushdie's *The Satanic Verses*, for example, food is used as a signifier for the liminality of boundaries: Hind, Sufyan's wife, who remains unchanged and traditional throughout the narrative, nevertheless

> cooked, and ate in increasing quantities, its food. As she devoured the highly spiced dishes of Hyderabad and the high-faulting yoghurt sauces of Lucknow her body began to alter, because all that food had to find a home somewhere, and she began to resemble the wide rolling land itself, the subcontinent without frontiers, because food passes across any boundary you care to mention.
>
> (Rushdie: 2006a: 246)

Food integrates and adapts: it is frontierless.

In Hanif Kureishi's *The Black Album*, moreover, a novel that largely tackles the aftermath of Rushdie's fatwa with the publication of *The Satanic Verses*, food can deliver a sense of home even in the most alienating conditions. Riaz, a radically enthusiastic writer, takes the protagonist Shahid, the novel's second-generation black Briton, to an Indian restaurant between a Caribbean wig center and a Romanian Café in London, and promises him he "will really feel at home" with all the "hot chapattis, soaking them in dhal and oily keema." Shahid wonders and questions nonetheless: "How did Riaz know he would feel at home in a place with five Formica tables and screwed-down red bucket seats, all as brightly lit under white neon as a police cell?" (Kureishi: 1995: 4). Also, when Riaz lectures Shahid that the word chilli is a South American one and was brought to India in the medieval times (Ibid: 5), it is clear that not just food, but the names of food are cultural signifiers with histories too. And when Chad, a Muslim radical, contrasts his own religious and loyally traditional identity with that of Shahid by ridiculing his buying, not Indian food, but a French baguette, food acquires cultural, ethnic, and national significations, for Chad presumes Indian food is "no longer good enough" for him (Ibid: 104). Shahid is accordingly considered a traitor of his own presumed Indian culture and identity. Descriptions of the interior decorations of rooms and houses also indicate the way in which food "sticks together" the heterogeneous fragments of a world. In contrast to Shahid's room with pictures of Madonna and Prince and paintings by Picasso, for example, Riaz's room is "cluttered with books ... pasted to the window-sill, perhaps by mango chutney or Lucknow pickle. Shahid was sure that some of the crispy-looking files were made of nan and dried chapattis, contained old poppadoms and were secured by cobwebs" (Ibid: 12).

In *Sour Sweet*, on the other hand, Mo uses food to highlight difference and dislocation in narrating the story of the Chen family: Grandfather Chen (first generation), Chen (first generation), Mui and Lily (second generation), and Man Kee (third generation). The Chen family establishes a Chinese takeaway that serves food that is changed, assimilated, and adjusted to Western cuisine such that it bears no resemblance to Chinese cuisine. "Cosmic repercussion," as Mo calls it, has been made to Chinese food. "Sweet and sour pork" was their staple, naturally (Mo: 1999: 111). The cosmically repercussioned Chinese cuisine was made by the Chinese seamen "who jumped ship or retired in East London a generation ago" (Ibid: 111). Lily suggests that chips should also be synthesized with sour and sweet sauce since it was "outselling" alongside the pork dish: "(potato, not bamboo) with sweet and sour sauce" (148). Food is also used to signify the difference between mother (first generation) and son (a second generation), Lily and Man Kee. Lily prepares a meal for Man Kee—beef, melon, and a nice shrimp omelette—which he, offending her, chews off and spits out demanding some mince, jam tart, and custard which he is usually provided with at the English-style school where he studies.

The novel revolves around three different generations, each of which deals with their experience of displacement differently. Lily seems to be the most hybrid and multicultural individual alongside her growing son, Man Kee. Born in England and raised within a Chinese household, Man Kee is described as happy as a child and "getting a fresh start. He had no history, no heritage to live up to, no goal to fulfill, no ancient burden to carry. Not one his father imposed, anyway" (116). Man Kee is born free therefore of an imposed, rigid hierarchy. He is free to choose and construct an identity without being tied to a singular system of cultural values.

Although Chen advises Mui, on the one hand, to "stick to what has been tried and don't adopt new ways just for the sake of them" (129), Mui, on the other hand, adventures and applies for British citizenship and establishes her own restaurant of, not Chinese food but fish and chips. This is not an indication of multiculturalism, however, as she does not understand her own culture and abandons it entirely for another. Mui does not translate but rather blindly assimilates. In other words, she does not balance the "yin and yang," the sour and the sweet. Although Mui suggests that Man Kee attends an English school, Lily realizes that her son cannot live without acknowledging both cultures at the same time. Thus, Lily sends him to attend a Chinese school twice a week so he can be familiar with his heritage while attending an English school for the rest of the week. Chen, the father, on the other hand, cannot achieve such a happy balance or think beyond his Oedipal territory, China. He "felt at home and yet not at home. He had been more comfortable rootless" (141). He does not mingle with or try to understand the English people or their culture. "Chen lifted Man Kee to the eyepiece. 'Do you see the ship, Son?,' he asked softly. 'It is a special little ship for people like us, Son. It is very little and very old but that is only what strangers see. We know better, don't we, Son, because it is the ship that will take us back home when we are finished here. It will take you to your homeland, Son, which you have never seen' " (162). Chen ignores the fact that "[f]irst lessons stick firmest" (174) and rather longs for a utopian return. *Sour Sweet* also uses language that is very rich with metaphors of cookery: "The English were peppery" (Mo: 1999: 88). For the Chinese, this comparatively meant that they were indifferent, careless of their own consequences of deeds, and careless of their elderly.

But most importantly the novel uses a language across a multiplicity of generations, where change and difference are bound to occur: "If one generation didn't climb, then the next declined, or the one after that; it would not maintain the level" (12). As in every other novel of migrant and exilic displacement, the themes of uprooting and metamorphosis, the migrant condition and the politics of home and identity reflect every man's condition in the modern age of technological advancement, economic turmoil, neocolonialism, and social and political disorder. In a community like that of London's, intermingling with international communities becomes unavoidable and this interaction can be conducive to promoting an understanding of the meaning of multiculturalism and a tolerant attitude toward cultural differences. But it could also have precisely the opposite effect: mingling with a new, changing cultural life might seem to some immigrants threatening and produce violence because of racial discrimination and sense of alienation.

Farrukh Dhondy portrayed exactly that London: a city of multiple faces, of both conflicts and integration, of opportunity and nightmares, of little cities within one, and of a space breeding of migrants. Dhondy, however, filled a gap in the market of literature and at the same time showed us the city from the point of view of its second generation, the working-class youths. He wrote the first fiction to use Asian and black British working-class youths as its subject: the insecure, politically naïve, confused, and culturally and linguistically displaced teenagers. Dhondy also "economically makes use of broken English or slang to convey the mentality." The stories also gain in their ironies from being told by youths whose mixed cultural values and perspectives result from lack of knowledge, inexperience, and pressures on them from schoolmates (King: 2004: 79–80).

East End at Your Feet is, for example, narrated in the first person by Kashyap, nicknamed Cashy. Telling his story, he would have called the story of the East End "A Tale of Two Cities": the working-class East End and the posh and expensive West End of London. Class differences are an evident feature in Dhondy's writings. A former resident of East London himself, he makes sure a contrast with the West end of London is cynically portrayed. Cashy tells a similar story; this time, however, it is about Bombay and London: two different tales of two different cities. Cashy is a second-generation immigrant of Asian descent. He does not know a lot of Hindi but nevertheless is forced to learn it in order to converse with his grandfather. Cashy represents second-generation Asians returning to India after settling in England and the dreadfulness caused by such return. He portrays linguistic and cultural difficulties and displacements:

I am young enough to learn, but he [his grandfather] ain't, and that's the reason I suppose I could learn to like Bombay. They say I will, I'll forget London. It's not London I'm worried about, it's just the whole idea of changing your life. At my age kids don't normally have plans for their lives, but you can see how you're going to grow up, you have a pretty fair idea. Now it's India and starting *all over again*, with friends, with *the language* and even getting used to the stinks.

(Dhondy: 1976: 52; my italics)

Cashy, reminiscing on his arrival in England with his uncle, also expresses dissatisfaction upon arrival/return:

My uncle said at the airport that it was a modern building they lived in. When we get here, it's all falling to bits, and he said there was beach in front, but the bloody rocks he was talking about are nearly a kilometre away even though you can see them from the balcony if you've got your specs on. (49)

Thus he expresses dissatisfaction and disappointment in both India and England. Talking to a lawyer, however, he stresses his hybrid identity as being of them both, in other words, a black British: "I'm sorry sir, I may be Indian, but I speak perfectly good English, but I haven't swallowed a dictionary and I was just wondering if you'd clarify your inquiry" (50–51). Language is represented here as a marker of cultural identity. He even expresses creativity as he improvises his own English proverbs, a new language: "Kashyap shows creative talent in his English lessons," the teachers remark (51). While his father hopes to see his son excel at maths, physics, and chemistry, all Cashy ever wanted was "that blue and claret shirt, West Ham forever" (52). He even looks for a toothbrush with West Ham colors in Bombay. Dhondy treats Cashy's problematic displacement with amused understanding.

Dhondy has learnt from Naipaul "the need to write truthfully from within a social group with attention to details and conflicts rather than sentimentalising, stereotyping, and making heroes of people: it helps if the characters, their problems and mistakes, are treated with amused understanding" (King: 2004: 79). He therefore exposes India's poverty as compared to England's relative wealth with such amused understanding and attention to details and with no sentimentality. Cashy compares London to Bombay and valorizes it for its economic advancement and better welfare:

it's not like London where you can be on the dole, there isn't any dole here. They just let you die in the street, them loving Indians, and I've seen it, I tell you. There's people sleep on the streets all over the city and some of them are just skin, like plastic bags stretched over their bones.

(Dhondy: 1976: 54)

The park in Bombay "isn't much of a park, just a huge empty space with a few palm trees tucked in a corner. Plenty of people about, all playing cricket and chucking stones about. There's a game of football too...These kids are playing without shoes" (Ibid: 55). Dhondy is clearly influenced by Naipaul's Conradian and bleak presentations of (post)colonial reality.

Leaving England for Kashyap was "[l]ike dying, really. Mullins said confusion, but there was no confusion before" (55–56). The confusion that is referred to here is the racial and cultural displacements black Britons are faced with in the East End. The confusion also refers to their not being accepted in England as British, nor being satisfied with India or being labeled as Indians. Kashyap admits, however, that his self-conscious identity relates, not to color of skin or origins; his identity is where he is at and the language he speaks, a Londoner: "I heard a lot about India this and India that from my mum, but it was never my business, because I reckoned on dying a cockney. It's what fourteen years can do to you" (59). Here, there is also an emphasis on the formative years of second-generation Britons that shape most of their identity, facilitate their integration into and being part of British culture, and present them as hybrid creatures of East and West. Sitting on the balcony back in India, as his uncle supposedly saved him from the cold weather of England, Kashyap reads a letter from England that tells him West Ham are playing Leeds and they are favorite for the Cup. As he sits there, a blind beggar sings a Hindi song, which Kashyap tries to translate into English as his Hindi improves and it ironically and appropriately reflects his own wish and desire: "Go away, fly away, bird/ Go to the home of singing choirs/ There's nothing for you here, my beauty..." (61).

In his second collection of short stories, *Come to Mecca* (1978), Dhondy develops his subject matter to involve more sexual encounters and images, as well as more violent scenes. *Come to Mecca* is narrated in the first person with the introduction of Shahid and his uncle, the Masterji, the school teacher back in the village. The setting is again the East End of London. Shahid is Bengali. He and the unnamed narrator work in a factory where Hindi workers work faster to the rhythm of Hindi songs. They are both sacked by the governor who is white, understands little Bengali, and irritatingly controls their pauses and breaks. Shahid and the unnamed narrator refer to their governor as the "gaffer." Dhondy always makes sure he exposes linguistic gaps among different generations of immigrants. He also introduces linguistic acquirements in different localities and in different situational circumstances. Dhondy exploits stereotypical images too to attract sympathy and to debunk such stereotypes at the same time. Bengalis, for example, were blamed for being late with their contract. Young workers are blamed for thinking of "heta" "a dirty word," we are told, while "the old ones thought of 'taka' (money)" (13). The Masterji holds a meeting and encourages the workers to go on strike because "[w]e didn't come to this country to be slaves" and be paid 50 pence a day (15). On strike, the placards read: "pay us fair rates," ironically in Bengali, to show how segregated Bengali communities are and how reactionary their responses are.

The boys, mainly Shahid and the unnamed narrator, were told by a white female reporter/translator that "we were not only part of the Bengalis but also we were part of the working class and we should forget about Bengalis only" (20). The unnamed narrator learns that "working class are third-class people" (20), whereas Betty, a British newspaper reporter, tells him that that is what newspapers wanted them to believe since newspapers such as *The Sun* were against workers. Dhondy uses Shahid's sexual desires here not to exploit him by white female characters, but to guide him to the right path, to make him understand that he is now part of the new British scene and part of its very working class. "It seemed to me that Shahid loved listening to her voice," the narrative remarks, "even though I'm sure he didn't understand half the things she was saying. She explained that all workers should be socialist and that communism comes after." Betty acts as their political and social advisor convincing them to join a union to fight against the National Front and fight for the rights of all Asians in England. The story ends with Shahid throwing a pile of papers calling for the fighting against the Nazi Front and declaring his disappointment that she was using him for her own political and journalist ends. Shahid is after all portrayed as a failure: unemployed, inferior, alienated, and sexually frustrated. The unnamed narrator also acts as Shahid's double character who comments on events with a critical distance. The title of the story paradoxically and ambivalently, like its characters' identity, refers not to the holy city in the KSA but to a British dance hall in London; thus, the title reflects the black Asian Briton's identity, paradoxical, and a synthesis of both East and West.

Dhondy's first novel, *The Siege of Babylon* (1978), is on the other hand divided into twenty chapters and tells the story of three Londoners from Brixton, Kwate (aged 28), Hurly (22), and Rupert (19), who take over a building called Babylon, take hostages, and fail to succeed in their demands that would instrument their escape to Algeria or Jamaica. They were committing an act of terrorism: a stereotypical image of Muslim characters that is narrated with unsentimental amused understanding. Lessons learnt in this novel vary: "the exploitation of black people is a class problem" (34); London "may be a dark satanic mill, but it's also a possibility of souls" (40); "Run Cap-it-al-ist/I and I want So-shyal-ist" (64); black music was a "new ground" (66); and that living in harmony, black and white, is not realistic but utopian. The novel ends in tragedy as Kwate and Rupert die and the only survivor, Hurly, is forever traumatized. What is most interesting in this novel is the effect of memory and how it functions. This is evident in the case of Hurly who cannot forget Babylon: he wants to remember while the only way to make peace with Babylon (a traumatic past) is to forget. Hurly, however, cannot forget; he learns that the past is always present and that "tomorrow drags along yesterday; it goes forward like a wounded animal dragging a trap" (Dhondy: 1978: 160). The novel therefore emphasizes the paradoxes of memory and forgetfulness, discussed in Chapter 2. It highlights the importance of the past and the present as a whole, as opposed to being two separate entities. It also examines black Britons' identity as it is caught between black and white, past and present. The novel, moreover, stresses how language provides authority. Rupert, for example, was fascinated by the power of language. Those who "talk black" found in language sources of power. To him, "language was identity" (37).

It cannot be ignored, however, that the novel revolves around an act of terrorism. This throws light on the increasing violence in the late 1970s onward, and the rise of (religious) fundamentalism. In an essay entitled "Our Islamic Fifth Element" (2001), Dhondy states that

> The affair of the [*Satanic*] *Verses* demonstrated that successive generations of Muslim immigrants to Britain, despite their broad Midland accents and their (admittedly rather curtailed) education in the Western intellectual tradition, identified themselves primarily as Muslims. They declared their allegiance not to the traditions that allowed them to settle, to worship, to have the Prince of Wales visit their mosques and proclaim himself their protector, but rather to a religious philosophy that emanates from a different place and different age. It was in the early eighties that this identity with a freshly militant universal Islam emerged as a politically distinct force in Britain. While the earlier generation of Muslim immigrants had gone their way without bothering to adopt Western dress, their children grew up wearing Air Jordan sneakers, baggy trousers, and Hilfiger tops, in imitation of American blacks. The great cliché of their generation, enshrined in endless articles and now in facile novels, is that they were caught between two cultures. Some of these second- and third-generation Muslim Britons resolved this tension by adopting the politics, philosophy, and culture of fundamentalist Islam.
>
> (Dhondy: 2001)

Dhondy's materialization of this view of religious fundamentalism and "five star Muslims" can be clearly seen in his debut adult novel *Bombay Duck*. Themes in this novel revolve around the rising dangers of religious fundamentalism, the celebration of hybrid, bicultural identities of young Asians in Britain between London and Bombay, belonging, the quest for roots, the breaking down of cultural barriers, and very evidently Dhondy's dissatisfaction with contemporary India. He portrays the violence that takes place within India's multireligious communities: in Punjab, Sikhs kill Hindus, and vice versa; Muslims are killing Hindus and Hindus are killing Sikhs. Dhondy stresses the idea—which is Naipaul's thesis originally—that these Pakistani, Indian, and Punjabi communities are converts to Islam in contrast to Arab countries to whom Islam was sent by God's prophet Muhammad. So "when he [Naipaul] says he catches people shitting in the streets it's all really so true, we are really disgusting people, but loveable too" (Dhondy: 1990: 108). Arabs are also converts, Naipaul suggests, and all converts had a history prior to the one that started after their conversion (presumably Jahilia: the age of ignorance) and that should be included and embedded into their civilization. This also resembles and echoes the immigrant whose past should not be totally ignored but should rather be embedded into their evolving identity.

It is also in this context that black Muslims are considered the most dangerous and fatal because they are the latest converts. They are "a five star Muslim." They "swear allegiance to Islam because they are not accepted by their own countries and are converting to this religion in the name of domination of other people in their country" (Dhondy: 1990: 135). It is very evident that Dhondy seems to be significantly influenced by Naipaul's ideas. Both Dhondy and Naipaul seem to also agree on the fact that "the idea of India is almost bigger than the experience of it" (1990: 110). India "the mob given national status, the ant hill searching for statehood, the font of philosophies, the overwhelming case for birth control, the place where square inches of land are overwhelmed by the pressure on them... the magnificent cliché" (126).

With such clichés, Dhondy tries to expose the stereotypicality of India, but he nevertheless seems to end up reinforcing them. The novel is full of stereotypical images of Africans, Asians, and even Chinese and Japanese. In Delhi, on his arrival from London, the first day in the hotel foyer Ali Abdulrahman, also known in the novel as Gerald Blossom, is "actually asked" whether or not he had "any Marks and Spencers socks or stockings or anything like that to sell" (Dhondy: 1990: 128). Chinese and Japanese are portrayed mimicking blacks and/or whites. They had no reggae, no black power, "just plenty rules" and "heavy education" (51). The British police are always racist (59). Ali Abdul admits that in India, and upon his return after his long residency in England, "everything freaks me. Everything. This is the place, mein Herr, the place. India, richest, poorest, they got guys without legs, just stump, talking to you from like a head and shoulders stuck on a cart and asking you whether you from the USA" (129).

Dhondy's *Bombay Duck* breaks with the realist mode to experiment making use of epistolary form (letters and notes), newspaper and journal articles, diary entries, fragmented narratives and subplots, direct speech, long monologues and short dialogues, and the shifting of narration between third-person narration and first-person narration. There is also a doubling or juxtaposition of the narrative structure with two independent stories and protagonists following two separate and yet interrelated paths. Thus, the narration is discontinuous and interrupted. As King notes, *Bombay Duck* "is a novel where everyone undergoes some change of identity, just like 'Bombay Duck': an

Anglicized pronunciation of a word for a fermented spicy fish (the 'dak') sent from Bombay on the colonial rail system under the British to inland India" (King: 2004: 82). Bombay Duck

> is not a duck at all. In fact it should be spelt Bombay Dak. What it is, is dried fish (known in Bombay as Bombil) and when the British introduced the railways system to western India under their Raj, it started going in wagonloads to the interior from Bombay. The crates stank of dried fish, like stale penises. They were marked "Bombay Dak" literally "Bombay Mail." At the time railway was run by whiteys. The English may call a spade a spade, but they don't call "stinking fish" by that name. They referred to it euphemistically as "Bombay Dak", the Bombay Mail.
>
> (Dhondy: 1990: 241)

Gerald Blossom, Dhondy's protagonist, is, like Kureishi's Karim, an actor: someone who has double characters, someone who interprets and mimics. He, an Indian, plays in an English narrative, like the naming of a Bombay duck dish, the role of Tony in a New Yorker adaptation of *Antony and Cleopatra*. The play "attempts to fight stereotypes, but falls into the trap of reinforcing them." Ali becomes an actor because he was fed up with being a bus conductor in the "badlands of London" (41). Gerry, or Ali, defines himself as a "nice British black boy" (11). Indian and West Indian displaced immigrants in London accuse Ali Abdul of being a traitor and of betrayal of his own culture, tradition, and "true" identity. They accuse him of losing "all touch with roots since he became a big actor and got on telly" and has become more indulged in a decaying liberal society. Ali sees in this a mentality of a colonized mind, a ghetto mentality, in contrast to what his fellow Indians accuse him, of being brainwashed (Dhondy: 1990: 80).

The Indian community is portrayed as working class in England; Anjali, an upper-class Indian, thought she was a black Briton until reality shocked and proved her otherwise; she emphasizes the effect of being culturally and psychologically displaced and in-between. Britain and its society had rejected her for the color of skin. "When I was a kid growing up in London," admits Anjali, "I used to go and cheer for the cowboys until Britain compelled me, culturally and spiritually to realise that I was on the other side, I was an Indian" (91). Anjali is doubly conscious, doubly marginalized as a black woman, physically alienated, and with an obvious split in her identity. Returning as an actress in the Indian play *Ramayana*, directed by British director David Stream, Anjali is accused by her own people of being a traitor to her own culture and its Gods. She was not considered a "real" Indian in India nor was she accepted as a black Briton in Britain. Anjali faces an existential dilemma that ends with her being murdered by her own people on her ancestral soil.

Like Rushdie's *The Satanic Verses*, *Bombay Duck* also promotes skepticism: the revision of a God-given past and traditions, the examination of the social group from which the narrative emerges, and doubt about all that is portrayed as absolute. Ali wishes to prove to the Indian nation that he is worthy of portraying Ram, "a God, a spirit which teaches the Indian nation how to live, the ideal of the perfect man, the valiant, the strong, the brave, the humorous, the whole in body" (137). The irony arises when Ali, the actor portraying God, is being physically tormented and injured by the Indians, his own people.

God is portrayed as something that is not immune or immortal, and unlike the actual end of the epic of *Ramayana*, God is not restored to his kingdom and does not return from exile. What the cast, directed by David and Sara, sees in the adaptation of *Ramayana* is what second-generation writing teaches its readers: "we teach people to see the trans-cultural, the human beneath the skin, the conflagration of nationalities, the global nature of bullshit and terror" (144). India, however, cannot see the human beneath the skin because it is deeply overwhelmed by religious beliefs, superstitions, and spirituals such as the superiority and almightiness of the fictional God of the *Ramayana* itself. God is insulted and the heart of India, its belief system is thus violated, for the protagonist is not "pure" Indian but a London-born one, and the director is English, and what does an English know about the Indian culture but its inferiority.

England is similarly represented, therefore, as a nation that cannot see beneath the color of skin because its identity is racially constructed and exclusive. Ironically, back in England, and in a reaction to playing the *Ramayana* by a non-Indian cast, Hindu fundamentalists physically assault British actors playing in a Leicester playhouse and a Hindu temple is burnt by neo-fascists warning Asians that there will be consequences. Bradford calls for an end to Shakespeare, and Hindus in Glasgow and Leamington Spa protest against any theatrical endeavors. Anjali herself is pilloried for being a British actress, which she is not. Holding an Indian passport, she is nevertheless adopted as British for her martyrdom. Being Western intellectually, she knew Joyce as good as an Irish did, Proust as good as a French, and Shakespeare as good as an English. Thus, *Bombay Duck* is an ironic and a cynical parody of British liberal multiculturalism in contrast to the realities of India and the so-called Third World. During the 1970s, "[e]xcept for Dhondy,

Indian writing in England diminished in bulk and interest as financial restrictions made leaving India difficult and migrants now preferred North America" (King: 2004: 83). Rushdie, Kureishi, Phillips, and others will soon emerge onto the stage, however.

This generation, however, is liminal: neither up nor down the stairs, but in the stairway. They are in the shadow of the doorstep. The second generation of immigrant writers shows "how newness enters the world." Newness, Bhabha tells us,

> is not part of the continuum of the past and the present. It creates a sense of the new as an insurgent act of cultural translation... it renews the past, reconfiguring it as a contingent "in-between" space, that innovates and interrupts the performance of the present. The "past-present" becomes part of the necessity, not the nostalgia, of living.
>
> (Bhabha: 2005: 10)

This establishes a major difference and distinction between the Windrush Generation and the Masala Fish Generation. In other words, while the Windrush Generation's past–present condition was overwhelmingly and melancholically daunting and hence nostalgia and memory were their way of resistance and surviving, for the Masala Fish Generation it was a style and an inevitability of living.

Rushdie's *East, West* provides a good illustrative example here. The book is divided into three chapters: it starts with East, then goes on to the West, and follows with the merging together of the two with a dividing comma that presents the immigrant's positioning in the past–present relationship, in the shadow of the doorstep: the liminal space. The structure also reflects the writer's identity: from East, observing from and living in the West, and eventually synthesizing the two together and yet drawing a line/comma between the two because each carries a unique, distinctive cultural experience. The displaced translates between both. In the last chapter, "East, West," the writer builds "a bridge between here-and-there, between my two othernesses, my double unbelonging" (Rushdie: 1995: 141). The "hidden realm... would grant me... harmony" (Ibid). The writer also emphasizes and highlights the influence England, the new cultural ambience, has had on him: "England has always been a breeding ground for our revolutionists," he writes. With historic evidence of the effect England and its empire had on formerly colonial Indians, Rushdie questions: "What would Pandit Nehru have been without Harrow? Or Ghandiji without his formative experience here? Even the Pakistan idea was dreamt up by young radicals at college in what we then were asked to think of as the Mother Country" (Rushdie: 1994: 164).

Eventually, the unnamed narrator of *East, West* declares a statement that reflects his own identity and that of the Masala Fish Generation. Despite being a British citizen, this unnamed narrator, thinly disguised as Rushdie himself, had

> ropes around my neck, I have them to this day, pulling me this way and that, East and West, the nooses tightening, commanding, choose, choose. I buck, I snort, I whinny, I kick. Ropes, I do not choose between you. Lassoes, lariats, I choose neither of you, and both. Do you hear? I refuse to choose.
> (Rushdie: 1995: 211)

Such a statement reflects a psychic fission in which Masala Fish writers started to think of themselves as neither black nor British, and both. They no longer thought of themselves merely as a part of a larger immigrant community but also as partly British, since they took roots, raised families, and integrated into British culture. They are not exiles or emigrants but black British.

Particularly with Rushdie, the writing mode starts to shift from careful realism to magic realism. For "[r]ealism can break a writer's heart" (Rushdie: 1995: 70). He also coins the concept "imaginary homelands." In *Shame*, a novel about postcolonial Pakistan, "my fictional country exists, like myself, at a slight angle to reality. I have found this off-centring to be necessary" (Rushdie: 1994: 29). One is reminded here of Bhabha's "[t]o be unhomed is not to be homeless, nor can the 'unhomely' be easily accommodated in the familiar division of social life into private and public spheres." "The world," he adds, "shrinks...and then expands enormously" (Bhabha: 2005: 13). India/Pakistan and England, in the case of Rushdie's displacements, "the private and the public become part of each other, forcing upon us a vision that is as divided as it is disorienting" (Ibid). Between past and present, hominess and homelessness, public and private spheres, Rushdie, like his hero in *Shame* Omar Khayyam, is "a translated man. I have been *borne across*. It is generally believed that something is always lost in translation; I cling to the notion—and use, in evidence, the success of Fitzgerald-Khayyam—that something can also be gained" (Rushdie: 1994: 29). Here, Rushdie is an object who is subjected to a process of translation. He is not only the translator but also a translated man. Therefore, he is able to interpret two cultures as an outsider looking in, and by virtue of multiple displacements he is able to interlink them contrapuntally.

Rushdie emphasizes that the past is never lost or abandoned but is rather reflected upon and preserved in memories, "in fragments of broken mirrors" and "I must reconcile myself to the inevitability of the missing bits" (Ibid: 69). With these missing bits and the surviving memories, Rushdie reinvents the past. Most second-generation writers therefore do not exclusively moan the lost past; they are rather more accustomed to change and celebratory of new beginnings. Rushdie for one reworks national identity under the light of his postcolonial migratory experience. His is an identity that is constituted by and through displacements rather than through a fixed "home." The latter, as explained in *East, West*, "has become such a scattered, damaged, various concept in our present travails. There is so much to yearn for." Homes, as displacements, "are metaphors of homeliness" (Rushdie: 1994: 93). *Shame* deals with such a notion of the multiplicity of displacements and homes. It emphasizes that there is no one single identity or home or history but it is rather "seen as a weave of narratives." "Rushdie's narrator characterizes telling (hi)story as piecing together the past." But most importantly, to narrate a history "that is opposed to the official one, he has to include what has been excluded. Rushdie links himself to women in Pakistan [in *Shame*] because he can be silenced" (Childs: 2005: 193). He, an outsider looking in, believes that history should be written by outsiders. The displaced's view resembles Gibreel Farishta's in *The Satanic Verses*, "floating up on a high crane looking down" (Rushdie: 2006a: 108). The past of Pakistan in *Shame* was also rewritten by displaced migrants in England in "Urdu and English, both imported languages. Pakistan was born in exile," too (87). Pakistan, "increasingly at war with itself... was just insufficiently imagined... a miracle that went wrong" (87). Rushdie then "sets himself up as an unofficial chronicle, someone who writes back to the past by writing overlooked or obscured elements of the past back into history" (Childs: 2005: 194).

Shame is about the conditions and corruptions of postcolonial Pakistan, the depiction of the Zia and Bhutto periods in Pakistan, the myths of national independence and nationhood, the myth of India and its Gods, and Third World writers living in the metropolitan city. It is also "a novel about postcolonial identity: a condition it debates in more terms than fragmentation, repeatedly using images of splitting, liminality, and hybridity" (Childs: 2005: 189). In this novel, as in *East, West*, Rushdie celebrates the off-centering. He states,

I am comparing gravity with belonging. Both phenomena observably exist: my feet stay on the ground, and I have never been angrier than I was on the day my father told me he had sold my childhood home in Bombay. But neither is understood. We know the force of gravity, but not its origins; and to explain why we become attached to our birthplaces we pretend that we are trees and speak of roots. Look under your feet. You will not find gnarled growths sprouting through the soles. Roots, I sometimes think, are a conservative myth, designed to keep us in our places. The anti-myth of gravity and of belonging bears the same name: flight. Migration, n. moving, for instance in flight, from one place to another. To fly and to flee: both are ways of seeking freedom.

(Rushdie: 1994: 86)

Rushdie resents overly stated concepts such as "roots" and "home." He promotes mobility and flights instead and fashions a country in his imagination, adding them to the remnants that already existed in the past. But like all migrants, Rushdie, "too, face[s] the problem of history: what to retain, what to dump, how to hold on to what memory insists on relinquishing, how to deal with change. And to come back to the 'roots' idea, I should say that *I haven't managed to shake myself free of it completely*" (Ibid: 88; my italics). Here, and despite his imaginary homelands and being a fantasist/fabulist, Rushdie emphasizes the solid existence of a beginning in the unshakeable idea of roots. He admits the enormous force of the gravity of having to belong, and of rootedness.

I tell myself this will be a novel of leave-taking, my last words on the East from which, many years ago, I began to come loose. I do not always believe myself when I say this. It is a part of the world to which, whether I like it or not, I am still joined, if only by elastic bands.

(Ibid: 28)

From the past the immigrant becomes loose, but which he does not completely lose. Rushdie evidentially does not leave Pakistan untouched and glorified but assesses and reevaluates the culture, the community, and its traditions through the eyes of the displaced traveler he became. He exposes the shamefulness about what Pakistan sees as "shameful": going to the pictures/cinema (because there are imported nonvegetarian westerns in which cows get massacred); the word "woman" automatically implies shame, peripherality, and dirtiness; and love is shame because it corrupts. In Pakistan there are also industrial programs that build nuclear reactors but cannot develop a refrigerator; there is anti-Semitism, smuggling, heroine exports, military dictators, venal civilians, bought judges, the appropriation of the national budget with focus on defense as opposed to education; and finally, arranged marriages, or shams (Rushdie: 1994: 69–70). Such an assessment of Pakistan would not have been as resourceful and proficient had it not been for the contrasting English experience of the West. As in every other novel too, Rushdie tackles the issue of religion, and of Islamist fundamentalism in particular. Rushdie, like Kureishi, sees in religion a constraint and a restraining of artistic creativity and expression.

Salman Rushdie, despite being raised in and coming from a Muslim family and background, is an agnostic. Or, at best, he is a secular humanist. "I am not, myself, a religious man," Rushdie admits (Rushdie: 1991: 376). In *The Satanic Verses*, Rushdie asks, "Question: What is the opposite of faith? Not disbelief. Too final, certain, closed. Itself a kind of belief. Doubt" (Rushdie: 2006a: 92). In *A Letter to the Six Billionth World Citizen*, he advises that "to choose unbelief is to choose mind over dogma, to trust in our humanity instead of all these dangerous divinities. So, how did we get here? Don't look for the answer in story-books." He continues,

> Only you can decide if you want to be handed down the law by priests, and accept that good and evil are somehow external to ourselves. To my mind religion, even at its most sophisticated, essentially infantilizes our ethical selves by setting infallible moral Arbiters and irredeemably immoral Tempters above us; the eternal parents, good and bad, light and dark, of the supernatural realm.
>
> (Rushdie: 2002: 157)

Rushdie promotes intellectual freedom and progressively continuous debate as opposed to closed, certain, and final systems of belief, i.e., religion. He invites the population of this planet as well as the six billionth world citizen to

> refuse to allow priests, and the fictions on whose behalf they claim to speak, to be the policemen of our liberties and behaviour. Once and for all we could put the stories back into the books, put the books back on the shelves, and see the world undogmatized and plain. Imagine there's no heaven, my dear Six Billionth, and at once the sky's the limit.
>
> (Ibid: 158)

This "letter" (1997) was incidentally written nine years after the publication of *The Satanic Verses* (1988) and eight years after Rushdie was sentenced to death by Khomeini's fatwa on Valentine's Day, February 14, 1989.

Although Rushdie's controversial and banned-in-Islamic-countries novel is best known for its critique of Islam and its promotion of doubt over the storybook that is The Qur'an, *The Satanic Verses* is also about migration and displacement. It is about the fact that in order "To be born again... first you have to die" (Rushdie: 2006a: 3). The falling of Saladin Chamcha and Gibreel Farishta from the sky down in London symbolizes rebirth and transformation: transmutation. This fall is described early in the novel as "angelic devilish fall": paradoxical, twofold. It is transitory and open, "because when you throw everything in the air anything becomes possible" (Rushdie: 2006a: 5). Ultimately, "great falls change people" (Ibid: 133). The fall also belittles the importance of the myth of return: time difference between east and west resembles the weather and climate change in each area, respectively; "turn your watch upside down in Bombay and you see the time in London" (Rushdie: 2006a: 41). A return thus would be an "inverting [of] Time" (Ibid).

The novel stands in opposition to the "bloody-minded," "mentally-ghettoized," "ramrod-backed type of damnfool" migrant who brings the past along, is boxed, and remains locked up and ghettoized in it. It objects to the type of migrant who does not open up, translate, or integrate. Upon his return to Bombay, Saladin Chamcha is tempted toward his old self, "but it was a dead self, a shadow, a ghost, and he would not become a phantom"; worse yet, it makes him feel "giddy because it feels like home and is not" (58). Thereafter, Saladin believes that an "adult chops down his childhood to help his grown-up self" (65). This, however, does not necessarily mean a total abandonment of the past, but rather a turn and a translation that gathers fragments of the past, reenvisions them a second time, and puts them in negotiation with the experience(s) of the present. To be locked up in the attic of the familiar/past/tradition in the midst of change/modernity/newness is like carrying "a brim-full pitcher of water through a holiday crowd without spilling a drop, on pain of death, so that when he returned he was unable to describe the day's festivities, having been like a blind man, seeing only the jug on his head" (42). The displaced migrant therefore is asked not to be a blind one and instead is invited to open both mind and eyes.

What is worth mentioning here is that Ahmad sees in Rushdie's turning from a self-exile into a forced exile a turn also in the "elasticity" of his bonding with origins and his subject matter.

The self-exile has no such irrecoverable bond; he is free to choose the degree of elasticity of that bonding, and the material consequences of his migrancy necessarily bring him into a much more accountable relation with the readership which is materially present within the milieu of his productive work. This one recognizes not as a weakness or strength of Rushdie's work but simply as one of its framing realities.

(Ahmad: 2008: 132)

Rushdie defines exile by its multiplicity and its wide range of possibilities. In *The Satanic Verses* he states that

> Exile is a vision of revolution: Elba, not St Helena. It is an endless paradox: looking forward by always looking back. The exile is a ball hurled high into the air. He hangs there, frozen in time, translated into a photograph; denied motion, suspended impossibly above his native earth, he awaits the inevitable moment at which the photograph must begin to move, and the earth reclaim its own.
>
> (Rushdie: 2006a: 205)

The exile thus resembles an amphibian: an adaptive creature that has the ability to live inside as well as outside natal and new cultural worlds and languages, adaptive to both known and/or changing environments. Instability, however, can cause disturbance and insecurity. Exile therefore is paradoxical; it is tragic as much as it is creative. Its ambivalent nature broadens the displaced individual's horizons, provides the displaced with a double insight; but it also forges and urges nostalgia and at times provokes national consciousness that might lead to nationalism or extremism.

Before the fatwa, Rushdie was a self-exile. Ahmad defines a self-exile as one who is "free to choose the degree of elasticity of that bonding" between self and place, home and identity. For Ahmad, the pleasures of self-exile are "much more often [exercised] than those of forced exile" (Ahmad: 2008: 210). Said, on the other hand, sees in the pleasures of exile "a particular sense of achievement in acting as if one were at home wherever one happens to be." He adds, "[m]ost people are principally aware of one culture, one setting, one home; exiles are aware of at least two, and this plurality of vision gives rise to an awareness of simultaneous dimensions, an awareness that—to borrow a phrase from music—is *contrapuntal*" (Said: 2001a: 186). Said himself expresses how he belongs to more than one culture and thus more than one world. Each of these worlds and identities are interchangeably interrelated. One influences the other. One draws from the other. He states: "I cannot identify at all with the triumphalism of one identity because the loss and deprivation of the others are so much more urgent to me" (Said: 2001a: 397). This teaches one that "cultural, national, or ethnic... identities are constructions, not god-given or natural artifacts" (Said: 2001a: 397). What these displaced and exilic figures also share is provisional homes lived partially in their writings, their stories, the long-lasting original expulsion of departure, and their off-centering.

Regardless of whether the displaced writers of this generation are self-exiles or forced exiles, born and bred English, or a result of family reunion, they are part of what Timothy Mo calls "the Renegade, those who through choice, rejection, or birth do not belong. They are hybrids, a sign of the new, the future, and are at the moral centre in an otherwise often divisive, tribal, and violent world" (King: 2004: 99). They have taken something presumably negative (melancholia, alienation, nostalgia, homelessness, rootlessness, and unbelonging) and turned it into something positive, creative, and celebratory. This also applies on the irregularity of unreliable narrators' narrative and memories. The falsification of events and dates is usually purposefully made for criticism and/or to avoid responsibility or shame. The unreliable narrator recalls false memories to displace the past and its narrative to suit their present. Sometimes this is also done to amplify events. Through the unreliability of the unreliable narrator, the reader finds reliability.

The unreliable narrator of Rushdie's *Midnight's Children* functions quite differently, however. In Saleem Sinai's misjudgment about events and their real and historical sequence (such as the year of Mahatma Gandhi's death), Rushdie reinforces the fact that memory is tricky and fragmented. The "slippages and distortions of memory" (Rushdie: 2006b: xii) prove that even if the displaced remembers things the wrong way and not as they actually happened, preference is often for the distorted version.

Rushdie's *Midnight's Children* is a novel of memories, semi-autobiographically narrated and is about a society he knew very well before the uprooting. Rushdie enjoys improvisation and thus his writing is "jazzy" (Reynolds and Noakes: 2003: 25). The novel was born out of his journey back to India in 1975 after publishing *Grimus*. This is a novel of childhood, "arising from my memories of my own childhood in Bombay" (Rushdie: 2006b: ix). Rushdie uses memory to invoke the past in order to understand the present. This process Rushdie calls filtration. Displaced from place and in time,

> migration placed a double filter between me and my subject, and I hoped that if I could only imagine vividly enough it might be possible to see beyond those filters, to write as if the years had not passed, as if I had never left India for the West. But as I worked I found that what interested me was the process of filtration itself. So my subject changed, was no longer a search for lost time,

had become the way in which we remake the past to suit our present purposes, using memory as a tool.

(Rushdie: 1991: 24)

For the displaced, the past ceases as a reality and becomes a reinvention. Looking back through the telescope of displacement(s), i.e., critical distance, the past is reconstructed to suit the present course. The here and now is not therefore eclipsed by the there and then. It rather feeds on it and uses it to see a better translated reality. Because, as Rushdie writes in *Midnight's Children*,

Reality is a question of perspective; the further you get from the past, the more concrete and plausible it seems—but as you approach the present, it inevitably seems more and more incredible. Suppose yourself in a large cinema, sitting at first in the back row, and gradually moving up, row by row, until your nose is almost pressed against the screen. Gradually the stars' faces dissolve into dancing grain;... illusion dissolves or rather, it becomes clear that illusion itself is reality.

(Rushdie: 2006b: 229)

The effect of a cinematic perspective on the perception of reality is a reoccurring theme in Rushdie's writings. For example, Saleem's grandfather, Aadam Aziz, with his old and long nose, was once an exile who left Kashmir. "Now returning, he saw through travelled eyes. Instead of the beauty of the tiny valley... he noticed the narrowness, the proximity of the horizon; and felt sad, to be at home and feel utterly enclosed" (5). "*Midnight's Children*" and its generation of those born and raised in a postcolonial period and place became "a familiar catch-phrase defining that generation which was too young to remember the Empire or the liberation struggle" (Rushdie: 1991: 26). They are second-generation immigrants, the children of first-generation emigrants: they are distant from a colonial history, with no vivid memories of a colonial past and for whom colonialism is an isolated knowledge as opposed to a recent experience.

Midnight's Children, however, is not completely a colonially involved novel; it is also a postcolonial narration. What connects both past and present in *Midnight's Children* is colonialism itself and Rushdie's looking back through fragmented memories of India under British rule. In other words, what came after colonialism has to be understood in relation and relevance to colonialism itself. According to Ahmad, a postmodern text should (a) "have enough modernism within it and (b) also to diverge sufficiently in a new avant-gardist way" (Ahmad: 2008: 124). Rushdie's avant-gardist predilection is evident in his introduction of magic realism, Urdu and Hindi, traditional Indian orature, and his chutnification of history and language. In this way he celebrates Britain's multiculturalism and diversity as well as the euphoria of multiple belongings as opposed to the melancholia of not belonging.

Midnight's Children highlights the so-called "too muchness" of India: its crowdedness, excessiveness, and diversity. Digression is also meant to reinforce Stuart Hall's theory of multiple histories as opposed to a singular one. Saleem says:

> there are so many stories to tell, too many, such an excess of intertwined lives events miracles places rumours, so dense a commingling of the improbable and the mundane! I have been a swallower of lives; and to know me, just the one of me, you'll have to swallow the lot as well.
> (Rushdie: 2006b: 4)

In other words, in order to understand the history of colonial and postcolonial India one has to understand the history of colonial and postcolonial Britain. Bombay, we are told, was named first by the Portuguese for its harbor where their merchant ships sheltered. Then it was a West India company officer named Methwold who saw a vision of British Bombay. Bombay was considered therefore the star of the east with an eye on the west.

Midnight's Children also reinforces this project's argument: we are not free-floating and nomadic creatures. We come from somewhere: "Nothing comes from nowhere" (Rushdie in Reynolds and Noakes: 2003: 28). In the novel, the Sterne-like narration of digression is always interrupted and "brought back on track" by Padma. She keeps pressuring him with her "what-happened-nextism" (Rushdie: 2006b: 45). The digression and too muchness of Saleem's narration are also used by Rushdie to say that we come to an already framed life, a structured identity: a family we did not choose, a geographical location we had nothing to do with, a religion and class, a race, a language that were all chosen for us. We live the presence of an absent past that happened before we were even born and by which we are influenced, judged, and sometimes from which we try to escape for the rest of our lives. And

the reason why in the book [*Midnight's Children*] there's so much that happens before Saleem is born, is to say, "We do not come naked into the world." We bring an enormous amount of baggage, so therefore, limitation. And that baggage is history, family history and a broader history too, and we're

born into a context, and we're born as the child of our parents, and as the descendants of our family.
(Rushdie in Reynolds and Noakes: 2003: 17)

The baggage (history, past, and family) can therefore be a limitation to the present: it slows the process of progress and translation, of transmutation. Rushdie's strategy of delaying and postponing the climax of the birth of Saleem Sinai is therefore an emphasis on the fact that "[m]ost of what matters in our lives takes place in our absence"; in this light, he narrates the prehistory of Saleem's existence to show how he is "handcuffed" to history before he is even born. Saleem is therefore absurdly handcuffed to, and twinned with, the history of India and feels he is the reason of its failures and tragedies. "I had been mysteriously handcuffed to history, my destinies indissolubly chained to those of my country" (Rushdie: 2006b: 3). At the end of the second chapter he is literally unhoused because his house is blown up and most of his family members are destroyed. The third part of the novel portrays Saleem being flung into history, no longer accompanied by family members and consoled by personal life. He is in the middle of history and he is not a master of it but rather a victim.

Rushdie's second novel is about (his Indian) childhood. But it is also a novel that is narrated from a postcolonial locus looking back at a colonial period and place: India's transition from British colonialism, toward independence and the partition, and the creation of the "pure" Islamic state of Pakistan; it is also about the fought-over Kashmir. "Kashmir, after all, is not strictly speaking a part of the Empire," Saleem clarifies, "but an independent princely state" (38).

The whole act of Saleem's writing his memories is to preserve them and prevent them from the decay that is forgetfulness. Ironically, the first thing Saleem smells with his "most delicately-gifted olfactory organ in history" is chutney (44). Saleem preserves memory against time in making sure that he is "letting no blood escape from the body of the tale." "Family history, of course," he adds,

> has its proper dietary laws. One is supposed to swallow and digest only the permitted parts of it, the halal portions of the past, drained of their redness, their blood. Unfortunately, this makes the stories less juicy; so I am about to become the first and only member of family to flout the laws of halal. (74)

Rushdie makes sure that he does not miss the bloody parts of Indian history, using discontinuous memory and narrative, digression, and magic realism as a tool.

Midnight's Children is a novel about historical and cultural displacement. Saleem's mother insists that despite Mr Methwold's furniture and belongings, which leaves them "sitting in the middle of all this English garbage... this is still India" (133). Methwold's, the house of the former colonizer, ironically becomes the household of Saleem's childhood. An Indian family living in the remnants of British colonialism is portrayed in the furniture of the house. Saleem admits, however, that India after the partition and the leaving of the British becomes

> a world which, although it had five thousand years of history, although it had invented the game of chess and traded with Middle Kingdom Egypt, was nevertheless quite imaginary; into a mythical land, a country which would never exist except by the efforts of a phenomenal collective will—except in a dream we all agreed to dream; it was a mass fantasy shared in varying degrees by Bengali and Punjabi, Madrasi and Jat.

Midnight's Children is also a novel about being away from India and, by virtue of an agonizing distance from it, an India of the mind is created. India is after all "a new myth—a collective fiction" (150). India for Rushdie is, as much as is Pakistan, an imaginary homeland. In *Imaginary Homelands*, he writes that no exile, expatriate, or emigrant can escape their past completely; the past keeps haunting the displaced with an

> urge to reclaim, to look back, even at the risk of being mutated into pillars of salt. But if we do look back, we must also do so in the knowledge—which gives rise to profound uncertainties—that our physical alienation from India almost inevitably means that we will not be capable of reclaiming precisely the thing that was lost; that we will, in short, create fictions, not actual cities or villages, but invisible ones, imaginary homelands, Indias of the mind.
>
> (Rushdie: 1991: 10)

Twelve years later, Rushdie writes in *Step Across This Line*: "The journey creates us. We become the frontiers we cross." He adds: "to cross a frontier is to be transformed" (Rushdie: 2002: 410–1). In this second volume, he does not talk about the past and imaginary homelands as much as he highlights the importance of transformation and crossing. Rushdie is ultimately known for themes of cultural translation, change, transformation, "celebration of the open road, and of the open frontier as well." He emphasizes here, however, the act of the crossing as opposed to memorization or forgetfulness. Displacement becomes in this sense

[t]he crossing of borders, of language, geography, and culture; the examination of the permeable frontier between the universe of things and deeds and the universe of the imagination; the lowering of the intolerable frontiers created by the world's many different kinds of thought policemen.

(Rushdie: 2002: 434)

In his story of 1,001 children of midnight, Saleem does not cross. He is caught in remembering, in history, and in language. Saleem's power or miracle, for example, functions only within the newly independent India bounded by its language, geography, and the baggage of history; he is powerful only within the India that is "bounded by the Arabian Sea, the Bay of Bengal, the Himalayas mountains, but also by artificial frontiers which pierced Punjab and Bengal" (Rushdie: 2006b: 271). After his exile to Pakistan, after his mother Amina left his father, Saleem loses his transmission power with the other midnight children outside of India.

Saleem also writes his story/memoir with a picture he buried at Buckingham villa in a squashed tin globe from his childhood in hand; the picture was all he had when he left for Pakistan with his family as a refugee. He does not think "outside of the box" of the past. Saleem is called baldie because of Mr Zagallo, the geography teacher, who pulled his hair as he was trying to convince him violently that he was an animal from the jungle and his face resembles the map of India, and Pakistan was a stain on it. The narrative, however, crosses the line and the frontier by bringing into the narration Saleem's son, Aadam, who is second generation and hence "would grow up far tougher than the first, not looking for their fate in prophecy or the stars, but forging it in the implacable furnaces of their will" (Ibid: 625). Rushdie ends the novel by reminding the reader that memory and remembering cannot be but distorted and fragmented, while the process of revision and translation should be constant and endless.

The writings of many of what are called here Masala Fish writers are influenced by Rushdie's own use of magic realism. Influenced by science fiction and Hollywood and Bollywood films, Rushdie introduces what King calls the "fabulous." The fabulous, he defines as, "a way to treat the political without sacrificing art to the literal." In this, Rushdie "modelled his digressive manner and extraordinary characters and events on the methods of Indian art, the fairy tale" (King: 2004: 141).

In her *Flights from Realism*, Alexander characterizes postmodern writings as quintessentially full of playfulness, treachery, and trickery; digression and outrageous subject matter; unreliable narrators;

emphasis on personal freedom, philosophical and moral enquiry; questions of human reality; religious unfaithfulness; subversion of received realities; and unsatisfactory conclusions. All of these characteristics are found in the magic realism of Rushdie's work. It is as if he combines the realistic and the surreal because he is intimately aware of the impossibility of recognizing, or for that matter creating a sense of a common reality. As Alexander says, he "employ[s] new conventions of magical realism, suggesting that there is a link between the culture and conditions of particular societies and the extent to which the novelist feels that he or she can present a stable view of reality" (Alexander: 1990: 13). In *Shame* he questions the reality of a Pakistani community and its cultural and religious values under a military government; in *Midnight's Children* he reinvents India after the departure of the British and examines its independence, combining autobiographical writing and historical narrative. In *The Satanic Verses* he continues to explore themes of alienation, displacement, immigration, and metamorphosis, providing an alternative reality for the representation of Islam and its history. Rushdie uses fantasy for political satire and the critique of religious absolutism.

But Alexander also draws on the fact that postmodernist writing can also invoke trouble and touch on sensitive issues like sexuality and religion. What came after the publication of *The Satanic Verses* (the burning of books and libraries and the fatwa) "confirmed the West's sense of the 'otherness' of Islam, and of its primitive handling of crisis." West and Islam are

> two irreconcilable systems of value in collision. On one side, the right to freedom of speech, observed by Western societies, has been upheld to the point where the British government is giving police protection to a writer who in this same book lampoons both the British Prime Minister (thinly disguised as Mrs Torture) and the British police force. On the other, behind Khomeini's death threat there is an absolute reverence for revealed religious truth which supersedes personal freedoms.
> (Alexander: 1990: 201)

This reactionary episode in the aftermath of *The Satanic Verses* shows that religion "has begun once again to insist on occupying a central role in public life" (Rushdie: 1990: 376). Rushdie's aesthetic response is to "describe reality as it is experienced by religious people, for whom God is no symbol but an everyday fact," but in the realization that "the conventions of what is called realism are quite inadequate" (Ibid: 376). He points out that religion in the Islamic world as opposed to the Christian West is national and not merely religious.

Soldiers have always been encouraged to die by the idea that they have God on their side. Khomeini's revolution was intensely nationalistic in character. The unity it forged between many widely disparate elements of Iranian society, from the high bourgeoisie to the oil-workers, was built upon the desire to depose a despot, to liberate a nation.

(Rushdie: 1990: 383)

This aligns and echoes Anderson's thesis in *Imagined Communities*. Born to a Chinese-Indonesian father and an English mother, and exiled from Indonesia in England, Benedict Anderson outlines, in his introduction to his *Imagined Communities* (1983), the definition of a nation as an "imagined political community." It is imagined because its members "will never know most of their fellow members" and "yet in the minds of each lives the image of their communion." The imaginary construction of a nation and its boundaries and perhaps of a citizenship encourages individuals to imagine its "inherently limited" boundaries. It is limited, he explains, because "even the largest of them...has finite, if elastic, boundaries, beyond which lie other nations." A dividing line and distinction between one nation and another, one race and another, one ethnicity and another is then invoked: us and them. Pan-Arabism is an example of such an all-encompassing nationalism from the Atlantic Ocean to the Arabian Sea, from Muscat (Oman) to Casablanca (Morocco). Although Arab nationalism is marginalized in Anderson's study, it is foregrounded in Rushdie's arguments about the fact that religion is being national and politicized.

Arab nationalism is one that is founded on the Arabic language, that is, the language of the Qur'an as opposed to Latin and the language of the Bible, Hebrew and/or Aramaic Greek, from which modern European languages stem. The difference here is that religion still defines the lifestyle and everyday lives of Arabs. Language in this case brings Muslims together because it is the language of the Quran. It is well known, for example, that Pakistanis can read Arabic and speak it unclearly in prayer, yet understand very little of it. Language nevertheless induces a process of gathering, based on an imaginary community that is being used for political reasons. In other words, Arab/Muslim nationalism is defined by cohesion that is based on linguistic and religious solidarity. Hence, Rushdie rationalizes the havoc caused in India over his *Satanic Verses* as it served the purposes of Islamic political parties, allowing them to become more powerful and acquire more votes in elections. What helped such communities to be imagined as unities "was the existence of sacred languages through which the religions could be mediated to many different peoples speaking many different tongues" (Rushdie: 1990: 381).

Acknowledging the shift in Britain's understanding of the Other and subsequently of its own identity, Caryl Phillips writes that

> Today there is a tacit understanding that Britain has changed. It has been a few years now since a Briton had the temerity to ask me, "where are you from" I take this a sign of progress. Sadly, however, I am coming to understand that despite these welcome changes, the constant questioning of those early years, and concomitant undermining of my sense of belonging, has inevitably affected my ability to embrace Britain as "home" with the degree of vigour that I might wish. Two years ago my lawyer asked me if I had any thoughts about how to "dispose of" my body. A chilly question, but I answered without hesitation. "I wish my ashes to be scattered in the middle of the Atlantic Ocean at a point equidistant between Britain, Africa and North America... a place that, over the years, I have come to refer to as my Atlantic home."
> (Phillips: 2001: 304)

Phillips is another significant writer of the Masala Fish Generation who writes from within the center and reflects its cultural synthesis and literary adventuring. His wide ranging essays in *A New World Order* (2001) establish a new world order that gives a significant role to the migrant and is characterized by cultural plurality, multiple belongings, and rootlessness, and the emergence of America as a new world power. This can be seen in the structure in which he divides the book: the United States where he moved to and lectures; Africa from which his family descended; the Caribbean where he was born and from which his family emigrated when he was five months old; and finally Britain where he grew up as a teenager, studied and graduated, supported Leeds United, struggled with, and was inspired by racial discrimination. "I am seven years old in the north of England: too late to be coloured, but too soon to be British," he declares (Phillips: 2001: 4). It is in England he read works of Sam Selvon and Derek Walcott as well as Shakespeare and Kipling. Phillips' book is dedicated to his father while the conclusion is triumphantly entitled: The High Anxiety of Belonging. Home, for Phillips, has come to be cultivated in terms of and across multiple displacements as "a plural notion" (Phillips: 2001: 304).

Phillips, as many other politically victimized members of the generation of the 1980s, "felt the desire to abandon Britain altogether. This feeling surfaced most powerfully in 1987 when Mrs. Thatcher achieved her third successive election victory. Her government's continued incantation of a discordant, neo-imperial, rhetoric of exclusion led me to the conclusion that I simply did not grief" (Ibid: 304). Post 1970, Britain was governed by three successive conservative administrations in Britain, by Margret Thatcher[3] and John Major. Thatcher fought unions and felt threatened by the coming of age of immigrants in England, believing Britain to be "swamped" with foreigners. Thatcher, thinly disguised as Mrs Torture in Rushdie's *The Satanic Verses*, was also scrutinized by Hanif Kureishi. He ends his *The Buddha of Suburbia* with Thatcher taking over power, and sets *The Black Album* in a time when she has remained in power successively. In the former novel, Eva Kay, Haroon's lover and eventual second wife, "is Kureishi's embodiment of Thatcherite ideals and capitalist energies, and she provides a stark contrast to the self-pitying inertia of Margret," the working-class wife (Buchanan: 2007: 18). Indeed, Eva is portrayed parroting Thatcher while conducting an interview with her Orientalist Buddha. "We have to empower ourselves," she affirms.

Look at those people who live on sordid housing estates. They expect others—the Government—to do everything for them. They are only half human, because only half active. We have to find a way to enable them to grow. Individual human flourishing isn't something that either socialism or conservatism caters for.

(Kureishi: 1990: 263)

It was during the Thatcherite era, however, that the "first black Members of Parliament were elected and non-white faces began to play for and even captain national sports teams" (Phillips: 2001: 278).[4] This is to say that "Mrs Thatcher's new idea of British nationality, with its dependency on economic virility and on codes of behaviour, was clearly to be culturally and not racially constructed" (Ibid). Thatcher's ideals were also colonial/imperial. "Put the 'Great' back into Great Britain again" was a popular Tory Party campaign slogan (Ibid: 279). Although there is no space here for a more in-depth discussion of the political upheaval and development post the 1970s or of its effects on immigrants, it is important to mention it in order to show that Masala Fish writers were deeply involved in their writings with radical political changes in British society and thus writing from within as a significant part of it.

Caryl Phillips is invoked here to illustrate that despite his traveling between the rectangle of his homes (Britain, the west coast of Africa, the New World of North America, and the Caribbean), his identity is rerooted in each home individually, and in relation to other homes simultaneously. Describing his journey to the four different countries, Phillips ends each visit with the same repeated statement: "I recognise the place, I feel at home here, but I don't belong. I am of, and not of, this place" (Phillips: 2001: 1–5). This repetition and his not belonging to one singular place reinforce the multiplicity of displacements/belongings. Nevertheless, Phillips believes that "[a]ll journeys have a beginning" (305) and his own nomadic traveling also starts somewhere: St Kittens. Although it could also be argued that his journey began in earlier historical context in Africa from which, through enslavement and the sugarcane industry, his ancestors were taken by the British to the West Indies; postcolonially, however, his begins in the Caribbean.

Phillips' debut novel (1985) *The Final Passage* is a good testimony to this fact. In other words, although Phillips was taken out of St Kitts at the age of five and primarily raised in Leeds, his first debut novel retracts to St Kitts, marking therefore a characteristic of second-generation writers: they still write and are inspired by their beginnings. It is also a satirical account of how the past should be translated within the context of the present as opposed to bemoaning loss; thereby, Phillips promotes a healthier dialogic translation by showing what otherwise can result.

The novel also reemphasizes earlier and yet ongoing conflicts and difficulties the displaced migrant faces in Britain. It highlights how far improved the situation in Britain has been since, because of their facing such difficulties. Phillips' highlighting the imperial past St Kittens had gone through indicates, moreover, that colonialism still affects second-generation writers and stresses its present economical and psychological impact upon its subjects and their so-called postcolonially independent nations. In *The Final Passage* (*TFP*), the grandfather with his colonial mentality reminds the now postcolonial grandson of the economic operation behind imperialism: "the economic of the world be soldered with my sweat and your sweat and his sweat and the sweat of every coloured man in the world" (Phillips: 1985: 41–2). In the face of the new and changing, however, Michael's grandfather asks him to remember him and remember the land and family. Phillips, it is worth mentioning here, and significantly inspired by Sam Selvon, brought back peasantry narrative into second-generation writing. He also writes a large part of the narrative in broken English, adding empathy. Upon arrival in England, emigrants "had nothing to declare except their accents" (*TFP*: 143). Before leaving for England, furthermore, people already had an imaginative landscape of England in place: "half-formed, half-truths, uncritical, myth, none of which could be verified except by trust" (*TFP*: 102). Some thought of it as "an education" and "a college for the West Indian" (*TFP*: 101). Others thought "England going put all coloureds in concentration camps" (*TFP*: 106). Being a novel about the 1950s, physical unaccommodation reflected racial discrimination. Edwin, Michael's West Indian colleague at work in London, lectures him about his expectations in England: any nostalgic memories of home will only cause one nightmares; West Indians are treated worse than dogs in England; and if Edwin has a son, he wants him to be a cricketer as opposed to a footballer, presumably because cricket emphasized his national and cultural West Indian identity (*TFP*: 168). Edwin also reinforces Fanon's argument about the psychological effects of fear and shame that were deliberately generated with colonialism: "It's how the white man in this country kills off the coloured man. He makes you beat up and blow yourself away" (*TFP*: 168).

With "Home" being the largest section of the novel, Phillips portrays Caribbean peasantry life in a postcolonial context. Michael, Leila's husband, is lectured by his grandfather on national identity and history. In food, he finds a cultural marker that is specifically agricultural but also divides the world continentally and politically: "Yam is African man tree, Mango is Indian man tree, Coconut is Pacific man tree" and "[n]ext time you see a piece of sugar cane ask yourself when the last time you did see a white man cutting or weeding in the field" (*TFP*: 40). In this he draws attention to the imperial past the island had gone through and the present time where "[y]ou must hate enough, and you must be angry enough to get just what you want but not more! No more! For, if you do, you just going end up hating yourself" (*TFP*: 41).

The novel is written in what this book has called an adventuring form in five chapters, starting at The End, Home, England, The Passage, and Winter. The novel is set at Home in a small village called St Patrick's in the Caribbean during the 1950s. Here, Phillips celebrates the past of a Caribbean diaspora to the Mother Country crossing the Atlantic on the *SS Winston Churchill*, a thinly disguised allusion to the famous *SS Windrush Empire*.

Leila, *The Final Passage*'s protagonist, is a teenager growing up in the West Indies and emigrates as part of a larger emigrant community to England, the mother country, to be reunited with her dying mother as she becomes more aware of her own identity and the world around her. She realizes that departure was "leaving the safety of your family to go live with strangers" (*TFP*: 11). Leaving the island, Leila "could see only half the island," emigrants on the deck, and a "small proud island...[which] had been her home" (*TFP*: 20).

As the narrative moves toward England, however, sceneries of nature fade. Hymn at the angelic church, food: "[p]lums, mangoes, sugar cakes, rice and meats, pears, ginger beer, soursop, lemonade, rum" (*TFP*: 50) were all highlighted at Home. In the same section, Phillips further portrays the town and its social life through a cultural event that is the wedding of Leila and Michael. During this, Leila comes to realize that she is doubly marginalized. "She got up, found a mirror on the wall and looked hard at herself. A wife and a woman. A woman and a wife. She shut her teeth tight with frustration" (*TFP*: 55). While still at home, Leila's double character can be found in Millie: a black girl who, unlike Leila, marries, wants to start a business, and settles down Home with her husband. She also tries to awaken Leila's consciousness as she describes her as "a coward" for not confronting her husband with the truth that he is having an affair with someone else (*TFP*: 60). Phillips' Leila resembles at the end of the novel Ali's Nazneen at the beginning of *Brick Lane*.

In the last chapter of the novel, Winter, Leila is imperiled by England and its women who pose nothing but a threat to her and her husband. Her skin she notices has gone paler as it was starved of the sun (*TFP*: 195) and she is physically and psychologically displaced and traumatized. Leila is the mad woman in the attic: her Other character and English Neighbor, Mary, "posed to Leila the hardest part of her new life to consider" (198) and in a moment of madness she "began to feed the fire with the objects and garments that reminded her of her five months in England" (*TFP*: 200). "Leila fell asleep, sure that she could hear the sound of the sea," which reminded her of home (*TFP*: 201). She was even "convinced that if she turned around quickly enough she would see her mother" (*TFP*: 201). Like Rhys's Mrs Rochester, Leila ends up romancing the past as a better place than the present. England is represented as a threat, with no hope, and it holds no attraction to her, especially after the death of her mother. Home offers her "safety and two friends" (*TFP*: 203). England, on the other hand, offers her nothing but threat and discomfort.

Leila is conscious of developing a new understanding of herself and her life as an emigrant away from home, nevertheless. She states: "everything up until now had been a preparation for knowing, not the knowing itself" (*TFP*: 132). She seems prepared for confronting difficulties, but fails to. Leila describes England as "bleak" and "overcast" (*TFP*: 142). Weather, as well as architecture and food, is once again invoked to reinforce the changing and emblematic nature of her displacement:

There were no green mountains, there were no colourful women with baskets on their heads selling peanuts or bananas or mangoes, there were no trees, no white houses on the hills, no hills, no wooden houses by the shoreline, and the sea was not blue and there was no beach, and there were no clouds, just one big cloud, and they had arrived.

(*TFP*: 142)

The meaning of the word "passage" in the title can be found in the section prior and on arrival in England. The passage is the physical crossing of the Atlantic for fifteen days by ship toward the shores of England. The passage is the crossing, the arrival at the cold, misty gray land of England through the English Channel. The passage is "more mental than physical discomfort, knowing the world she had left behind no longer held anything of interest for her save Millie and Bradeth. The world she was choosing to inhabit might hold even less if she could not share it fully with her mother" (*TFP*: 137–38). The passage is the leaving behind of a world of familiarity and familiality toward estrangement and the unknown. It is the starting of the physical realization of psychological detachment too. The world left behind is to presumably be neglected and is no longer interesting, whereas the air of doubt and suspension is all about the place of arrival that might hold any interests or excitement for the emigrants of the passage. The passage to England therefore involves knowing the culture of the country, the knowing and exchanging of histories.

It is also about beginning to change. Failure to cope with the new, to adapt and change, Leila ends up lonely with her son during Christmas. Typical of a second-generation writer, Charlie, her son, is a second-generation character raised and bred in England to Caribbean parents. His first words are in English and of racial speculation: "Why is Santa Claus white?" *The Final Passage* can be read as a cynical narrative of first-generation emigrants who were locked up and ghettoized in the past and could not move forward or take a cultural turn. Second-generation writers, despite the moving away mentally and physically from the parental homelands, however, still draw on them for their material and reflect upon them for inspiration—let alone visiting them on annual basis. They are their starting points from which they take a cultural turn.

While for Rushdie, Dhondy, and Mo identity reconfiguration takes place outside England, however, for Hanif Kureishi it takes place completely inside it. While offering a fertile soil for second-generation writers to draw on, for Kureishi the past (memory and nostalgia in particular) simply did not exist. It is replaced nevertheless by rootlessness and instability. In both cases, however, the melancholy of non-belonging is replaced by a celebration of multiple belongings: a rerouting of pluralistic displacements.

While Rushdie, Mo, and Dhondy wrote with some memory and experience of the past and tradition and its culture, Kureishi had to invent it. Born and bred English and raised up in a mixed-race household with a Pakistani name and brown skin, "if he were to survive he would have to construct everything from scratch, would have to invent the ground beneath his feet before he could take a step" (Rushdie: 2006a: 132). His identity, like the narrative of his first novel *The Buddha of Suburbia*, is "a narrative of growing understanding and awareness" of who he really is (Childs: 2005: 143). Kureishi shifts the focus from origins, beginnings, exile, and cultural conflict to present complexities of contemporary England and British society, popular culture, and sexuality. Since he focuses on British society and the complexities it involves, Kureishi cannot avoid, in his earlier works, the presence of large numbers of Asian and black immigrants in England: their class distinctions and generational differences as the children of first-generation emigrants became part of English society. His later work, however, turned in focus to the intimate, the loss of excitement, love and aging, and sexual desire. Despite being half black, Kureishi does not find solace or comfort in black separatism and sees in religion an unappealing restriction because it restrains and represses artistic freedom and creativity. It is also well known that instead of seeing himself as being part of the black diaspora, Kureishi accepted being British and started writing as one.

In Kureishi's writings, the desire for change and renewal is expressed among other things through sexuality. Sexuality is linked to personal freedom and autonomy, to individual expression and identity development, and it is about the journey from repression to liberty. Individuals in Kureishi's novels do not resort to the tropical islands of sun, familiar cuisines, and memories to resolve their unsettled identities; they resorted to drugs and sex, music, and fashion. Through sexual and love relationships, Kureishi's characters try to escape constraint, borders, subvert class, and enlarge themselves. "They're trying to find out who else they may be, or who else might be inside them, or what identifications with other groups are possible to enlarge the sense of self... 'Who can I become?', 'What are the possibilities of life for me?' " (Buchanan: 2007: 112).

In both *The Buddha of Suburbia* and *My Beautiful Laundrette*, the half brown half white protagonist is portrayed as advancing into social and cultural life through sexual encounters. Sexuality to an extent liberates their traditionalism. Kureishi's portrayal of sexuality, especially of Pakistani, Muslim characters, as gay (Omar in *My Beautiful Laundrette*) or lesbians (Jameela in *The Buddha of Suburbia*), was considered adventurous. Other adventurous writings are also those of *The Body* and *The Penis*.

Furthermore, Kureishi is, like some aforementioned writers, a humanist and sees that differences (age, sex, gender, religion, and geography) are less significant than they might seem. He believes that society should have no hierarchy of class, but should rather be fluid and with free movement between classes. This obsessive portrayal of class and sexuality is for a reason: because "the two biggest influences on my generation and my time were Freud and Marx, sexuality and class, to put it simply" (Kureishi in Buchanan: 2007: 113). In class, however, Kureishi finds constraint. In sexuality, he finds escape and freedom. Class is about "what you can and what you can't achieve, where you can and where you can't go" (Kureishi in Buchannan: 111). He adds, "in the sixties... you were slightly liberated from your sense of class, because the pop stars that we knew, who were mostly lower-middle class, like John Lennon or The Who, who had liberated themselves from the straightjacket of class. We identified with them" (Ibid: 111).

Through sexual and love relationships, on the other hand, Kureishi's characters try to escape constraint, borders, subvert class, and enlarge themselves. They go through different (geographical and psychological) displacements, become influenced by these experiences, and thus are changed by and through them. Kureishi evokes Freud as he explains that "we grow up identifying first with our fathers, then with our uncles, then with the wider family, and then with the wider world" (Buchannan: 121). In saying this he also alludes to Said's theory of affiliation: from the familial filiation to the worldly affiliation.

Kureishi does, however, reinforce previous themes and subject matters from previous and former generations. The most evident of all is the way England and Englishness has changed under the influence and presence of the formerly colonized emigrant in the metropolis. Kureishi writes about immigrants as a part of an international community as opposed to a particular enclosed racial or ethnic one. In other words, instead of presenting East against West, or in contrast to one another, he shows them meeting, integrating, and negotiating through difficulties. In *The Black Album*, Shahid oscillates between black and white cultures: between fundamentalist rebels and his liberal white lover. To the fundamentalist, Shahid is expected "to adhere to a cultural tradition that has very different expectations and ethics to himself" (Childs: 2005: 157). Instead of following in the steps of Asian cultural traditions, he questions, is very skeptical, reinforces freedom of speech, and celebrates imagination and literature. Kureishi also celebrates hybridity. In a conversation with Buchanan (2007), Kureishi states that the "concept of hybridity is more universal than genes and genders. It is everywhere. Even in psychological terms. A baby is conceived by sexual intercourse of a male and a female" (Kureishi in Buchanan: 2007: 118). The very novel's title, *The Black Album*, celebrates Prince's identity. Prince is "half black and half white, half man, half woman, half size, feminine but macho too. His work contains and extends history of black American music, Little Richard, James Brown, Sly Stone, Hendrix." Prince "is a river of talent. He can play soul and funk and rock and rap" (Kureishi: 1995: 21). In this Kureishi emphasizes hybridity and change, synthesis and adventuring, diversity and adversity, multiplicity and newness.

Unlike other writers who were writing back to the center, Kureishi is now inside the center writing from within. Like every other mixed-race writer, however, Kureishi wanted to learn about the places his father came from. This means that the image of Pakistan for Kureishi is completely imagined as opposed to lived, experienced, and intensified through past memories or evoked by nostalgia. While there is no nostalgia in Kureishi's work, for there is no foreign/different past from which he emerged or emigrated, there is a celebration of hybridity/syncreticism, of a new ethnicity: his being a black Briton. It is this doubleness/hybridity/syncreticism and new ethnicity Kureishi celebrates in *The Buddha of Suburbia* (*TBS*). Childs writes that doubleness/hybridity/syncreticism in Kureishi's *The Buddha* is presented as a handicap but what he does with this traditional logic is to invert it, "arguing that hybridity means doubleness not homelessness, addition not division." Ultimately, Indian and English identities are not exclusive, and Karim "can be part of an ethnicity that is both English and Indian" (Childs: 2005: 148–9).

Karim is not a nomad, nevertheless. He is aware of two identities. He is racially abused for being something he does not understand at the beginning and from which he wishes to disassociate himself: race. Eventually, however, he comes to realize that he can be partially Indian/Pakistani and British at the same time. Leaving for New York, Karim returns to his starting point, London. For Karim, London "was the extent of my longing" (Kureishi: 1990: 121). Although Karim "felt directionless and lost in the crowd," London was his "new possession" (*TBS*: 126) because it is full of "disoriented people" with whom he identifies (*TBS*: 127). Karim is portrayed as a nomad inside the city of London and its suburbs: he is never fixed in one place, is always on the move, like his identity, from Eva's house, to Anwar's, to Changez's.

This also reflects London's bottomless temptations (*TBS*: 8). In the city of London, almost all characters in the novel relocate. *The Buddha* is about dislocation, about taking on different displacements and about change and transformation. Anwar, Haroon, Jameela, Charlie, Karim, and Eva, all lived permanently nowhere: "the excitement of increasing life...as if each day was an adventure that could end anywhere" (*TBS*: 117). The metropolitan city therefore continues to be portrayed as the city of opportunity and open possibility. In London, Karim deconstructs and reconstructs his identity moving between places geographically, between identities culturally, and between two selves psychologically. Karim's Indian past is his father's, not his own. Shadwell, the theater director, embarrasses Karim as he raises issues of rootlessness and racism. Karim feels embarrassed because of a past and a color of skin for which he had no choice. Karim would overcome the fear of future but loath the past and childhood. He therefore blames the "prejudice and abuse I'd faced being the son of an Indian" (*TBS*: 147). Pyke also tries to turn Karim into someone he is not. He wanted a Mowgli: an Indian identity with an Indian accent. "Try it until you feel comfortable as a Bengali" (*TBS*: 147). Feeling uncomfortable and totally ill-at-ease, Karim wants to run "back to South London, where I belonged" (*TBS*: 148). Indeed, Karim had been struggling since childhood to "locate" himself and had failed. This, nevertheless, however painful and disturbing, offers him more a multiplicity of choices and diversity. He is a product of two histories, black and white, the product of divorce, of counterculture revolution, of the British class system, of multicultural London, of racism, and of rootlessness and homelessness. Karim's identity is constructed and reconstructed through different experiences, through different displacements. "Kureishi sees identity both as 'performative' and as subject to 'active negotiation', and his work chronicles not a straightforward clash of fixed identities but a complex interplay of many cultural movements" (Buchanan: 2007: 14). Karim is therefore no nomad: he starts, longs for, chooses, and returns to London. He is a result of multiple displacements and moves freely between his Indianness and Englishness without any fixed centrality. He is creamy: neither white nor black, but both, almost.

Similar themes to Kureishi's and Rushdie's writings in particular and second-generation writers' in general are Zadie Smith's debut novel *White Teeth* (*WT*), published at the beginning of the twenty-first century in 2000. The story starts with a failed attempt at suicide. Archie Jones's Italian wife, Ophelia, returns to England with him and cannot cope with the new life order. She therefore divorces him. The story begins with a gloomy opening: a negatively received return, suicide, divorce, and nostalgia. It is 1973 and Samad Iqbal, a Bengali Muslim, joins with his twenty-year-old wife, Alsana, his wartime friend Archie, a Londoner, in the same borough of London. Both Archie and Samad share a memory of the war, their "biggest memory" (Smith: 2000: 14). The banality of war proves to be evident as both of them were not aware the war was over even two weeks after it had finished. During that war, however, they befriended one another crossing class and color. Archie calls Samad "Sam." Their friendship resembled a friendship taking place on holiday, "a friendship that takes as its basis physical proximity and survives because the Englishman assumes the physical proximity will not continue" (*WT*: 96).

While the novel's most radical lesson lies, however, in its epilogue, "The past is prologue," *White Teeth* ends with an emphasis on the importance of moving away from the past without losing sight of it, nonetheless. It promotes multiplicity over singularity: the Many over the One. For "multiplicity is no illusion" and immigrants, and particularly second generations like Samad's twins Magid and Millat, "will race towards the future only to find they more and more eloquently express their past, that place where they have *just been*. Because this is the other thing about immigrants ('fugees, émigrés, travellers): they cannot escape their history any more than you yourself can lose your shadow" (*WT*: 466). Immigrants therefore prove once again that we are not history free and that we come from somewhere. History will always shadow us: the past should be examined in terms of the present. People "do not shimmer down staircases. They do not descend, as was once supposed, from on high, attached to nothing other than wings. Clara was *from* somewhere. She had *roots*" (*WT*: 27). Clara, Archie's wife, is a second generation who is born in "Lambeth (via Jamaica)." To Archie, Clara is not therefore "*that* kind of black" (ibid: 54); Clara was a black Briton. Samad and Alsana "were not *those* kind of Indians" either. In fact, they were "not Indian at all but Bangladeshi" (ibid).

Samad's wife Alsana was becoming as open and liberal as Gladstone Park: "a park without fences, unlike the more affluent Queens Park (Victoria's), with its pointed metal railings" (*WT*: 62). But at the same time she emphasizes the idea of roots. People like herself will always have "One leg in the present, one in the past. No talking will change this. Their roots will always be tangled. And roots get dug up. Just look in my garden—birds at the coriander every bloody day" (*WT*: 80). Alsana and Samad, however, find difficulties in integrating to the British society and therefore remain alien and alienated, feel marginal and marginalized, and fail to start anew and dwell in England. Clara, on the other hand, is influenced by her relationship with Ryan, a Londoner, who is introduced to black culture as her mother becomes interested in knowing more about English culture.

Archie's daughter, Irie, on the other hand, tries to escape roots as she is happy to a certain extent that the father of her child will remain ambiguous between the twins Millat and Magid with whom she has sexual intercourse. Thus, her child will not have to go through the complexity of roots. In becoming a dentist, Irie also looks for a unifying element across different peoples within society: white teeth. For white teeth represent equality and shared human values: no matter how big the differences are: different religions, different colors of skin, different roots and backgrounds, all people have white teeth. Teeth symbolize people. Teeth are white regardless a person's race, color, background or religion, making them a universal symbol of humanity. And although teeth are rooted in gums, they still go through certain changes and metamorphoses over time.

White Teeth also emphasizes the fact that food transcends age and gender, color and class, and different migrant generations. Old and young generations of migrants, for example, are portrayed to be meeting together in the story "with a little condescension; with low expectation of the other's rationality... and with the feeling that they must arrive with something the other will like, something suitable. Like Garibaldi biscuits" (*WT*: 162) whose raisins suit the old as well as the young. *White Teeth* promotes, as in the biscuits, compromise and negotiation across different generations as well as hybridity. It is a narrative of multiple generations aware that earlier generations have paved the way to later ones, earlier generations whose "accidents will become their destinies" (*WT*: 102). This is evident, for example, in Joshua's rebellion against his father's scientific experimentations by joining FATE (Fighting Animal Torture and Exploitation). Furthermore, Samad sends Magid to Bangladesh to grow up learning traditional Muslim values; instead, he becomes an Anglicized atheist and devotes his life to science. Millat, his twin brother, on the other hand, pursues a rebellious path that is detoured to militant fundamentalism.

Feeling South Asians are marginalized within English society, Millat demonstrates against Salman Rushdie in 1989 as he joins KEVIN (Keepers of the Eternal and Victorious Islamic Nation). We are informed in the novel that "the idea of KEVIN had been born within the black and Asian community. A radical new movement where politics and religion were two sides of the same coin...a splinter group frowned on by the rest of the Islamic community" (Smith: 2000: 470). What is learnt here is that first-generation parents' lives and traditions are disrupted by the existence of their sons and daughters: this second generation lives a present, which diverts and reroutes away from their father's at times and at other times is itself disrupted by their parents' past. Past and present should work in tandem, in a fluctuating dialogue as opposed to in contrast to one another. Smith delivers this message through the Iqbal's and Jones's.

Furthermore, while Selvon and Lamming emphasized the coldness of England, and how one had to melt the frozen words to hear them once they parted one's lips in contrast to the tropicality of the Caribbean, Smith contrastingly proves to come from a different generation who leans more toward the celebratory. "On cold days," she states, "a man can see his breath, on a hot day he can't. On both occasions, the man *breathes*" (*WT*: 103).

The most interesting of characters in Smith's narrative, however, is Samad Iqbal. Samad, a first generation, is crippled by his blackness. Doubly conscious of his identity and color of skin, he wonders: "Who would have such an Englishman there [in Bengal or Delhi]? To England? Who would have such an Indian? They promise us independence in exchange for the men we were" (*WT*: 112). Samad is conscious of being double: an outsider in England as well as "back home" in Bangladesh. He furthermore becomes more aware of the impossibility of retrieving the past, of going back and the necessity of moving forward. This manifests in the statement with which Smith opens Samad's section in the novel. Quoting Tebbit, Smith writes: "Are you still looking back to where you came from or where you are?" (*WT*: 123). Samad's answer to this is his wonder and questioning of his existence: "Why, in the name of Allah, am I here?...Because I simply cannot be anywhere else" (*WT*: 153). Samad's existence is therefore blinded by a blanket that is despair and helplessness, homesickness, and alienation beyond which he cannot see or think despite his intellect. Samad is ghettoized within religion and the sphere of the past. Despite his intellect, his naivety, like that of Nazneen's father in *Brick Lane*, overwhelms his being. What frustrates Samad most importantly is the irreconcilability of return simply because an immigrant is "particularly prone to repetition... Even when you arrive, you're still going back and forth" and you "can't help but re-enact the dash they once made from one land to another, from one faith to another, from one brown country into the pale, freckled arms of an imperial sovereign" (*WT*: 161–12).

What differentiates between Western urban metropolitanism and Bangladeshi peasant life according to Samad is religion and community. Religion is being marginalized in the West, and religious events such as Christmas are celebrated simply for socialization purposes rather than for religious significance. A man's position in Western communities has to be earned, whereas in the East it is more reliant on blood relations. Samad's son, Millat, for example, grows to believe that sexuality is exaggerated in the West where "women are men! I mean, they've got the same desires and urges as men—*they want it all the time.* And they dress like they want everyone to know they want it" (*WT*: 373).

Samad is presented as incapable of breathing. He always opted for tradition because "tradition was culture, and culture led to roots, and these were good, these were untainted principles" (Ibid: 193). He sees in assimilation corruption; he sees the west as tainting, corrupting, and threatening and feels he has to protect his children by sending them away to Bangladesh. A physical return to Bangladesh was a must; a return to "deep roots that no storm or gale could displace" (*WT*: 193). Alsana on the contrary believes that "second generation... you always... need to let them go their own way" (*WT*: 346). Samad does not share such views. He sees his sons as lost second-generation brown people, neither here nor there. "They are strangers in strange lands," in both England and India. They are "stuck between a rock and a hard place, like Ireland, like Israel, like India" (*WT*: 425). Samad is totally unaware of what Smith calls the "resourcefulness" and "footloosity" of the immigrant which enable him/her to, echoing Rushdie's eclecticism, "use what they can when they can." Because "immigrants are constantly on the move, footloose, [they should be] able to change course at any moment, able to employ their legendary resourcefulness at every turn" (*WT*: 465). Immigrants are ideally "free of any kind of baggage, happy and willing to leave their difference at the docks and take their chances in this new place" that is England (*WT*: 465). Culturally displaced in a new language and place, Samad, however, is burdened with tradition and constantly bemoaning western liberality and democracy; he ends up a "faulty, broken, stupid, one-handed waiter of a man who had spent eighteen years in a strange land and made no more mark than this. It just means you're nothing" (*WT*: 506).

Finally, England at the end of the novel is therefore represented as the land of white teeth: the "green and pleasant libertarian and of the free"; it is

> the "Happy Multicultural Land" out of which passive, untransformed immigrants leave "neutral...as they had entered it: weighed down, burdened, unable to waver from their course or in any way change their separate, dangerous trajectories. They seem to make no progress, the cynical might say they don't even move at all."
>
> (Smith: 2000: 465)

This stillness and inability to progress is further discussed below where the poetics of multiculturalism in England prove to be far more fruitful, despite many problematics.

Promoting Cultural Diversity/Multiculturalism Post-9/11: A Conclusion

I

The Prime Minister of the current British government has expressed resentment toward not only mass migration but, as he categorizes it, "bad immigration"—as opposed to a "good one." The speech (Cameron: 2011) came in conjunction with the French prime minister's ban of the burka/niqap amidst political uproar and acceleration in policies aimed at the large Muslim and Arab population in France in particular and Europe in general. A predecessor speech by Germany's chancellor had already announced: *multikulti* has failed in Germany (Merkel, October 17, 2010). Reading these speeches, one feels, on the one hand, a sense that West European societies, cultures, and values are being threatened, or to use a less harsher term, challenged by the existing nonnative population as well as the rapid influx of immigrants (especially now North African and Middle Eastern countries) to Europe. On the other, and whether there is a certain policy being set toward immigration or mere intimidation toward the foreign, such political speeches and attitudes toward the formerly colonized have created anger and inflamed extremism and strong opposition of migrant Asian and African communities in Britain, Algerians, Tunisians, and Moroccan in France, and the majority of Turks in Germany.

What connects and is shared by the three major immigrant populations (namely Turks and Kurds, Pakistanis and Indians, Algerians and Moroccans) targeted in the speeches of the top three West European leaders is that they all come from the so-called developing or Third World countries; the majority of these immigrants' religion and mother tongue are, respectively, Islam and Arabic; they are all of a dark(er) skin color; and they come from a colonial past and living a postcolonial present where neocolonialism is evident as yet another manifestation of imperialism—not necessarily military but more economically and culturally driven.

In a neo-colonial, global homogenization, however, seeking old traditional symbols becomes necessary. "One way to defend yourself against the sense of an all-encompassing global atmosphere... is to return to comfortable symbols of the past. In the Islamic world, for example, more people are wearing traditional dress, not necessarily as a form of piety, but as a way of affirming an identity that resists this global wave" (Said: 2002: 14). Some of these resisting, displaced migrant communities have managed to integrate into the class system of the host society and develop a new language that is very different from their mother tongues; others see in their religious faith an act of resistance and survival: an identity. While some Easterns see in extreme religion and/or vulgar nationalism an anti-imperialist identity and refuge, the West sees it as an extreme threat.

Labeling immigration or even dividing immigrant influx into two parties or groups, good and bad, black and white, good and evil, favorable and unfavorable, seems discriminatory and offers little understanding of postmodern hybrid societies. But it also expresses paranoia: "The old imperial powers, such as the British, have found it hard to adapt to their new, diminished status in the post-colonial world." In Empire's aftermath, "they have been pushed back into their box, their frontiers have closed in on them like a prison, and the new opening of political and financial borders in the European Union is still viewed by them with suspicion" (Rushdie: 2002: 424). The drunken Sisodia says in Rushdie's *The Satanic Verses* that "[t]he trouble with the Engenglish is that their hiss hiss history happened overseas, so they dodo don't know what it means" (Rushdie: 2006a: 343). To this Phillips adds that Britain should not be intimidated by continuous waves of immigrants that presumably threaten its national cultural identity; "the truth is that it needs some very great fortune such as continual waves of immigration to *create* a national culture" (Phillips: 2001: 281). He also emphasizes the fact that migrants urged Britain to "think beyond Derby Day, Wensleydale cheese and the Boat Race as signifiers of national identity." He adds, stressing the importance of first and second generations of migrants on the critical change of Britain's cultural and national identity, that "While it was the pioneer generation of Caribbean migrants who helped to introduce Britain to the notion of Postcoloniality, it is their children's and grandchildren's generation who will help Britain cross the Rubicon of English Channel and enter the European age of the twenty-first century" (Ibid: 282).

Undoubtedly, migration has been an inevitable part of the process of globalization and it has had cultural consequences. This, however, has not been perceived open-mindedly or tolerantly, neither has it been widely welcomed. Migration has formed large networks and communities within the Quartet: Turkish in Germany; Caribbeans, Middle Easterns, Pakistanis, and Indians in the UK; Algerians and Moroccans in France; and a commingling of different ethnicities within the United States. Without migration and displacement, "Western civilisation," as Said puts it, is an "ideological fiction, implying a sort of detached superiority for a handful of values and ideas, none of which has much meaning outside the history of conquest" which today gives its metamorphosed capital cities their interracial, multicultural identity (Said: 2003: 349). Said wonders:

Who in India or Algeria today can confidently separate out the British or French component of the past from present actualities, and who in Britain or France can draw a clear circle around British London or French Paris that would exclude the impact of India and Algeria upon those two imperial cities?
(Said: 1994a: 15)

Displacement has created, in Rushdie's words, a "whaleless world" where "there can be no easy escape from history"; a world that "lacks not only hiding places, but certainties. There is no consensus about reality between, for example, the nations of the North and of the South." Displacement has exposed all hidden places of both East and West to one another and drew a picture of the world from within the metropolis. Rushdie stresses that it is "imperative that literature enter such arguments, because what is being disputed is nothing less than *what is the case*, what is truth and what is untruth. If writers leave the business of making pictures of the world to politicians," he insists, "it will be one of history's great and most abject abdications" (Rushdie: 1991: 100).

The conclusion of this project promotes the concept of multiculturalism and its cultural diversity as a positive, tolerant way forward for a multiracial British society which has developed over more than fifty years, subsequent to the end of the Second World War and the decolonization of the former British colonies. Hence, the arrival of the intellectual displaced migrant in the heart of the metropolitan city of London debunked former conceptions of British identity. This subsequently changed the map of the metropolitan literature of England, or, in other words, the literature written in English by England's former subjects and their children. A rapidly evolving chain of displaced migrants has made the black population an unavoidable part of its cultural, political, and social life. The displaced migrant and diasporic mobilization open doors for geographical and cultural awareness and promote a more liberal multicultural society that celebrates diversity and multicultural individuals. It is undoubted, however, that "the rise of multiculturalism has been accompanied by a parallel rise in racism and racial violence. The question therefore remains: Is there some way of learning to live with difference?" (Hall: 2001: 7).

Multicultural societies, such as the metropolitan city of London, have demonstrated that different cultures and races can indeed live and coexist peacefully together not despite but through difficulties. In London, there is what Rushdie calls "the new empire within Britain" (Rushdie: 1991: 129). While one feels obliged by human necessity and justice to encourage, stimulate, and defend cultural diversity and antiracism within a metropolitan city like London, where the world feels at home, one cannot neglect the individuality and specificity of religious rituals and cultural codes that create each particular individual. Cultural diversity is necessary, however, to build human societies and sustain the survival and continuity of human culture. Said states:

> The idea of separating people simply cannot work—it hasn't worked. The moment you start boxing people in, you give them a sense of insecurity and produce more paranoia. You produce, in my opinion, more distortions... So the idea of different but intertwined histories is crucial to a discussion—without necessarily resolving them into each other.
> (Said: 2002: 26–27)

Rushdie's case, for example, promotes the concept of eclecticism in the face of plural and diverse possibilities and the entrapment between past and present, old and new, familial and changing. "Eclecticism, the ability to take from the world what seems fitting and to leave the rest, has always been a hallmark of the Indian tradition, and today it is at the centre of the best work being done both in the visual arts and in literature" (Rushdie: 1991: 67).

It is commonly thought that every culture bears an authentic personality and has an internalized privacy. Such privacy and personality can be seen by Other cultures as closed and ethnically exclusive, which ultimately leads to what has been supposedly termed the myth of what Samuel Huntington called in his 1992 lecture "the clash of civilizations" (Huntington: 2002: 570) and expanded it in his 1996 book titled *The Clash of Civilizations: Remaking of World Order*. This myth is one that assumes cultural, as opposed to political or economic, conflict between Western and non-Western civilizations. The supposed clash is based on the fact that "about more than a billion Muslims, scattered throughout at least five continents...are all enraged at Western modernity, as if a billion people were but one and Western civilization were no more complicated a matter than a simple declarative sentence." It is mostly outraging, however, because Huntington, Said suggests, writes aggressively and chauvinistically a "prescription for what the West must do to continue winning" (Huntington: 2002: 570). The concept of clashing civilizations assumes that both civilizations are "unchanging" (Huntington: 2002: 572). While Huntington suggests the superiority of Western civilization over an "inferior" one (Islamic and Confucian), Said asks: "Doesn't this method [of producing a simplified map of the world] in effect prolong, exacerbate, and deepen conflict? What does it do to minimize civilizational conflict? Do we *want* the clash of civilizations? Doesn't it mobilize nationalist passions and therefore nationalist murderousness?" (Ibid: 573).

To take extreme pride in one's culture at the expense of other cultures builds an invisible barrier and wall that pushes one and societies toward exclusive centralities, resulting in the marginalization of Others. It builds ghettos. What can be seen as cultural ghettoization facilitates the peripheralization of Other cultures. The purpose of any kind of a ghetto, Rushdie believes, "is to confine, to restrain. Its rules are basically conservative. Tradition is all; [and thus any] radical breaches with the past are frowned upon" (Rushdie: 1991: 68). Advocating cultural diversity as opposed to monochromatic cultures and mental ghettoization, this book has sought to contribute to an ethic of the valuing of cultural inheritance, the preserving of its continuity, and also the promotion of the sharing of cultural values. To respect Other social and cultural practices of one nation and race does not necessarily mean the elimination of other religious or political beliefs, or indeed any other forms of cultural practices. While military assault facilitates domination, cultural dialogue, or indeed eclecticism and translation, should prevent conflicts. "I believe," states Daniel Barenboim in conversation with Edward Said, "that in cultural matters—with literature and, even better, with music, because it doesn't have to do with explicit ideas—if we foster this kind of a contact [amongst cultures], it can only help people feel nearer to each other" (Said: 2002: 11).

Edward Said conducted a workshop with Mr Barenboim and Yo-Yo Ma for young Arab and Israeli musicians in Weimar, Germany, in 1999 and from this project The West Eastern Divan Orchestra was established (an orchestra of Palestinian, Israeli, and other Arab musicians). The WEDO takes its name after Goethe's book of lyrical poetry, inspired heavily by Islamic religion and Persian poetry, West–East Divan (West-östlicher Diwan: 1814–1819). Goethe is incidentally the German philosopher who coined the concept of World Literature. World literature, Bhabha writes,

> could be an emergent, prefigurative category that is concerned with a form of cultural dissensus and alterity, where non-consensual terms of affiliation may be established on the grounds of historical trauma. The study of world literature might be the study of the way in which cultures recognize themselves through their projections of "otherness." Where, once, the transmission of national traditions was the major theme of a world literature, perhaps we can now suggest that transnational histories of migrants, the colonised, or political refugees—these borders and frontier conditions—may be the terrains of world literature. The centre of such a study would neither be the "sovereignty" of national cultures, nor the universalism of human culture, but *a focus on those "freak social and cultural displacements"*... in their "unhomely fictions."
> (Bhabha: 2005: 17)

Said, Barenboim, Bhabha, Goethe, and the WEDO all promote cultural translation, hybridity, dialogue, and contrapuntal histories. A discourse of a world of postcolonial literatures (literatures written in appropriated english) might therefore model itself on such a dialogue and take on a rather symphonic wholeness with an appreciation of theoretical individuality, meanwhile keeping in mind a picture of the whole. It should develop a discourse that shares diverse experiences. As an academic discourse taught in universities and being part of their faculties and curricula, a world of postcolonial literatures should offer a "creative making of place for works that are otherwise alien and distant" (Said: 2003b). Instead of focusing on the clashes of civilizations and the superiority of one culture/civilization over another, a world of postcolonial literatures demonstrates that a "study of all literatures of the world as a symphonic whole... could be apprehended theoretically as having preserved the individuality of each work without losing sight of the whole" (Ibid). To function as a piece of world literature, a work has to be circulated, printed, translated, read, and written in multiple locations and languages; it also has to be worldly in its subject matters, themes, and language which compare geographies and cultures to become part of both a national (individual and private) and an international (whole and public) narrative. A work of world literature today means it engages with postcolonial studies, migration, displacement, exile, nationalism, and multilingualism.

Teaching different writings of world literature or a world of postcolonial literatures (literatures of the world written in and/or translated into English by the formerly colonized, Commonwealth literature/Third World literature) and its discourse across educational institutions (universities, colleges, and schools) displaces an image drawn by an exclusively Western discourse and brings cultures closer. The teaching of a world of postcolonial literatures helps debunking what Said refers to as "imaginative geographies," that is, a language that "legitimates a vocabulary, a universe of representative discourse" (Said: 2003b: 71–72). It uses a language that is "inaccurate" in order to "characterise the Orient as alien and to incorporate it schematically on a theatrical stage whose audience, manager, and actors are for Europe, and only for Europe. Hence the vacillation between the familiar and the alien" (Ibid). While such theories as "the clash of civilizations," imaginative geographies, and the mass media facilitate conflict, teaching a model of a world of postcolonial literature across educational institutions mobilizes multiculturalism, facilitates understanding of cultural differences, assists in the spreading of (an)Other image of the world, and translates different images to the mainstream. Since the *SS Windrush Generation* docked at Tilbury and discharged 492 Jamaican migrants, the (hi)story is being written by Others. And, "[i]nstead of reading in the real sense of the word," writes Said,

> our students today are often distracted by the fragmented knowledge available on the internet and in the mass media. Worse yet, education is threatened by nationalist and religious orthodoxies often disseminated by the media as they focus historically and sensationally on the distant electronic wars that give viewers the sense of surgical precision, but in fact obscure the terrible suffering and destruction produced by modern warfare.
>
> (Said: 2003b: xxvi)

As discussed in Chapter 2, the problem with immigration is in essence racial. "Immigration is only a problem," Rushdie states, "if you are worried about blacks; that is, if your whole approach to the question is one of racial prejudice" (Rushdie: 1991: 132). In this he foregrounds the fact that multiculturalism can be an antiracist, progressive hybrid system, but that it has the potential to be, if regarded otherwise, a negative reactionary political system that results in cultural and social segregations and religious and national extremism. Like assimilation, integration, or even racial harmony, the concept of multiculturalism can be read as a superficially westernized, Orientalist concept that "means little more than teaching the kids a few bongo rhythms, how to tie a sari and so forth. In the police training programme, it means telling cadets that black people are so 'culturally different' that they can't help making trouble" (Rushdie: 1991: 137). This therefore reinforces the western viewpoint and Orientalist perspective on blacks/Others as culturally backward and racially inferior. Rushdie sees in multiculturalism a method for tolerating the Others' backwardness and difference. He sees in multiculturalism another "token gesture towards Britain's blacks, and it ought to be exposed, like 'integration' and 'racial harmony', for the sham it is" (Ibid).

Paul Gilroy sees in multiculturalism, on the other hand, a way of calling for an end to Britain's entrapment by the problem of assimilation. Some of the early writers of Caribbean origins realized in Britain that ethnicity was a vital determiner of identity. The migrant formed within Britain a multiracial community whose identity questioned those fixities and determinants. Multiculturalism should be set against "Powellite themes" such as "immigration as invasion" (Gilroy: 2001, 2007). Displaced people, refugees, and immigrants are unwanted, as Gilroy suggests, because of what he calls "melancholia"; in other words, the newcomers "maybe unwanted and feared precisely because they are the unwitting triggers for the pain produced by memories of that vanished imperial and colonial past." What multiculturalism actually does, he suggests, is try to make Britain like the rest of the world and this threatens and intimidates the British monoculture and ethnic absolutism (Ibid). But a "truly multicultural society," states Phillips,

> is one which is composed of multicultural individuals; people who are able to synthesise different worlds in one body and to live comfortably with these different worlds. In order for a society to tolerate such individuals the society must by definition be open, fluid and confident. In other words, the society must be everything that Britain was not when the first Caribbean migrants stepped off the ships in the 1940s and 1950s.
>
> (Phillips: 2001: 281)

In other words, multiculturalism as translating cultural differences starts with and projects from multicultural individuals who themselves translate cultural differences and consequently become translated. London, for instance, has offered a very fertile soil for those who have made it a place where the world is at home. National identities for the host and the immigrant are insecure and always seem to be under threat. Living in the midst of different cultures will always cause cultural conflicts as the gap between East and West culturally widens rather than narrows. To live as part or in good knowledge of these two cultures is to bring the two closer while living as part of a larger community. Hence, multiculturalism, or what Cameron calls "the state doctrine of multiculturalism," is not a disjointing act that creates segregated communities. Multiculturalism has opened windows to closed ghettos; it has brought people from across the world closer on a fertile soil of metropolitan cities like London which has given birth to incredible numbers of literary masterpieces. The British model of multiculturalism has answered Hall's question above with an affirmative yes. Through difficulties, it has promoted a space for freedom of speech, eclecticism, religious freedom, and humanism, and most importantly, offered a fertile soil for artistic vocation and aesthetic creativity.

II

The bombings of 9/11 in New York and July 7 in London have intimidated many and have unfortunately once again reinforced the stereotypical image of Muslims, particularly in relation to Muslim extremist groups, and generally that of the faraway Orient, anew. They have also shifted the gravitation of the politics of identity from the national to the religious, a fact that has added insult to injury. The bombings of July 2005, however, and not coincidentally,

> followed the US invasion of Afghanistan and Iraq in which the UK participated as a subordinate ally, and were initially framed in terms of 9/11 as an incident in the larger "war on terror" declared by Bush administration. But when it transpired that those responsible for the July bombing were British Muslims... public discussion was immediately focused by establishment politicians and the mainstream media on the alleged failure of multicultural society in Britain and the need to reassert a unified British identity.
>
> (Macphee & Podder: 2007: 3)

Manifestly, what happens to Muslims abroad and externally matters as much as it does to British Muslims internally in Britain. After all, the "supposed failure of multiculturalism is not only cultural, but also political: the involvement of Western power in former colonies (Africa, the Middle East and Asia)" (Ibid: 3–4).

The displaced migrant, geographically dislocated, culturally alienated, psychologically in exile, and physically (by virtue of skin color, facial features/traits, accent, and so on) under scrutiny, finds refuge and reconciliation in the familiar and known as opposed to the changing and foreign. Recoiling into ethnicity and/or religion becomes a reactionary weapon to shield attacks, for European tolerance toward the immigrant alternates with suspicion. Hence, one can find two types of migrants: not good and/or bad, but rather a progressive, adaptive one; and another traditionally defensive and conservative. "As a migrant myself," writes Rushdie,

> I have always tried to stress the creative aspects of such cultural commingling. The migrant, severed from his roots, often transplanted into a new language, always obliged to learn the ways of a new community, is forced to face the great questions of change and adaption; but many migrants, faced with the sheer existential difficulty of making such changes, and also, often, with sheer alienness and defensive hostility of the peoples amongst whom they find themselves, retreat from such questions behind the walls of the old culture they have both brought along and left behind.
> (Rushdie: 2002: 415)

In *Shame*, for example, one finds two types of emigrants: those who take a cultural turn from the past and translate between past and present, and those who do not: those who are "locked up in the past," in another time, and remain ghettoized there and then; and those who are flexible and open, translating, and consequently become translated. Passive migrants are those who receive change and newness as a threat and resort to tradition for stability and safety, and clutch onto national or religious identity as a refuge and as a means of resistance and self-assertion. Others are active immigrants who are challenged by newness and change but not threatened by it. "All migrants leave their pasts behind, although some try to pack it into bundles and boxes—but on the journey something seeps out of the treasured mementos and old photographs, until even their owners fail to recognize them, because it is the fate of migrants to be stripped of history, to stand naked amidst the scorn of strangers upon whom they see the rich clothing" (Rushdie: 1994: 63). These two types can also be found in *The Satanic Verses*. Migrants are of two kinds: (a) "the kind that compromises, does deals, accommodates itself to society, aims to find a niche, to survive"; and another (b) "the cussed, bloody-minded, ramrod-backed type of damnfool notion that would rather break than sway with the breeze" (Rushdie: 2006b: 335). The second kind is ironically and cynically portrayed in the novel in the character of the Ayatollah Khamenei, as he is exiled from Iran, and keeps the curtains shut in his hotel room because the place outside is foreign, "abroad," and alien. He is threatened by the "harsh fact that he is here and not There, upon which all his thoughts are fixed" (206). He is portrayed as being fixed in the past and tradition and thus loathes exile because he wants to remain "ignorant, and therefore unsullied, unaltered, pure" (207).

Signs of extreme nationalism and Islamism post-9/11 became a result of cultural misunderstanding, alienation, stereotypical imagery, facing difference with violence, and monatomic cultural maintenance. Since the simplest way to describe multiculturalism is cultural diversity then it is fair to suggest that neither submission to nor total rejection of one culture for another is an option within such a cosmopolitan community like London. Cultural translation and revision of one's culture within the other are, however, necessary. What pushes cultural diversity toward either regression or progression is either racial and cultural resistance and opposition, or accommodation. The tolerance and understanding of racial differences provide the dynamics of integration and translation, whereas the accommodation of racism leads to havoc. Racism "is still there," writes Gilroy, "souring things and debasing our public culture, but it is not what it was in the rivers of blood days. Its political geography is, for example, very different. Tokenism has had important effects. Sport, pop, reality TV, advertising and the House of Lords are all superficially integrated" (Gilroy: 2004).

Multiculturalism has diversity at its heart, a fact the global free market opposes since it seeks singularizing a global culture. Hall believes that "the postcolonial world had to be shaped by our understanding of difference, by the need to rub along with each other" (Hall in Adams: 2007). He also contributed to this understanding by establishing the first cultural studies program at a British university in Birmingham, in 1964. Furthermore, he established Rivington Place Art Gallery "to diversify the mainstream of art organisations" and contribute to an "optimism of an ongoing cultural dialogue: in films, literature, or at street level outside" (Ibid). For him London can be "the example of this tolerant debate," where "despite Brown's and Cameron's definitions of Britishness, it is a more genuine multicultural society than New York" (Ibid). Two years prior to Hall's essay, however, Sivanandan, another fellow displaced intellectual and founder of The Institution of Race Relations, wrote in the same *Observer* column an article entitled "Why Muslims Reject British Value," where he shares a similar viewpoint despite continuous racial and violent encounters: "no country in Europe could be prouder of its multicultural experience than Britain" (Sivanandan: 2005). This also echoes Lamming's earlier emphasis on the intimate, colonial–colonized relationship between Britain and its former colonies.

Other bodies and institutions (World Music, World art, World Cinema, and so on) should not be of a lesser importance, nonetheless, as they work to "diversify the mainstream of arts organizations... to give space to show people who are being left out of the Tate, to create a context for the wider understanding of our worlds" (Hall in Adams: 2007), and to cover news, music, and events from British Asia and South Asia (including India, Pakistan, and Sri Lanka) by such institutions as the *BBC Radio Asian Network*.

Drawing on such diversity of mainstreams, Kureishi questions monolithic cultures and ethnicity: "Who exactly is of one's kind and what kind of people are they? Are they only those of the same 'nation', of the same colour, race and background?" Witnessing the racially motivated political speeches by Enoch Powell, Duncan Sandys, and Roger Scruton, Kureishi saw in them a "feeble, bloodless, narrow conception of human relationships and the possibilities of love and communication that [they] can only see 'one's kind' in this exclusive and complacent way!" (Kureishi: 2011: 26). Ironically, when black British detainees told of their Caribbean detention in Guantanamo Bay, they, "in articulating their strongest desires for freedom and relief from the Camp regime," said that "what they really craved was a packet of [Scottish] Highland Shortbread biscuits!" (Gilroy: 2004). Black British youth, sons and daughters of the Masala Fish Generation, has heavily invested in cultural plurality; in other words, "they are able to synthesise Wordsworth with Jamaican patties, or Romeo and Juliet with the music of Bob Marley" (Phillips: 2001: 280).

III

To conclude with Monica Ali's *Brick Lane* here is rather fitting since it is one of the few novels that incorporates four different generations of displaced migrants (Mrs Islam, Chanu, Nazneen, Razia, and Shahana) in a detailed narrative across different cultures and geographical spaces (East Pakistan, Bangladesh, and England), particularly after 9/11. It also follows up from and recaps themes that were introduced in the second half of the twentieth century and exemplifies subject matters that have been discussed in this book, such as mental and cultural ghettoization, memory, representations of identity, the meaning of home, and the thriving multicultural society within London. *Brick Lane* furthermore evidences the geographical, linguistic, cultural, and most importantly psychological displacements across different generations.

Nazneen goes through a series of successful and considerable transitions: a displaced female who is brought to a foreign land; a wife to an unappealing, traditional, culturally ghettoized emigrant husband, Chanu; she is also a Bengali and an idea of "home" to Karim, her black Briton lover; a mother to Shahana, a black Briton; and a daughter-in-law to Mrs Islam, an earlier arrival and emigrant. Nazneen's identity is therefore bound by culture, race, and gender. The divide between Mrs Islam, Chanu, and other first-generation displaced migrants and Nazneen's children is split according to their conception of what and where home is. Nazneen's decision eventually to stay in London with her children demonstrates how, as discussed below, her concept of home and who she is evolves and develops as the narrative carries on. The development of Nazneen's identity from a silenced, informed object to a speaking, voiced subject also illustrates how a displaced migrant can translate from being a closed, passive migrant to an open, active one. The novel moreover articulates and marks the shift from national to religious identity post-9/11, manifest in the character of Karim.

Brick Lane (*BL*) retraces themes in relation to migrants living in the metropolis of London: nostalgia, cosmopolitanism, and loneliness as "everyone [is] in their own boxes" (Ali: 2003: 24) and as the city "would not pause even to shrug" (*BL*: 59). It reinforces the "myth" of return as Razia advises Nazneen that "[y]ou can never go back and do it a different way and see if that would have been better" (*BL*: 424). Melancholia is turned inward as Nazneen feels like she is being "locked in the attic" and hammered (*BL*: 24). Group consciousness is also evident as people from the same past always stick together in the present, forming a kind of ghetto (Brick Lane itself is a Bengali district within London) beyond which Nazneen discovers liberty. The so-called going home syndrome, one of the most celebrated themes in postcolonial literature, is thematized as "[t]he pull of the land is stronger even than the pull of blood" (*BL*: 32). Ghetto mentality is also demonstrated as most migrants "don't even really leave home. Their bodies are here [in England] but their hearts are back there" (*BL*: 32). Instability and desolation are depicted as Nazneen is overwhelmed in her everyday life and "did not want to run, but neither did she want to sit still" (*BL*: 102). The hauntingly seductive pulling of the past wakes Nazneen up from her dreams thinking she was back home and then she is shocked by the reality beyond the ghetto of Brick Lane: Nazneen feels she is "caught in a net of dreams and dragged up to the surface, and the sun hit the water and sliced her eyes and she saw everything in pieces as if in a smashed mirror" (*BL*: 324).

Memory also plays a significant role in the novel. For Nazneen it is very strong as she associates it with the sense of smell: it is very "vivid; so strong she could smell it. More often, she tried to see and could not... She began to rely on a different kind of memory. The memory of things she knew but no longer saw" (*BL*: 217). Her memories, moreover, are "like a lump in her throat... a thing without substance but with an undeniable presence" (*BL*: 329). The significance of memory is represented through flashbacks/analepsis that interrupt Nazneen's engagement with the present and at times imprison her in an isolated and still zone. They also indicate to the reader how strongly Nazneen is longing and nostalgic for the past and hence not totally engaged with the now and here. The epistolary format, represented in letters from Nazneen's sister, nevertheless, gives her hope and confidence. In the structure of the narrative, moreover, the realism of the memories, portrayed through the letters, contrasts starkly with the magic realism of her nightmares, ghosts, and dreams.

As a female displaced migrant, born in Bangladesh and brought to England in an arranged, sham marriage, Nazneen is alienated by the men in her natal community. She is also doubly displaced and marginalized by her husband who sees her as inferior and the English community who sees her as a foreigner. Nazneen's growth as an individual is demonstrated through the novel's traditionally linear narrative from start to finish. Nazneen's translation between a Bengali identity and another in displacement is certainly stimulated by Karim's place in the world. He introduces her to the outside world with which she becomes more engaged. She is puzzled but also provoked by his own hybrid identity that is evident in his language, clothes, behavior, and mentality. Nazneen slowly realizes, however, that she is not the same naïve girl motivated by written fate, but rather a new person in the making. This very change is stimulated by Karim's making her feel "at home." But it is also significantly awoken by her sexual consciousness and her surprising ability to reject Karim later on as he embraces a Muslim identity and becomes part of the Bengali Tigers. Nazneen's growth is furthermore secured through her financial independence, obtained through the sewing work she acquires. Just as she pieces together fabric with sewing, she also starts putting single pieces of her life together to produce a whole self. With her productivity and channeling of creative energy she is soon empowered: she stops being influenced by her mother's voice/behavior, the fact that she committed suicide and was not there for the children, and her mother's voice in her dreams. She repeatedly says, "Amma used to say," but then Nazneen realizes that "the world is changing and me with it."

The silenced and marginalized Nazneen is not allowed to speak at the beginning as her identity is preconstituted and given and as all the characters around her suppress and prevent her from speaking. But when the situation changes and she is encouraged to open up (by Razia, Karim, Mrs Azad, and London itself), she finally speaks and most importantly makes sure she is heard. "I will decide what to do," she screams (Ali: 2003: 405). Her distant past is no longer capable of interfering with or maintaining the coherence of her identity in the present as she no longer relies on fate, no longer listens to her mother's ghost, and no longer awaits her future to reveal itself. Nazneen takes action and adapts to a new identity that is not centered around or stems from the authority and strength of men and/or national or religious settings. She liberates herself, gains self-authorship, and certainly does not feel she has to assimilate like Mrs Islam advises her to do when she says, "you have to give up your culture to accept theirs" (Ali: 2003: 29). Rather, Nazneen is influenced by the Anglicized Mrs Azad who travels and chooses between Bengali and English cultures freely and at will.

Nazneen sees herself in her daughter Shahana: she exposes generational differences between herself and father, and herself and mother. Her use of language is a significant marker in her resistance as she corrects her educated father grammatically; she lectures him and informs him that he is still locked up in the past and mentally ghettoized, whereas the rest of the family have managed to integrate and learn how to fit in. Shahana also bemoans how the absent presence (the past that happened before her birth) has condemned and determined the rest of her life. She angrily and frustratingly confesses that she has had no choice in becoming what she is: "I didn't ask to be born here" (*BL*: 181). Shahana does not want to listen to Bengali classical music and her written Bengali is shocking. Her clothes are loathed by her conservative father (jeans as opposed to a sari). Precisely because Nazneen also sees herself in Shahana, she takes her children's side as opposed to Chanu's. The latter always lectures her that in order to go forward, one must look back first. And this is a valuable lesson in Nazneen's course toward self-authority. For Shahana, moreover, Bangladesh is not a real country back to which she could travel: it was a punishment. In Bangladesh "they don't have toilet paper," she complains (*BL*: 398). Nazneen's feeling of guilt toward Shahana also prevents her from a return. "I'm from London," Shahana identifies.

One last reason why *Brick Lane* is a good example here is the fact that it shows how the focus has shifted from the question of national identity as depicted in the previous two chapters to religious identity post-9/11, with the rise of religious fundamentalism and the impact this has on displacement. The Bengali Tigers, for example, assemble different Asians and non-English groups from different areas in London and bring them together under the umbrella of Islam. In doing so, they seek refuge, security, unity, and identity; however, at the same time they are creating a segregated community, a village of Bangladeshis inside a multicultural capital. *Brick Lane* is therefore "about the clash between Western values and our own... the struggle to assimilate and the need to preserve one's identity and heritage... [and] the feelings of alienation" (*BL*: 113). *Brick Lane* shows that after September 11, a Utopian multicultural life in the Babylon of difference is ultimately faced with many obstacles and difficulties, and that the gap of difference widens as opposed to narrows. It also shows, however, that a possible multicultural society can indeed live through and not despite differences. Nazneen after all does not gain her own self-authorship, liberty, and self-consciousness through political parties, adultery, divorce, or abandonment of family and/or traditions. She achieves these things by becoming a multicultural individual herself: through cultural translation, integration, hard work, experience, and open-mindedness. She becomes a multicultural person within herself and hence becomes part of and also reflects the multicultural British community which, despite difficulties and obstacles, presents a better example of a multicultural society than elsewhere in Europe. This is England, as Razia says: you can dance on ice wearing a sari.

IV

It has been asserted throughout this book that the concept of displacement is in part defined here within the context of the Palestinian displaced narrative and its exilic experiences of dispersions. *Nuzooh* therefore acts as a critical tool that can also act as a compass helping us to find interesting points of reference with the Caribbean, Indian, and African experiences of displacements.

Between the Oedipal and the anti-Oedipal, the Palestinian develops an identity that entertains difference, rejects a presumed hierarchy, and is always, by virtue of exilic displacements, in transit. The Palestinian is very adaptive, robustuous, and multicultural at heart. The Palestinian, however, is not even recognized as one national being neither inside nor outside of Palestine. Gazan? A West Banker? Coastal? An "Arab Israeli"? *Nazih*/Displacee? *Laji'*/Refugee? The irreconcilably irredeemable memory and loss of place deems all Palestinians a sense of nationhood, of brotherhood, of oneness, then, "You learn to transform the mechanics of loss into a constantly postponed metaphysics of return" (Said: 1986: 150).

Between 1956[1] and 2003, that is, the timeline of this book, the Palestinian exile has also shared with the Caribbean and Indian migrant, and to an extent, the African slave, a British (an Ottoman and Zionist, too, in the case of the Palestinian) colonial history, an ongoing globally American capitalist regime, historical displacements, a growing sense of national consciousness, double consciousness, "an imbalance in consciousness" (Said: 1985: 129), the going-home-syndrome, the myth of return, desolation and profound psychological displacement, overlapping identities, the crossing of frontiers, the metaphoricity of the postcolonial individual toward home and identity, transnationalism, transcendence of the nation-state borders, a homeland with no borders, remembering and forgetting, a bipolar mentality, a vantage and vintage point, an ethical and aesthetic distance, amnesia, a reconstructed national identity through difference, a political, national, transient, and resistant identity, a narrative of multiple narratives, adapting to rapidly changing landscapes, violence, "writing back," a collective forced and voluntary exodus, and a growing national literature reflective of all this.[2]

Although the majority of the Palestinians' historic circumstance and color of skin are different compared to the Indians and Pakistanis, the African, the Indians of the Afro-Caribbean Diaspora, and the West Indians, they all share a history of colonization and racism; they are all postcolonial subjects whose homes have become imaginary constructs, undergone cosmetic reconstructions, and whose present identities are still burdened with a colonial past. They are all subjects of a postmodern, twentieth-century prevalent phenomenon of displacements and migration and an existential predicament.

Palestinian nationalism under colonial rule, however, was the first during the twentieth century to be constructed way before the First and Second World Wars. Palestinian identity was the first to demonstrate significant nationalism in the early Mandatory period[3] and, similarly and paradoxically, also remains the only colonially occupied territory hitherto. Furthermore, there "is clearly a paradox here. Its core is that Israelis, many of them descended from victims of persecution, pogroms, and concentration camps, have themselves been mistreating another people. We thus find that the sins done to the fathers have morally desensitized the sons to their sins toward others, and have even sometimes been used to justify these sins" (Khalidi: 1997: 5).

For the Palestinian, as well as for the other members of displacements in this book, home remains a relatively distant memory, an idea that is much bigger than the geography, and is continuously reterritorialized elsewhere. Palestine, in this context, remains that one thing around which "memory needs to organize its chaos" (Darwish: 2010: 57). Moreover, a Palestinian finds meaning in this very continuous striving for a possibility of an envision of a Palestinian identity that is always in transit and elsewhere. The Palestinian is adaptive, enduring, and always turning. Probably this is why the Palestinian fled in 1948, 1956, and 1967 without attempts at or feeling urged to changing circumstances: to accept defeat and move on. Besides its literature, there has probably been no stronger imperative through and in which a Palestinian identity could be and have been ensembled or articulated thus far.

With their de facto national anthem, oratory, national press and media, national literature, imagined community, suffering and exilic displacements, through this "imbalanced balance" (Said: 1986: 129), however, a Palestinian national identity develops in spite of, and in some cases because of, the obstacles it faced and still faces. Palestinian identity cannot be represented or spoken for, nonetheless, because it is a collective narrative of individual narratives and of different generations, of diverse losses. Furthermore, a lost homeland can never be recollected within borders or reassembled within books in libraries, neither is the Palestinian here a mere object for academic research, but rather a human subject, with memories and aspirations. This academic research only aspires, therefore, to act as an agent to speak to postcolonial displacees of India, Pakistan, Africa, China, and the Caribbean generally, and particularly the different displaced generations of the Palestinians.

Notes

Placing Displacement: An Introduction

1. The difference between origins and beginnings is that with the former the starting point is a romanticized, fixed point, whereas with the latter it is "the first step in the intentional production of meaning" and could be rerouted elsewhere (see Said's *Beginnings: Intention and Method* (New York: Columbia University Press: 1975)).
2. english is used here with a small letter to accentuate the English language's reappropriation by postcolonial writers. It is also to highlight the fact that there has been a move from what was known previously as English literature to literatures written in English.
3. See Khalidi, R. *Palestinian Identity: the Construction of Modern National Consciousness*, 1997.
4. From Mahmoud Darwish's *The Earth Is Closing on Us*. See *Victims of the Map*: 2005.
5. I am German by nationality, Jordanian by birth, Palestinian by descent, and spent my twenties in England. I am a third-generation Palestinian exile to a first-generation Palestinian refugee/Laje' father (born in Palestine in 1938, a few years before and left subsequent to The Nakba, The Catastrophe of 1948) and a second-generation Palestinian displaced/Nazeh mother (born in Palestine in 1964, right before, and left subsequent to the Naksah, The Six Days War of 1967).
6. See Philips, M. and Trevor, W., *The Windrush Generation: the irresistible rise of multi-racial Britain*, 1998.
7. "Masala Fish" is the title promoted and demonstrated in Chapter 4 to cover the second generation of displaced writers mentioned below. Masala (Oriental, colorful, hot) and fish (Occidental, cold, white) are combined or "infused" to offer a syncretic reflection of the displaced's hyphenated identities. Food is particularly used here as a metaphor for displacement and migration, for food is a signifier for the liminality of boundaries: food passes across any boundary: it is adaptive, integral, and frontierless.
8. See George, R. *The Politics of Home* (1996).
9. See Bhabha's *The Location of Culture* (2005: 13).
10. Bhangra is a Punjabi, South Asian genre of music, a genre that has become internationalized. From a folk music of rural India, and with

an increasing Asian population in England, it turned into a fusion of the old and new, of Punjabi and Pop music.
11. Psychoanalytically, the concept of displacement starts out in the twentieth century as a Freudian concept (*Verschiebung*). See Freud's *The Origins and Development of Psychoanalysis* (Montana: Kessinger Publishing, LLC: 2010, p. 29).
12. See Buchanan (2008: 28–34).
13. That is, when it is cast more broadly outside the Oedipal framework that is a rigidly imposed hierarchy, restricted, closed, and familial.

CHAPTER 1

1. It is worth mentioning that "British" here stands for an open description of cultural and political identity: "British" is not an exclusively ethnical term, whereas "English" is a rather local experience and a racially exclusive one.
2. It is worth mentioning here that the words *Heim* and *Heimat* are German concepts which broadly speaking mean homeland. But since the word long originated before the existence of Germany as a nation, it is usually associated with a region, district, and is distinguished by a particular dialect, such as Bavaria for example. A German therefore is connected to his/her *Heimat* by emotional ties as opposed to the political. Furthermore, Hitler once tried to masculinize the feminine term *Heimat* to serve his nationalistic ends: *Vaterland*.
3. Mental and cultural ghettoization is to "forget that there is a world beyond the community to which we belong, to confine ourselves within narrowly defined cultural frontiers" (Rushdie: 1991: 19).
4. It is worth mentioning here too that Jordanian occupation of the West Bank of Palestine ended by 1967 and in 1988, Jordan renounced its claims to the West Bank (with the exception of guardianship over the Muslim holy sites in Jerusalem), and recognized the Palestine Liberation Organization (PLO) as the legitimate representative of the Palestinian people.
5. See Kaplan's *Questions of Travel: Postmodern Discourses of Displacement*: 1996: p. 138.
6. See Du Bois's *The Souls of the Black Folk*, 1994.
7. See D & G's *Anti-Oedipus*, 1983, p. 112.
8. See Marshal McLuhan's *Understanding Media* (1964).
9. According to Stuart Hall, a cultural turn is a

> process [that] continues in the direction in which it was travelling before, but with a critical break, a deflection. After the turn, all of terms of a paradigm are not destroyed; instead, the deflection shifts the paradigm in a direction which is different from that which one might have presupposed from the previous moment.
>
> (Hall: 2001: 9)

This suggests that while Palestinian exilic displacements always register a beginning, they are not necessarily ghettoized in it, and rather deflect from it as opposed to the Jewish one and its salvation through a physical return to it.

10. It is worth mentioning here that neither did the Oslo Accords/Peace Process of 1993 nor 1995 grant the Palestinians statehood, nor did they cease Israel's ongoing building of settlements. For further reading, see Said's *The End of the Peace Process: Oslo and After* (2001).
11. It has already been clarified in Chapter 1, Section 2, that the concept of displacement is in part defined here within the context of the Palestinian displaced narrative and exilic experience of dispersions. The Arabic translation of the word displacement is *Nuzooh*. The latter is the noun that is derived from the verb Nazaha, which literally means to forcibly (e)migrate, to evacuate. Within the Arab world, this particular concept/verb (to evacuate, to be displaced) has always been particular and exclusive to the Palestinian experience after the Nakba, the Catastrophe of 1948, which signaled the return of the Jewish diaspora and consequently triggered the mass Palestinian displacement.
12. See James Clifford's pluralized title *Diasporas* in *Cultural Anthropology*, Vol. 9, No. 3, *Further Inflections: Toward Ethnographies of the Future* (Aug., 1994), pp. 302–338. Clifford's essay focuses on Jewish Diaspora and its return (as well as the Armenian and Greek) without any explicit mentioning of the subsequent Palestinian displacement. Written in 1994, however, Clifford does highlight the importance and the consequences of the PLO's signing of the Oslo Accords.
13. Palestinian and Jewish experiences of scattering are particularly invoked here in contrast because Palestine was a British colony and thus fits within the context of this project along with other colonial histories of the Caribbean, India, and Pakistan; also because Palestinian exilic displacements are ongoing and current. Furthermore, contrasting the two particular experiences here is partly because the historical context of the word Diaspora instinctively refers to and resonates with the destruction of the Holy Land that is Jerusalem: the center of the old as well as existing Arab–Israeli conflict.

Chapter 2

1. See Hoffman in Aciman's *Letters of Transit* (1999).
2. For further reading, see Rushdie (2002: 159–60).
3. It is worth mentioning here that when Said first introduced himself to others upon his arrival in America, he introduced himself as an Egyptian. "'I'm from Cairo,' I said enthusiastically" (Said: 1999: 228).

4. It was W. E. B. Du Bois who first coined the term double consciousness in the context of describing the experience of African-Americans in which they were constantly looking at themselves through white eyes. This sense of two-ness, and of warring ideals also applies to the black British migrant and it carries with it an equivalent ambivalence in terms of identity: is one black or British?
5. Although at Du Bois' time America was emerging as a new world power and Britain was going through major changes in its identity, politics, and culture, the American Negro example does not map on to or emulate the black British migrant's experience. It is contrastingly evoked here because it was during the 1960s that the black displaced migrants in Britain were immensely inspired and influenced by the American Civil Rights revolutions across the Atlantic.
6. Since the 1960s, the West Indian community color the streets of Notting Hill and London for three days. The Caribbean flavored carnival was to an extent a response to the Notting Hill racial attacks and riots (1958). The festive carnival promotes cultural diversity and tolerating difference. It celebrates London's multiculturalism. A carnival also signifies the interaction of different people together, freedom of expression, unity, and eccentric behavior.
7. Thatcherism is understood here as Thatcher's addressing Britain as an imagined community, her nostalgic language of Empire, and her fear that Britain was going to be "swamped" by foreigners.
8. Ian Wright (MBE) first played for Crystal Palace in 1985 before moving to Arsenal at the peak of his career. Captain Paul Ince, on the other hand, is allegedly the first black player to captain the national team of England and the first black Briton to manage an English team in the Premier League.
9. World heavyweight boxing champion Muhammad Ali (Cassius Marcellus Clay, Jr.; 1942–) visited a children's home in Notting Hill, London, May 15, 1966. Converting to Islam in 1964, Ali protested against the Vietnam War and hence refused to join the US Army. His boxing license was suspended. Four years later, Ali won an appeal in the US Supreme Court. Ali was not only an Afro-American athlete and The Greatest boxer of all times but also a social activist and an idolized cultural icon.
10. To an extent, this also echoes the Palestinian's experience of exile. The Palestinian is exiled twice too: in and outside Palestine by virtue of ethnic cleansing, colonialism, and displacement.
11. One is reminded here of Frantz Fanon's psychological services of shame and fear, where if the colonized gives in and does not resist, the colonized is helpless and coward. And if the colonized does resist, the colonized is a barbaric savage. Unlike Fanon's speech that always addresses the black man, however, Du Bois's speaks to both audiences, black and white. To the whites, it challenges the

"colour-coded civilisation and national culture" (Gilroy: 1993: 127) while to the black, it explains how double consciousness emerges from three modes of thinking (racially), being (nationally), and seeing (diasporically).

Chapter 3

1. *Him* since most Windrush Generation writers were male adult emigrants.
2. See Frantz Fanon's *The Wretched of the Earth* and *Black Skin, White Masks*.
3. See Tayeb Salih's *Season of Migration to the North* (1966).
4. See Aime Cesaire's *A Tempest* (1969).
5. By the time *Moses Ascending* was written in 1975, Enoch Powell's infamous "River of Blood" speech had been delivered.
6. Subalterns are those politically, socially, and geographically outside the hegemonic structure and therefore without human agency by virtue of their social status: the peasant farmers, unorganized labor, Third World women, other Third World women, and migrant laborers in the West.

Chapter 4

1. This applies to an extent to first generation and second and third generations of Palestinian exiles. The historic land of Palestine to the former is a colonially lived experience the Palestinian exile glorifies romantically, whereas to following generations it is reterritorialized in the imaginary.
2. Multiple as opposed to "excessive" since the adjective "excessive" seem to imply emptiness and redundancy which could slide toward nomadic rhizome.
3. More than 10,000 people marched through Central London from Hyde Park to Trafalgar Square to protest against the proposed Nationality Bill, April 6, 1981. The March was organized by the Campaign against Racist Laws. Some placards read: Deport Her Now!
4. Diane Abbott, November 1987, was one of the first black politicians, under Welsh politician and leader of the Labour Party, Neil Kinnock.

Promoting Cultural Diversity/Multiculturalism Post-9/11: A Conclusion

1. Incidentally, 1956 does mark not only the year *The Lonely Londoners* was published but also the year Britain failed to take over the Suez Canal and subsequently intensified the so-called Arab–Israeli conflict.

2. Mainly those who formed the beginnings of a national Palestinian literature and born before the Nakba/Catastrophe: national poet Mahmoud Darwish, writer and journalist Ghassan Kanafani, author Edward Said, caricaturist Naji al-Ali, writer Emile Habibi, author Khalil al-Sakakini, poets Fadwa and Ibrahim Touqan, photographer Karimeh Abbud, among many others.
3. See Khalid's *Palestinian Identity: The Construction of Modern National Consciousness*, 1997.

BIBLIOGRAPHY

Achebe, C. (2000) *Home and Exile*, Edinburgh: Canongate Books Ltd.
Achebe, C. (2001) *Things Fall Apart*, London: Penguin.
Aciman, A. (ed.) (1999) *Letters of Transit: Reflections on Exile, Identity, Language, and Loss*, New York: The New Press.
Adams, T. (2007) *Cultural Hallmark*. The Guardian [online] September 23. Available at: http://www.guardian.co.uk/society/2007/sep/23/communities.politicsphilosophyandsociety [Accessed April 13, 2013].
Ahmad, A. (2008) *In Theory: Classes, Nations, Literatures*, London: Verso.
Alexander, M. (1990) *Flights from Realism: Themes and Strategies in Postmodernist British and American Fiction*, Kent: Edward Arnold.
Ali, M. (2003) *Brick Lane*, London: Black Swan.
Anderson, B. (1991) *Imagined Communities: Reflections on the Origin and Spread of Nationalism*, London: Verso.
Appadurai, A. (1996) *Modernity at Large: Cultural Dimensions of Globalisation*, Minneapolis: University of Minnesota Press.
Ashcroft, B., et al. (2002) *The Empire Writes Back: Theory and Practice in Post-colonial literatures*, London and New York: Routledge.
Auerbach, E. (1993) *Mimesis: The Representation of Reality in Western Literature*, Princeton, NJ: Princeton University Press.
Bammer, A. (ed.) (1994) *Displacements: Cultural Identities in Question*. Bloomington and Indianapolis: Indiana University Press.
Barghouti, M. (2004) *I Saw Ramallah*. Translated from Arabic by Ahdaf Souief, London: Bloomsbury.
Barry, P. (2002) *Beginning Theory: An Introduction into Literary and Cultural Theory*, Manchester: Manchester University Press.
Bhabha, H. (1990) 'Introduction: Narrating the Nation' in Bhabha, H. (ed.) *Nation and Narration*, pp. 1–7, London: Routledge.
Bhabha, H. (2000) 'The Vernacular Cosmopolitan' in Dennis, F. (ed.) *Voices of the Crossing: The Impact of Britain on Writers from Asia, The Caribbean and Africa*, pp. 133–142, London: Serpent's Tail.
Bhabha, H. (2005) *The Location of Culture*, London & New York: Routledge.
Brick Lane. (2008) [DVD] London: Film 4, Ingenious Film Partners and the UK Film Council.
Brodsky, J. (1994) 'The Condition We Call Exile' in Robinson, M. (ed.) *Altogether Elsewhere: Writers in Exile*, pp. 3–12, London: Harcourt Brace & Company.

Brown, S. (ed.) (1999) *The Oxford Book of Caribbean Short Stories*, Oxford: Oxford University Press.
Buchanan, B. (2007) *Hanif Kureishi*, New York: Palgrave Macmillan.
Buchanan, I. (2008) *Deleuze and Guattari's Anti-Oedipus*, London: Continuum International Publishing Group.
Cameron, D. (2011) *David Cameron on Immigration: Full text of Speech.* The Guardian [online] April 14. Available at: http://www.guardian.co.uk/politics/2011/apr/14/david-cameron-immigration-speech-full-text?fb= native#_= _ [Accessed April 13, 2013].
Cesaire, A. (1994) 'Discourse on Colonialism' in Williams, P., et al. (eds) *Colonial Discourse and Post-colonial Theory: A Reader*, pp. 172–180, London: Longman Pearson Education.
Cesaire, A. (2000) *A Tempest.* Translated by Philip Crispin, London: Oberon Books.
Chaudhary, V. (2003) *The Big Bhangra.* The Guardian [online] August 15, 2003. Available at: http://www.guardian.co.uk/music/2003/aug/15/shopping.popandrock [Accessed April 13, 2013].
Childs, P. (2005) *Contemporary Novelists: British Fiction since 1970*, New York: Palgrave Macmillan.
Clifford, J. (1994, Aug.) *Diasporas* in *Cultural Anthropology*, Vol. 9, No. 3, Further Inflections: Toward Ethnographies of the Future, pp. 302–338.
Cohen, R. (1997) *Global Diasporas: An Introduction*, London: UCL Press.
Conrad, J. (2002) *Heart of Darkness and Other Tales*, Oxford: Oxford University Press.
Darwish, M. (2010) *Absent Presence.* Translated by Mohammad Shaheen, London: Hesperus Press Limited.
Deleuze, G. and Guattari, F. (1983) *Anti-Oedipus: Capitalism and Schizophrenia*, Minneapolis: University of Minnesota Press.
Deleuze, G. and Guattari, F. (1988) 'Introduction: Rhizome' and 'Treatise on Nomadology: The War Machine' to *A Thousand Plateaus: Capitalism and Schizophrenia*, London: The Athlone Press.
Deleuze, G. and Guattari, F. (1992) *A Thousand Plateaus: Capitalism and Schizophrenia*; translation and foreword by Brian Massumi, London: The Lions Press.
Dennis, F. and Khan, N. (2000) *Voices of the Crossing: The Impact of Britain on Writers from Asia, The Caribbean and Africa*, London: Serpent's Tail.
Dhondy, F. (1976) *East End at Your Feet*, London: Macmillan Education Ltd.
Dhondy, F. (1978a) *Come to Mecca and Other Stories*, London: Fontana and William Collins Sons & Co Ltd.
Dhondy, F. (1978b) *The Siege of Babylon*, London: Macmillan.
Dhondy, F. (1990) *Bombay Duck*, London: Jonathan Cape.
Dhondy, F. (2000) 'Speaking in Tongues' in Dennis, F. (ed.) *Voices of the Crossing: The Impact of Britain on Writers from Asia, The Caribbean and Africa*, pp. 163–174, London: Serpent's Tail.
Dhondy, F. (2001a) *C.L.R. James*, New York: Pantheon Books.

Dhondy, F. (2001b) *Interview: V S Naipaul talks to Farrukh Dhondy*. Literary Review [online]. Available at: http://www.literaryreview.co.uk/Naipaul_04_06.html [Accessed April 13, 2013].
Dhondy, F. (2001c) *Our Islamic Fifth Column*. City Journal [online] Autumn, 2001. Available at: http://www.city-journal.org/html/11_4_our_islamic.html [Accessed April 13, 2013].
Dhondy, F. (2008) V S Naipaul: The Man and His Mission. *Journal of Caribbean Literatures*, 5 (2): 181–200.
Domin, H. (1994) 'Heimat' in Robinson, M. (ed.) *Altogether Elsewhere: Writers in Exile*, pp. 129–131, London: Harcourt Brace & Company.
Du Bois, W. E. B. (1994) *The Souls of Black Folk*, New York: Dover Publications.
Eagleton, T. (1970) *Exiles and Émigrés: Studies in Modern Literature*, London: Chatto & Windus.
Edward Said: The Last Interview. (2005) [DVD] England: ICA Projects and Drakes Avenue Pictures Limited.
Fanon, F. (2001) *The Wretched of the Earth*, London: Penguin Classics.
Foreword and Introduction in Levi, E. & Scheding, F. (2010) *Music and Displacement: Diasporas, Mobilities, and Dislocations in Europe and Beyond*, Plymouth: Scarecrow Press.
Freud, S. (2010) *The Origin and Development of Psychoanalysis*, Montana: Kessinger Publishing, LLC.
George, R. (1996) *The Politics of Home: Postcolonial Relocations and Twentieth-Century Fiction*, London: University of California Press.
Gilroy, P. (1993) *The Black Atlantic: Modernity and Double Consciousness*, London: Verso.
Gilroy, P. (2002) *There Ain't No Black in the Union Jack*, London: Routledge.
Gilroy, P. (2004) Melancholia and Multiculture. Open Democracy [online] August 2, 2004. Available at: http://www.opendemocracy.net/arts-multiculturalism/article_2035.jsp [Accessed April 13, 2013].
Gilroy, P. (2007) *Black Britain: A Photographic History*, London: SAQI.
Graham-Yooll, A. (1986) *A State of Fear: Memories of Argentina's Nightmare*, London: Eland.
Hall, S. (1994) 'Cultural Identity and Diaspora' in Williams, P., et al. (eds) *Colonial Discourse and Post-colonial Theory: A Reader*, pp. 392–404, London: Longman Pearson Education.
Hall, S. (2001) *Modernity and Difference*, London: Institute of International Visual Arts.
Harasym, S. (ed.) (1990) *The Post-colonial Critic: Interviews, Strategies, Dialogues, Gayatri Spivak*, London and New York: Routledge.
Hawley, J. (2005) *Amitav Ghosh: Contemporary Indian Writers in English*, Cambridge House: Foundation Books Pvt Ltd.
Hoffman, E. (1994) 'Obsessed with Words' in Robinson, M. (ed.) *Altogether Elsewhere: Writers in Exile*, pp. 229–234, London: Harcourt Brace & Company.

hooks, b. (1989) 'Choosing the Margin as a Space of Radical Openness', *Framework: The Journal of Cinema and Media*, 39(36).
hooks, b. (1994) 'Postmodern Blackness' in Williams, P., et al. (eds) *Colonial Discourse and Post-colonial Theory: A Reader*, pp. 421–427, London: Longman Pearson Education.
Hosain, A. (2000) 'Deep Roots, New Language' in Dennis, F. (ed.) *Voices of the Crossing: The Impact of Britain on Writers from Asia, The Caribbean and Africa*, pp. 19–28, London: Serpent's Tail.
Hugo, V. (1994) 'What is Exile' in Robinson, M. (ed.) *Altogether Elsewhere: Writers in Exile*, pp. 67–84, London: Harcourt Brace & Company.
Huntington, S. (2002) *The Clash of Civilizations: Remaking of World Order*, London: Free Press.
Joyce, J. (2001) *A Portrait of the Artist as a Young Man*, London: Wordsworth Classics.
Kaplan, C. (1996) (2005, 2nd edn) *Questions of Travel: Postmodern Discourses of Displacement*, Durham and London: Duke University Press.
Khalidi, R. (1997) *Palestinian Identity: The Construction of Modern National Consciousness*, New York: Columbia University Press.
King, B. (2004) *The Internationalisation of English Literature: The Oxford English Literary History, 1948–2000*, Volume 13. New York: Oxford University Press.
Kureishi, H. (1990) *The Buddha of Suburbia*, London: Faber and Faber.
Kureishi, H. (1995) *The Black Album*, London: Faber and Faber.
Kureishi, H. (1999) *Midnight All Day*, London: Faber and Faber.
Kureishi, H. (2002) *The Body and Other Stories*, London: Faber and Faber.
Kureishi, H. (2011) *Collected Essays*, London: Faber and Faber.
Lamming, G. (1953) *In The Castle of My Skin*, Essex: Longman Drumbeat.
Lamming, G. (1954) *The Emigrants*, London: Allison & Busby.
Lamming, G. (1960) *The Pleasure of Exile*, London: Michael Joseph.
Landry, D. and Maclean, G. (eds) (1996) *The Spivak Reader*, New York: Routledge.
Lavie, S. and Swedenburg, T. (eds) (2001) *Displacement, Diaspora, and Geographies of Identity*, Durham, NC: Duke University Press, second printing.
Macphee, G. and Poddar, P. (eds) (2007) 'Introduction: Nationalism Beyond the Nation-State' to *Empire and After: Englishness in Postcolonial Perspective*, pp. 1–19, New York and Oxford: Berghahn Books.
Matar, D. (2011) *What It Means to Be Palestinian: Stories of Palestinian Peoplehood*, London and New York: B. Tauris.
Mcluhan, M (1964) *Understanding Media: The Extension of Man*, New York: McGraw-Hill.
Mishra, V. and Hodge, B. (2005) 'What Was Postcolonialism?' *New Literary History*, 36 (3): 375–402.
Miyoshi, M. (1993) A Borderless World? From Colonialism to Transnationalism and the Decline of the Nation-State *Critical Inquiry*, 19(4): 726–751.

Mo, T. (1999) *Sour Sweet*, London: Paddleless.
Naipaul, V. S. (1969) *The Mimic Men*, London: Penguin Books.
Naipaul, V. S. (1973) *In A Free State*, Middlesex: Penguin Books Ltd.
Naipaul, V. S. (1987) *The Enigma of Arrival*, New York: Vintage.
Naipaul, V. S. (2002) *A House for Mr Biswas*, London: Picador.
Naipaul, V. S. (2003) *The Writer and The World*, Knopf: Canada.
Nevid, J. S. (2011) *Psychology: Concepts and Applications*, Belmont: Cengage Learning.
Phillips, C. (1985) *The Final Passage*, London: Faber and Faber.
Phillips, C. (2001) *A New World Order: Selected Essays*, London: Secker & Warburg.
Procter, J. (2003) *Dwelling places: Postwar Black British Writing*, Manchester: Manchester University Press.
Procter, J. (2004) *Stuart Hall*, London: Routledge.
Reynolds, M. and Noakes, J. (2003) *Salman Rushdie: The Essential Guide*, London: Vintage.
Rhys, J. (1966) *Wide Sargasso Sea*, London: Penguin.
Rhys, J. (1979) *Smile Please: An Unfinished Autobiography*, London: Harper & Row.
Rhys, J. (1988) *Voyage in the Dark*, London: Penguin Books.
Robertson, G., et al. (1994) *Travellers' Tales: Narratives of Home and Displacement*, London: Routledge.
Robinson, M. (1994) *Altogether Elsewhere: Writers on Exile*, London: Harcourt Brace & Company.
Rushdie, S. (1983) *Shame*, London: Vintage.
Rushdie, S. (1991) *Imaginary Homelands: Essays and Criticism 1981–1991*, London: Granta.
Rushdie, S. (1995) *East, West*, London: Vintage.
Rushdie, S. (2002) *Step Across this Line: Collected Non-fiction 1992–2002*, London: Vintage.
Rushdie, S. (2006a) *The Satanic Verses*, London: Vintage.
Rushdie, S. (2006b) *Midnight's Children*, London: Vintage.
Said, E. (1983) 'Introduction: Secular Criticism' and 'Travelling Theory' in Said, E. (ed.) *The World, The Text, and the Critic*, pp. 1–30 and 226–247, Cambridge, MA: Harvard University Press.
Said, E. (1986) *After the Last Sky: Palestinian Lives*, New York: Pantheon Books.
Said, E. (1994a) *Culture and Imperialism*, London: Vintage.
Said, E. (1994b) *Representations of the Intellectual: The 1993 Reith Lectures*, London: Vintage.
Said, E. (1999) *Out of Place: A Memoir*, London: Granta Books.
Said, E. (2001a) *Reflections on Exile: And Other Literary and Cultural Essays*, London: Granta.
Said, E. (2001b) *The End of the Peace Process: Oslo and After*, New York: Vintage Books.

Said, E. (2003a) *A Window on the World*. The Guardian [online] August 2. Available at: http://www.guardian.co.uk/books/2003/aug/02/alqaida.highereducation [Accessed April 13, 2013].
Said, E. (2003b) *Orientalism*, London: Penguin Books.
Said, E. and Barenboim, D. (2002) *Parallels and Paradoxes: Explorations in Music and Society*, London: Bloomsbury.
Salih, T. (2003) *Seasons of Migration to the North*, London: Penguin Books.
Selvon, S. (1985) *A Brighter Sun*, Essex: Longman.
Selvon, S. (1993) *An Island is a World*, Toronto: TSAR.
Selvon, S. (2006) *The Lonely Londoners*, London: Penguin Books.
Selvon, S. (2008) *Moses Ascending*, London: Penguin Books.
Selvon, S. (2009) *Moses Migrating: A Novel*, London: Lynne Rienner Publishers.
Simpson, J. (1995) *The Oxford Book of Exile*, New York: Oxford University Press.
Sivanandan, A. (1990) *Communities of Resistance: Writings on Black Struggles for Socialism*, London: Verso.
Sivanandan, A. (2005) *Why Muslims Reject British Values*. The Guardian [online] October 16, 2005. Available at: http://www.guardian.co.uk/politics/2005/oct/16/race.world [Accessed April 13, 2013].
Smith, Z. (2000) *White Teeth*, London: Hamish and Hamilton Ltd.
Snead, J. (1990) 'European Pedigrees/African Contagions: Nationality, Narrative, and Communality in Tutuola, Achebe, and Reed' in Bhabha, H. (ed.) *Nation and Narration*, pp. 231–248, London: Routledge.
SOURSWEET. (2010) [DVD] London: National Film Trustee Company Limited and Film Four International.
Spivak, G. C. (1992) 'Interview with Gayatri Chakravorty Spivak: New Nation Writers Conference in South Africa' *Ariel: A Review of International English Literature*, 23 (3): 29–47.
Spivak, G. C. (2002) 'Discussion: An Afterword on the New Subaltern' in Chatterjee, P. and Jeganathan, P. (eds) *Subaltern Studies XI: Community, Gender and Violence*, pp. 305–333, New Delhi: Permanent Black.
Sterne, L. (2009) *The Life and Opinions of Tristman Shandy, Gentleman*, London: Wordsworth Classics.
The Buddha of Suburbia. 2007 [DVD] London: BBC Worldwide Ltd.
The Mystic Masseur. (2003) [DVD] Merchant Ivory Production Ltd and Pritish Nandy Communications Ltd.
Thiong'o, N. (1994) 'The Language of African Literature' in Williams, P., et al. (eds) *Colonial Discourse and Post-colonial Theory: A Reader*, pp. 435–455, London: Longman Pearson Education.
Trousdale, R. (2010) *Nabokov, Rushdie, and the Transnational Imagination: Novels of Exile and Alternate Worlds*, New York: Palgrave Macmillan.
Walia, S. (2001) *Edward Said and the Writing of History*, Cambridge: Icon Books.
Williams, Z. (2012) *The Saturday Interview: Stuart Hall*. The Guardian [online] February 11, 2012. Available at: http://www.guardian.co.uk/the

guardian/2012/feb/11/saturday-interview-stuart-hall [Accessed May 31, 2013].
Williams, P., et al. (1994) *Colonial Discourse and Post-colonial Theory: A Reader*, London: Longman Pearson Education.
Wilson, J., et al. (2010) *Rerouting the Postcolonial: New Directions for the New Millennium*, London: Routledge.
Wong, F. C. (2000) *Kazuo Ishiguro*, Devon: Northcote House Publishers Ltd.
Young, R. J. C. (2003) *Postcolonialism: A Very Short Introduction*, New York: Oxford University Press.

Index

9/11, 9, 11, 118, 121, 173, 175, 176, 177, 180

Aboulela, Leila, 69
Achebe, Chinua, 34, 35, 62, 110, 115
Africa, 5, 18, 19, 31, 35, 46, 50, 60, 61, 62, 65, 68, 69, 71, 72, 75, 78, 84, 90, 91, 94, 105, 106, 112, 120, 131, 149, 150, 151, 152, 165, 173, 180, 181
(Afro-)Caribbean, 3, 5, 11, 18, 23, 31, 32, 35, 40, 46, 47, 49, 50, 54, 61, 62, 69, 71, 72, 78, 80, 81, 85, 86, 87, 90, 94, 95, 96, 97, 99, 101, 103, 105, 106–11, 122, 123, 149, 150, 151, 152, 154, 161, 166, 167, 172, 176, 180, 181
After the Last Sky, 6, 43, 44
Ahmad, Aijaz, 11, 39, 118, 119, 139, 140, 142
Ali, Monica, 2, 8, 9, 11, 117, 176
Ali, Muhammad, 72
amnesia, 37, 69, 181
An Island is a World, 19, 21, 83, 86, 99
Appadurai, A., 26
Arab, 3, 6, 23, 24, 30, 43, 47, 48, 52, 54, 65, 69, 71, 81, 130, 146, 148, 165, 169, 170
Arab-Israeli war, 23, 43, 52
Arab peninsula, 30
Asia, 18, 40, 47, 49, 54, 65, 70, 71, 79, 120, 122, 125, 126, 129, 130, 131, 133, 155, 157, 161, 165, 173, 176, 180
assimilation, 32, 37, 51, 82, 94, 99, 106, 121, 162, 171
Aswad, 71
Auerbach, 15, 37, 60
authenticity, 47, 69, 82, 94
autobiographical, 11, 37, 97, 110, 114, 141, 147
Avant-gardist, 142, 143

Babylon, 2, 55
Baldwin, James, 71
Bangladesh, 32, 118, 159, 160, 161, 162, 176, 178, 179, 180
Barenboim, 42, 43, 65, 169, 170
Barghouti, Mourid, 24, 25
BBC, 71, 81, 88, 176
beginnings, 1, 2, 6, 18, 20, 28, 39, 62, 65, 74, 107, 136, 151, 155
belonging, 1, 15, 19, 21, 22, 38, 39, 42, 60, 64, 65, 66, 67, 73, 83, 90, 97, 98, 101, 108, 109, 111, 118, 119, 121, 130, 134, 136, 137, 141, 143, 145, 149, 151, 155
Bengali, 128, 145, 158, 159, 177, 178, 179, 180
Bhabha, Homi, 4, 8, 9, 13, 18, 27, 28, 41, 51, 59, 62, 91, 105, 115, 134, 135, 170
Bhangra, 11, 70, 71
bipolar mentality, 19, 181
Birmingham, 175

The Black Album, 123, 150, 156, 157
black British, 2, 18, 68, 71, 120, 121, 125, 126, 135, 176
body, 37, 38, 74, 123, 133, 144, 149, 156, 172
The Body, 37, 74, 144, 156
Bombay, 8, 11, 37, 45, 62, 86, 126, 127, 130, 131, 132, 136, 139, 141, 143
Bombay Duck, 11, 37, 130, 131, 132, 133
Booker Prize, 9, 71, 81
botanic multiplicity, 20
Brick Lane, 2, 11, 32, 34, 37, 120, 121, 153, 161, 176–80
Brixton, 68, 129
The Buddha of Suburbia, 11, 19, 32, 37, 120, 121, 150, 155, 156, 157

calypso, 81, 89, 99, 114
Cameron, David, 165, 172, 175
capitalism, 13, 57
Caribbean, *see* (Afro-)Caribbean
carnival, 69, 77, 105, 107
Cesaire, Aime, 88
China, 19, 46, 84, 125
citizenship, 1, 69, 70, 74, 76, 83, 110, 124, 148
civil rights, 68, 72, 74, 81
clash of civilizations, 168, 169, 171
class, 12, 25, 43, 50, 53, 59, 85, 96, 100, 104, 105, 109, 120, 121, 125, 126, 128, 129, 132, 143, 150, 155, 156, 158, 159, 160, 166, 179
Clifford, James, 46, 47, 49, 50
Cohen, Robin, 46, 49, 51, 54
colonialism, 3, 10, 18, 23, 24, 57, 62, 79, 90, 92, 94, 107, 112, 125, 142, 144, 145, 151, 152, 165
commonwealth, 68, 69, 77, 81, 85, 93, 171

Conrad, Joseph, 12, 85, 86, 111, 112, 127
consciousness, 3, 13, 14, 26, 28, 33, 34, 35, 36, 38, 40, 42, 45, 47, 48, 49, 52, 57, 60, 63, 67, 68, 72, 73, 74, 75, 81, 83, 85, 88, 89, 90, 94, 95, 99, 101, 103, 108, 140, 153, 177, 178, 180, 181
contrapuntal, 35, 38, 44, 62, 105, 135, 140, 170
cosmopolitan, 28, 29, 32, 33, 36, 43, 77, 78, 82, 100, 102, 110, 175, 177
creole, 35, 95, 97, 106, 107
creolite, 28, 170
cricket, 87, 88, 127, 152
critical distance, 18, 22, 26, 33, 51, 129, 142
criticism, 3, 4, 19, 20, 33, 52, 67, 141
cultural identity, 1, 40, 57–67, 73, 91, 95, 106, 126, 166, 167
cultural paralysis, 22
cultural studies, 3, 14, 69, 175
cultural translation, 1, 7, 29, 58, 107, 134, 145, 170, 175, 180
cultural turn, 7, 47, 58, 61, 62, 154, 174
culture 2, 4, 5, 7, 9, 12, 13, 17, 18, 19, 28, 29, 30, 32, 33, 34, 35, 36, 40, 41, 47, 49, 51, 52, 54, 55, 57, 58, 59, 60, 61, 62, 63, 66, 67, 68, 69, 70, 71, 72, 73, 77, 78, 79, 81, 82, 84, 92, 93, 96, 97, 99, 100, 106, 107, 110, 111, 112, 115, 116, 117, 118, 119, 120, 122–7, 130, 132, 135, 137, 140, 146, 147, 154, 155, 156, 158, 160, 162, 165, 166, 168, 169, 170, 172, 174, 175, 176, 177, 179
Culture and Imperialism, 4, 47

Darwish, Mahmoud, 3, 22, 23, 24, 41, 42, 44, 45, 47, 54, 182
decolonization, 10, 72, 81, 90, 93, 101, 106, 108, 110, 167
Deleuze and Guattari, 6, 10, 13, 14, 15, 17, 20, 21, 116
deterritorialization, 2, 17, 29
Dhondy, Farrukh, 8, 9, 11, 88, 111, 112, 117, 120, 125, 126, 127, 128, 129, 130, 131, 132, 133, 154, 155
dialogic, 7, 15, 40, 41, 59, 63, 118, 151
diaspora, 3, 5, 13, 18, 23, 24, 25, 28, 29, 30, 32, 40, 42, 46–55, 61, 71, 72, 88, 152, 155, 181
double consciousness, 38, 40, 60, 67, 68, 74, 181
dreams, 13, 36, 37, 82, 94, 95, 119, 177, 178
Du Bois, W. E. B., 38, 60, 62, 67, 72, 73, 74, 75, 76
duality, 27
dwell, 4, 20, 47, 86, 90, 158, 160

Eagleton, Terry, 12
eclecticism, 45, 162, 168, 169, 173
education, 28, 78, 90, 130, 131, 137, 152, 171
empire, 3, 8, 11, 19, 78, 79, 80, 81, 85, 87, 91, 94, 107, 109, 117, 122, 134, 142, 144, 152, 166, 168
England, 1, 8, 9, 12, 30, 31, 32, 46, 68, 69, 70, 76, 78, 79, 80, 81, 84, 86, 87, 88, 90, 91, 92, 93, 94, 95, 97, 99, 105, 107, 110, 111, 117, 118, 120, 121, 122, 124, 126, 127, 128, 129, 131, 132, 133, 134, 135, 136, 148, 149, 150, 151, 152, 153, 154, 155, 156, 159, 160, 161, 162, 163, 167, 176, 177, 178, 180
The Enigma of Arrival, 37, 110, 112
enlightenment, 14

enunciation, 20, 36, 75, 108
epistemology, 18
epistolary, 45, 131, 178
ethnicity, 2, 9, 28, 46, 52, 54, 69, 75, 77, 85, 118, 120, 148, 157, 172, 173, 176
ethnoscapes, 26
etiology, 15
European Union, 166
exile, 38, 39, 42, 43, 44, 45, 46, 47, 50, 53, 58, 63, 64, 67, 72, 73, 74, 80, 85, 90, 91, 98, 110, 111, 113, 115, 121, 128, 133, 134, 155, 159, 160, 161, 162, 165, 168, 175, 193
exilic displacement, 3, 4, 6, 23, 24, 30, 31, 36, 37, 38, 46, 47, 48, 49, 51, 52, 53, 54, 125, 180, 182
existential, 133, 174, 181
existential homelessness, 21
expatriation, 4, 6, 22, 32

Fanon, 92, 106, 108, 115, 152
fascism, 14, 60, 112
fatwa, 121, 123, 138, 140, 147
feminist, 95
films, 115, 146, 175
The Final Passage, 151, 152, 154
food, 118, 120, 121, 122, 123, 124, 152, 153, 160
France, 66, 80, 90, 95, 165, 167
freedom, 1, 59, 89, 100, 101, 137, 138, 147, 155, 156, 157, 173, 176
free-floating intellectual, 19
Freud, 1, 2, 6, 13, 14, 15, 38, 39, 50, 156
frontiers, 18, 22, 26, 28, 33, 34, 49, 60, 64, 65, 67, 70, 123, 145, 146, 166, 181

gay, 156
Gaza, 24, 47, 52, 180
gender, 66, 69, 156, 157, 160, 177
generational conflict, 121

geography, 14, 22, 30, 36, 49, 66, 82, 86, 146, 156, 175, 182
Germany, 43, 80, 165, 167, 169
Ghana, 62, 74, 81
Ghandi, Indira, 134
ghettoization, 1, 19, 27, 58, 67, 123, 169, 176
Ghosh, Amitav, 49
Gilroy, Paul, 27, 40, 75, 76, 77, 172, 175
globalization, 9, 30, 167
Goethe, G. W. von, 170
Guantanamo Bay, 176
The Guardian, 70
Gurnah, Abdulrazak, 69

Hall, Stuart, 7, 51, 52, 60, 71, 122, 143
Harris, Wilson, 12, 88, 101
Heart of Darkness, 32, 105
Hindu, 130, 133
hip hop, 70
historical displacement, 30, 31, 90, 122, 181
history, 1, 2, 3, 5, 6, 7, 11, 13, 15, 18, 19, 22, 23, 25, 27, 30, 36, 40, 41, 42, 50, 51, 52, 61, 62, 63, 64, 69, 70, 76, 78, 79, 80, 84, 88, 92, 93, 94, 100, 105, 107, 109, 110, 116, 122, 124, 130, 136, 137, 142, 143, 144, 145, 146, 147, 157, 159, 166, 167, 174, 181
home, 3, 6, 10, 18, 19, 21, 23, 25, 27, 28, 31, 33, 34, 37, 38, 41, 42, 43–52, 58, 60, 73, 77, 78, 81, 82, 89, 90, 91, 92, 94, 96, 97, 98, 102, 108, 114, 117, 118, 119, 123, 125, 135, 136, 137, 139, 141, 145, 149, 150, 151–4, 157, 170, 172, 177, 178, 181
homeland, 6, 18, 28, 31, 37, 43, 44, 49, 52, 54, 60, 65, 71, 85, 95, 97, 99, 101, 104, 118, 125, 135, 137, 145, 154, 181
homelessness, 21, 22, 26, 27, 31, 76, 94, 110, 135, 141, 157, 158
Hong Kong, 8, 78, 117
Hosain, Attia, 82
Hugo, Victor, 25
hybridity, 1, 7, 27, 40, 41, 51, 52, 63, 120, 121, 122, 136, 157, 160, 170

identity, 2, 4, 5, 7, 9, 11, 15, 17, 24, 26, 28, 29, 32, 35, 36, 38, 40, 43, 48, 50, 52–6, 57–67, 72–5, 77, 79, 88, 90, 92, 94, 99, 100, 101, 104, 106, 108, 114, 118, 122, 124, 127, 129, 130–4, 149, 150, 155, 158, 166, 172, 173, 176–81
imaginary homelands, 31, 135, 137, 145
imaginative, 2, 25, 31, 36, 49, 53, 57, 62, 86, 91, 93, 96, 98, 118, 151, 171
imagined community, 182
Immigration Acts, 68, 69, 85
imperialism, 4, 18, 22, 47, 64, 66, 67, 73, 85, 106, 151, 166
India, *see* (West/East) India
individualism, 92
insomnia, 37
institution of race relations, 175
integration, 32, 50, 104, 110, 117, 120, 121, 125, 127, 171, 172, 175, 180
internationalization, 29
Intifada, 24, 47
I Saw Ramallah, 24, 25
Ishiguro, Kazuo, 71
Islam, 48, 112, 121, 130, 131, 138, 144, 147, 148, 161, 165, 166, 169, 170, 175, 176, 177, 179, 180

Index

Israel, 3, 23, 24, 42, 43, 47, 48, 49, 50, 52, 65, 162, 169, 170, 180, 181

Jamaica, 32, 62, 72, 77, 81, 89, 94, 95, 129, 159, 171, 176
James, C L R, 87, 88
Japan, 84, 118, 120, 131
Jazz, 71, 81, 141
Jerusalem, 42, 43, 50, 62
Jewish Diaspora, 23, 24, 25, 30, 42, 43, 46–55
Joyce, James, 12, 21, 22, 133

Kaplan (*Questions of Travel*), 20, 21, 22, 31, 33, 39, 52, 109
Kapoor, Anish, 51
Kashmir, 142, 144
Khomeini, Ayatollah, 174
Kunzru, Hari, 105
Kureishi, Hanif, 8, 9, 11, 19, 37, 71, 117, 118, 120, 121, 123, 132, 134, 138, 150, 154, 155, 156, 157, 158, 159, 176

Lamming, George, 8, 9, 11, 27, 47, 72, 80, 82, 83, 84, 85, 86, 87, 88, 89, 90, 91, 93, 109, 111, 112, 115, 161, 175
Leeds, 69, 81, 128, 149
lesbian, 156
liminal, 123, 134, 136
linguistic displacement, 4, 30, 32, 34, 115
literary displacement, 10
locality, 41, 43, 48, 55, 83, 109, 128
London, 2, 4, 8, 9, 10, 12, 18, 29, 32, 34, 35, 46, 47, 54, 68, 70, 71, 73, 75, 76, 78, 80, 81, 82, 85, 86, 87, 88, 89, 92, 94, 98, 100, 101, 102, 103, 104, 106, 107, 109, 110, 113, 115, 117, 118, 121, 123, 124, 125, 126, 127, 128, 129, 130, 131, 132, 133, 139, 152, 157, 158, 167, 168, 172, 173, 175, 176, 177, 179, 180
The Lonely Londoners, 2, 10, 11, 32, 34, 35, 37, 46, 77, 86, 98, 99, 101, 103, 105, 106, 107
Luther King, Martin, 72

Ma, Yo-Yo, 169
magic realism, 9, 37, 71, 117, 121, 135, 143, 144, 146, 147, 178
Malcolm X, 72
Marley, Bob, 69
marriage, 8, 137, 178
Masala Fish, 2, 8, 69, 117–63, 176
melancholic paranoia, 27, 39, 40, 98
melancholy, 27, 36, 38, 39, 40, 41, 58, 112, 119, 155
memory, 1, 2, 10, 18, 23, 24, 31, 37, 38–47, 53, 69, 70, 80, 92, 93, 97, 100, 107, 108, 113, 129, 134, 137, 141, 142, 144, 159, 178, 182
metaphoricity, 27, 181
Middle East, 18, 24, 43, 44, 47, 53, 165, 167, 173
Midnight's Children, 37, 45, 71, 141, 142, 143, 145, 147
migration, 5, 9, 13, 27, 29, 32, 40, 44, 46, 67–78, 85, 90, 95, 103, 108, 122, 137, 139, 141, 147, 165–73, 181
The Mimic Men, 11, 22, 37, 65, 100, 109, 110
mimicry, 32, 82, 94, 99, 100, 112, 115
mixed race, 100, 105, 121
Mo, Timothy, 8, 9, 117, 118, 120, 121, 124, 141
modernism; modernity, 1, 7, 39, 41, 61, 62, 139, 142, 169
monism, 10
Mukherjee, Bharati, 61
multiculturalism, 107, 124, 125, 133, 143, 163, 165–81
multinational, 29, 30

202 INDEX

multiracial, 81, 105, 107, 167, 172
music, 3, 42, 43, 69, 70, 71, 75, 81, 89, 106, 114, 121, 129, 140, 155, 157, 169, 170, 176, 179

Naipaul, V. S., 8, 19, 71, 83, 87, 109, 110, 112, 115
Nakbah (Catastrophe of 1948), 3, 23, 47, 52
Naksah, 23
National Front, 129
nationalism, 1–3, 8, 27, 48, 55, 57, 60, 65, 66, 67, 73, 74, 86, 94, 106, 140, 148, 166, 170, 175, 181
nation-state, 2, 35, 50, 66, 181
negro, 68, 73, 74, 76, 77, 80, 92
neo-colonialism, 57, 125, 165
newness, 26, 36, 52, 64, 76, 134, 139, 157, 174
new world, 5, 14, 27, 36, 83, 149, 150
New World Order, 5, 14, 149
New York, 110, 117, 132, 157, 173, 175
niqap, 165
nomadic, 5, 6, 7, 10, 11, 17, 19, 20, 21, 22, 27, 29, 47, 61, 65, 110, 119, 143, 151, 157, 158
nomadology, 1, 2, 5, 6, 7, 17, 18, 22
nostalgia, 3, 6, 10, 15, 21, 34, 38–46, 88, 97, 100, 108, 119, 134, 154
Nuzooh (Evacuation), 3, 23, 48, 180

oedipal, 1, 6, 7, 14, 17, 28, 47, 51, 70, 79, 89, 125, 180
Okri, Ben, 71
ontology, 18, 75
oriental(ism), 36, 115, 122, 150, 171, 172
out of place, 1, 43, 53, 74, 76, 96

Pakistan, 3, 18, 23, 30, 32, 54, 61, 62, 64, 78, 112, 118, 120, 130, 134, 135, 136, 137, 138, 144, 145, 146, 147, 148, 155, 156, 157, 165, 167, 176, 181
Palestine, 2, 3, 4, 20, 23, 24, 30, 31, 43, 46, 47, 48, 49, 50, 53, 62, 81, 180, 182
Palestinian literature, 48
partition, 30, 61, 82, 144, 145
peripherality, 29, 137
Phillips, Caryl, 5, 8, 9, 12, 32, 54, 67, 77, 80, 85, 112, 113, 114, 117, 118, 120, 134, 149, 150, 151, 152, 153, 166, 172
pluralism, 10
pluralistic openness, 119
politics of home, 2, 8, 50, 52, 95, 120, 125
pornography, 38
post-colonial, 4, 10, 11, 166
postmodern, 20, 21, 32, 39, 40, 52, 62, 95, 142, 146, 147, 166, 181
post-structuralism, 62
Powell, Enoch, 68, 69, 114, 172, 176
psychoanalysis, 1, 5, 8, 14, 15, 17, 25, 30, 36, 37, 38, 39, 63, 80, 81, 86, 87, 92, 93, 95, 96, 97, 98, 100, 114, 119, 132, 151, 152, 153, 154, 156, 157, 158, 173, 176, 181
Punjabi, 70, 130, 145

R&B, 70
race, 2, 9, 12, 17, 27, 28, 60, 65, 66, 67, 68, 69, 70, 71, 75, 79, 85, 95, 100, 105, 112, 121, 143, 148, 155, 157, 159, 160, 166, 168, 169, 175, 176, 177, 178
racism, 2, 8, 27, 57, 64, 67–78, 94, 96, 107, 114, 158, 168, 175, 181
Ramayana, 132, 133
representation, 2, 4, 6, 9, 15, 27, 28, 32, 36, 42, 51, 52, 74, 85,

93, 111, 113, 115, 116, 121, 147, 176

resistance, 5, 24, 32, 38, 47, 48, 57, 63, 66, 67, 77, 108, 115, 134, 166, 174, 175, 179

return, myth of, 27, 50, 78, 139, 177, 181

rhizome, 1, 5, 6, 10, 17, 18, 19, 20, 21, 47

Rhys, Jean, 8, 11, 22, 62, 85, 86, 87, 95, 96, 97, 98, 109, 110, 114, 115, 153

Rivington Place Art Gallery, 175

rootedness, 17, 40, 83, 109, 110, 137

rootlessness, 18, 31, 110, 118, 141, 149, 155, 158

Routledge, 3, 4, 69

Rushdie, Salman 6, 7, 8, 9, 13, 19, 20, 26, 27, 29, 31, 35, 42, 43, 45, 51, 53, 58, 63, 64, 66, 67, 71, 73, 75, 76, 79, 82, 99, 107, 112, 113, 117, 119, 120, 121, 122, 123, 133, 134, 135, 136, 137, 138, 139, 140, 141, 142, 143, 144, 145, 146, 147, 148, 150, 154, 159, 161, 162, 167, 168, 169, 171, 172

Said, Edward, 2, 4, 6, 19, 20, 22, 23, 24, 26, 33, 36, 42, 43, 44, 47, 48, 51, 53, 59, 60, 62, 65, 66, 74, 105, 110, 113, 115, 140, 156, 167, 168, 169, 170, 171

Salih, Tayeb, 71, 108

The Satanic Verses, 11, 26, 37, 63, 71, 75, 119, 121, 123, 133, 136, 138, 139, 140, 147, 150, 166, 174

satire, 84, 111, 147

schizoanalysis, 14

Schizophrenic, 4, 26, 27, 39, 40

Scottish, 100, 176

Second World War, 1, 3, 10, 28, 29, 64, 84, 85, 87, 88, 90, 167, 181

Selvon, Sam, 2, 8, 9, 10, 11, 19, 21, 27, 35, 37, 46, 47, 62, 71, 77, 83, 84, 85, 86, 87, 92, 94, 95, 97, 98, 99, 100, 101, 102, 103, 104, 105, 106, 107, 109, 110, 113, 115, 118, 120, 122, 149, 151, 161

sexuality, 3, 37, 38, 121, 147, 155, 156, 162

Shame, 19, 72, 84, 92, 108, 111, 135, 136, 137, 141, 147, 152, 174

Sivanandan. A., 175

Smith, Zadie, 8, 9, 117, 118, 121, 159, 161, 162

Soueif, Ahdaf, 24, 69

Soul II Soul, 70

Spivak, G. C., 51, 115, 116

stereotype, 39, 63, 104, 128, 132

Sterne, 37, 143

subaltern, 51, 115, 116

Suez, Canal, 78, 81

Susheila, Nasta, 101

syncreticism, 27, 63, 122, 157

Thatcher, Margret, 68, 69, 149, 150

Things Fall Apart, 35, 95

Thiong'o, Ngugi Wa, 34

third world, 33, 39, 115, 133, 136, 165, 171

tourism, 4, 22

transient, 18, 181

Transjordan, 30

transnational, 6, 13, 29, 35, 38, 40, 46, 49, 54, 71, 170, 181

travel, 4, 6, 7, 19, 20, 22, 26, 28, 33, 42, 43, 44, 51, 54, 55, 58, 61, 64, 75, 80, 84, 85, 93, 111, 112, 113, 137, 142, 150, 151, 159, 179

travel writing, 4

tricontinental, 18, 19

Trinidad, 8, 11, 21, 31, 32, 46, 62, 72, 81, 83, 84, 89, 95, 99, 100, 102, 103, 105, 107, 109, 110
two-ness, 72, 74

unhomely fictions, 10, 11, 12, 170
the United States of America, 5, 20, 149, 167
unreliable narrators, 37, 40, 113, 141, 146
uprootedness, 17
Urdu, 35, 120, 136, 143

violence, 50, 72, 73, 78, 104, 120, 125, 130, 168, 175, 181
Voices of the Crossing, 82

Walcott, Derek, 88, 149
(West/East) India, 18, 23, 30, 31, 32, 35, 46, 50, 54, 61, 62, 64, 70, 72, 75, 77, 78, 80, 81, 82, 83, 84, 86, 87, 88, 89, 90, 92, 93, 94, 95, 99, 100, 103, 104, 105, 106, 110, 111, 112, 118, 119, 120, 122, 123, 126, 127, 130, 131, 132, 133, 134, 135, 136, 141
White Defence League, 77
Wide Sargasso Sea, 11, 22, 32, 37, 95, 97
Windrush generation, 2, 8, 32, 62, 72, 78, 79, 81, 83, 85, 87, 88, 89, 91, 94, 97, 99, 109, 113, 114, 117, 118, 119, 134, 171
World Cinema, 176
world literatures, 24, 170, 171
Wright, Ian, 71
Wright, Richard, 88

Young, Robert, 18

The manufacturer's authorised representative in the EU is Springer Nature Customer Service Centre GmbH, Europaplatz 3, 69115 Heidelberg, Germany. If you have any concerns regarding our products, please contact ProductSafety@springernature.com

Printed and bound by CPI Group (UK) Ltd, Croydon, CR0 4YY

23/03/2026

02076682-0011